✝Aíno

José Barreiro

✝Taíno

A Novel

José Barreiro

FULCRUM
GOLDEN, COLORADO

First published by Arte Publico Press, 1993

Library of Congress Cataloging-in-Publication Data
Barreiro, José.
    Taino : a novel / José Barreiro.
        p. cm.
    ISBN 978-1-55591-761-6 (pbk.)
    1. Indians of the West Indies--First contact with Europeans--Fiction. 2. America-
-Discovery and exploration--Fiction. 3. Columbus, Christopher--Fiction. I. Title.
    PS3552.A73257T35 2012
    813'.54--dc23
                                    2012015996

Printed in the United States of America
0 9 8 7 6 5 4 3 2 1

Design by Jack Lenzo

Fulcrum Publishing
4690 Table Mountain Dr., Ste. 100
Golden, CO 80403
800-992-2908 • 303-277-1623
www.fulcrumbooks.com

For my tía Lilina and my abuelo Joseíto,
who taught me to value the old ways

And for my father and mother,
who pointed me to my future

Contents

Author's Introduction: A Fabulous Find 1

Folio I: Our Reality and Theirs 9

Folio II: Losing Everything 45

Folio III: To Go Forth and to Return 123

Folio IV: A Visit to the Rebel Camps 177

Folio V: Cohoba Dreams............................. 235

Folio VI: The First Good Treaty 267

Folio VII: Last Testaments 305

Postscript.. 319

Glossary *321*

About the Author *328*

Author's Introduction

A Fabulous Find

From 1988 to 1990, while I was completing research on a doctoral thesis, I endeavored to locate descendants of the aboriginal people of the West Indies. I visited the island nations of Santo Domingo/ Haiti, Puerto Rico, Cuba, Saint Vincent, Trinidad, and Dominica. My research led me to interview numerous informants on family oral and documentary history, lifestyle, and the genealogical foundations of the islands. This exhilarating work—fueled, in part, by the occasion of the Columbus quincentennial, in 1992—led to a number of adventures, some personal revelations, and the fulfillment, twenty years late, of a doctoral thesis. However, that thesis, "The Indigenous Caribbean," which became a curriculum, was not the only revelation of those years of research. A far greater discovery resulted, the dream of this researcher: the manuscript that follows this introduction.

In January 1990, during a research visit to Cuba, a friend from the Oriente region of the island told me of a fabulous find in the remote city of Baracoa, among the elder members of a family of Amerindian descent. My friend, an archaeologist of Indo-Cuban descent (from Santiago), insisted that the manuscript was a long-lost set of notes made by Father Bartolomé de Las Casas in preparation for his historic book *Brevísima relación de la destrucción de las Indias* sometime during the 1530s. He said two investigators from the University of Havana had visited the family in the early 1980s but had only been allowed to view portions of the manuscript. "The family is very guarded," my friend said.

Such documents have often been found among Indian descendants, so I was not surprised by my friend's assertions. Throughout the Western Hemisphere, the Amerindian peoples have revered and tried to keep safe such material legacies as they have been able to secure. Researchers have often reported otherwise destitute Indian families who could produce old chests full of intricate and high-quality breastplates, quill- and beadwork, ceremonial bundles and written testimonies and treaties dating back generations, materials sometimes several hundred years old. In fact, there is presently a generalized movement among Indian peoples to recover spiritually important museum pieces. In several places, tribes have reburied human remains taken by archaeologists and have established their own museums or asked traditional societies to hold artifacts, religious icons, and other objects retained from the past.

Indeed, I was soon to be pleasantly surprised when the two researchers, both doctoral candidates at the Department of Anthropology of the University of Havana, confirmed that the family had shown them six of the pages, written in Old Spanish script. They had judged that the paper was probably old, perhaps the log of a merchant sailor, but they had declined immediate work on the subject, having found the material unsuited to their own research on early colonial sugar mills. My friend, whom I had no reason to distrust, assured me that they had viewed but a minor part of it. He surprised me further by informing me that he had translated and read to the Indian family an old article of mine about Indo-Cuban persistence in the Baracoa area. They judged my perspective to be respectful, he said, and asked him to contact me about reviewing their prized possession.[1]

A week later, I was in the village of Guarikén, in the sierra of Baracoa, overlooking the central valley of the Toa River, where I visited the family of Don Francisco Suárez Padrón, a native of the same village. The Suárez Padrón clan is a peasant mestizo/*indio* family that, for several generations at the end of the eighteenth and the beginning of the nineteenth century, worked for the estate of a Cuban scholar, Don Ernesto Bosch Samoa near Guarikén, still one of several small Cuban Indian communities.

After sharing a cup of Cuban *cafecito* and reviewing my credentials, Suárez produced a copper box, twelve by eighteen inches in size and almost four inches thick, which he placed on a small wooden table. He said that except for the few pages shown to the Havana investigators, he had never revealed the inside of the box to anyone outside his family. Suárez recited how he had been entrusted with it by his grandfather, who had received it from his own grandmother.

That matriarch from five generations ago, according to Suárez, had said that the box and its contents came to her family via a great-aunt from the Dominican Republic, a migrant to Cuba, who had received it herself as a young woman from a Catholic friar. The friar was a member of the Dominican Order, one of a long line of friars dating back to the turn of the sixteenth century in Santo Domingo. Remembering that Friar Bartolomé de Las Casas was a member of the Dominican Order, I took careful note of all the names and their family connections. Suárez then ushered me to the table, where he placed the box. He took my hand and put it on the stack of papers.

"Most of it is written by an Indian," Suárez said.

I told him I had been informed it was a Las Casas manuscript.

"Yes," he said, "there are letters from Las Casas, but the bulk is by a Taíno Indian who claims to have known Columbus." He pronounced it "Colón," as in Spanish. Suárez claimed to understand only about a third of the material, as he found the Old Spanish, written in an elaborate twirling script, hard to decipher.

The copper box was indeed full of sheets, pressed tightly. It gave every indication of being quite old. The box had been lined inside with fine wood, of which only a slip remained, dry as last year's tobacco leaf. With great care and under Suárez's watchful eye, I took out one section and then another. There were two types of paper, both fifteen inches long but one slightly thicker than the other. The thinner papers were blank and had been placed between the sheets of writing for protection. Many of the sheets appeared blank to the eye, but about halfway into the manuscript a blotting effect had occurred and much of the ink was stenciled onto the thinner sheets, reading backward to the eye but discernible. I could immediately see that the papers were old. The script was indeed elaborate, in the ornate style of Spanish calligraphy used in the 1500s. Having held in my hands and closely studied verifiable documents from that period at the General Archive of the Indies in Seville, Spain, I could indeed sense that these pages were likely to be a genuine find. Later, in 1990, radiocarbon tests at the Bureau of Ethnology in Washington, DC, dated the paper and wood to the period 1450–1550.

Encouraged by this potentially important find, I rented a room at a *pensión* near the Suárez home, and thus began a six-month process of photographing, reading and deciphering the tiny script, and determining the authorship of the documents.

I found that the contents consisted of letters, some notes, and a manuscript of some 440 pages handwritten in very small script. There were indeed letters by Las Casas, two of them, both addressed to a Diego or Dieguillo Colón at the Dominican convent in Santo Domingo, a long, rambling note by an unnamed friar, dated 1659; a short note by Don Ernesto Bosch Samoa, dated 1864; and the long manuscript of notes and journal entries, comprising the bulk of the papers by a Diego Colón, who I initially assumed would have been either the brother or the son of the discoverer Christopher Columbus. However, the note by scholar Bosch Samoa seconded Suárez's assessment, guiding me toward a truer analysis. After a short paragraph explaining that he came to read the manuscript on a request from his aunt, Bosch writes, "This is not the writing of the son nor of the brother of the Great Mariner. Neither the argument nor the exposition corresponds with the point of view of the Colón family. This is likely a fraud, though admittedly an old one, judging from the paper stock."

Immensely intrigued, I read the manuscript pages. Signed by Diego Colón, they were obviously not by a Spaniard, since the journal entries spoke from the point of view of a Taíno or Arawak Indian, one who claimed to have sailed with Christopher Columbus during the Caribbean phase of the contact period. The manuscript of 440 pages, each signed by Diego, was written in a descriptive and natural Spanish. It tells of events lived by the author, mostly around the period 1532–1535, but with episodes that recall the first encounter at the island of Guanahaní, site of Columbus's landfall and the writer's home island. Thus, the entries tell of memories from the early conquest history of the island that the Spanish named Española, now divided by the countries of Santo Domingo and Haiti. They tell also of the conquest of Cuba and of Puerto Rico.

The full translated text of the Diego Colón journal, plus the two letters from Las Casas, follow this introduction. However, I leave out Bosch Samoa's and the friar's notes, as they are largely unreadable. I am thankful to the eminent Caribbean scholar Professor Juan Mateo (Harvard emeritus), who helped me translate the manuscript and authenticated dates used by the author. Professor Mateo, an indefatigable tracker of the Caribbean's Taíno roots, was extremely helpful in deciphering the meanings of Taíno words. However, the final translation is my full responsibility. For the sake of readability, I have sometimes introduced modern usages, such as Puerto Rico (named San Juan Bautista in Diego's time), and I use the contemporary term *Kwaib* interchangeably with the more historical *Carib* or *Caniba*. The term *Taíno* refers to the broader Caribbean indigenous culture that blanketed the Greater Antilles. The two letters of Father Bartolomé de Las Casas, one left for Diego and the other sent from Barcelona, are placed at the end of the volume, as they are in fact dated from 1534 and 1543. Diego's final entry, dated 1546, in shaky handwriting, comes after a full three years of silence following the last of the Las Casas letters. It provides a proper postscript to the narrative and comes after a final encomendation of Diego's worldly goods.

Diego Colón: Points in the Trajectory

After a cursory search of the early chronicles, I found the historical personality named Diego Colón, who was indeed a Taíno Indian. Diego Colón was a young man, twelve years old, when taken captive by Columbus at the first landfall at Guanahaní. A quick study, Diego became Columbus's primary Taíno interpreter within weeks of the first contact. He would not only remain at the center of events throughout the first ten years of the Spanish colonization of La Española, but he lived to full maturity in Santo Domingo. Diego Colón was a native witness to the first half century of that fateful encounter.

Among the early chroniclers, Las Casas himself mentions the Indian interpreter Diego Colón several times in his *History of the Indies*.[2] Dr. Álvarez Chanca, who sailed in the Columbus voyage, mentions him twice (though not by name) in his famous Letter to the City of Seville. Both Gonzalo Fernández de Oviedo,[3] the king's historian, and Columbus's son Ferdinand[4] refer to Diego in their books: in Oviedo's definitive *General and Natural History of the Indies* (1535) and in Columbus's biography of his famous father, respectively. Diego also turns up in the infamous letter of Michele de Cúneo,[5] raconteur and friend of Columbus, and in Pedro Mártir de Anglería's *Décadas del nuevo mundo*[6] (1530).

There are references to a Diego Colón at the General Archive of Indies that twice place such a person in Española in 1514; he is also mentioned by an *encomendero* (Spanish grantees who were ceded lands holding whole Indian communities) in Cuba in 1515. Among twentieth-century historians, Columbus's preeminent biographer Samuel Morison provides several anecdotal references to Diego in his books *Christopher Columbus: Admiral of the Ocean Sea* and *The European Discovery of America: The Southern Voyages*.[7]

In a twentieth-century novel, Cuban writer Alejo Carpentier twice mentions a "Dieguito, the only one of them to learn some of our words."[8] Writing in Columbus's own voice, Carpentier reflects the final thoughts of the legendary admiral: "Through Dieguito, the last one left to me, I learned that those men neither liked us nor admired us; they had us for treacherous men, liars, violent, choleric, cruel, dirty and foul-smelling."

But that was fiction and in a European (Columbus's) voice. Diego's manuscript reopens the historical record and his is an indigenous voice. Sitting in the coastal breeze of the eastern Cuban mountains, under palm and *ceiba* trees and surrounded by the sounds of *inriri*, the Cuban woodpecker, Diego's words resonated in my ears with a vibrancy that is a researcher's dream. Diego's journal narrates a moment in that early history of encounter when, for a brief decade, the Taíno people regrouped under the leadership of the young chief Guarocuya (Enriquillo's Taíno name) and actually won a war against the Spanish Crown, one that resulted in capitulations that constitute the first treaty between a European power and an American indigenous people.

In any case, Diego's folios provide us with the story of Enriquillo's war and many other historical incidents as well. A narrative written in journal style and making full use of descriptive elements, it can be read for itself, making these explanations already long enough. Except for a glossary that explains Taíno and Spanish words, readers will rejoice that this introduction constitutes the only words extraneous to the noted translator's journal and the letters he saved from Father Las Casas. Without further delay, then, five centuries overdue, we directly proceed to the translation of Diego's text.

José Barreiro
Crows Hill, NY
December, 1992

Notes

1. José Barreiro, "View from the Shore: Toward an Indian Voice in 1992," *Northeast Indian Quarterly* (1990).
2. Bartolomé de Las Casas, *History of the Indies*. Ed. Andree M. Collard. New York: Harper and Row, 1971.
3. Gonzalo Fernández de Oviedo, *Historia general y natural de las Indias*. Asunción: Editorial Guaraní, 1956.
4. Ferdinand Colón, *The Life of the Admiral Christopher Columbus by his Son Ferdinand*.

Trans. Benjamin Keen. New Brunswick: Rutgers University Press, 1959.
5. Michele de Cúneo, "Letter of the Second Voyage," *Universidad de la Habana*, 1972.
6. Pedro Mártir de Anglería, *Décadas del nuevo mundo*. Trans. Joaquín Torres Asensio. Buenos Aires: Editorial Bajel, 1944.
7. Samuel Morison, *The European Discovery of America: The Southern Voyages*. Oxford: Oxford University Press, 1974.
8. Alejo Carpentier, *El arpa y la sombra, Obras completas de Alejo Carpentier*. Ed. Maria Luisa Puga. Coyoacán, Mexico: Siglo Veintiuno Editores, 1979.

9

Folio I
Our Reality and Theirs

The good friar Las Casas requests my witness of the early years... A reason to remember so much pain... An introduction of myself... The good friar's argument... The story of Enriquillo... My own truth I pledge... What the friar wants... Starting out... I begin with the return... A route home denied... The trip to Cuba, barbecuing on the beach... Bayamo and Macaca: not a discourse but a curse... The Castilians change everything... The admiral is cursed... Hard to explain our Indian religion, even to a good friar... Enriquillo's conditions and vigilance... The Bible guides Las Casas...

April 12, 1532

ONE. *THE GOOD FRIAR LAS CASAS REQUESTS MY WITNESS OF THE EARLY YEARS.*

The Castilians call this the Year of Our Lord 1532, and today they call the twelfth day of the month of April. This is the day I start.

I write from a small square room in the convent of the Dominican Order, in Santo Domingo de la Española, where I have resided for six years. These journal pages, where I will inscribe my memories, are a manifest of the kindness of a great man, a priest of the Catholic faith, Don Bartolomé de Las Casas, of whom I am a grateful servant and to whom I am greatly in debt for my life and my well-being.

I have had a quill pen, acquired many long years ago, and ink, too, I obtained on my own. But paper has been nearly impossible to come by. The great man of robes, just a few days ago, gifted me with a sheet-book of paper, blank pages for me to fill. Now I have it and today I begin to scratch these Castilian symbols on the page, these drawings that talk. For that, and for his unceasing labor on behalf of my people, I am very grateful to His Eminence. I add here, of course, a certainty: that as always in my dealings with the Castilians, the ones my elders called the covered men, I am aware that the friar has a reason for granting me paper. Don Bartolomé writes now the story of Don Christopherens and the taking of the islands. He requests that I put down on paper the stories of my times with the admiral.

"Write it now before your mind forgets," the friar told me. "However you want, what you remember, note it down. The actual landfall—how the admiral first set foot on the New World. You were there, Dieguillo." And this is true. I am the only one left who remembers the first landing, from the beach on my home island, my *bohío* of Guanahaní. And I do remember. I remember the ships, their sails like giant gulls; I remember the strange men with coverings like crabs and hairs like frayed rope on their faces. I do, I remember even the clouds, how they formed and what they said to us that day. I remember now, I feel now, a great sadness about that day. It pains me now as I relive it, reminded to remember it by a great man that I love as I come to hate, every day more and more, the twisted ways of his race. I am pleased to do this for Don Bartolomé, though I did warn him he might not like my words.

April 14, 1532

Two. *A REASON TO REMEMBER SO MUCH PAIN.*

Much too busy with convent duties for two suns, today I rush to continue this work, and I am quickly flushed in the greenery of my memories. In this little room that the monks have allowed me, stiff-legged as I am, soft stomach, aching teeth, I still have my mind. For six years, as we have shared an existence in this convent's stone buildings, the friar has asked many questions, bringing up old times and writing down my stories. But now I feel the freedom of my hand, I draw my words on this paper, these words that will carry and be read by others.

I put pen to paper, close my eyes and I am there, almost forty years ago, but now fresh in my sudden memory, during those first days when close behind young Rodrigo, my new friend and captain's servant, I snuck under the poop deck of the *Santa Maria* (*Marie Galante*, the admiral always called her), anchored still on the small bay of my home island of Guanahaní, right into his master room. The admiral was bent over a table and quietly Rodrigo and I watched him from behind. He never took notice. That was the first time I saw him scratching the ink marks in his ship's log, engrossed in his mind, resembling one of our *behikes* in full ceremonial prayer. That act of the admiral's I pondered even at my early age. Later, as I learned their different ways, this writing on paper that could be taken over long distances and read directly again and again appealed to me. I think on that: that I, too, now can write, and it warms me.

I confess to the sky and I hope the friar can forgive me when he reads these words. I do intend to tell, to write on paper, what I did see and how I do see it. For the good father and for whomever else might read these pages, I will stall my anger, restrain my hate, retain my *cagüayo* lizard spirit, my revolving eye, the coolness in my body to see them clearly, and I will write what I have learned of their actions, their speech, during the early years and on to the present. But I confess: I am no longer enchanted by anything Castilian, anything Iberian, Portuguese, anything Genoese, or whatever else they have across the great open waters. Even as I write, and freely, I still ponder: How will these, my own words scratched on paper, how will they free my spirit? Or will they capture my thoughts, my heart? Will they betray me?

I am nervous to write of those times and those places where once flourished my Taíno relatives. The wounds of these forty years

cut deep into my heart and so will mostly these pages. So I sit and
I cry, and hurriedly before he returns, I sit down to pen these few
words of a beginning, on my own. Many things I can say about
the admiral that he will not like. And many things I can tell, too,
about the great world of my ancestors, the people of the islands that
the Castilians call Antilles but which to the eye of my mind I see
as our long Cuban lizard (Caymán-Cubanakán), the land of great
mountains (Haití-Bohío), the center of dancing (Borikén) and the
little Carib turtles, *hicoteas*, in our language, arching south to the
great forest.

And I start with this: What I do for this friar, our great
defender, I do because I know what he endures for my people. But
it is for my people, too, for that world in which we lived and which
we lost, that I want to write also what I know of who we were, how
we felt and believed, and what has happened. I want to be this friar's witness, by Yucahuguama Bagua Maórocoti, great spirit of my
ancestors, I do, and even by the baby Jesus, I do, but in my witness
I will write for you, my Taíno-ni-taíno, natural *guaxeri-ti* relatives,
for those of you who will survive, for those of you in times to come
who will remember that your fathers and your mothers, your grandfathers and grandmothers were a people.

April 15, 1532

THREE. *AN INTRODUCTION OF MYSELF.*

My Christian name in the Castilian language, from the time of my adoption by the admiral, is Diego or Dieguillo Colón. Fifty-two is the count of my rains. Of origin, I am from Guanahaní, the first land sighted in my world by the covered men of Castile. I am of the Taíno people and in my native language my name is Guaikán—the remora fish. My mother was Nánache, from the canoe-building clan of the *yukaieke*, or village, called Old Guanahaní. My father had several names but was most prominently called Cohobanax, after his functions and title in the council of the Cohoba. He was from our island's central village, called Guanahanínakan, but he lived on the coast with my mother's people, who esteemed him as a fisherman of great skill.

I think now of my father's death, only weeks before the admiral's arrival, in a moment of joy, climbing lazily on the overlapping branches of a palm tree, reaching over to the tree of the fruit called *mamey*, his tight muscular body, like the great *mahá* snake, with a stick he struck down two, three bundles of ripe *mamey*. Then, stretching for one more fruit, arm extended, body extended along thick, broad leaves like a brown *cagüayo* lizard, a sharp crack and how he dropped, long and hard and with no sound, all silent but the snap, the crack when the flat branch broke, as he dropped fast and hit rock.

My first sadness comes back to me now, the worst and best, and I must stop. Thinking of my parents, of their generation and their elders, fills me with longing.

This is all in me. I pull away now, lift the pen. I leave my father be. Slowly, I will approach it. There is so much. Again today my mind swims with colors and faces, turns of words and the many smells of the sea. The friar's request has filled me with force, my chest is warm and my mind turns. Even the pain of my right side, past injuries I carry from the time of my betrayal, when even his name that I still carry could not protect me, even the old pain that stiffens my arm and leg, even my tired limbs, have warmed so that my heart can almost feel glad.

April 21, 1532

FOUR. *THE GOOD FRIAR'S ARGUMENT.*

At lunch today the good friar took his meal, as I usually do, with the Indian servants of our convent. We shared with him our *cassabe* tort, *axiaco* soup, and a fresh red snapper caught out in his canoe in the early morning by young Silverio. Don Bartolomé comes to eat with us quite regularly. Today, before taking seat, he was already agitated with our cause. As part of his prayer, he said, "Almighty God, help us condemn the *encomienda* system, brutal destroyer of our good Indian brothers."

The good friar is very forceful. Once he intends to go in a certain direction, he will not be dissuaded. Every day, for his ideas about our Indian people, he suffers. Today, I watched him mop around his soup bowl with a piece of *cassabe* as we heard the first yeller. The shouting came from the stone road that runs down the hill by the convent, and you could hear the culprit hurrying by. "Las Casas, the great whoreson! Boogs the she-dogs and their sons!" he yelled.

Two or three come by every day. They shout their insults to the friar and run away before the younger monks can have at them. Most are sons or guards of *encomenderos*. They hate Don Bartolomé. Once, he was in the vegetable garden, picking our Taíno peppers that he loves so much, when several of the criminals pelted him with stones. They truly hate him and I believe would kill him if given a chance.

As usual, today Don Bartolomé sat quietly through the insults, his hawk's face and nose tilted down over his bowl with only the slightest of furrows lining his ample forehead. Two monks came back from a brief chase, empty-handed, and Don Bartolomé ignored them. He put his plate away and requested I follow him to my little room.

"How is the writing?" he asked, walking straight to the window as I closed my door.

"I am only starting," I said.

"I need your memory," he said. "I intend to sail to the kingdom soon. I will pretend to go to Puerto Rico. But from there I will go before the court in Castile. The king will hear my case."

"Why now, Father?" I asked.

"These bastards have no backbone. The whole island is terrified."

He spoke the truth. As we stood and talked today in the convent at Santo Domingo, a young countryman of mine, Enriquillo, the warrior chief of the Bahuruku mountains, remains at large. For thirteen years, Enriquillo and his warriors, among them his war captain, Tamayo, have been free in remote camps in the southwest mountains of the island.

"Enriquillo's warriors attacked a farm this side of La Maguana just eight days ago," Father Las Casas continued. "The governor is trying to keep it quiet, but four soldiers were killed and their weapons seized."

I asked the good friar if perhaps now the king might not be angrier with the rebel *cacique*, thus complicating his mission.

"The king will be upset. But with whom? Enriquillo's case is now well-known. Everyone wants the mountains pacified, including the king. My intent is to remind him that Enriquillo is a baptized Indian, a Christian. And he is at war for very good reasons. Others have argued with the king on that account. It is the brutal abuse of the *encomienda* that caused Enriquillo to war."

The good father was right and as always I was glad to hear him say it, but what he said pricked me. Indeed, Enriquillo was baptized. But, this I do not see as so great an achievement.

I know the story of Enriquillo. I knew his father and his uncles, including his great aunt, the *cacica* Anacaona, hereditary tribal mother of the Xaraguá region, sister of the wise old *cacique* Bohekio and widow of the feared warrior *cacique* Caonabó. All are now dead, victims of betrayal, victims of slaughter, almost thirty years ago.

"At the court they call you idolaters, heathen, barbaric people," he pressed me. "I want to argue that your people's beliefs were actually a form of Christianity, that you worshipped under similar ideas. Do you see? As Christians we are to conquer and war upon heathens at will; but a people who have had a measure of Christianity can command more consideration..."

I nodded, though not with the vigor he wanted.

"Yes or no?" he persisted. "Do you agree with what I maintain, that our best argument to the court is on religious grounds?"

"In truth, Father," I told him. "I do not hope so much for that argument as you do."

The good friar meant to press on. "I may convince the monarchs by asserting that your own religious beliefs before our coming are not so different from the Christian catechism," he said.

Deeply in my heart of palm I refuse to accept this argument from Don Bartolomé. I like what he tries to do, how tirelessly he argues on our behalf, but it angers something deep in me.

"The closer to Christianity you are, the more the kings must care for you. Among all the abhorrent practices of your old *behikes*, I know some Christian notions were apparent. The idea of Heaven and Hell, for instance, maybe thoughts about a celestial trinity, things like this, which could lead to a king's recognition. A royal declaration is what your people need."

"We need only to be left alone," I said, in an eruption of words. I must confess that his inquiries and assertions have triggered my memory. I am agitated. I do not mean to be blunt with the good friar, but he speaks sometimes without thinking.

The good father listens to me sometimes, and I feel his acceptance of my truth. But other days he walks as in a waking trance, like a guilty man smitten by the *cohoba*. Then, he admonishes me: "Only through the Lord Jesus Christ can you find salvation." Or he says: "Bringing Christ on the cross was our mission to you. Before, it is true, you were lost." When he is like that, when he must own not just my memory but my very own spirit, I shrink from his verbal embrace. Today, at first, it was like that. We couldn't talk. I withdrew into my silence rather than argue, and my good Castilian friend, this brother of Christ who so much has suffered for my people, he, too, withdrew, mumbling quietly to himself, his gaze roaming the valley beyond my window.

FIVE. *THE STORY ON ENRIQUILLO.*

A full hour went by before the good friar continued.

"Let's stick to Enriquillo," he said. "As I understand it, twice before going to the mountains, Enriquillo filed complaints. He tried to use the lawful means to achieve justice."

I know that story, too. I know exactly who Enriquillo is and how he comes to have hundreds of Indians in the bush mountains of the Bahuruku, how he has changed our lives, and what he means to the Indians and African Negroes of this island.

"And he is a Christian, is he not?" Las Casas said, to pull my tongue.

I reminded the priest that Enriquillo is a survivor of the Massacre of Anacaona's Banquet, which in 1503 destroyed the last major Taíno *cacicasgo* on Española. I myself saved Enriquillo's father, then took his young boys at my side, though I did not say so. That was the time when Governor Nicolás de Ovando, a friar and, in my estimation, an assassin, pretended friendship and accepted Anacaona's hospitality. Then, on his signal, Castilian soldiers attacked the friendly village, shooting and hacking and stabbing. I did remind the good friar of my presence at that massacre.

"But I didn't know Enriquillo was there," he said.

"Yes, he was," I said. "And, you should know, before he was taught the catechism, he was brought up for the *cohoba*."

"Leave the *cohoba* aside. It is a drunkenness by any other name."

This is a regular conversation between the good priest and me. He knows I will defend our *cohoba* ritual to him. I won't attack him, but I will argue with him.

"You have your wine. And you use it in ceremony, in communion with the Christ."

"This is not fruitful, Dieguillo…"

"With *cohoba*, our *behikes*, our priests, communicated, too, with our Yucahuguama, our supreme God."

"Enough. You are going too far and twisting my intention. Tell me about Enriquillo's life."

"After the massacre dictated by Fray Don Nicolás de Ovando," I said, to irk him by reminding him that the assassin was one of his brothers in the cloth. "Enriquillo was educated by the Franciscan fathers, as you know. Then, along with what remained of his village, some eighty or ninety people, he went to an *encomendero* named Valenzuela. When old Valenzuela died, his son, Andrés, received Enriquillo and his people for his own *encomienda*."

"So he was inherited by Andrés Valenzuela from his father?" Las Casas asked.

"Yes," I explained. "The old Valenzuela, named Francisco, died. And, you know, he was a calm man and not given to fits of temper like so many of the Iberians. Enriquillo's people paid labor tribute but kept their own *conucos* and much of their dignity under him."

"Nevertheless, by the king's law of 1517, an Indian was to have been freed upon the first *encomendero's* death. It was an illegal inheritance."

"So it was," I said. "Like so many, even today."

I saw Enriquillo occasionally at the convent until 1505 or 1506, when I myself was *encomended* and lost touch with him. He was only seven years old then, but I remember his serious eyes and his alert mind.

It was late in the year of 1518 when the story changes for

Enriquillo and his people; that was when they took their fate in their own hands. Young Andrés Valenzuela, an obscene profligate who lives in Santo Domingo even today, took away Enriquilo's mare. The mare was special, a deathbed gift to the young Taíno *cacique* from Andrés's own father. Enriquillo complained, but Valenzuela claimed it as his own father's inheritance to him. His overseers overtook Enriquillo in a field and beat him down, bruising his ribs and breaking a finger. A month went by. To fulfill his prescribed obligation, Enriquillo took a group of his *guaxeris*, his working men, to the mines for a four-week period. While he was thus occupied, Valenzuela came to his home and lewdly demanded sex from Doña Mencia, his wife.

"This I had heard," Las Casas said. "It was the rape—how Doña Mencia was raped."

A boy was sent for Enriquillo, and he returned immediately. He complained to Valenzuela and demanded an apology to his wife. "I love my wife," he is said to have told Valenzuela, who replied: "Neither Indians nor dogs know how to love. What would an Indian know about love?"

"Valenzuela said that?" Las Casas said, taking detailed notes as I spoke. He knows I know the Indian side of this story.

"Of course, he did. And this is well known, how Enriquillo and his wife love each other. Those two were close since early childhood and were brought up together by their families."

"They are lineage?"

"Yes, an arranged marriage. But let me finish. Because Enriquillo, an Indian like me and educated to his legal rights by friars, followed the good course and took his complaint to the lieutenant governor, Pedro de Badillo. And again, Badillo laughed him out of court in San Juan la Maguana. Then he had him arrested for public insubordination and beaten severely."

"It's a miracle he survived!" the friar said.

"It took Enriquillo weeks to recover, but when he did and could get around, he went to the court in Santo Domingo, where he hoped the *oidores*, or judges, would hear his complaint. But they, too, laughed at him. He stood up, again and again, in court, insisting that they hear his complaint. They placed him in chains for a week, then sent him home, where, at the courthouse of San Juan la Maguana, once again, three Castilian peons jumped him and beat him severely."

"'I went to them three times,' Enriquillo then told his people. 'All the talk of the priests is for nothing.' This time, when Enriquillo recovered, he rounded up the families under his care and took to the bush mountains of Bahuruku. Valenzuela pursued him with eleven foremen, but Enriquillo easily ambushed them, killing two of the men outright. He caught Valenzuela and stripped him naked, but merely chased him away. 'You are lucky I don't kill you, Valenzuela,' he told his former *encomendero*. 'Don't let me see you again in these parts or I will.'"

The friar laughed heartily, contentedly. "I have always heard that Enriquillo is not blood thirsty," he said.

No, Enriquillo is not blood thirsty, but he is tough. As I write now, thirteen years later, Enriquillo and his many warriors, who number into the hundreds and include African men, have this Española island near paralyzed. Christians, whether Castilian or Indian, dare not travel the roads without strong guard. The Spanish are not as numerous as they once were on these islands, many having gone on to the mainland, although the *encomiendas* that remain are quite large. Not a few have lost great sums paying for useless expeditions against Enriquillo, who is one Indian cunning beyond the Castilians and forceful enough to frustrate them at every turn.

"I think all authorities want to kill Enriquillo," I told Don Bartolomé. "I will do all I can do to save him."

SIX. *MY OWN TRUTH I PLEDGE.*

I write this now in a late night of full moon and calm waters. I feel the sea breeze enter my room, lick at my lips. Crickets chirp their long rasp, again and again, and the tree frog bellows back. Beyond earshot but not far, the waves, I know, caress our shore, once and again, an ancient stroke by which my people breathed. What our world was, how we saw life, how we lived by our heart, by the belly button of belonging and the memory of ancient teachings—this of my blood and my heart, it seems, the friar does not hear. He has an argument that we were almost like them, nearly Christian, as if this proves us a better people, we who were Taíno—"the good people." No, I respect him, but I have lived too long. I know what we had, the personality of our people that was like a gentle breeze, how they saw only seed in the rotting fruit, what would come forth. But, in forty years, I have yet to hear a Castilian priest express such a thought. Yes, I have seen too much, and now, in my time of illness and pain…my arm and leg on the right side stiffen with their own memory of injury and travail…[illegible]…in this providential gift of paper, I pledge my own truth to the mysteries, even if in the foreign language of Castile, which I have commanded since my first weeks with the admiral.

April 22, 1532

SEVEN. *WHAT THE FRIAR WANTS.*

I worked the garden all morning, ate lightly at lunch, attended a Mass, then napped. I was washing up after waking when the knock came and my benefactor, Don Bartolomé, pronounced by King Ferdinand "Protector of the Indians," entered forthrightly. He announced the continuation of what he called our "historical witness," and requested I take notes.

"I remember a story told by Michele de Cúneo," the friar began, and he must have seen me grimace, because he said, "I know you did not like Cúneo—but you were there in his story. It happens during Columbus's second trip, when he explored the southern coast of Cuba."

I remember the trip, during the admiral's second voyage, in April to September of the Christian year of 1494. Don Bartolomé has brought up this episode before. I can tell he wants this episode because of his argument about our Taíno people being almost Christians in their old beliefs.

"Cúneo told my father about that trip. He said that a Cuban *cacique* spoke of a heaven and a hell among his people..."

It was not quite so. However, I held my tongue. Cúneo was a total bastard, abusive, deceitful, a man who let his balls squeeze his mind, a rapist of women and buggerer of boys. Cúneo was on board only because he was a boyhood friend of Don Christopherens, from his own city of Genoa. He came back from Castile with us, on that second trip, a guest of honor of the Grand Admiral of the Ocean Seas.

"It was the trip to the south of Cuba," the friar continued. "Cúneo told my father that a prominent Cuban *cacique*, chief of a large *yukaieke* called Bayamo, feasted the admiral, then had long words about his own spiritual doctrine. Cúneo said you translated at the meeting."

"I was translator," I said, and I felt faint to remember that time. The friar went on but, again, he had thrown my mind back. That was the voyage of the miserable, when I confirmed for my thick-skulled self that the Castilians were not only cruel and violent men but also liars and crazy. It was during that voyage, too, that Don Cristopherens lost his own mind for weeks at a time.

"Cúneo said the *cacique* spoke in Christian terms about Heaven and Hell, and expressed his belief that good people go to Heaven and bad people go to Hell," Don Bartolomé repeated.

"Cúneo is full of shit, Father, with your permission," I actually said. I could not help myself.

"He was a loyal friend to my father," Don Bartolomé responded solemnly. "Though he was a rake."

"A perverted man, Father, with your permission," I said.

The good friar looked past me for a few moments. He admonished me finally. "You speak with vehemence again, Dieguillo."

"Yes, Father," I said. "With your forgiveness, Father."

He was right. I insulted him, and I do not mean to do that. But my breast was a sail taut with wind.

"I beg your forgiveness, Father. I only meant to say it was not like that. Cúneo did not understand the language, and in any case he was not there during that talk between the *cacique* and the admiral."

"Where was he?"

"He was exploring, Father."

"Exploring what? The coast?"

"Yes," I told him. "The coast." I did not need to tell him that Cúneo was, as my people would say, emptying his fleshy gourd all through that evening. Chasing for a place to stick his *yuán* was always the main occupation of Monsieur Michele de Cúneo.

"And well then, did the two men discuss the existence of Heaven and Hell?"

"It happened," I said. "But it did not mean what you think it meant."

"Write about it anyway, Dieguillo. It could be very important."

I told him: "That was the time Don Cristopherens lost his mind."

The good friar shook his long face. "No wild stories now, Dieguillo. I can take your testimony to the king. I need something new from that time that will help him sympathize with your people."

EIGHT. *STARTING OUT.*

The problem is: I remember so much more.

The trip to Cuba of Don Bartolomé's question came after our return from Castile, during the admiral's second voyage and four months into the settling of the new colony of Isabela.

But for Don Bartolomé's insistence, I would not begin my narrative there. My inclination is to start at Guanahaní, when we first saw the admiral. That would be the proper sequence. I would start that first morning, with my father-uncle, Cibanakán, who was the first to see the giant seagulls and tell how in the company of six of my kin, I sailed away in the Castilian ships through our small islands of the Bahama, how we guided the admiral to Cuba, then to Bohío, now the island Española, where he lost a ship, was embraced by Guanacanagari's people, and left forty men at Fort Navidad.

I saw Castile in my youth. I would write about that next, how I traveled through Spain in 1493. Then I would write about our return, the shock of what we encountered at Fort Navidad. All that and more would come before, in my story, because from the time I met the admiral to the time we sailed to Cuba and met Bayamo, the *cacique* who cursed Columbus, it was a year and more.

Now, it is forty years since that morning at Guanahaní, when after a night under lock in the hatch of the *Santa Maria*, I heard the pilot, Sancho Ruiz, holler the order to pull up anchors, and the three caravels hoisted up sails, gliding swiftly as they let the seven of us Guanahaní-ti, or as they called us, Indians, come out on deck just in time to see our beach disappear, our little turtle island of Guanahaní, become a sliver in the horizon, gone from our eyes.

NINE. *I BEGIN WITH THE RETURN.*

Later in this journal, I will take up the proper order. I want to tell my own stories and I have plenty of paper. But first I will let the good friar guide my pen.

In Castile, the admiral was received as a hero, but when we arrived again at our shores, that time with seventeen ships and more than fifteen hundred men, it was a not a good moment. The colony Don Christopherens left behind, Fort Navidad, was destroyed and everyone killed. Trouble brewed.

I remember well those first nightmare days of the new Isabel town, when all Castilian eyes were nervous and distant, weapons always at the ready and quickly used. The admiral's authority was daily challenged. The Castilian captains and the priest, the buzzardhead Buil, disdained him as a mere Genoese. Daily were the fights and contentions between Castilians themselves and against our Indian people.

A simple thing: the taking without permission of a cutlass from a sleeping Christian man. For that I saw the broad ax come down and a fourteen-year-old Taíno boy hopping and hopping as blood poured from his wrist, as the admiral, walking the ship's deck in long steps, shrugged his long shoulders, nodding, "It is the lesson we must teach, Diego. Always understand, I myself have no bloodlust, but the lesson must be sharp (*tajante*) to be understood." His hair was still red, that marvelous red hair we all had wondered at. I remember now how I told myself over and over that the bloodletting had its reason: *The Guamíquina knows what he does, I cried against hope that night. The Guamíquina knows what to do.*

April 26, 1532

Ten. *A ROUTE HOME DENIED.*

Columbus was by then my adopted father, this having happened in Barcelona, after his triumphant reception by the queen. And I still loved him, though it was a love in its final instances. Nevertheless, those first few days sailing, the openness and natural generosity of the sea made my heart soar. Too, Don Christopherens was a man who came alive on a ship. A thing to behold was his certainty of signal from wave and wind and cloud. I admit I sailed happily off with him from Isabella, still as his main interpreter, escaping the troubles of landlocked men.

The hope of my innocence that time was to once again arrive home at my island of Guanahaní. I rejoiced in the possibility of return to my own village by paddling home around the Maisí Point of Cuba. That first night, starting out, when I mentioned this wish to the admiral, he said: "It is possible to do so, Dieguillo." I envisioned rounding Cuba's easternmost point and heading north. Night after night I dreamed myself in a canoe, paddling home those last few suns to arrive at Guanahaní in the early morning, where I would make fire for my mother and awaken her gently by stroking the skin of her face.

Sighting Cuban land, our three ships indeed hugged the shore but turned west, not to round the Maisí tip of Cuba and out to my little island of Guanahaní. I questioned not the admiral, but waited; he spoke soon enough. To the officers and crew that very evening he asserted that this land of Cuba, which he renamed first Juana and then others called Fernandina, was not an island but a peninsula of the mainland of China. He meant to determine this thesis, he said, by exploring the southern coast going west. Don Christopherens got that distant look in his face, a dreaminess, when speaking of Cuba this way. So we sailed around the southwestern point of Cuba, which the admiral renamed Cape of the Cross.

In my heart I despaired I would never again see my mother, my village, or my people. Suddenly I felt the loneliness that would be with me the rest of my life. Yes, stingray jolt was for me that trip to Cuba, that trip that exploded my wonderment about the admiral, this arrogant man that renamed the world at will, changing the nature of everything, mixing what was ours with what was to be theirs. Yes, that was the moment. My beckoning like a son to this man we believed could cross the barriers to the Spirit World shattered. My heart was as the dried out carapace of the great sea turtle left out in the midday sun.

ELEVEN. *The trip to Cuba, barbecuing on the beach.*

On the beach in southern Cuba, from the distance, we could see Indian fishermen cooking. Then on the open sea in front of us, we saw two men in a canoe. They turned out to be brothers, and one fished with a net, the other by means of a guaikán, or sucker fish, which I am named after. This clever method of my people was unfamiliar to the Castilians on board. It makes use of the powerful circle of suckers on the guaikán's flat head, by which the fish attaches itself to larger fish and even bigger turtles. The fishermen tied the fish's tail with a long, thin *bejuco* string and asked us to slow our approach as they were then pulling in a big turtle.

I talked to the brothers from aboard ship. They gave our ship four large *caguama* turtles and invited me to the beach in their canoe. The ship's boat followed us to the shore, where we found other men cooking hundreds of smoked lobsters, yellowtails, barbecued *hutías* and iguanas, most of it wrapped in *maize* husks and stacked in small huts.

The men were of *cacique* Bayamo's village. Immediately they stated that from there to Baracoa, on the northern coast, and including all the mountain ranges of the region, their *cacique* and his line of *behikes* were respected. Their *cacique* had told them to prepare food for visitors. They said Bayamo was a seer who knew many things. Believing that we must be those expected visitors, they directed us to a place up the coast, a fishing village of a lesser *cacique* named Macaca, where we would find Bayamo. They gifted me with many foods for our ships. When the sailors thanked them, they shrugged, and said together, "We'll catch more." Since they had seen me emerge from the caravel's hold, the brothers were sorry to see me go, for they wanted to hear my stories about the hair-faced men who traveled in wooden caves.

TWELVE. *Bayamo and Macaca: not a discourse but a curse.*

The next day, I sat next to the admiral in the rowboat going to the shore. The three caravels sat behind us in the thick of the bay.

Waiting on the beach, hundreds of men, women, and older children surrounded the *cacique*, an old man, frail but spry, who carried a woven tunic over his shoulder. In one hand he carried a basket of small *guayabas*. The admiral spotted him. "Regard thou this Indian his apparel," he said to Captain Juan de la Cosa, his mapmaker, who sat behind us. I, too, was impressed. The old *cacique* of Bayamo watched sternly as his men pulled our boats to shore, then waved us to him. The admiral stiffened but went to the old man, standing before him a few seconds, then offering his hand. Old Bayamo grasped the hand and held it, peering directly at the much taller Don Christopherens.

Bending slightly toward me, the admiral said: "Tell him he may kneel and kiss the ring, which is granted me by the sovereigns of Castile and Aragon, now the united Christian Kingdom..." But, before I could begin to put that into our language, another old man, the local *cacique* Macaca, came up and took the admiral's other hand. The two *caciques* turned and began walking fast, the multitude closing behind them and suddenly it was all we could do to keep up, Don Cristopherens, myself, Captains Herrera and Navarra, a dozen soldiers and sailors, plus the braggart Cúneo, walking for half a league, the soldiers hacking a trail through the greenery, sweating gourds before arriving at a deserted *yukaieke* of twelve *bohíos* built in a square.

Their round *bohíos* were very well made, with tight thatch ties in the roof poles and bamboo and palm board walls fastened so sunlight could not penetrate. All had good dimensions and some large ones were forty and fifty feet wide. The square was recently swept. Large woven mats made from palm fronds lay covered with baskets of sweet fruits, pots of cooked corn ears, *ñame*, *boniato* soups, barbecued duck, lobster, iguana, and a fragrant herbal tea, freshly squeezed with cool mountain stream water. It all had been left out, smoking and steaming in the empty village, awaiting our arrival. Immediately I felt at home. This was the way it was done among our Guanahaní people, to leave food out like that, as if dropped from the sky. Even among small *caneys* of three or four families, often a family might return from harvesting or fishing and find a meal prepared like that, all warm and freshly made and no one around. As we sat and feasted on the *axiaco* and *cassabe*, I felt a great homesickness grip my chest.

Thirteen. *The Castilians change everything.*

I promised, good friar, to tell about the meeting and not get too involved in my own story. You say we were like Christians in our ways of worship, that we believed in similar spirits. I will say it is true, that our people had some similar ideas to yours. But another truth is you came from a world other than ours. And that world you brought with you, and with it you saw everything of ours, and with your words you renamed and changed everything that was obvious before.

At Bayamo's open-air *batéy*, or plaza, a dance was held. First the young men drummed and sang, then the women and all children joined in, holding hands in two long rows on both sides of the fire, singing long and melodic *areito* songs. They gave a beautiful rendition of the *areito* of Bayamanacoel, which they would, of course, being the Bayamo people. They did this in greater detail than I had heard before or since. Bayamanacoel was the first maker of *guanguayo*, our sacred *cohoba* paste and the *areito* tells how Bayamanacoel found *cohoba* the first time, what great trials he suffered to gain its favor and the favor of fire itself to prepare its powers for creation. Later, in one part of the story, he spits this paste on the back of Deminán, another of our ancestral grandfather-creators...

A Taíno such as myself could appreciate this offering, which was ceremonial and spiritual. Truly, I have loved reclining in the wide hammocks of my mother and grandmother, listening to the *areitos* of our Taínos that can go on and on, night after night, and never lack for songs. Bayamo's *areito* was so intricate, so ancient, that it ended after almost two hours where the same *areito* of other places would begin. Then, four old men and one old woman, all wearing the white, woven tunics, joined the great *cacique* Bayamo in reciting ancestral stories for our ears. These doings put through by the old *cacique* represented a great honor and normally would have been reciprocated with several days of ceremony.

Sitting next to me, the admiral was impatient to be back in his ship as night was falling and a bright moon was our only fighting advantage. I knew and informed the admiral that his turn to speak, as honored guest, would surely come, and thus he waited quietly, observing everyone at the same time that his agonized mind calculated everything. Here, he had been seated by our people in a *duho*, or ceremonial chair, his back placed against a wide root that protruded, tall as a cathedral wall, from a huge tree that towered over the clearing. Here he was feasted and sung to and offered the hospitality of the village, but in his mind that I know so well, he was in his mission, calculating possession and achievement.

Asked to speak, the admiral stood. This is what he said, as I remember it. "I am here to claim the lands we stand upon for the sovereigns of Castile and Aragon, whose loyal subjects you are now become," he began. I stood next to him to interpret and yet consciously moved a bit apart to establish my own stance before Taíno people.

"We are Christians," he continued, "and we are led by the most revered Catholic queen, our beloved Isabel of Castile, who, along with her own sovereign husband, King Ferdinand of Aragon, sent us to these lands. If Bayamo wants to be among the good people who go to Heaven when they die, he and his people should accept what I am telling them. But by our Christian law, once you have heard our doctrine, not to accept it is to be damned eternally, and you would force my armies to war upon you without mercy."

I translated as well as I could the words of the admiral. My instinct was always to let my people know as clearly as I could the intentions in the Castilian's words, but often they could be so drastic that I had to refrain from giving their full tenor.

Thus, at first, the *caciques* smiled at each other over the admiral's words, hearing only favored points. "Taíno-ti-Taíno," they said, one after another, meaning: "Good, we are the good people, too, the nice-minded people."

The admiral listened to their words with distant demeanor, until a reference was made to their own land by a young leader, whom Bayamo asked to speak. "This is our island," the man said clearly, "which we share with the Çiboney villages, not far from us down the coast. Our own people, guided by ni-Taíno that we understand in our language, extend from here to the small Lucayos and to the Bohío land, to Borikén and Xamayca."

I knew this would cause me trouble, although, of course, among our people we have always known Cuba to be an island. All of our pilots who ever guided the admiral—all—always referred to Cuba-cubanakán as a land that can be circled by canoe. But when I loudly translated the young man's description of Cuba as an island, the admiral reddened in the face and widened his eyes at me with a terror that frightened me.

Old Bayamo, I could tell, saw the heat of the admiral and watched intently. The Castilian captains and sailors had also heard me say "island." Looking at the admiral, I knew that he knew I had consciously betrayed his idea. From that moment on, the admiral always saw me as a potential betrayer of his intentions. Because I did know his intent.

In Barcelona and Seville that previous winter, I sat next to the admiral at the many dinners given in his honor, where he claimed to have touched the lands of China by sailing west. Thus, he called Cuba, which he renamed Juana, a peninsula of the distant mainland ruled by the Grand Khan. I knew the sovereigns granted him one in ten of all the wealth generated from lands he discovered and claimed for the Crown. Thus the noblemen who wined and dined him and who would finance his return made much of his assertion that Cuba might, indeed, be that main motherland of the rich and vast Mongol Empire, a gold-hued heathen civilization.

FOURTEEN. *THE ADMIRAL IS CURSED.*

It is true the admiral felt great pressure in his mind to find the nearest source of gold. He said directly to *Cacique* Bayamo: "In the most powerful land of Castile, my queen hurts deeply in her breast with a pain most horrendous. Only one thing can cure her: the shiny metal we call gold." I translated the Spanish *oro* for Bayamo as both *guanin* and *caona*, "copper" and "gold" in our language. "My queen and her king will love dearly any people that can provide them with the shiny metal, and they need much of it to quench their heart's pain," the admiral said.

Those words I remember distinctly. Since by then I knew how gold is used by the Castilians, what it means to them, I was daunted by his expression. It made everybody wonder just what he meant and how it could be that the shiny metal might help a sick person, which, interestingly enough, was also our custom. We did not know yet, not even I, the lengths to which the covered men would go to secure the gold.

When Bayamo stood to speak, I translated his words for the admiral. Bayamo called the admiral by a Taíno name, Guamíquina, which means something like "main chief." He was direct and, again, I remember his words quite well, as they still bounce in my ears.

"Tell the Guamíquina that in these parts we have our kind of people. The good people, Taíno-ni-Taíno, are peaceful. We share what we have, what the land and the sea give us. As you can see from our many foods, we are a fortunate people. Our spirits are plentiful. Because we are good, our spirits like us. They fortify our plantations. Thus the *yucca*, thus the *maize*, the *aji*, the beans, fruits of the trees, fish, turtles, and iguanas. In the sea, the Kaçi, our eldest Mother Moon, guides the women and the snappers..."

"What spirits is he referring to?" the admiral interrupted, out loud. His voice was accusatory. Bayamo fell deeply silent and looked surprised. I could tell he had never been interrupted in his life. In our people's ways, an elder is never interrupted, much less in mid-sentence. Young Taíno faces turned away out of respect for Bayamo, who patiently heard my translation. "It is a natural curiosity for spirit men," I added by way of excuse, although I had no doubt by then that the covered men were not spirit beings.

"What spirits would I speak about?" Bayamo responded. "I speak of the grandmothers and grandfathers, the Taíno who are in us. I speak of no one else. I mean only our old ancestor spirits, the spirit of the sea, the spirit of the mountain, the spirit of our incense and our tobacco, spirit of our *yucca* and our corn, those ones that forever have helped us..."

I interpreted. The admiral responded thus: "This that he says is mistaken. Tell him his faith is misplaced. Tell him he would fare better by accepting our Lord, Jesus Christ, and baptism in the true faith. Then he could travel the road to Heaven and Life Everlasting. Tell him those who do not accept Jesus Christ as lord and savior will go to Hell, tell them their souls will roast and burn for ever and ever."

My translation was more gentle and included an apology for the whole interruption.

"Tell him about Hell. He must understand how the punishment works," the admiral insisted.

I translated. The *cacique* peered silently at the admiral. At that moment I saw Don Christopherens rear back slightly, detecting the intensity of the *cacique*'s *goeiza*, or living spirit, which emanated that light hummingbird tremor.

Cacique Bayamo was truly of the elder men of our people, of the ones that spoke to the earth directly, keen with the certainty of our Taíno love and common spirit with the living world.

It is true that the Castilians have reduced us, have just about destroyed us. I admit that our fighting skills could not match their furious thrust. Truly were they decisive and resolute when we, in

ɔur habitual and cyclical understandings, took forever
⌐ᵧ ᴄhing but what our culture dictated, responses so slow
that they still hurt. But I know this: the superb among our people,
those most steeped in our traditions, were men and women who
could spark response in wind and cloud, could converse with plants
and trees, could hear the animals speak, could even be heard by
snake and *caimán*, turtle and *manatí*.

For generations on generations were our Taíno guided by those
conversations, held by our elders with the dream-time leaders of the
reptile and bird nations, with the leaders of trees, the *ceiba* and the
guásima, with the discernible snake motion of the long fish runs, the
passing of the flocks, with the very swell of the sea.

Bayamo himself was of the snake. His neck and sloping shoulders on a thin body, his flattened forehead, carefully manipulated
from his birth by grandmothers of his line, a practice for precisely
such babies in whose reptile eyes could the great mothers feel the
cold, penetrating, never-forgetting, never-ignoring justice of the
snake, who can snatch time from the quickest prey.

Such men and women among our people were extraordinarily
powerful. And I can state with certainty that there never was and
never will be even one such as those among the covered people,
whose very best can forge wide roads out of forest and cross worlds
of water and command huge quantities of death and mayhem, but
cannot ever hear the adjoining voices, the surrounding and constant
conversation from our living world.

Cacique Bayamo began the shaking in Columbus's Christian
heart. I saw it, and I was glad to see it and, now, to remember it. It
was in his look, how he transferred to the admiral's eyes his own
body's terrifying inner shaking. Yes, at that very meeting it was that
the hummingbird medicine grasped the admiral's heart.

"We have guided you in our world," the *cacique* talked on. "So
you would not be lost. And now you know us. We are a people that
stay to our islands, fishing and visiting, mindful of the present business of our foods, our *bohíos*, our *conucos*, and our ceremonies. We
have been here for a long time, drink the same water, eat the same
food. Always, in our gatherings, amongst us, we love the children.
And our children, in turn, love and respect us. Even our dead, our
opías who come through the treetops from the Coaybay, House of
the Dead, and have no belly button, sometimes they stay around us
and dance with us. We are good, Guamíquina. We don't raid. We

never raided, always build and fish and plant, do for ourselves. In our way, we feed everyone. If a man comes from other islands and he accepts our peace, we take him in, marry him into our people, exchange names with him. In this way, we extend our houses, our *bohíos*, and give roof to everyone. Our ni-Taíno circles and the outlier *guaxeris* listen to each other. That way we have grown strong and are growing still on these islands." (I translated *islands* as simply *lands* this time).

"The bad men, Kwaib, thigh-eaters, heart-eaters, from the south and some raiders from the north, are mean-spirited," Bayamo continued. "They raid for women, raid for our young ones. Among them even, some are very, very bad, *caniba* warrior bands that leave their women on their own islands—the Matininós—and raid for the joy of killing, bent on tasting human flesh. My old people said, 'Watch out when you see those uglies coming!'"

The other headmen all laughed, out of habit, at the *cacique*'s joke. As I translated, the admiral smiled, but very lightly. He liked it that our Taíno had their longtime enemies and made much of it to the king and queen. I myself always thought Bayamo and other *caciques* who said such to the admiral exaggerated their old enemies' cruelties. However, it appeared Bayamo had someone else's cruelty in mind.

"The giant seagulls that carry you across the ocean, your garments and sand-skin, these things I have heard of," Bayamo continued. "Our brother-cousins from *Cacique* Baracoa's villages, over the mountains on our northern coast, they told us about you. Many things were told when we met them at our common *areito*, the dance for Yucahuguama Bagua Maórocoti. They even said you came from the skyworld and could fly away. They also said that when you left, you took ten of their people, those you put in a cave hole in your floating house."

Columbus stood up with a bound as I translated the words. Again, he interrupted.

"All people are lost without the knowledge of Christ. Those taken are better because of it."

"He is agitated," I said in Taíno, trying to bridge the minds and minimize the impact of his eruption. "He is a great captain but he is not well."

The admiral spoke hurriedly. "The light of the Lord has now come to your lands, headman. Innocence cannot save you from eternal torture. The word of God is in your ear now and only the Holy Doctrine will capacitate your people to enter the Kingdom of Heaven..."

Bayamo began to talk for himself. I stopped listening to Columbus, who predicated for another full minute, and listened to Bayamo.

"I have a question of yourself, great lord—are you *caniba* that your giant seagulls eat Taíno people?" Bayamo asked. "Are you a cousin of thigh-eaters who kidnap our people? I ask the question: Are you good or are you bad? Because if you are bad to my people, you will go to that hell you have mentioned. If you believe every man answers for his deeds into death, then you will not harm those who do not harm you, or you will certainly go to that fire place of hell."

Having said that, the *cacique* sat down and the admiral stopped in midsentence. The silence left behind by the sound of Bayamo's voice seemed to dumbfound him.

I translated the *cacique*'s words then and did not tone down the directness, seeking to maximize the impact. But the admiral had regained his composure. He was not Admiral of the Ocean Sea, Christ-bearer, and grand navigator to be without the capability for an answer.

"Tell him again," the admiral said, looking to his own captains and twirling his finger to signify a closure to the parley, "that the people taken are meant to serve us and in return are instructed in the true faith of our Catholic kings."

I translated this as gently as I could. However, the precision for terms of bartering in our language made obvious the faults of the admiral's proposition.

The old men of Bayamo understood and did not like the admiral's reasoning. "What if we don't want to be taught?" one asked. "Why that place of burning?" another one asked. "Why is that necessary?"

An old man who was gnarled and had not aged gracefully, like Bayamo, stepped into the circle in front of the *cacique*. He looked to a line of elder women, mostly sisters and aunts in Bayamo's line, standing together behind the seated line of men. The women all had a rearing-back look, fixing wary eyes on the admiral. The old-timer raised his palm and pointed toward the women with his open hand. "Be careful," he said. "When you counsel your *cacique*, be careful of the hair-faces."

I translated bluntly again, and the admiral smiled bitterly. "He should fear us more," he said plainly to no one. It was not meant for translation.

The old man had stopped. Now Macaca, the village chief, joined him and they went to stand by a tree. I noticed the old man wore a thin belt of caracol shells around his hips and held a small gourd in his hand. Now he took a plug of rolled leaves from the gourd and put it in his mouth. I could tell he was a medicine man, a *behike*, and that, like his *cacique*, Bayamo, there was no fear in him.

The *cacique*, Bayamo, stood again.

"Tell my words to the Guamíquina," the *cacique* said, and I stood by him to hear him better.

"The fire is sacred to us," the *cacique* said. "We talk with our sacred fire. In fire we think not of death but of life. As for the Spirit World, as I said, our grandparents await us there."

The *cacique* himself nodded at the admiral, but warily.

Again, I translated his words and, again, the admiral was taken aback. Momentarily, his face looked flush and his eyes darted about.

"We are going now," he announced, standing, though with a slight wobble. He stared at the *cacique*, who stared back. "The fire is good," the old *cacique* said. I translated. The admiral stared at him. "Tell him that fire burns," he said.

Then the curse was pronounced upon him.

The gnarled old man, the *behike* of Bayamo standing by the women's council, cleared his nose and throat, then coughed into his left palm. Cupping the thick snot with his right hand, he walked between the fire and the admiral, suddenly showing the gob directly to the admiral. "With this I will teach you humility," he whispered harshly, in Taíno. "The door to your dreams, I close." The admiral turned quickly to face him and our soldiers stepped up too.

The old man had no fear in him at all, his palm and fingers slicing through space at the admiral. "Hell is in your dreams if you, a far-seeing man, commit the deeds that are in your mind," he said.

A soldier drew his sword, sensing the old man's hostility.

"Don't quarrel here," the admiral told the soldier.

With the growing sense of threat, the admiral regained his composure. He felt the men of Bayamo might overcome our small troop of not quite twenty. "Our business is over here," he said and ordered Captain Herrera to organize the troop. The soldiers and sailors surrounded the admiral, and as we began to walk, he asked what the old man had said at the end.

"He said to watch your dreams," I said. "It was a kind of farewell gesture."

The *guanguayo* had power, I knew, particularly for Bayamo's people. *Behike* men like the gnarled old-timer meant everything they said. For myself, I knew they would not attack us under the circumstances, and indeed they lit resin torches and thick, rolled tobaccos and led us down to the shore, singing once again. They carried dozens of baskets full of foods for the ships. But the admiral had been shown a *guanguayo*, *cohoba* medicine, teacher of our people, veil of water between the worlds. Don Christopherens moved stridingly, in measured long steps, but even so, walking to the boats he stumbled several times. Later, climbing on ship, he tripped and had to hang by an elbow from a net while sailors hauled him on board.

We sailed on for many more weeks during this journey, the admiral intent on proving Cuba a peninsula of the mainland. The weeks dragged on and fewer and fewer of his officers believed him. Twice, out of spite, I reminded him of the words of Bayamo's young chief on the island nature of the Cuba. He had me flogged the second time—five swift ones from the many-tailed whip. For that I cursed him myself and intoned the *guanguayo* of the dark over him as we sailed for long weeks among the islands. And it happened that as the weeks rolled on, he slept less and less, and I believe that special curse, which he now and forever carried from the people of Bayamanacoel, blocked the doors between his waking and dreaming selves. Truly, the navigation was difficult through the channels of the smaller islands and the admiral became extremely nervous. Finally he got sick and brittle. And for weeks, in feverish deliriums, he exclaimed how much the queen would like it that the Indians believed in a heaven and a hell, evidence to push the enterprise of their Christianization. "For the use of their labor," he half sang sometimes, "we will bring them the true Faith!"

I would add, good friar, that from hearing these ravings (which later became law), Cúneo must have picked up the reference to Heaven and Hell, as he helped nurse the admiral during that voyage.

May 1, 1532

FIFTEEN. *HARD TO EXPLAIN OUR INDIAN RELIGION, EVEN TO A GOOD FRIAR.*

Don Bartolomé read my pages of the admiral's meeting with Bayamo. He shook his head at me. "Cúneo mentioned nothing about a warning or curse. In fact, he said that the *cacique* wanted to go with the admiral to visit Castile. He said the admiral had gone ashore to hear Mass when the *cacique* approached him. And that he was very happy when the admiral mentioned that he would help the Taíno against raids by Kwaibs."

"No," I said. "What got the admiral that time was how clear the *cacique* and his *behikes* were about the fate of our Taíno people."

"It would seem so, from your pages."

"I was there. I saw it. The admiral was fashioning the idea of the *encomienda*."

"Yes, I admit that. Your perception on Indian servitude being exchanged or requested for Christianization, that is a very good, Dieguillo. And you remember that from the meeting with *Cacique* Bayamo?"

"Oh, yes. He said that even then. And Bayamo knew what it meant. We all did. Even I, as dense as I can be, I finally understood they meant to own us forever. All of us were to be their *naboria*, or worse, their complete slaves…"

"A great sadness you must have known."

"Indeed, but for that little revenge of the *guanguayo*, which I confess, Father, lifted my Taíno spirit."

"That's witchcraft, Dieguillo. You would persist otherwise?"

"Father, please, trust my character, which you have known. There is no devil in it. The *cohoba* was at the center of our minds. It was the veil of water for us, it was the passageway between this world in our hands and the one of our memories, in our dreams."

"You still believe in that, Dieguillo? And you, a baptized Christian, and so knowledgeable in our sacraments?"

"This is what I mean. Even now, the Christian owns everything. Even you, the best of Christians, would choke my little space. Let me have a moment with this. Or would thou call the Inquisition on me for explaining my people's beliefs?"

"Very well. I try to understand you. Proceed and forgive me."

"Understand, they were angered. And they did have a power. In our way. Now, let me finish, Father. Don't start again. Because they

did curse him, directly. And never again would he be as certain. He
began losing his way then, after his encounter with Bayamo. By the
time we arrived on ship, he looked graven. It was our old medicine,
good friar. It was one connection that we Taíno had, a power that
existed here even before your word of the Christ and the Supreme
God with no mother who begot a man-son with no father. You see,
even in that, ours was an opposite way. Our Supreme Being, Yucahuguama, had spirit mother but no fathers, no grandfathers."

"You help yourself not with these fancy notions."

"Let me tell you, Father. Because, it does not deny your way. It
is opposite, yet it is also true. Our *behikes* used to say, the opposite of
everything is also true. What would you say to that thought?"

"Perhaps if you could just answer my question, Dieguillo. I
don't want to get lost in too much detail. The thing is: did the *cacique*
believe in Heaven and Hell?"

I shook my head.

"But do you not see the importance. It makes your people nearly
Christians, even before hearing the gospel. We can argue that the
Indian can reach Christ directly, through the clergy, without need of
overseers and masters."

I have grown used to his thick-headedness. The friar's cause
before the Spanish court has lingered for twenty years to little avail.
Our people, those who are not in active rebellion or who, like me,
have received special dispositions, have remained miserable slaves—
killed and raped, cut at will. No, I do not care to prove that our
people were like Christians before the coming of the first Iberians.

We were not a perfect people; I only look in the mirror to prove
that. But, I know the truth of what was. So, in my poor health, as I
am become nearly a dried up man, my family lost and my heart on
the ground, I no longer need to please anyone. I respect the friar,
yes, and I am obliged for the many gestures he has had with me, but
what I saw and heard I know and remember.

"He did not mean Heaven and Hell, as you say it," I told him.
"Bayamo used the admiral's own words to warn him to stop stealing
our people. Good friar, our world here was very different. We did
not just talk of the Spirit World as an afterdeath; it was not a place
faraway. We could walk in and out of it, our ancestors danced with
us, even as we lived."

"Don't speak of pagan things," he snapped at me. "I won't
allow it in my presence."

That was his precise response, and at that moment I felt a nausea from this greasy-smelling, thick-headed Spaniard. Truly, sometimes I wish to *macanear* this priest, smash his head like pineapple.

I stared out my window for a long while. The friar assumed I was in meditation and scribbled away at my desk, copying selected paragraphs from my manuscript. I don't like to displease him. I know we need him, and, in fact, I respect him very much. Presently, he wiped his pen, folded his papers, and stood up to go.

"You should confess yourself soon, my son," he advised as I lowered my head to receive his blessing.

May 2, 1532

Sixteen. *Enriquillo's conditions and vigilance.*

He came again in the afternoon.

Father Las Casas is dark for a Spaniard. He had the cowpox as a child, in Seville, and it scarred him. His nose and face are long and he is thin but for a bulge at his belly, like the *mahá* snake after swallowing one of our tree muskrats. He sat on a three-legged stool next to my cot and, as always when excitation takes hold, the bulge of his stomach wiggled. His torso truly resembled the *mahá* with a meal still living in his guts.

"Enriquillo is much the topic again at the government house," he said. "They are obsessed with pacifying him. Another delegation has gone already to king's court about it, even as I would go."

Enriquillo himself will not parley anymore with officials on the island, as the troops here have tried to sniff out his hidden camps while pretending peace. Once, shortly after taking to the bush, we met at the ranch of friends. He told me: "On our island all are thieves and liars. If the king is just, as they say, he cannot know what is going on."

Another time, I was sent to him by the governor general, Don Diego Colón, son of the admiral, with a partial offer of amnesty. Then, Enriquillo would not let the Castilian official with me within four leagues of his camp. Even I, who once saved his life, did not visit the main camp myself, though he did greet me properly with a feast at the edge of the Lake of the Encomendador. There I met Ciguayo, his allied chief, as well as the one called Romero.

"Vigilance guides my every step," Enriquillo told me then. "I trust not a one of them but the good friar, and even he I would hang if I had to."

I acknowledged that the good friar and some others among the Dominicans and the Franciscan priests were indeed trustworthy, but advised him equally. "Learn from the fate of your fathers," I told him. "The Castilians are masters of treachery."

"The king might capitulate now because their campaign to ensnare Enriquillo has absolutely collapsed," Father Las Casas said today. Again, he told the truth. The island government has fielded ten experienced captains to root out Enriquillo's camps, causing him no end of trouble. Enriquillo retaliated by destroying the *encomiendas* of the specific captains sent against him, burning several and forcing the other four captains to stay close to their haciendas. I can say without any exaggeration that in the past year, Enriquillo's prestige among our own people and among the Africans here has grown. Since the failure of the last campaign against him, many Spaniards are talking about returning to Spain or migrating to the mainland.

"I am informed the king reasons he risks loosing the island if he does not interfere," said the good friar.

"Enriquillo has never asked for more than the king's intercession," I said.

"Intercession in freeing all Indians," he said. "Fray Remigio, when he saw Enrique in the mountains, reports that among the *cacique*'s demands is an end to the *encomienda* system in Española."

"He is a true hero," I said, though I suspected the good friar was exaggerating. "It concerns me, Father, that he may ask for too much. All-out war from the king will come next if a peace is not reached."

"Not at all," the good friar said. "He must do no less than demand an end to the *encomienda*."

SEVENTEEN. *THE BIBLE GUIDES LAS CASAS.*

Tonight, one day later, Father Las Casas stopped by again. He leaves in the morning for the monastery at La Plata, where meetings to discuss the Enriquillo negotiations are being held. Together we read a chapter from the Old Testament, one in Ecclesiastes where the good book tells of misbegotten gifts, how property and goods obtained immorally are not acceptable to God. He read it out loud after we read it silently and then reminded me of how he released his own Indians in Cuba, in 1514, to begin his work on our behalf.

"The truth of our Bible guided me, Dieguillo," he said. "The good book I have given you before. Read it. As you know how to, read the gospels. Read Matthew. This you must do every day, on three occasions. Empty your head of the things of *behikes*. The Devil can control that. You may not think so because you have a love for your people's things, this is natural. But beware that the Devil can control them and you will fall prey. He will damage your soul. He will steal you from us. Fill your head with Christ, my son, Dieguillo."

"Yes, Father," I agreed, though I hate to be spoken to in this manner. As I wrote before, I am past the point where I have to please anyone. But I said, "It is only that my memories exist, Father."

Before he left, Don Bartolomé took my hand. "Resist bad memories," he said, forcefully. "Think of our Holy Trinity, think of our Christ on the cross."

Folio II

LOSING EVERYTHING

Thinking of the elders, after my father's death... First sight of the admiral, first greetings... Meeting Rodrigo and the Castilians, my turn of life, and leaving Guanahaní, my home... Report to the elders and pubescence... The old cahobaneros' *vision on the night and morning of my short farewell... Last words, for a while... Enriquillo sends his messengers, request of* cohoba *peace pact... A message and words of instruction... A letter to Las Casas... Useful Castilian things, paper, horses... News from Cuba, death of the Guamax rebellion... Remembering the elder Guamax... Jiqui, a warrior, escapes... Sojourn in Cuba, along the northern coast, searching for the Great Khan, the curse of Old Guamax, days of early reverence... Embassy to Camagüey... Caréy's doubts and my certainty... Meeting Baigua, a ni-Taíno of Camagüeybax, the old ladies call for* jaguajiguatu*... Torres reports to the admiral, Cuba as mainland... Cibanakán, my father-uncle, comes on board... The old man Guamax, his curse on the admiral... Life on board and learning Castilian ways; out from Punta Maisí, at one with the admiral... Ignoring the feelings of my own people... Getting closer to the admiral... Even closer to the admiral... The good friar returns from La Plata... Preparations for his trip to court in Spain... Jiqui is captured... The execution of Jiqui... Cruelty is the province of the covered men... Pressing "the Indian cause" could get Enriquillo killed... Las Casas wants to end the* encomienda; *I want Enriquillo to live... A message for Catalina Diaz, midwife and friend... A note for later writing... Reminding Las Casas of Enriquillo's first cause... The townsmen have reasons for peace... Dissimulated romancing with Catalina... Catalina believes in both us and them... The meeting ends... Good-bye to Las Casas, ashamed of my writing... Breeding my mare... Survival in humility... Our ways were respectful of reproductive powers... I do not really feel shame... Indians* *tell Columbus to look elsewhere for women and gold... Diving for yellowtail with Rodrigo and Caréy... Cibanakán faces the hammerhead, impressing the sailors... A generosity of parrots... Guacanagari, first Taíno sachem to meet Columbus... Columbus's ship* Santa Maria *sinks on Christmas night... Guacanagari saves the day and provides the first gold... The white man's industry is as impressive as his hunger for gold is immense... They get more gold from us... Spirit men remain behind as we sail off from Fort Navidad...* Escarmiento—*the fight to leave a warning... Sailing out to the great water...*

June 14, 1532

Eighteen. *Thinking of the elders, after my father's death.*

The good friar has been gone ten weeks. Twice in early May he was roughed up while walking through the square. Fortunately, Obispo Cisneros, as well as the governor general, have pressed him into the negotiating embassy soon to discuss the parley with Enriquillo. For now, he is in study at the convent on La Plata, a much more quiet place than this hellhole of Santo Domingo. Despite our difficulties, on his departure he asked me to continue writing. I took the opportunity to request more paper, but, in all sincerity, I grew weary of the writing. It is only today, after an afternoon watching fluff clouds dancing through a light blue sky, that the wish to speak arises. The sky carries messages, as does now my pen.

Today I ask my pen: how can I pass on what I have in me but by telling the truth about myself? And I say, reader of my words: do not think my story more important than another; it is just the only one I know how to tell. Those among my people of whom I have some knowledge, those remarkable among my *guaxeri* countrymen, I will try to recount here so that their names and their deeds might be known.

From a young age I liked the feel of words; always I could make pictures from my eyes to your eyes. I remember *cohoba* nights that were full of that prettiness, when the chiefs described their old stories, told of our past, how everything came alive again, again and again, our village dreaming in unison, sometimes for days after an *areito*, sharing their words. I would pick up turns of phrases then and repeat them for my mother, her sisters, and for the boys in my group. I was well named as a boy, and often elders would remind me that my being was truly *guaikán*—keeping ahold of things, bringing them back with my head, as the *guaikán* fish will, never letting go. The elders liked me for that willingness of mine to repeat their old things, and in my village I was one of the youngest men ever to participate in the *cohoba*.

After my father's death, the old men cried for me. They loved me very much but they revered my father. Many would call me to their backs, as my father had, during the first round of *cohoba* songs, this for eight nights, and I would, out of my need, hug the backs of my two great-uncles, as they sang those beautiful songs I have not heard in forty years. During that time, my father was already drying in the sun, on the small bluff on a hidden bay called the Cove of the

Dead. Night after night, following the double snort of the barrel
sticks, chief after chief would talk and talk and they would cry to
my father for me, telling me again and again his four great deeds,
always recalling how our Taíno people came to be. The old people
told many stories and sang many songs. Mind full of words that I
have, I never picked up the songs, but I do remember the stories.
I feel grateful for this time with my elders, when they showed me
their love and gentility.

After the nights of *cohoba*, ceremonies full of emotion, the old
men prescribed for me eight days of rest. I slept and slept again and
I was well fed, in the spiritual way, by my mother and two aunts.
Twice in my dreams my father visited, once walking the rim of the
sky, another time sitting with me, leaving me clear minded, physi-
cally recovered from his death and its condolences. Not two moons
later, when the three giant seagulls of our destiny appeared on the
horizon and bearded men covered with cloth first came to our shore,
it was natural the old-timers would send for me, requesting that I
take a group of men to meet them. They could not tell me if I would
be in danger or not, they said, because they had never heard of such a
thing as the giant seagulls described to them very early that morning.

NINETEEN. *FIRST SIGHT OF THE ADMIRAL, FIRST GREETINGS.*

More than thirty young men, most older than me, followed me
down to the shore. I admit I would not call myself a brave man. I
have survived enough perils, have been wounded, both in incidents
of war and as a slave, but seldom have I dared physical danger if it
could be avoided.

We walked toward the shore up and down sand dunes formed
behind a line of brush. Gaining height on a dune, I could see the
giant gulls were actually huge sails, and men climbed atop long poles
while others pulled on long *bejucos* (ropes) from below. I motioned
our men to lay low. "They are something like people," I whispered,
as they too preened over the top. Crouching now, we spread across
the dune and made our way to the brush line, very near the shore.

Maybe an hour went by and presently we saw three small boats
emerge, one from each of the bigger ones. Two men paddled each
boat, though, curiously, they sat backward as they rowed their vessels around the bigger caravels. Rope nets were lowered, and other
men descended onto the rowboats. Presently I remember seeing the

admiral for the first time, at the rudder of the larger rowboat, his slender back arched like a Ciguayo bow and that magnificent head of flaming red hair.

Closer and closer their boats came and then thudded home on our sands. They were not sixty feet away from me. I watched the admiral directly as his eyes scanned the beach from the boat and saw us. Immediately two men went to assist him but he ignored them, jumping to the dry sand. All the covered men often looked his way, as if to check their actions. He held a long staff, banners blowing in the breeze.

I am forced to say that the man they later called *el descubridor* vibrated at that moment. I saw it myself how he held that staff high, such as our own *behikes* might, and intoned a voice for the skies, how he spoke to the heavens in a harsh but resonant language.

We were all stupefied, eyes wide like seashells. "How does one greet such beings," Xiquí, my brother-uncle, whispered in my ear. "Where could they be from?" Cibanakán, my father-uncle, responded: "Perhaps the sky. Perhaps they have arrived from the sky."

It was the admiral I watched. He was totally clothed, along with six of the others. The rest of them, bare chested, wore short pants and on their heads, red stocking caps. One man in particular was very hairy, large tufts covering even his shoulders, and all their faces, except the admiral's, were hairy, too. As he finished his oration, the admiral handed the staff to two sailors, who jammed it solidly into the sand and then took positions around him, weapons at the ready, as he walked toward our brush.

I must admit something now that still confuses me. As I looked at Don Christopherens the first time, I felt a great glow of warmth, a happiness inside my chest I have never been able to explain, and it drew me out of the brush and onto the beach, pulling a dozen of my men. As if enchanted, we walked toward the admiral, directly and without fear. Suddenly the two sailor-soldiers brandished swords, running forward menacingly and we all jumped back. They ran toward us, and we ran, a powerful terror in the calves. Then they stopped. We stopped and I could hear laughter from them. I spotted their red-haired chief, their Guamíquina, whose palm was raised toward us and the soldiers now dropped behind him. So I walked toward him again, and he came toward us with palm raised as my father-uncle, Cibanakán, properly walked before me to pronounce our people's formal greetings.

June 19, 1532

TWENTY. *MEETING RODRIGO AND THE CASTILIANS, MY TURN OF LIFE, AND LEAVING GUANAHANÍ, MY HOME.*

Today, I think of young Rodrigo, and it is indeed a very proper day to think of my dear friend. One of my two twins, born on this day, named Heart of Earth in Taíno, I named Rodrigo in the Castilian, after my good friend. Among the Castilians, I value no one higher than Rodrigo, not even the good friar.

Rodrigo was there on the first day, a young man of fourteen years, kind and soft-spoken. I remember how he came to me, a hawk's bell dangling from his fingers. "*Para ti*," he said. I responded, "*Taíno-ti.*" And though we spoke different languages, we understood each other immediately. I took the hawk's bell, a great wonder as it would ring when shaken, rather as one of our *maracas*, or gourd rattles, but with a high, metallic pitch. Then I cast around to spot one of our men who held a *jaba*, or cord sack, full of fruit. I pulled several *guayabas* and returned the gift, indicating with my hand that he should crack it open and eat. Rodrigo followed my instructions, whereupon Don Christopherens came toward us and I also offered him a *guayaba*, cracking it quickly to expose the sweet part as he extended his hand.

Thus we stared at each other and smiled. More hawk's bells were offered, more *guayabas* and other fruits were returned. Three men from a coastal village situated around the bend of the cove now joined us. Don Christopherens spoke out loud, locking into our eyes as we crowded around him. Several times Don Christopherens raised his arms toward the sky. Then my father-uncle, Cibanakán, also spoke. "The spirit men of the skies have arrived," he said. "Tell your communities to bring them food and other gifts." Turning toward me, he said: "We must go and tell our elders. They have instructions for such a day. Where these men come from there is no death. We may be very lucky today."

By instinct I now looked for Rodrigo. I spotted him by the sea brush, urinating. "*Para-ti,*" I called to him in our new language. "Guaikán I am, and I go now." He looked at me in wonder, then pointed to my chest and his ear. "*Nombre?*" he asked, and though I did not know the word, I understood him. I said again, "Guaikán, Guaikán." He repeated: "Guaikán." Now he said: "Rodrigo." I said: "Oligo." He smiled and nodded his head to affirm my word. He put his hand on my shoulder. "*Amigo,*" he said. "Oligo," I said. We laughed.

I looked him up and down. He was all covered with clothes, even his feet were crisscrossed with rope. I caught myself staring, and he read my thoughts, grabbing his groin and pointing at mine, again nodding. I laughed, as I had noticed him passing his waters. Our men, of course, went naked. My *yuán* was free. Everybody, both our men and theirs, stared a lot that day. Then, while some remained to stare a while longer, most of us walked away.

Twenty-one. *Report to the elders and pubescence.*

That night we had a meeting at Old Guanahaní village. Everyone came, even the oldest of grandmothers, crowding around the *cohoba* elders as the inhaling mixture was prepared and the men lined up at the edge of the trees, inserting vomiting spatulas to cleanse themselves.

The old-man title holder of Guanahaní, whom we called the Guanahabax, chose the opening song. Appropriately the song told of Deminán and his three brothers—the dual set of spiritual twins— our spirit forebears who traveled the clouds, enduring adventures and creating the sea and islands of our world. Yucahuguama Bagua Maórocoti, Grand Spirit of our sustaining world, was thanked for the creation of the mother of the four brothers, but it was the four, the doers and makers, who were intoned. Significantly, the *cohoba* was not touched to start. The old men had opted to inhale only after the reports of the greeting on the beach.

Everyone was so greatly excited, waiting in anticipation for the reports, even the food was neglected. The song ended and there was a pause in expectation of what we called, in our ceremonies, the little feast, which did not materialize, as the women food preparers and all their assistants were intent on listening. Aware of the anticipation, the nimble Cibanakán stood, holding his open palm out to the group.

"I will start," he said, as the old men nodded, "to tell of the wondrous day. A Guamíquina has come, I saw today. A Guamíquina and three vessels, full of hair-faced, covered beings. Nothing I have ever seen prepares us for this day. Yet I saw them smile, mostly. They traded gifts with us, and everything they have is wonderful, just wonderfully wonderful. Small rattles, made of *guanin*, pretty, pretty noise. A cloth so smooth I wanted to eat it. A long sharp edge, so sharp and heavy my cousin Turey was cut in his hand as he tried to hold it."

Everyone looked at Turey, who stared shyly at the ground. A bandage made by the red-haired Guamíquina himself was wrapped around his hand. His old mother, next to him, took the hand and raised it up and Turey smiled.

"The Guamíquina," Cibanakán continued. "He speaks to the sky, and his men murmur with him as he intones orations. It sounded nice, very nice. His hair is red like the inside of a parrot's wing and wavy like the sea. And he has a very quick way to strike fire. Amazing. A click on a click and there is flame, red like his hair."

Something wonderful and strange was happening to me. The sun was low on the horizon, one of those beautiful afternoons, red on the water, red in the sky, the end of a day so full of wonder I could hardly sit. Yet the elders had opened the meeting and it was impolite to fidget. So I sat still though my heart raced, flapping in my chest like a fish in a canoe, and a warming glow covered my abdomen, my inner thighs, my *yúan*.

I want to be truthful, so much I have seen and endured since that evening. But that night, after Cibanakán's story was discussed and digested, as my turn came to speak, a great honor considering my age, I felt myself stiffen as I stood and in my chest a heat, an excitement I had never imagined could happen.

I write this because it truthfully happened to me. That very day and moment, my body came of age. Everything in my heart and body and in my mind expanded at once. As we are used to among my people, especially in those days, I paid no attention to my nudity, I only felt my heart expand. "I love the new people," I said quite forcefully. "They are of the sky and of the earth, too. They have wonderful things, and as my father-uncle relates, they think of fire and flame erupts." I admit that I rhapsodized, and with an eloquence I did not know I contained: words of love, excitement, reverence, and wonder flowing from my delirious heart. I recalled the oldest of *areitos*, how they expressed the beauty of our ways, how happy must be the far-gone spirits (everyone, of course, thought of my father), how the wonder of Deminán and his creative hand must have guided the covered men here, how lucky we were. They are friendly, I kept repeating, there is nothing to fear, they smile and bring wonderful gifts, and we should love them so very, very much.

Old Guanahabax finally raised his finger, as if to slow me down, and though mildly embarrased, I could only smile. I felt so certain of my words and could see the people's eyes were sparked.

When I sat down again, my body had relaxed but I felt incredibly alive, as if for the first time I was experiencing the world.

After me, others wanted to describe the day, but Guanahabax cut off the speaking. "We have heard the essence," he said. "Now the old men will smoke. Then we will snort our *cohoba* powders. The spirits will advise us. Of one thing I am certain: the life of our people has changed forever."

Only the old men sat in Guanahabax's circle that night. His women assistants brought them the big and small *hícara*, the big one brimming with the sacred powder. Twice before I had snorted with them, gestures of sympathy with a bereaved boy. Both times I simply slept and afterward remembered nothing. Guanahabax told me this was proper, as I was not yet a man. "Their messages will come later, in your dreams. All at once, at your age, it would kill you."

Sleep took me in a hammock in my mother's thatch-roofed *bohío* as I surrendered my hold to the sounds of the *cohoba*; the wheezing and coughing, the snorting and the whacking, the loud wails and thick laughter, and the early morning songs blending with my dreamtime thoughts. Once, turning over, I caught glimpse of my mother's gentle face, gazing enchantedly at me. I was the light of my mother's eye. All of my young life, except for times at sea with my father, I always took sleep in my mother's gaze. She would often sing me an old mothers' oration. It went: "I sense your breathing with my eyes, I collect the motion of the distant waves into my ears; blowing my loving breath toward you, I wish you into your dreamtime peacefully, with all the love of a mother's heart."

The sun was just up when the urge to piss awoke me. I walked to the brush with such a terribly stiff *yuán* I could not force it down to piss. I had to nearly hunch over on all fours to direct my spray at the ground.

Some eyes were already watching, and company soon gathered to greet the day. But I was sleepy and dived into my hammock once more, barely clutching in my mind the scene of sleeping *cohoba* elders, curled up as babies where they had fallen around the fire. A man who had seen me take the dog stance in my morning predicament walked by. "Sleep, puppy," he teased me.

And I slept. And thus it happened for me, a dream I have always remembered. I dreamed a rare woman, light of hair and complexion, not on a hammock but on long, white sheets on a wooden bed, in a cool, moist room, my *yuán* growing like a *yucca*, old in my spirit and young in body, and she held me tightly in her sand-colored arms in a place very far away, a place I had to go to, a place of huge caves, and her body so appealing, and suddenly the dissolving sensation, full release, sounds and smells of *yucca* starch popping from the squeezing of the *yucca massa* in the long squeezing net, what they called the *çibucán*.

I woke up sticky with the generational water. It was my first time, and I understood that the time of turning had come upon me. It was not very strange, as many times I heard the men talk, my brother-cousins and father-uncles, about how it happened to them. Since we come from the earth, they always said, it is a natural thing. I felt not strange thus that morning, but oddly weakened, yet agreeable with myself.

Nearby, a group of women did squeeze *yucca* juice out of a *çibucán*. I could smell its starch. My mother was among them. She had eight women working in rhythm. As always, I felt respectful of the sight of women's hands squeezing out the *yucca*'s sticky white sap, powerfully poisonous yet a great preserver of food. Across the *batéy*, at the ceremonial fire, several elders huddled, whispering with a sharpness that pulled my gut. I washed at the stream and joined them.

Twenty-two. *The old cahobaneros' vision on the night and morning of my short farewell.*

"I found confusion in our Spirit World, nothing was familiar to me, except the wailing of an owl. I heard loud, sharp noises, booming like thunder. I heard strange voices, a strange loud singing, and I heard Taínos, men and women, with voices like ours, also wailing," old man Garaboy reported. He was a hearer. In the *cohoba* this was his gift. Often he heard old songs, orations, even conversations. Spirit frogs would talk to him, and snakes and, not long before this day, a grandfather *manatí*.

Sometimes Garaboy returned from his *cohoba* journey with great stories. All day he could tell us tales. He would say: "Only the fish do not speak; only their world is silent." Then he would tell about the pregnant *manatí* who fooled two hungry sharks, "just a few suns ago," and he would say exactly where this had occurred, on what reef of what cove of our little island. We were always enchanted by his recounting of events from the lives of our relatives in the sea and the forest. "The secret of the pregnant *manatí*," he would wink. "She stiffens like a log in the water. You see, sharks are so easily fooled."

The fish would not talk to Garaboy, so he would not hunt them. He accepted their meat, though sparingly, as gift food from men he had raised, such as my father. But he would not kill a being to whom he could not apologize in the *cohoba*. Even in my excitement to go, I felt a great love for old Garaboy, who was so keen and could blend into trees like a flat brown vine.

Sad this morning, old Garaboy spoke little this day of a *cohoba* night full of wailing. I struggled to appreciate what he had said, holding back my impatience to arrive at the beach, to greet again my friend Rodrigo, the Guamíquina, and their many wonderful things. Old man Garaboy looked truly old to me, flabby thin legs that he now crossed, dropping like a sack upon his haunches.

Axeax was even older than Garaboy. He reported his experience next. "I saw a large number of grandfathers," Axeax said. He as a seer in the *cohoba*. "They were crying, too. They scratched at themselves. One stood forward and put on a garment, covering his arms. Then, he put on a garment that covered his legs. I was walking closer when suddenly this man pulled his garments off and threw them at me. He was young but very bony. He had scabs on his face and puss came out of his eyes..." Axeax stopped in midsentence. He cried softly. Lifting an old, wispy hand, he showed that it trembled. "There was much fear in my dream."

Axeax went on at length, repeating his *cohoba* dream. What he related would scare anyone, and it touched me to my spine, but I couldn't find a place for it in my reflecting heart, vibrating on that special day with my great recent discoveries, both on the beach and in my hammock. Yes, I was impatient with the old men's stories. They seemed remote compared with a run to the beach and the sight of the marvelous mountain canoes and the many shapes and colors the covered men gave their things. I loved my father's uncles and grandfathers but I felt at that moment I would have them forever.

Guanahabax felt my impatience and called me to him. "You must stay with us a while this morning," he told me, much to my dismay. Guanahabax knew me the best. He had backed up my mother's midwife when I was born, praying with my father for strength of my mother's and me over several nights. Guanahabax grasped my knee firmly, and as always I felt a great deal of love from him. He called on Ayragüex, the third old man who had snuffed *cohoba* the previous night.

Ayragüex smiled as he pushed a staff into the earth to help himself up before casting it aside. His thin, muscular forearm was extended into a fist, which now made a slow lizzard-head bobbing motion. "I saw them fucking," he said. "The new men have white haunches, hairy white haunches. They are spirits, I am certain. But they are the fuckingest spirits," he said in a chuckle that stopped suddenly. "It rains until it stops. They fall on our women like logs. My advice is: nothing sacred should take place today." Ayragüex stopped talking and stood silently a few moments. I lost concentration until I found him staring at my eyes. He moved slightly toward me, whispering with a smile, "Guaikán." Ayragüex stepped up to my ear. He was serious now. "I saw the white-skinned woman who touched you last night. She walked through our camp and straight to your hammock."

Guanahabax leaned into me with his shoulder and put his cheek on mine. Even old man Garaboy moved toward me. They looked determined to do something with me, but Guanahabax spoke. "There are twelve suns of ceremony prescribed for you in the *cohoba*, if you are to ready yourself. But we can see you are impatient to go. You have all of your life ahead but not twelve days to give us, not even one."

Guanahabax asked me to wait for him while he went inside his *bohío*.

I was embarrassed by their directness, even mildly scared, but their knowledge of my intimacy was actually reassuring. I was overwhelmed with the need to run, fast as a panicked iguana, to the shore. Mind you, I had yet no sentiment that I would leave with the Castilians. I didn't know then that I was never to see my uncles again.

Guanahabax came out of his *bohío*. He put a bundle in my hand, my father's *cohoba* bundle. "Take this bundle of *cohoba*, your own spatula and rattle, your gourd and two-pronged sniffer, your feather fans. Remember that *cohoba* loves you. As you walk, do not turn back. We will speak to your mother and her house. Take our hearts with you. Take our dreams."

A sadness passed over me as I percieved the farewell, but Guanahabax yanked my shoulders and pointed me toward the beach. "No more speeches," he said. "We know there is no more time for Guaikán."

As I walked away, he said: "Go, young son of our beloved Cohobanax. Don't look back. Go to your destiny with the covered men."

I ran and ran and ran, bundle in my *macoutí* pack. At the beach, relieved to find the ships still there, I noticed little of what was going on. With Rodrigo's help, I snuck in early and hid out in the hole of the Guamíquina's ship. Not only men now, but many of our young women were on the beach, swimming and paddling canoes. By midafternoon, half of the Castilian sailors were swimming naked, too. I could see them through a porthole near the food bins, where Rodrigo had found me a cubbyhole. As Ayragüex said, the "fuckingest spirits." The Castilians kidnapped six of our Guanahaní people as they left our shores the next morning, but I was not one of them. Drunk with the pull of adventure, I pressured Rodrigo to hide me—and was the first to go in. No one else can I blame for my captivity, not even Rodrigo. I captured my own self that day, choosing to cast my lot with the Castilians. It was the last free decision of my life, as I now consider it.

August 2, 1552

TWENTY-THREE. *LAST WORDS, FOR A WHILE.*

It now astounds me that I have written the above scenes. I reread these papers, and I feel the urge to vomit. I don't want to remember so much, by Yucahuguama, by Itiba, my mother, it hurts. I remember the heart behind the heart now. Once I catch the thread, the words come pouring out. I relive the moments, I see them pass before me, and always, afterward, I cry. Truly, these should be my last words for a while.

August 3, 1532

TWENTY-FOUR. *ENRIQUILLO SENDS HIS MESSENGERS, REQUEST OF* COHOBA *PEACE PACT.*

How quickly things change. But twenty-four hours ago I forsook to write further. Now the heart thumps. That was yesterday morning. Today I am a different man, a man with a mission.

It was yesterday, after vespers, I left the convent. Reading these papers in the morning, prior to the last entry, uncontrollable pain wracked me all day. Searching solitude, even death, I walked past the convent gate. I wished to die because I never saw my people again ... because I have seen the destruction of the world ... because I should not have lived so long.

Looking a *mánso*, a pacified Indian, attired in white shirt and knee-length pants with my straw hat on, I walked without notice down the lane that passes the convent, cut across a field of grazing cattle, and entered woods that immediately begin the climb up a ridge. The ridge overlooks the ocean and the road to the eastern sugar plantations.

Reaching the top, I sat and rested. My leg ached at the knee so I could hardly open my eyes. All the way I ignored it, punished it, heart and vision darkened deep. Now, I read the clouds a while. They came in soft puffs and calmed me some. "My grandfathers," I said to the directions, "tell me why I should be alive. Why am I not dead, too?" The pain behind my knee I cherished, happy to offer the simple gift of my suffering, though small compared to so much I have seen.

In this island of Española, where finally my days are counted, how many have I not seen die? Thousands upon thousands so there is not one in ten, nay, not one in fifty, not one in one hundred, of what there were the first time I came here with the admiral. Yes, I hate what I have seen. But I will not falter now; today I do want to tell it, because a young man named Enriquillo is now at large, imposing his own Taíno liberty, and his act gives me life.

TWENTY-FIVE. *A MESSAGE AND WORDS OF INSTRUCTION.*

Late evening found me walking toward the docks. The grog of the sailors called me now that the sun was gone. God knows what I might have done had any old sailor from the days of early voyages spotted me and offered his bottle. Deadly with hurricane eye, I was ready to kill, forthrightly, as I have done twice before, take the Castilian unawares and cut him deep. Such were my thoughts at that moment, and timid as I am, and bent, yet capable I was of so much damage, as I carried my good fishing knife and much *Ya*, our spirit of movement.

But feeling the ocean close by, I naturally approached it, leaving aside thoughts of the sailors' cantina and walking to sit on a rock by the waves. There I sat a while, until the laughter of whores and drunkards disturbed me. Walking west along the shore, leaving the buildings in the dark and searching the line of the sea, I suddenly heard men walking in the sand behind me.

"*Taíno-ti, Cacique Guaikán, tao caraya guatiao,*" one said in Taíno. "Good evening, brother Taíno. For you we have been looking."

They were young men of Enriquillo. I answered them in our language, and they came forward. "Guarocuya sends us," the speaker of the two said, using Enriquillo's Taíno name.

I spoke at length with the young ambassador and his fellow runner. The speaker had a long report for me, a speech he had memorized from Enriquillo himself. I was to listen carefully, as they would return to the bush immediately after delivering the speech. As with all our Taíno memorized messages, he spoke in sections.

The young warrior started:

"Guarocuya said to tell you that these are his words, though out of my mouth they will come now.

"Our *cacique* trusts you and respects you, he said. Your gesture with him at the Massacre of Anacaona's Banquet he remembers, and your many favors over the years."

He paused briefly. "Now I continue," he said.

"A hard campaign has been fought, the *cacique* of Bahuruku wants you to know. Guided by our own *mánsos* in the dry season five years ago, Captain San Miguel sniffed out three of our larger camps and destroyed them, killing many of our people. Since then we are much weakened to defend against other major assaults."

He paused again.

"That time, Guarocuya struck back. We moved deeper into the mountains, to the last good places of retreat. Then did our *cacique* send our warriors to the enemies' ranches. When the rains started, we followed the Castilian captain home. That night, we burned his ranch and strangled three men who had done the guiding. Many horses we took, many cattle, and weapons, and tools. His bulls and boars, rams and stallions we decapitated and left to rot. All progenitors he lost. He and three other such captains all lost their ranches, one by one, destroyed for their aggressions against our free villages."

He paused again briefly.

"Guarocuya said to tell Guaikán these important words: We are strong, more than two hundred tested warriors. But camps and even villages we must sustain, and war raids we must withstand as well. A coordinated campaign, such as the emperor king could unleash, which might all at once send eight or ten fighting squads against our territory, would be difficult to avoid or repel. We depend on surprise and the willingness to punish our tormentors. Thus, we are feared. But, we are mortally threatened if the king's armies should turn fully against our cause."

He paused again. I counted twelve waves lapping at the shore before he continued.

"Many tongues make talk about an embassy from the emperor king. Our *cacique* asks—is it only words to roll up time? Or is there sincerity in the wish for peace?

"The king must learn, he says, that the *cacique* is man of peace. The king should know the *cacique* is a man of his word when he says that he would serve the king, who is a fair man, but not the local *cajayas*, the man-shark captains of the islands. The *cacique* is a firm man. Negotiations will not happen with island authorities, only with the king's embassy.

"I carry these instructions: Five conditions are required, according to our *cacique*. The safety of the *cacique* and his chiefs and captains must be the king's first words. The location of our camps and villages he must not inquire. Pardons must be granted for all his people, the Africans among our people included. Good planting land could be offered for a settlement and gentle peace. Then, if need be, the *cacique* should police his own. He wants men among his captains deputized, so arms they can hold legally."

The young envoy stopped. He walked a few steps into the oncoming waves, and I followed him. The three of us stood in the water, caressed to our ankles by the waves. He meant to say by that: the sea mother cleans my next words. It is an old way of ours.

"Now about the good friar, our great protector, and your convent companion all these years, the robed man called Las Casas. I am to tell you that he has been in touch, but with disorienting effect. He sends messages suggesting sites for a parley, as such. He sends lists of conditions and offers to come and put up a Mass, give us the many sacraments. This is not good. Messengers open paths that soldiers follow. And, for certain, all parleys with Castile at this moment are death traps. So, the good friar is to know: deciding where to meet is for later and the site will be chosen by the *cacique*. And our *cacique*, who watches over all of us, he says the friar might go to the king's court. This would be good. Yes, indeed, he should go and report for us, nay, demand for us that a king's embassy is required for a true parley to take place."

Enriquillo's messenger-warrior stopped abruptly, a final pause. He had a very alert face, proud of his memory.

"As for you, uncle, the *cacique* asks Guaikán to walk our mountain way. The steps to peace must be reviewed, he said, and you are requested to remember the time of Guarionex, the way of his peace pact. You are to remember how your old father-in-law conducted his alliance-making *areito* ceremony. In three new moons, we will come to guide you. And you must let us know when you are ready."

His message delivered, the young Taíno lowered his head to receive my warmest blessing, then they both ran off without another sound.

August 7, 1532

TWENTY-SIX. *A LETTER TO LAS CASAS.*

I sent a letter today to Father Las Casas. It went with young Silverio, who took my mare. He rides to the monastery at Puerto de Plata to deliver my letter himself. I wrote to the good friar of my contact with "the boy held in the bosom." This is a reference to how I held the boy Enriquillo during the Massacre of Anacaona's Banquet, carrying him to the only safe spot, in Commander Ovando's own tent. His older brother I led by the hand, but a soldier drunk on blood killed him with a sword. I then held the four-year-old Enriquillo to my chest, protecting him as I ran. This story Father Las Casas knows from me.

TWENTY-SEVEN. *USEFUL CASTILIAN THINGS, PAPER, HORSES.*

I marvel at the usefulness of paper to carry the message. Young Silverio was brought up *manso*. I would not wish to trust his memory, much less his ability to hold a secret. The mare, too, is a Castilian thing. I have had her six years. She was a gift of Don Diego, the admiral's real son, upon his return to Castile, after his time as governor of the island. "For your service to my father, during the early years," he told me.

My little mare is a sturdy brown Andalusian and has a white face. I call her Cariblanca, in Castilian. I don't ride her much, for the old leg wound just under my left buttock can be irritated and sends horrendous burning pains down to my knee and up my back. I rent Cariblanca to messengers and occasionally to travelers, but only if they treat her gently.

August 10, 1552

TWENTY-EIGHT. *NEWS FROM CUBA, DEATH OF THE GUAMAX REBELLION.*

Sad news this week from Cuba. The rebel *cacique* Guamax is dead. A Castilian patrol attacked his main *rancho*, near Baracoa, on the northeast coast of that island. But the *cacique* died of an old wound weeks before they broke up his main camp. When they rode into his clearing, Guamax's widows were placing his bones in a funerary basket. They say that for all the running and killing, the two women continued their work until captured inside their *bohío*.

I heard a version of this story at the dock today from Juan Martín de Ayala, an old sailor of Hojeda's, who now commands his own caravel. He sailed in from Santiago with a boat full of slaves, including some of Guamax's captured men. Ayala said the skull of Guamax was stuck on a spike at the entrance to the village of Baracoa, as were the severed heads of his chiefs and principal women.

"Our good Carlito [King Charles V] lost his patience with that one," he told a group that gathered later to hear his story at the Pensión Marinera. "Guamax burned our forts to the ground at Sancti Espiritus and Puerto Principe. But the king sent new troops, well-heeled with harquebus. Damn Indian kindling were blasted with shot all over that plain. What's left of them are deep in the forest, still running."

I could not call Ayala publicly on his equivocation, so now with pen and paper I will set the record straight. Guamax of Baracoa went to war in 1522, less than two years after Enriquillo took to the bush here in Española. Three years ago, in August of '29, he nearly defeated the Castilians in Cuba, burning down several towns, as Ayala recounted, though Ayala made it sound as if it happened recently. It wasn't the king's soldiers that got Guamax either. It was the smallpox, which got to his large war camps as they moved through the mountains to lay siege on Baracoa and Santiago. They say his warriors and women advisors dropped all around him by the hundreds, nine out of ten of them, over the course of but a few days. Guamax's campaign was destroyed by the pox—that son-of-a-bad-mother disease. Guamax himself was heartbroken by the death that seemed to come in the wind, though his surviving warriors continued to raid. Beyond the raiders, too, other *guaxeris* just moved away to the high ground or back to the coast.

Ayala and the group discussed Enriquillo next, but I eased away for fear that Ayala or another one from those times of

Commander Ovando might remember my actions of then. I owe my peace of recent years to an instinct for evasiveness. Sailors, soldiers, and *encomendado* peons, even some *patrones*, all hang together in Santo Domingo. They pray at the same church and frequent the same whorehouse. In both, they damn to Hell the good friar, of whom I am a devoted servant, and in both they relish in descriptions of punishments for Enriquillo and his men. Tonight, they will be toasting the death of Guamax.

TWENTY-NINE. *REMEMBERING THE ELDER GUAMAX.*

I never met the younger Guamax, though once, at the beginning, I was in his territory of Baracoa. It was with the admiral, not many days after leaving Guanahaní in the ship *Santa Maria.* That time, forty years ago, the Guamax who died of recent would have been a crawling boy. Another Guamax, an elder *cacique*, held the title then. We did meet him and, now that I think of it, in a rather peculiar way. While I await the good friar's return, I will take up that tale next, how I sailed to Cuba with Don Christopherens after hiding on his ship at Guanahaní, what we did and how we later arrived at this island of La Española, or, in our language, Haiti-Bohío, or Quisqueya, the big mountain country.

THIRTY. *JIQUI, A WARRIOR, ESCAPES.*

Word today that one of Guamax's warriors among the prisoners sold by Ayala has escaped. His name is Jiqui. He jumped a guard, then bolted for the woods. Two *cuadrillas* with mastiff hounds took up his trail early this morning.

August 11, 1532

THIRTY-ONE. *SOJOURN IN CUBA, ALONG THE NORTHERN COAST, SEARCHING FOR THE GREAT KHAN, THE CURSE OF OLD GUAMAX, DAYS OF EARLY REVERENCE.*

I still remember the Yunque of Baracoa, in Cuba—that wide, flat mountaintop that can be seen from the bay. I remember the Cuban coast, how thick and lush it was, how big the island felt that first time. The admiral was very excited. A land more beautiful human eyes have never seen, he said—words I heard him repeat many times later in his discourses with nobles, bishops, and powerful merchants of Spain.

In Cuba, we from Guanahaní knew Cubanakán, a *cacique* from the center of the island whose fishermen made the journey once a year to Guanahaní. And once a year our own men (my father and uncle Cibanakán among them) would reciprocate, visiting also on their shores. They traded woven *jenikén* ropes produced from maguey grass at Cubanakán for our good fish catchers, hookers, and spearpoints, made from the shells on our great caracol beach on the northeast corner of Guanahaní. The great hemp twine woven in Cuba from tall savanna grass was much requested, particularly their very fine long ropes that made the best reinforcers of fishing nets. In good weather, it took the men six days to make the trip to Cubanakán; in my memory, they never lost anybody during those journeys.

Many times, encouraged by Rodrigo, I mentioned that *cacique*'s name, Cubanakán, and the island's name, Cuba, to Don Christopherens, who wrote it down and had his secretary, Escobedo, write it down, comparing the writing to my sounds. Caréy, a man of my village and a cousin of mine, was forced on board as we left Guanahaní. He was a *guaxeri* in the fishing with my father, and he guided Captain Pinzón and the admiral. Caréy had made the trip to Cuba for several years.

We sailed into Cuban waters on the thirteenth sun after leaving Guanahaní, my home. By the Castilian calendar it was October 27, 1492. I remember it rained all night, drops pounding flat on the decks like frogs falling from trees; the ships hove to, drifting in the bay, and all night rain fell. The morning sky was so clean, the eyes drank from it, the kind of day my elders would have deemed "swept by Coatrisquie," the spirit *cemi* who, in our Taíno mind, ruled the heavy rains and assisted in the cleansing of the skies.

Cuba was different from the beginning. The coastal *caciques* were not forthcoming. As he had done on four other islands, the admiral landed the ship's boats. He liked the many small and large bays and took boats himself up the wide rivers, but for days the local Taínos fled from him. This excited him even more, as I could tell he had grown tired of the hundreds of people that had swarmed his ships in the smaller islands. When he found two very large and well-carved traveling canoes, one with capacity for more than 150 people, the admiral paced and paced and many times showed me, Caréy, and others a bracelet and a chain made of fine gold. Rodrigo's agile hand signals interpreted for us: the Guamíquina wants to see other great *guamíquinas*. The Guamíquina wants to see them wear their gold.

Thirty-two. *Embassy to Camagüey.*

Caréy, though he was resentful of his captivity, which I yet was not, offered to guide the admiral to Cubanakan's shore. However, the admiral declined to sail that far west on the Cuban coast and at a bay near Puerto de Mares, around November 3, decided to send an embassy inland. Both Caréy and I were chosen to go on this mission, to assist Luis de Torres, a converted Jew, and Rodrigo de Jerez (a former crusader, not my young friend Rodrigo Gallego), as they led us inland.

Only years later did I learn the true reason for our trip inland to Camagüey, but I will state it now. Cubanakán, our *cacique* brother from Cuba, the great *caimán* island, was mistaken by the admiral for the Great Khan, a chief of the Mongol people in the land of China, with whom he wanted to trade. Nothing else interested him that day. The few Indians who had pulled up to trade, mostly canoes from the islands we had passed, he now ignored. "*Caona, caona*," (gold, gold) he repeated to the dozens of canoes that had now caught up with us. Or he would say "*Turey, turey*," another Taíno word, meaning "sky," which he at first believed meant also "gold." But the *lucayo* Taínos offered no *caona*, only cotton nets, food, fresh water, and fruit.

The search for the Great Khan had been planned in Spain and the admiral ceremoniously entrusted Torres, the poor converted Jew, with gold samples and types of spices and a letter for the Mongol from King Ferdinand and Queen Isabel. "I am convinced we are on the mainland, near the cities of Zayto and Quinsay, a hundred leagues more or less distant from one or the other," he told Torres. Instructing him to take no more than five days, the admiral said: "Find the Great Khan."

Thirty-three. *Caréy's doubts and my certainty.*

Caréy plotted to leave the Castilian ships as soon as possible. He hoped at Cubanakán's village he could slip away to the forest and later make his way home. But now we were barely on the edge of old Camagüeybax's territories, with whom we had no particular relations. "What do the Castilians want, really?" he despaired, as we walked thin trails south over the coastal hills into Camagüeybax's plains. "They want to see Cubanakán but won't sail west; now he sends us here. I do not like this, Guaikán, and I don't understand what you find so curious about them."

It was true. I was still intrigued. I still liked the Castilians. What's more, I believed them to be men-spirits, sent by the Spirit of Spirits, first Creator, Yayá, first grandfather to us, in the Castilians' words, "Our Father, Who Art In Heaven." The Castilians, I felt, were wonderfully superior and clever, and anything they said was bound to be right.

"They have done you no harm, Caréy," I argued with my *guaxeri*.

"They take me against my wish," he responded.

"Don't worry so much," I remember I told him. "We'll all return home safely."

Thirty-four. *Meeting Baigua, a ni-Taíno of Camagüeybax, the old ladies call for* jaguajiguatu.

We walked two days, joined by crowds that reached into hundreds, arriving at the village of a secondary *cacique*, one of old Camagüeybax's ni-Taínos, by the name of Baigua. Baigua's village was the largest by far that we had encountered, and he had been preparing a feast for a day before we arrived. Along the way we had seen small clusters of *bohíos*, maybe four or five together, but Baigua's *yukaieke* was made up of more than fifty *bohíos*, probably a thousand people, and it was where Torres finally decided to stop.

Baigua greeted us with great courtesy, in the open Taíno style. He was the sweetest of *caciques*, only middle-aged but doted upon by grandchildren and old ladies and appeared to have not a care in the world. He had a kind face that stood out for its gentility, even among Taíno. All around his large *yukaieke*, as far as you could see on a valley of rolling hills, there were planted *conucos* (raised beds) of *yucca*, *ñames*, potatoes, and other types of tubers, much *maize*, pineapple, herbs, and edible grasses, all interwoven with fruit stands of *guayaba, mamey, caimitu, anon, guanabana* and other fruit and nut trees. The *batéy*, or main plaza, had been recently swept clean. Around the *cacique*'s central fire, several Taíno ceremonial seats, *duhos*, were arranged for us.

After exchanging gifts and eating (they served much meat of the delicious *yaguasa*, the Cuban tame duck), Caréy let me do the talking. As I was by then accustomed, I conveyed my heart-felt views that the covered men were truly special, sacred, that they had come from the sky in huge canoes with wings like seagulls, and they could guide a ship against the wind. Instructed by Torres, I inquired after the Great Khan. They responded that they knew him but that he lived farther west. I asked, too, after *caona, gua-nin*, or any other metal, of which they claimed to have none. Torres was obviously disappointed with the second answer but gratified by the first, although, certainly, they only referred to Cubanakán, the Cuban *cacique* and not the Mongol ruler. Torres showed profound relief when informed that the walk to the "Khan's" towns would take more than fifteen suns, as it excused him from continuing the exploration. With an air of great solemnity, he announced we would spend the night at Baigua's village and return to ship at first light.

Poor Torres, whom I came to like very much, was a sensitive man, and could read and speak several languages. On ship, he was under constant suspicion for any lapse in his Catholicism, as he was a first-generation converted Jew. He compensated for his fate with a very light foot and quiet demeanor. Among the Castilian men, he was one of the very few who had abstained from lying with our women, making it a point to be at the admiral's side at all prayers, although he was a man of fine features and liked to gaze nonetheless.

The speeches over, Baigua had large gourds and clay pots of water brought in for us to wash. All the men first and then some of the women smoked large tobaccos. Torres was curious about their smoking and they showed him the tobacco plant, our *coxibá*, sacred offering to the Creator Beings and all *cemis*. The older women, who liked the tone of his words, then whispered to the *cacique* a request that I had anticipated by the manner of our reception. Our own Guanahaní people had the same custom whenever, quite infre-quently, visitors arrived at our villages.

"*Jaguajiguatu*," the old women whispered, meaning, literally, "fire in the loins," an old right of the housemothers to mix into the village life, and their bloodlines, the potential contributions of men visitors. Baigua, gentle chief, was delighted, even enthusiastic at the request, which I explained to Torres as best I could as the older matrons ushered out their selected young women, who commenced to wash our feet and, in Torres and Jerez's case, to pull and half-carry them into a large *bohío* scented by a thick floor of freshly cut pine boughs. I never looked in on them all night, but I laughed with Caréy at Torres's ever-weakening admonitions as the women swarmed him and silently urged from him his traveler's duty to our Taíno grandmothers, ever watchful for their future generations. Jerez, the old slaving hog, needed little prodding, though he was a peculiarly ugly man, short of leg and long of torso, little neck. "What good seeds you'll get from Torres, you are losing with the no-neck," Caréy kidded, in his sardonic way, and we laughed with Baigua's old woman *bohío*-mother, who said, "We've never seen anything like those two. They look strong. I truly hope some of the girls will take."

August 14, 1532

THIRTY-FIVE. *Torres reports to the admiral, Cuba as mainland.*

Not ten minutes back from Baigua's village, while waiting for Don Christopherens to complete his meal service, Jerez had told the *Santa Maria*'s pilot, Sancho Ruiz, about his night of abandonment. Torres's participation in the overnight adventure came out in the telling, and, immediately, several sailors made the most of it. Three men in particular, bad characters from the ship's home port of Palos, made a song about "the converso's hiccups of ecstasy, how the old rabbi must have left something for him to use, after all."

Finished his dinner, the admiral came out of his cabin. "Torres!" he called. Torres was before him as the sound faded.

"Did you meet officials of the Khan?"

"No, my captain."

"What did you see?"

"A very large village, sir, very large."

"And the people?"

"About the same as our guides, sir."

"No slipper shoes, head casks?"

"No, sir, they were all naked as their mothers birthed them, sir."

"The way Torres likes them!" someone shouted, from starboard, causing some laughter. It was Clavijo, a nasty character who was one of three convicted criminals granted clemency to join the expedition.

The admiral would have none of it. "*Alguacil!*" he ordered, quieting everyone. "Arrest that man."

Clavijo was led down the hatch by three men.

Don Christopherens asked next about geography and the Great Khan's whereabouts. "It's a long way," Torres told him. "Two weeks' journey, maybe more."

"Maybe much more," said the admiral. "Probably many leagues, wouldn't you say?"

"Probably, my captain."

"I am convinced this is mainland," Columbus said then. He had learned that *Cuba* means "large territory, well planted" in the Taíno language. "We are at the southern extensions of the Great Khan's dominions," he pronounced. "Cuba of the Great Khan."

Torres, of course, knew better, as did Jerez. Caréy and I had even told the admiral, several times, that Cuba can be rounded by canoe. It is a very large land, indeed, but an island. The admiral never quite conceded the point. He kept insisting it a mainland, and, as I have written earlier, insisted on it completely on the second voyage, as we traveled Cuba's long southern coast.

THIRTY-SIX. *CIBANAKÁN, MY FATHER-UNCLE, COMES ON BOARD.*

We sailed east from there, as the admiral decided to round the cape of Cuba at Maisí Point and strike southward to explore the large island of Bohío, now Santo Domingo or Española. Touching points on the coast of Cuba, the ships took in sixteen more Taínos, chosen from the crowds to be kept as captives. This new action disconcerted me. Like our own Guanahaní people taken by force, the Cuban Taínos were selected for their strength and physical appeal. Of our own men, three had already slipped overboard at appropriate moments, hitching rides on the canoes of friends. In one case, the rescuer was none other than my uncle, Cibanakán, who later returned to get me, talked at length with me, and ended up staying. Cibanakán being at the time some forty-five years of age, we made up a story about his wife and children being aboard in order to obtain the admiral's permission. "He should work with you to keep our captives calm," he told me.

THIRTY-SEVEN. *THE OLD MAN GUAMAX, HIS CURSE ON THE ADMIRAL.*

I promised to tell about the elder Guamax, the old *cacique* of Baracoa who held the name at the time of the first voyage. I believe he was related to the other great *cacique* of eastern Cuba, Bayamo, whom we met in the first of my pages.

As the Taíno men and women taken on the Cuban coast numbered twenty or more, the story of the takings spread on land. From coastal promontories, signals of smoke that told of seaborne danger (very black smoke from the resin of the *jobo* tree) could be seen, and for days after a taking, shore after shore turned up empty. Once our sailors, ashore to search an empty village, found the skull and bones of a grandfather, as customary, resting in a basket near the ceiling of a tall *bohío*. After the admiral inspected it and both Caréy and I explained its significance, the sailors played with it on the beach, in sight of his hidden relatives, who watched from a hill out of reach. Two sailors tossed the skull around by its long hair, finally discarding it into a river. I remember being sickened by their game. This occurred, I am reasonably certain, near the end of November 1492. I had been with the admiral six weeks.

On December 3, as I count suns in my memory, after three days of absolutely contrary wind, the caravels moved east along the coast of northern Cuba, entering small coves as they made their way out of the Baracoa area. That day, as we took final pass of a wide river mouth, the local ni-Taínos, despite their fear of the Castilians, perceived us to be leaving and several dozen canoes came out. One of our captive Indians, taken days before, pointed out to me an old man, tall and thin and wrinkled, wearing a wide headdress, who directed his young paddlers round the stern of the *Santa Maria*, where Columbus was standing. "*Taíno-ti, Guamax-cacique*," I heard a captive man say, next to me, by way of greeting the old man.

The old man who at that time held the title of Guamax pointed directly at the admiral, took off his headdress, and slipped into the water. Kicking against the current, he rubbed himself with sudsy *digo* herbs all through his body and, when cleansed, swam to just below the admiral, who looked down at him. Guamax spoke.

"Here I am in the water, a fish in my river. Understand that my words are clean, like my body in this river. Now hear me: my sons and daughters you have in your canoe. I know they have been swallowed. You are to let them go. Those are my children who belong to me. Now, you must respond."

The admiral understood not a word, and I wasn't much help. I was getting so I could understand many of their Castilian words, and I could interpret their wishes for my people, but old Guamax's speech shocked me dumb, speaking as it did to the only secret doubt in my immense (at that moment) reverence for the Castilians.

"Respond!" the *cacique* demanded, when the admiral, who perceived the scolding tone, stared at him.

"Do not take them, for I will curse the Guamíquina his red hairs," old man Guamax said. "You will be crazy among our trees and rocks. You will die a fool."

At this moment, another man taken from us, Manaya, yelled back from the boat. "You will be the one that dies, if you threaten the Guamíquina." Manaya took up a sword and a crossbow, showing them to old man Guamax, who was still in the water. "This big knife, it slices a tree in half. This arrow shooter will pierce the clouds. Don't make the sky-men angry, old *cacique*."

Old man Guamax made no answer, swimming slowly away and slipping into his canoe. From the canoe, he stared at the stern of the *Santa Maria*, then ordered his men to paddle away. I remember Caréy standing next to me on the *Santa Maria*. He was more trusted now and had the run of the ship after his trek into Camagüey. Increasingly fearful to be lost among Taíno angered at the loss of their relatives, he had not dared run away. At that moment, like many times during those first days, Caréy took my hand in friendship and held it tightly. "I hope you are right about our getting home safely," he would say.

August 17, 1552

THIRTY-EIGHT. *LIFE ON BOARD AND LEARNING CASTILIAN WAYS; OUT FROM PUNTA MAISÍ, AT ONE WITH THE ADMIRAL.*

All us shipboard Indians, as the admiral had begun to call our people, were closely watched. No more escapes were to occur. We were to sail to Haiti, the Bohío, a major Taíno homeland. Among the captives, and even myself, an intense fear arose, moving now as we were to lands beyond our usual realms. We knew of the Bohío land, of course, as we knew of Borikén and Xamaica and all the many islands in our fecund sea, but we feared the added distance from our home. A fearful outcry now began among three women from the village of Quiribe, across my island from Old Guanahaní village. I had not known them much before this trip and had kept my distance as they were harsh to strangers, even people from the same island. They wailed about not going home, about their fate to be eaten by our legendary enemies, the Kwaib "thigh-eaters/heart-eaters," who were known to raid our coasts.

By day's end, the outcry affected the men so that everyone was sad and crying, and the leaders took the job of imploring for their liberty, for canoes to make the trip home, for guarantees of return. "We are heading for the heart-eaters' islands, the thigh-eaters. Bad men who eat other men," our people claimed to the admiral. I seconded them, though timidly, but the admiral had made up his mind that we would sail across the (windward) passage to Bohío, and there was nothing to be done.

THIRTY-NINE. *IGNORING THE FEELINGS OF MY OWN PEOPLE.*

I am chagrined now, asking myself what kept me hopeful about the covered men. Yes, many of us were taken forcefully, I would think, but no one has been harmed. It did not seem so to me, in any case, and, then too, I was busy every moment on board. I kept with young Rodrigo and often Caréy joined us. Among our men, six were learning ship's ropes, and they included three from Guanahaní—Cibanakán, Caréy, and myself. Those of us on the ropes, or, in my case, often at the admiral's side with Rodrigo, had little contact, for days at a time, with the huddled group in the holds that came on top to sit together in the sun and, without task, could only wonder on their fate.

FORTY. *GETTING CLOSER TO THE ADMIRAL.*

Rodrigo was grommet, cabin boy, and, with my arrival, Castilian instructor. He taught me the daily routines, their timings and sequences and commands, and he taught me to never disturb the admiral's habits of prayer and dining, so that his mood of fatherly disposition toward young men could be sustained. That was the knack of the early Don Christopherens, I think, that fooled my tender heart. Going through his day, particularly when busy with stellar calculations and the making of knots and sea leagues, the admiral could be a most happy and pleasing personality. The day he saw me keep the *ampolleta*, the hourglass, for the first time, he worked at his desk, writing and yet noticing my attentiveness. Rodrigo had set me up to the task of turning over the glass as the sand ran out every half hour. I took the shift from three to seven in the afternoon and was strictly attentive throughout my eight spins. "Excellent," Don Christopherens commended, talking to Rodrigo, who came to relieve me. "Your friend has a sharp eye."

Don Christopherens liked chickpeas and lentils in soups, took to using our *cassabe* bread almost immediately (for mopping his bowl). Near shore, he was always pleased to get a basket of fresh fruit, which I would get for him at least once a day, and often he would have me sit and look out his small porthole as he wrote and napped, then wrote again. Not often, but occasionally during those first days, in the reverie of long tropical afternoons, he would pull my head to his shoulder and sing me a song or recite a poem or tell a story from the Bible. He never reached that kind of intimacy with Rodrigo, who served him zealously, but would with me, which endeared me to his instinct and his ways and added to my considerable resolution at the time to champion the covered men's mission to my people.

Even Caréy and Cibanakán, who followed my lead but wearied of the experience, could not help admire the admiral his way with a ship or any kind of boat. Although we helped him a great deal to navigate our channels and reefs, it was always uncanny the way he could immediately size up shoals and sandbanks, depths and winds, and the landfall ahead. Long after I too knew the Castilians were no good at all, I would be startled awake by the certainty of his directions, that quality he had to pull my heart, to make me want to cling to his back. That certainty of his word during storms and

dangerous moments at sea later carried me through my second season of servile stupor with the Castilians; truly, he projected a God
of Destiny, a naming God, his suddenly distant eyes focused on the
far point of the horizon.

FORTY-ONE. *EVEN CLOSER TO THE ADMIRAL.*

Don Christopherens was quiet and dignified in his personal habits
but sharp and severe in his judgments. Everything about him was
steeped in his Catholic faith and devotion. The day's prayers, from
the morning Salve Regina to the vespers and its Ave Maria, he led
or watched over with intense attention. He missed nothing about
a religious service, how it was done, who was respectful, penitent,
or devout. Once, I saw a man laugh quietly during a Mass. Next
day, he was worked mercilessly until he dropped and then set in
the filthy bilboes of the ship for a fortnight. Don Christopherens
was somber in correcting waywardness among Christian men and
would always turn them over to the worst elements among the marshal's enforcers for severe punishments.

Those days of his first voyage to our sea, as I knew the admiral,
he never changed his mind about anything. He was easy to follow
and obey. Much beyond the other covered men, Don Christopherens gathered into himself a mystical force that seemed to carry him.
All the early Castilian captains were hardheaded and single-minded
and would strike out at long distances; they were tough and mean
and powerful. But one had to see the admiral in his long mantle
on deck in a misty evening to also see his *goeiz*, his personal spirit,
surrounding him. Even his keenness for gold, which later turned to
virulence and *sinrazón*, was during those days a detached inquiry,
something investigated but not coveted. At least, that was his style.
Often he delighted in odd little things, like cakes of wax, the smells
of particular woods, or the counting of each and every number of
flocks of parrots or doves, such as the ones that can blacken out the
sun of our islands for days sometimes.

More than a *guaxeri*, our word for the common independent
man, even among the totally uncommon covered men, he was Guamíquina, principal man, the flaming hair who commanded everything, spirit driven by spirit. I would look at him standing among
his officers and think: spirit man, what wonders you must behold.
Take me to your spirit lands, take me to your shining cities of gold.

I want to see, I want to hear and smell your world. This, as we sailed to the island of Santo Domingo for the first time. It didn't yet touch me how the disturbance of my people had already begun. The repercussions were slight yet compared to my wonder. And I was clever, too, easily adept at projecting devotion at his Mass. His crucifix I revered and learned to genuflect before. I quickly learned the Ave Maria, with Rodrigo's tutoring. One afternoon, standing at the admiral's side, I joined the singing. He touched my shoulder proudly, for all the men on ship to see, and next morning he gave me a long shirt to wear. A few times, with the shirt hanging to my knees (as did his cape on him), I found myself standing on the poop deck, in the posture and position of the admiral, watching the horizon. I could feel the shape and power of his spirit at those times, a "greeting of *goeizs*," as the old people would say, calming a longing in my own soul.

August 29, 1532

FORTY-TWO. *THE GOOD FRIAR RETURNS FROM LA PLATA.*

Father Las Casas came in last night. He rode my Cariblanca back to me, having sent young Silverio by ship with several letters to the mainland. The letters were to his Dominican friends in Mexico, who have appealed to the king on behalf of Enriquillo. The good friar is a hurricane of activity, his mind raging. I could tell by the state of my poor Cariblanca, girth swollen and head hanging low to the ground as he dismounted in the convent stable. "We must talk," he said, shouldering his own pack. "The final campaign begins."

FORTY-THREE. *PREPARATIONS FOR HIS TRIP TO COURT IN SPAIN.*

In my room, by candlelight, the good friar discoursed on his strategy to move court and king on Enriquillo's behalf. It was hours before he stopped reviewing the arguments and only then did he wonder about the message in my letter, "Something about a young boy," he said.

I reminded him about the Massacre of Anacaona's Banquet, how I carried the young Enriquillo. He smiled. Father Las Casas seldom smiles. "God bless you, my son. You did save his life."

But when I told him about the messengers Enriquillo had sent me, he was peeved. "I spent two months trying to contact him! Why did he not answer me?"

I said that Enriquillo could not afford too many contacts.

"Enrique is too independent," he said. "He must work with our groups. We must work together."

Father Las Casas reviewed his strategy. A friendly cardinal has the ear of the emperor king, who might consent to settle with Enriquillo. Las Casas feels now is the time to go and present the evidence of the *encomienda*'s horrible results and call to the king to settle the injustice once and for all.

"But I have to know what he is going to do," Las Casas complained. "Enriquillo must follow the required steps."

The good friar explained that in 1530, after meeting with the Spanish court and the emperor king himself, he had returned from Spain to a place in the mainland called Nicaragua, where he met with and delivered an ultimatum to Pizarro, new governor of the Peruvian lands. It was a royal decree by Emperor King Carlos V declaring the Peruvian Indians his vassals, not subject to slavery. Pizarro was shocked, the good friar said, and now all the colonists, from Peru to Nicaragua to Mexico, were of one mind in wishing death upon Las Casas.

"The good queen tried the same in 1502," I reminded him. "It made no difference."

"This king will impose himself, one way or the other. He wants this war here ended."

"The war, yes, but not the *encomienda*."

"Without pushing, nothing moves."

"At the cost of our young *cacique*'s head?"

Las Casas grimaced at me in exasperation.

"I can tell you now. Before I came this last time I was under siege all over the mainland. Pizarro told me on his way back to Peru: 'That is what I came here to do is subjugate Indians, work the mines, and clear the lands. If I put my sword to their throats, it is for that reason, or there is no reason.' Others said worse. They cursed me as an interloper and have given assassins orders to kill me. But this time it was the new governor of Hispaniola himself, Don Sebastian Ramirez de Fuenleal, who wrote to me from here, asking my involvement in the matter of Enriquillo. He has appointed *oidores*, or hearing judges. Now I can tell you, because the news of an impending embassy is fully known. Tomorrow, I will go meet with the *oidores*. We will start to set up the covenant and the particulars of the meeting."

All this information the good friar gained directly from the newly appointed island governor Sebastian Ramirez de Fuenleal. Word was, he said, King Carlos V would pursue a peace negotiation with Enriquillo. However, Enriquillo must agree to a time and a place, and the terms of his peace offer must be clear. He must give up his weapons and horses and accept a degree of justice against some of his men.

"We have them on the run this time," Las Casas said. "If the king will capitulate here, with Enrique, who has a pitiful band, think of what the royal proclamations could mean for the mainland. The *encomienda* could be ended here."

"I am of your group, Don Bartolomé," I reminded him. "But in the matter of Enriquillo, we each know our half."

This much smells: one of the *oidores* is Juan de Vadillo, a crony and, I think, relative of Pedro de Badillo, the lieutenant governor who had Enriquillo beaten and jailed when he petitioned his court against Valenzuela's attempted rape of Doña Mencia in 1519. That same Pedro de Badillo later commanded a troop of eighty men against Enriquillo, who trailed them around that hard sierra for two months, picking off Badillo's soldiers from ambush. They tell that Badillo got so mad he started to hack his own *mánsos* to death.

I trust not these Vadillos or Badillos who hang in with my old tormentor, Pero Lopez, as well as with the *cacique*'s old master, Andrés Valenzuela; all of them would relish Enriquillo's head. Neither do I trust the king. I am certain Enriquillo will be assassinated unless we are very careful. Don Bartolomé would save all Indians but sometimes is a bit careless about just one.

"Our rebel *cacique* requests a Taíno peace-pact ceremony at the negotiations," I said. "The way Guarionex used to do them, what we called the opening of hearts or exchange of hearts ceremony."

"Guarionex of La Vega, who was attacked by Bartolomé Colon around 1498?" Las Casas asked. "Who would remember that?"

I nodded, pointing to my own heart. Suddenly, he smiled kindly, again, a rare sight. Thus he recognizes my participation in the earliest days, prior to his own arrival here in 1502. He remembered that Guarionex was my *cacique* by law, as I married his sister Ceyba and lived in his village for more than a year prior to his sad demise, more than thirty years ago.

I told the good friar about Enriquillo's conditions. It also occurred to me that my old friend Rodrigo Gallego, now a captain of the court of Seville, might be assigned to the negotiations. Las Casas agreed to carry my letter to him; then, listening to me more carefully, the good friar nodded on all my suggestions for protecting Enriquillo. He understood that Enriquillo's life was at stake, that he might be assassinated, even as the king's ambassador might come to sit with him.

"Dieguillo," he said, and this is the part of this old priest that I truly love. "We are meant for this moment, you and me. We will gather a crew, all our best people and help Enriquillo win his freedom."

August 31, 1532

FORTY-FOUR. *JIQUI IS CAPTURED.*

Guamax's young warrior has been caught. Spanish hounds made short work of the chase and cornered the poor boy yesterday, near a swollen river. His name is Jiqui, same as one of my uncles I left behind at Guanahaní. They have him shackled outside the jail, next to the House of Contracts. His execution is set for two o'clock this afternoon.

FORTY-FIVE. *THE EXECUTION OF JIQUI.*

I write now by candlelight, at the end of a horrible day. This is the Heaven the Castilians have brought us.

After lunch, the good friar and two other monks accompanied me to the square. The heat was intense today. Nevertheless they wore their brown robes and I, too, was dressed, wearing a *mánso* hat low over my eyes.

Many people were out, including the town ladies and their children. Sailors, soldiers, peons, and town merchants crowded about half of the square. Two local *encomienda* farms brought all their Indians, more than two hundred men and women. The execution of Jiqui would be a lesson to them. The two groups sat idle for most of the afternoon, a rest day for their tired bodies, waiting for a torment dedicated to their minds.

Santo Domingo is a large town now. Two times ten thousand Spaniards, Indians, African Negroes, and mestizos live here. There are few "free Indians" like myself, but there are some. We are the ones with peculiar histories, given some refuge from the torment of the *encomienda* by the interest of high officials. In my case, it was Don Diego Colón himself, my namesake and actual son of the admiral, who freed me from all formal servitude in 1522. I am ever thankful to him for the act, which allowed me to recover a measure of my health and no doubt has prolonged my life until now.

The *encomienda* Indians are pitiful. I walked near to see them fully and recognized not a one from the old days. As always, they were thin, almost all. Several men had open sores from whip lashes and *planazos*, blows by flat saber. I saw only two children and no old people. They ate *cassabe* and fruit, packed in among themselves, and many slept in profound stupor before lining up to witness the prisoner's final torture.

Jiqui stabbed a guard in the leg when he made his getaway. That guard, leg bandaged, sat immediately behind the planted post, next to the jail, as two other guards brought Jiqui to the post. The *oidores* were out with a rather large group. The bishop was with them.

Everyone was asked to sit, except the farthest out. Oidor Suazo, who is to arrange the Enriquillo negotiations, gestured with his hand, and the sentence was read by the marshal.

"Punishment will be exact," said the marshal. "The crime was not merely escape. The heathen rebel cut a Christian. And why? So he could go join the devils in the hills. And why? So he could flee to kill and torture other Christians, wherever he may go."

For this persuasion of mind and for his aggression against an officer of God and king, the young cannibal would be: 1) cut across the back of the calves; 2) set upon by two mastiff dogs; 3) raised up above a fire and slowly roasted until dead.

This happened today. I write it now, only hours afterward, and I will tell it now if I must write all night. I saw the cruelty, one more time, and Las Casas was with me.

There was little in particular about Jiqui. He was young, short in stature, and sinewy. He did not look badly beaten and had treed himself before the dogs got to him. As per the formal Spanish custom, he was fed well before his execution. He was tied chest and face to the thick post, his arms hugging around it, but I could see his face. His eyes scanned the crowd. The post itself was of the *xikí* tree, a tough wood that will not burn once charred and hardened. Many poor Taínos have hugged that post before, but Jiqui was actually named after his death tree.

The wounded guard, whose name was Carrasco, got to do the cutting. Two men carried his chair to the back of the prisoner, and the marshal gave him a short razor-sharp dagger. Carrasco, a small, thin man with a goat's beard, held up the dagger and offered the Ave Maria. Then he thanked the marshal and the principal *oidor* for the privilege. Leaning over, he then poked the boy, Jiqui, in one buttock, getting a piece of the skin and slipping the dagger in a half inch. Jiqui groaned, then Carrasco's dagger scraped bone and he yelled aloud, "Aiiii!!!"

The crowd gasped, and the soldiers and sailors laughed. Among the guards, several laughed loudly. One yelled to the lined-up Indians, "Hear the devil yelp, you dogs!"

Carrasco looked up proudly. I could tell he was a nobody among the guards before this. Smiling, he raised the dagger to the guards, then put the point at Jiqui's anus. Jiqui gasped and the guards began to titter loudly, but the marshal barked at Carrasco to "Stay with the sentence." Dutifully, Carrasco cut the calves then, two deep slits across each, just under the knees. Blood began to flow. Finished with the calves, Carrasco took a stab at the thick of one calf, and Jiqui yelled again.

I wished he wouldn't yell. It cut into my heart. Searching the crowd, his eyes came to rest on me. I think he could tell I loved him. He was at the age I remembered my twin sons, how I have pictured them since I lost them. But I emphasize that I love all my Taíno-ti, even the ones who have betrayed me. I would kill anyone of them that threatened my Enriquillo, or the cause of our freedoms, but I still love them for being mine and I hold us all to be victims together.

Carrasco was carried away in his chair as two men with dogs on short leashes approached. Mastiffs of war, they sniffed blood excitedly and lunged for Jiqui's bloody calves. The handlers held the dogs, up on hind legs, inches away from the calves. I wished to yell my love to the boy but was silent. Next to me, I could tell the good friar was praying. At a signal from the marshal, the mastiffs were allowed close enough to lick the blood with their extended tongues, snarling up on hind feet. At a second signal, they tore in, one on each calf, tearing flesh in sharp bites as Jiqui yelled and yelled and yelled.

The dogs were yanked away when they bit into bone. The two balls of the calves were gone. Two men with hot irons burned into the cavities left by the mastiffs and Jiqui slumped as if dead, but his eyes stayed open. Jiqui was untied and lashed by wrist and ankles to a thick iron bar, which was propped between two Y poles with dry brush gathered underneath. He was washed with water, and as he did move his head, he was made to drink copious amounts of it. Then the fire was started.

All watched intently. Jiqui dangled by hands and feet six feet above the fire. His back blackening slowly, his hair singeing, and the horrible smell hung like a mist throughout the square. The sun grew intensely hot, and you could feel the heat of the fire itself. He groaned for two hours before he expired, but no one left the square. Many Indians, including myself, cried quietly for Jiqui as he burned, and among the women in the slave group I did hear the hummed refrains of our *areito* song of death, to accompany the separation of the *goeiz* from the body and the birth of the *opía*. Poor boy. How happy he might have been but for the existence of the Castilians on our lands!

I remember Hatuey, who was burned to death and did not utter a sound. I remember the groups of thirteen burned by Ovando after the Massacre of Anacaona's Banquet. Ovando, here on this island, and later Vasco Porcallo de Figueroa, in Cuba, burned us in groups of thirteen to celebrate the sacred thirteen of Christ and his twelve apostles.

Father Las Casas himself offered extreme unction to the dying young man. For once, there was no attempt to turn him away, although many in the crowd murmured as they recognized him, and someone did yell, "Leave the heathen his route to hell!" However, no one interfered as the guard himself did not. Suazo, the other *oidores*, and their group, waited for the termination of the rite and then approached the good friar. All nodded and greeted him, somberly but politely. Suazo invited the friar to walk with him a ways and Las Casas went with him. Following that group, Andrés Valenzuela and Pero Lopez, the former *encomenderos* of both Enriquillo and I, actually walked together. They stood back and watched as Suazo exchanged words with the good friar and led him away. Lopez's whole group had mean eyes. Several men in their company stood by Jiqui's charred cadaver for a while, one actually poking it with a stick.

FORTY-SIX. *CRUELTY IS THE PROVINCE OF THE COVERED MEN.*

The Christians, the Castilians, have been so cruel. I say, as a people, they have been very cruel. Never among my people did I ever see that kind of meanness. I admit among the Spanish I have good friends and some of them have been very good to us; but as a group they have imposed themselves violently. Tonight, Jiqui, charred and twisted, lies in the heap of ashes of the fire that consumed him. I curse them all for that. I curse the soldiers for what they will do as they drink their wine and spirits tonight, which is they will piss all over the charred remains and call on their favorite saints to bless their deed.

I have heard many stories of the thigh-eating Kwaib, how they ate our Taíno people, how they took our women. But in all of my childhood, only once did a strange canoe sail our Guanahaní waters, paddled by two men who would have kidnapped a woman. They were discovered in the act, paddled away, and were caught within one day by our fishermen. I know of other such incidents, some more violent, among our Caribbean peoples. And, of course, I have witnessed how some of our own *caciques* attacked others of our peoples, both here and in Cuba, usually in disputes over fishing and planting grounds. But even the worst of those fights I only saw at the urging and the service of the Castilians. The Taíno *caciques* seldom went to war against each other anymore by the time the Castilians came. No, all of our hatreds are as a drop in the ocean of Castilian cruelty. Suffering is what they like; even their God-man, who spoke with them as another human—what they adore is his bleeding heart; in their most sacred ceremony, they drink his blood, again and again, even the young children. Truly, the Christians find salvation in the spilling of blood. They did today to that poor boy what they have done many times. Tonight, as I write, Jiqui's body grease is in my nostrils. I can see yet how his life oozed out of him and hissed on the fire. The Castilians are taking all the fat, from the rivers and mines, from the land, and from our very bodies.

September 1, 1532

FORTY-SEVEN. *PRESSING "THE INDIAN CAUSE" COULD GET ENRIQUILLO KILLED.*

Much before the light of morning, I found the monk in our chapel. I knelt next to him and knew that we shared great disgust. In the darkness, brightened faintly by a faint moon, the events of the afternoon seemed a horrible dream. We prayed together for the soul of poor Jiqui, for him and for the many others. I prayed too for my *jimaguas*, my twin boys, that they always be happy and fresh-feeling Taíno, here or in the Spirit World. Done with my prayer, I felt like walking, wanting to work a kink out of my leg. The good friar stayed with me, walking behind me, staring blankly, and thumbing the pressed-rose beads of a big rosary that dangled from his right hand.

Morning found us facing the ocean, catching the breeze of the outgoing tide. We stood on the promontory that overlooks the coastal road. Mornings like this one, facing the ocean, palm trees, fruit trees all around, the gentility of our Caribbean islands reveals its imprint on my people. The sea wind speaks to me. It blows me soft kisses from the mother waters; it whispers the hopes of past generations. This wind that parts on my face, cupping my ears, blasting against my chest, my thighs, I can say to this wind, "Treat me well; make me well; carry away my pains, carry away my aches." This wind that came today will do that for me.

I caught my calm; the world once again returned me to myself. I could see the good friar struggling with his pain. His horror stays within and his fury consumes him. He is a good man but the wind speaks not to him, so on his knees he says his Ave Marias and his Pater Nosters in a strong and steady murmur. The way he closed his eyes and prayed I could tell he knew not how to talk to the sun, which was appearing strong from the sea at our left. I do not know how to pray without acknowledging the sun, the moon, the four creator winds of the earth, the mother waters. But I have always seen in the priests and monks that they pray through the image of Jesus Christ on the cross, or through a face of the Virgin Mary, in statue or painting. Also, they like to pray indoors, inside the church. Even today, as we moved our service outside, with the sun and sea, with the wind at our faces, he prays to the image of Christ in his mind, nothing else. I have noticed this in all the Christians: they seek not the world in their prayer, but the man-god on the cross.

Walking back to the convent, Las Casas announced his

vehement commitment to destroying the Spanish conquistador circles, to achieve the complete renunciation of the *encomienda* system.
He was very forthright and spoke for most of the way. "The time is
ripe to line up the pressure," he kept saying. "It is the moment."

His vehemence bothered me. As he leaves soon for the court, I
felt again the need to reaffirm the importance of the peace negotiation with Enriquillo.

"This work with Enriquillo must be precise," I said. "His concern is for the safety of his mountain groups."

"They will be safe," he said. "I guarantee it. But these negotiations, at this time, also mean everything to the mainland, for Peru,
Guatemala and Nicaragua, for Yucatán and Mexico, even for Borikén and Cuba. We must push for everything we can. I insist that
if we apply all the pressure now, we can overturn the *encomienda*."

Again, his response bothers me, especially throwing in the two
islands, which I could tell was an afterthought. His impatience to
overturn the whole colonial law continues. No doubt his concentration is stimulated by witnessing the execution of Jiqui. It bothered
me that he can claim to guarantee Enriquillo's safety, as we have
just witnessed an execution without hope of influencing the case.
I asked him about the attitude of Oidor Suazo and the *señores* of
Santo Domingo. Again, he was casual.

"For one thing, they are loath to finance more military expeditions and even less willing to actually serve on any of them. So they
would opt for peace."

"What they did to that boy yesterday is what they would do to
Enriquillo," I said.

"What they have done many times in many places," he said.

"But yesterday, condoned by those same authorities, we
witnessed…"

"They are butchering in the mainland like that, Dieguillo.
Peru, Nicaragua, Yucatán, the Valley of Mexico. Many hangings
and burnings, like the early massacres here. No, we must destroy
the *encomienda*, which is the law and the justification."

The *encomienda* is what Taíno slavery is called by Spanish law.
The *encomienda*, which started with the early *repartimientos*, or the
giveaways, of Taíno people imposed after the first battles, granted
to specific conquistadors the right to use Indians as laborers in the
farms and mines, on sea, and anywhere. This followed the admiral's logic that in return for their labor, the Spanish masters would

Christianize the Indians. It was an argument that the queen, who tried to prohibit outright slavery for Indians, could accept.

"Just remember, the *encomienda*'s promise was to teach us Christianity."

"Well, it goes back to that savage Ovando," Las Casas said, seeming to accept my comment. "And he was a man of the church."

"But the idea goes back to Columbus himself," I said.

"The admiral reasoned it out, but Ovando formalized its structure."

"Yes, we gave our freedom and our lands; in return, you gave us the new faith." I said.

"But, Dieguillo. It is not the Christianity as it is meant to be lived, as our Lord Jesus taught."

FORTY-EIGHT. *LAS CASAS WANTS TO END THE* ENCOMIENDA; *I WANT ENRIQUILLO TO LIVE.*

The good friar needed to discourse, as I had piqued his polemical mind.

I will write down here the good friar's discourse on the institution of the *encomienda*. I was impatient to review our plan on Enriquillo, but I like what I learned from the priest, who has, among his many documents and books, the admiral's ship's log of the first voyage, letters from Michele de Cúneo and Dr. Alvarez Chanca, on the second voyage, and many court documents detailing the history of the dreadful institution.

Las Casas said: "The admiral had to pay for his excesses in describing the wealth of the Indies. Unable to find sufficient gold, he set about the justification for capturing Indians and selling them as slaves. This is where he clashed with Queen Isabel of Castile.

"When Columbus sent his first Indian slaves to markets in Spain, Queen Isabel denounced the Admiral of the Ocean Sea. 'These are my vassals,' she said. 'Who is Columbus to sell my vassals?' She ordered the Indians freed, though, truthfully, few of them ever made it back to the islands.

"Nevertheless, the Great Discoverer invoked the rights of war and conquest, justifying imposition of Christian sovereignty over heathen peoples. He continued to capture and send Indians to Iberian markets. As infidel prisoners of war could be sold as slaves, any excuse for war was welcome.

"Queen Isabel pressed for the work of evangelization. And in this she was convinced by Columbus and others that the Indians were 'roamers' who would avoid Christianity unless secured and held to a place. Thus, as the slave trade back to Spain dwindled, the conquistadors proposed the "burden" of granting upon themselves titles to lands and to the Indians that came with the titled land, in order that the Indians could be properly instructed in the Chistian faith. To recompense the conquistadors for the burden of Christian instruction, the Indians would be made to work, in the farms and in the mines, to support the upkeep of the Castilians in their island and to fill up the coffers of the royal court."

What the good friar says is true. The conquistador's argument about settling down the Indians in order to Christianize us was a trick for the queen to accept the *repartimientos*—the giveaways—of the Taíno population of the island among the early *señores*. Afterward, all notices received by the court were contradictory and even led to laws to protect my Taíno people, but their enslavement was just as total and brutal as were the assertions to her majesty by the delegates from the islands that everything was kind and good for the Indians. Queen Isabel's concern for our people was little avail as her health was failing and our islands so far away from her.

After Queen Isabel's death, in 1504, I say, there was little more to be done at the courts on our behalf. King Ferdinand was disinclined to consider the fate of heathens. Only the good friar and his allies defended our people. And to refute him, many calumnies and half-truths were divulged against us—assertions that we were indolent, could not feed ourselves, that we were idolaters, that we were sodomites, that we had no law. "Beasts that talk," Las Casas said. "That's what they called your Indians."

Las Casas's review of these events and assertions fueled my anger, bringing forth words and curses, arguments and anecdotes, but by late afternoon, as we took the final uphill trail that would bring us to the rear of the convent, I was again tired of the polemic and history; I wanted to plan for the survival of Enriquillo and his people.

"Father," I finally said. "The way my people have died, again and again, no one knows better than you and I. But what of the Guarocuya, how can we help him?"

"That is my point," he responded. "I believe there is room for reform. I believe we can still turn the *encomienda* around. Through the righteous stand of Enriquillo and our Christian faith, our religious orders are building pressure toward a major investigation..."

"Father, please," I said. "Enriquillo may want to discuss the *encomienda*, but it is the last one of his points. I know his strategy. He is most concerned for the fate of his people in the Bahuruku, how to bring the war to an end so he can settle them."

"You must understand, Dieguillo, that this is already beyond Española. We truly have the orders behind us. In Peru, the *encomienda* is in a chaos. A new investigation, conducted by the religious..."

"Father!" I said sharply to him. "If we mix up Enriquillo's needs with the demands of mainland strategies, we may get him killed."

"That is a precisely Indian problem: thinking too small. Our strategies must cast a wider net."

"What about Hieronymites, Father, remember that farce of an investigation?" I said. "What about the free Indian communities? What happened to them?"

Immediately, I knew I had hurt him. Those two projects of earlier campaigns are dear to his heart. Their demise, through corruption and greed, is a deep wound in him. I am sorry to do it but there is no other way to get his attention. We walked silently after that, climbing the wooded east side of our convent. Two flocks, one of parrots and one of doves, swarmed together overhead, moving through the trees just ahead of us. As we talked I had not noticed them. But as we settled into our silent walk, slowly the woods surrounded me; I followed the birds, sniffed the lairs of serpents and iguanas, noted trees and plantations of fruit. On the way, too, on a knoll, I saw a *guasima* tree with two identical trunks, beautiful, with equal branches on both sides, almost perfectly resembling each other. I love our forests; I love this world that speaks to me still.

September 6, 1532

FORTY-NINE. *A MESSAGE FOR CATALINA DIAZ, MIDWIFE AND FRIEND.*

The past several days I worked on the building crew for the convent of La Merced, which is finishing a wing on its church. I learned to swing a hammer years ago, so they always call me for their building sessions. By good fortune, two *mánsos* who work for Valenzuela were there. Young men of Anacaona's line, they helped carry planks and ran for things. I shared food with them and they conversed with me in Taíno. They agreed to carry a message from me to Catalina Diaz, an old friend who is Valenzuela's senior house servant and who has helped her nephew Enriquillo before. My message merely stated that I had some baby powders for her, made from the ground-up cranium of *manatí*. The young men are to let her know I will be at the town meeting in Santo Domingo scheduled for the fifteenth of September and will have the powder there for her.

Catalina Diaz is a midwife, one of the old-timers who still remembers many of our cures. Even the Spanish ladies go to her with their ailments. She uses the *manatí* cranium powder in a broth to strengthen the women after childbirth. However, my message was cryptic. With Catalina, whom I have known for more than thirty years, I use the term *baby* when refering to Enriquillo. I mean to ask Catalina to be my ear in the Valenzuela household, so she might learn what those vile minds plot against her nephew. Two of Catalina's daughters also serve the household. All three of these women conduct themselves humbly and piously, seldom talking, so that their *señores* hardly know them to understand and speak the Spanish language, but they do. Among them they are bound to hear most of the talk in the house of Valenzuela.

FIFTY. *A NOTE FOR LATER WRITING.*

Rereading my conversation with the good friar, I note my reference to the mission of the Hieronymites and also to his project to set up free Indian communities. I will explain both of these events as they come up in my recollections. I brought them up to him to remind him how his ideas have failed in the past, at other times when he was stronger and hoped for total solutions to our people's misery.

September 15, 1552

FIFTY-ONE. *REMINDING LAS CASAS OF ENRIQUILLO'S FIRST CAUSE*

I write this in the late evening. Tonight the grand men of Santo Domingo met at the House of Contracts. The fifteen major sugar cane plantations were represented. The large cattlemen were also there, even Bishop Bastidas, reputed to have more than twenty thousand head of cattle in ranches from here to the Bahuruku.

I met the good friar at the convent gate. More than a dozen monks were already congregated, and we started to walk down together. I paired off with Las Casas. "Will you be speaking tonight?" I asked in his ear. "Yes," he answered.

"Speak please of Enriquillo's cause."

"Of course, I intend to."

"He has always wanted peace, to live in harmony," I said. "He has kept his Catholic sacraments, even in the mountains, fasting his Fridays and even hearing Mass whenever possible."

"Do not worry, Dieguillo, we will speak of the *cacique*'s character and of the justice of his cause. But you tell me: will Enriquillo come to a parley? Can I hold his promise in my hand that he will come in? "

"Enriquillo trusts you, Father," I said. "But can he forget the parley at Anacaona's, Ovando's dirty trick? We must remember, Father, how each of the major *caciques*, one by one, were tricked and killed."

"I will be there to guarantee Enriquillo's safety."

"And your safety. Who would guarantee that?"

He shook his head. Las Casas is totally fearless. Always ready for martyrdom, he is not quite impressed by arguments about safety. But for a chief like Enriquillo, this is preeminent. His first loyalty as *cacique* is precisely for the safe settling of the dispute and the accommodation of his people in their own community.

"It is complicated to guarantee the safety of our people on the Bahuruku. You know they will try to kill him."

"What brutes they would show themselves to be!"

"Yes, and our young *cacique* would be dead."

We walked. To impress him again I told him, as we neared the House of Contracts: "While you speak, I will try to find out when they intend to kill him."

He vacillated a step and turned to me, as if awakened abruptly. "Strength, Father," I reassured him. "I am praying for your success."

FIFTY-TWO. *THE TOWNSMEN HAVE REASONS FOR PEACE.*

The House of Contracts is a two-story building. It has a large meet-ing hall that was crowded with more than eighty people. On the platform, the *oidores*, with Judge Suazo at the head and Vadillo to his right, looked over the hall. Some thirty or forty servants waited on the street, verandas, and stairways of the large government building, half of them *mánso* Indians, half of them Negro Africans. More than twenty of the permanent guard milled about outside, interspersed but not mixing with the servant group. Only four, led by a lieutenant, had stand-up duty, two inside and two outside. The commander of the permanent guard was inside also, sitting in a second row on the platform, behind Suazo.

When Las Casas came up to the door, the lieutenant quickly saluted him and kissed his ring. Immediately, the good friar was ushered toward the raised platform and seated next to the vicar and bishop. All greeted each other graciously, though not a one of them respect the other. Las Casas took his seat, and I could see his face through the window as he lowered his friar's hood to the shoulders. Then the various *señores* came in and many, almost all, approached Father Las Casas, offering polite greetings. I found this completely remarkable because to a man they all hate him deeply, as he has harassed their persons and insulted their endeavors many times.

Of the meeting, I heard the first part, up until the good friar's intervention, when Doña Catalina got my attention. After the bish-op's blessing, Suazo called it to order, explaining the contemplations now before the king's court, relating to the troubles of the Bahuruku Indians, under *Cacique* Enriquillo. The meeting got started with a recounting of the Enriquillo affair through its thirteen years of hostilities and campaigns. The lesser *oidores* read testimonies from important people in the island expressing the wish to settle a peace with Enriquillo. I looked at Valenzuela, Enriquillo's pushed-aside master, who sat silently as even Suazo acknowledged the early griev-ances of the young *cacique*. The *oidor principal* even spoke of some "lack of understanding" shown to Enriquillo when his complaint came to old Vadillo's jurisdiction. The *oidor* Vadillo, brother-cousin of the early magistrate, also sat silently.

The commander of the guard reported next. He informed the *señores* that Enriquillo's fortresses had been attacked by half a dozen well-stocked campaigns. Not a one had been successful, he said.

The loss of Castilian men was more than two hundred, counting all the campaigns. Several major estates had gone to ruin pursuing the military destruction of Enriquillo. There was considerable fear that more and more Africans, slaves, would take the *cimarrón* trail and join Enriquillo. "The Indians are very hard to pursue," said the commander. "They eat anything, anywhere, and somehow always manage to survive and keep going. Our troops must be supplied and are not used to the constant climbing. The Bahuruku mountains have many ridges and tall points. The only attack that might succeed would be to penetrate the Bahuruku with fighting *cuadrillas* from at least fourteen directions at once. Such a crusade would be very expensive, and even that could fail. Were a major campaign to fail now, I am afraid many Indians and Africans would determine to join the armed camps."

Perhaps not too long ago, that commander would have been called for cowardice and lack of spirit, however, tonight there was considerable approbation in the assemblage. One cattleman said: "Give the *cacique* his due; bring him to a peace, negotiate with him. We shall give the group a tract and be done with the damnable war."

A merchant man added: "Not only are the armed campaigns ruinous for our townships and estates; while the Indians are in the bush, all merchandizing is reduced. Little of consequence travels overland anymore. And even docking ships have been attacked. Our commerce is at times paralyzed by the nuisance assaults. I say as the cattleman from Juan de la Maguana, make peace with the devils and be done with it."

When Judge Suazo introduced Las Casas, he was most generous, crediting the good friar his steadfast search for a more just treatment of the natural race of the islands. An acquaintance of the rebel *cacique* in his youth, said Judge Suazo, Las Casas should be recognized for his providential demeanor to make himself available to help secure the peace that is sought. I prayed silently as Las Casas stood to speak that Enriquillo's safety would be at the center of his thoughts and words.

"Many of you no doubt believe the Indian to be inferior to our race," he began, and my heart sank as my mind paid attention. "You are incorrect. The Indians of these islands and over most of the mainland are a race of innocents, pure and gracious people, who had their own beliefs. The original inhabitants you hold now as servants and slaves met us in a state of grace. They have ancient stories, like the Greeks of our ancestry. They are still endowed with that nature. But our own ancestor, Adam, only lasted six hours in that state before the Lord kicked him out of paradise."

Everybody murmured at once. Las Casas was so brazen it made me shudder. "Sodomites," I heard a guard say at a nearby window. "That priest is still a puker."

The good friar further demanded that the assembled *encomenderos* guarantee their Indians sufficient food and other benefits "if you are not ready to give them up, although that is precisely what you should do if you would respect the doctrine of Jesus Christ." He reminded them, "I have not absolved anyone holding Indians for almost twenty years. Wolves thou shalt not be among these sheep. I believe it is wrong in the eyes of our Lord."

More murmuring was heard, some quite loud. One phrase I agreed with: "Stick to the issue, *cura*. What about the *cacique* Enriquillo, in the Bahuruku?"

"Peace with Enriquillo, yes. Respect Enriquillo. But free all the Indians, as the king would have them do in Peru and Nicaragua, where he sent word via my own person, to dissolve the *encomienda*."

From the center row, immediately before the *oidores*, a rather stout man in a long blue shirt stood and reared his head. He said: "The good friar, as he is called, protector of the Indians, will forgive a mere writer and servant of the king if he takes issue with the friar's usual misbegotten logic."

It was Oviedo himself, I could tell, as the speaker approached the platform. Gonzalo Fernández de Oviedo, the official historian and enemy of Las Casas—I had heard he was a recent arrival on a caravel from Spain. He went on: "The king, whom I have seen frequently, has not renounced the *encomienda* and has in truth congratulated the *encomenderos*, I heard him say so just this past summer, for the dutiful task of imparting Christian doctrine to Indians. Your information is old, Father Las Casas. Or maybe it simply does not apply to Española."

It was at this moment that Catalina called to me from the street through her daughter Julia, who simply walked by and gained my attention. I was sorry to have to go, as I was both fascinated and chagrined by the widening debate the good friar had aroused. The anti-*encomienda* talk, as I had anticipated, bothered everybody. I could see the discussion was going to get heated.

FIFTY-THREE. *DISSIMULATED ROMANCING WITH CATALINA.*

For an extra moment, I watched the clique of Vadillo, Valenzuela, and, not far distant, Pero Lopez, the man I hate most in the world. I stared at Lopez that extra moment, thinking quickly in my mind as usual how much I have wanted to kill him. I could see Father Las Casas's face reddening, too, and said a silent prayer for him to stay with Enriquillo's cause. Then, lowering my hat and showing a bit of limp to give the appearance of a smallpox-scarred *mánso* Indian, I went looking for Doña Catalina.

The street was quite crowded, but I found my old friend around two right-hand corners, sitting in a group of young women in a crowd of *mánsos*. Catalina wore a long cotton skirt and blouse and, as usual, held a baby in one arm. She was small and thin but wiry and alert. As I found her, she was instructing the baby's young mother, no more than fourteen years old, in the use of an aloe salve for a case of butt rash. In the moonlight, my eyes watered, as I had not seen her in more than three years.

Catalina had loyal people around her, including several Negro girls who challenged me directly with their eyes. But Catalina jumped up to greet me as I lowered my head to get her blessing. "Diego," she said. "My old boyfriend."

I had to laugh. I had never been her boyfriend, but it is true she is not ten years older than me, and once, when I knew her after the Massacre of Anacaona's Banquet, we shared a common adventure. At that time I still had Ceyba, my wife, and our twin sons, all of whom I hid with Catalina for several months before being pressed into Diego Velazquez's service in 1505. Later, we toiled at the same *encomienda*, survived it, lost track of each other, and reencountered around 1520, by which time we both had gained a semblance of freedom, I as monk's servant and she as housemaid in the Valenzuela estate. Time and again we have seen each other, which I truly enjoy, as she is the closest person I have for a relative; Catalina is like a mother-aunt to me, or maybe like an older, distant cousin.

Tonight, for this *guajira* of mine from an earlier life, I had a present. She received it graciously. It was the ground *manatí* brain bone, not for the baby, so much, but our own best cure for side pains, which Catalina and the women she cares for often suffer. She had something for me, too, a good stack of tobacco leaves, selected for low aroma and consistent dryness, the kind to be mixed in our *cohoba*.

Slowly, without any overtness, we walked into the darkness, where we held hands. Nearby, in door frames on both sides of the street, pairs of lovers embraced in the darkness. One man was a guard, and it seemed safe to assume that other guards would not disturb couples there. "We are not a sun's walk from each other," she said. "But I never see you."

"In my moon walk, I see you," I said. " I will always do that for you, and for your line."

The moon walk is a ceremony I acquired through Catalina, in the days of our bush run with Ceyba and the boys. Already a midwife to her people, Catalina took Ceyba in and nursed her ailments through that nightmare of violence and persecution. More than once we gave thanks together, and it was during one of those times she taught me the midwife's moon walk as a thanksgiving to the women's medicine and a way to bind our spiritual lines.

"My concern is for your nephew," I said, contemplating that no one else around us would know whom I meant. But I leaned Catalina against the wall, facing me.

"The baby boy is in danger," she whispered. "There is talk of striking him at the first opportunity, at the earliest point of actual contact, before getting to the stage of sitting down together."

"Why early?" I said.

"They would commit the act in the moment of confusion between war and peace. They are certain that he will be drawn out of the Bahuruku this time, maybe into the fields or the lake shore."

"Who would do it?"

"My master's talk is to pay two guards to strike him quick. Valenzuela, as rightful holder of the nephew's *encomienda*, would be easily validated to attempt an apprehension or a punishment. Your former holder, Pero Lopez, has made visits to the Valenzuela house."

"And if the king mandates different? If he mandates a clear peace offering? Such is the good friar's claim."

"You know these *señores*, *mi* Diego. They blaspheme the king his goiter. They believe in cutting off the head, then finding the body. It is true that many are for peace, but only because Enriquillo has proven so costly in war. And they are desperate to quiet the island and attract more ships."

"What you tell me may save the nephew's life," I said.

"I will think of everything I remember and hear everything I can," she said.

She worried that Enriquillo might expose himself prematurely and offered the use of one of her daughters as a go-between that the young *cacique* could trust. I reminded her such an offer would divulge her relationship to him. Maybe, she said, but if the negotiations are final and conclusive, it will not matter. We all want to help in my family, she said. We would be offended, especially Inez (her own name for Julia), if we could not help in every way we can.

I agreed to set up the deal with Enriquillo and to use her daughter Inez as both currier and message. I mean by this that her actual identity will tell the *cacique* whether an ambush is expected or not. If an ambush is planned, we would not send Inez but a Castilian as a messenger.

FIFTY-FOUR. *CATALINA BELIEVES IN BOTH US AND THEM.*

Catalina. She is so keen. How good it was to talk to her again. How good to hold her and pretend to be lovers.

We agreed to meet in church, at the earliest Mass each Sunday. She is a *beata*, a church matron. Her Catholic vocation has saved her life many times and has given her a certain respect among the Castilian ladies and even the *señores*. But she has given up nothing of our peoples' beliefs. "I believe what they tell me about the Jesus, but what they say about us, that our *cemis* and *areitos* are the devil's works, that I don't believe," she says. Before we parted, she stroked my right leg, always sore. Her thin hands are strong. She massaged the muscle at the front of the leg but directed the strength to the back of the thigh, where the Cuban *caimán*'s long tooth dug deep into nerve and muscle nineteen fateful years ago. When she was done, I stroked the back of her neck and shoulders. "Take bark from the *jobo* tree," she advised. "Boil it thick and make a jelly. While still warm, rub this jelly into the back of your thighs and calves. If you cannot, I have some. We could meet someday, and I will do this for you."

FIFTY-FIVE. *THE MEETING ENDS.*

It is late in the evening. I tire now of writing, although I like it more and more. I find I enjoy the telling of actual happenings and think to preserve these memories for my boys, if they would ever return. This is the hopeful part of me. Catalina is one of my old ones; I have been a fool not to look for her more. She is an ally, a sister, a doctor, a knower of my heart.

The meeting was still going on as I got back to my place by the window. Judge Suazo, *oidor principal*, was giving the summation. On the platform, Las Casas looked one way, and from his chair on the main floor Oviedo looked the other way. Suazo pressed the question of peace with Enriquillo, and he once again praised Las Casas for enlisting in the endeavor. I chuckled that he admonished Las Casas as I had, although for different reasons. "The protector of the Indians is perhaps too persistent in his opinions about the *enco-mienda*," Suazo said. "But we all thank him for his involvement now and continue to encourage his assistance in bringing the Enriquillo to a negotiating parley." It seemed that despite Las Casas's antagonistic words, the group was more than agreeable to a peace settlement on the Enriquillo war.

"Enriquillo will come in," Las Casas said. "He is a man of peace."

"Yes, a treaty of peace from the king will bring the Carib out," Vadillo responded for the *oidores*, using an ominous word, *Carib*, that signaled dubious intent. Las Casas simply nodded back, and just past him Pero Lopez wore a thin smile as he stood to go join the crowd around the *oidores*.

A toast of wine was made for the *oidores* by the major *señores* and the meeting was concluded.

September 20, 1552

FIFTY-SIX. *GOOD-BYE TO LAS CASAS, ASHAMED OF MY WRITING.*

I helped Las Casas embark for Puerto Rico, Borikén in our language, this morning, ferrying his trunks to the docks on the convent wagon. I know he means to go to Spain from there but dares not anounce it beforehand. We spoke while the ship's servants loaded up water and high stacks of freshly baked *cassabe* bread.

All Spanish here eat our *cassabe* bread now, although I remember a time when, except for the admiral, most of them disdained it, "Like eating chalk." If kept dry, the *cassabe* lasts a long time and is good food. Our sacred torts complement any type of meat soup or gravy and will fill your gut, even by themselves. I say they are sacred because to us our main foods were all appreciated in ceremony, and among them the most appreciated was the *yucca*, which had its own *areito* songs and was represented in our principal *cemi*. I looked around this morning, as the *cassabe* was loaded on ship, and had to remark how much of our Taíno ways the *España* people (the good friar taught me this word) have taken up. Looking back from the docks, nearly all of the houses, including the tavern, are actually *bohíos*, walls of palm wood tied together with wet, hard-drying *bejuco* vines and roofs made of palm thatch. In the interior and along the coasts, the small Spanish settlements all rely on the *bohío* construction. Many a Spanish fisherman now sails our waters in our Taíno canoe, and lots of them sleep in our hammock.

"Temporary matters," Las Casas commented back, cutting my argument. "For all its ills, our Christian civilization will impose itself. It is inevitable. For instance, you don't see many thatch-roofed churches or government houses anymore."

"You don't hear many *areitos*, either," I said. "Not after Velazquez, for one, beheaded every *behike* holy people he could find."

"The *behikes* were idolators," he said. "I disagreed with their execution, but I worked many times to convince them to Christianity."

I felt particularly proud of our Taíno ways this morning. Yesterday afternoon I prepared Catalina's recipe for *jobo* bark liniment to rub on my legs, and it greatly lessened the stiffness. I admit, too, that seeing Catalina has rekindled many sentiments. But I did not want to fight with the good friar today, particularly as he was about to board ship, so I held my tongue.

Las Casas cleared his throat. He had a way of doing that when he wanted to change the subject. My reference to the execution of *behikes* he clearly found discomforting. My "for one" recalled a particular event, from the time of the campaign after the Massacre of Anacaona's Banquet, in 1503, when Diego Velazquez, sent later to conquer Cuba, beheaded two *behikes*. Las Casas, before becoming a priest, was a soldier in that campaign and witnessed the murders without objecting.

In front of us, several sailors watched as two muscled Negro dock workers struggled to load a recently fixed anchor. "I have read your pages on the discovery and your first look at Cuba," Las Casas said, as we walked up the dock to kill a bit of time. "Some of the detail is interesting, but your memory is a bit clouded. For instance, you don't mention the Pinzóns at all, Columbus's other captains. Pinzón left him, you know. Took off for Jamaica or God knows where, while the admiral made his way here to Española."

"But I haven't gotten that far," I protested. "I planned to write something about Pinzón taking off like that."

"The other thing is you make them sound so wise and good—I mean your old people."

"Yes, that is how I remember them," I said.

"No doubt, but try to be more true, more realistic. You have to tell the bad with the good."

For some reason I felt his commentary on my writing like a slap on my forehead. I felt revealed and vulnerable to the priest.

"Finally, don't write so much about yourself," he continued. "You embarrass me with your midnight ejaculations…"

I wanted to run. I had forgotten what I actually wrote, and it was something very private as I wrote but to hear it spoken revolted me. I felt trapped by my words, and I didn't like it.

"Writing is very much like confession," Las Casas commented, softening, as I think he could see my chagrin. "But the best writing goes beyond one's own person to describe the sequence of events accurately."

"Yes, I believe in sequence…" I said.

He admonished me: "The intent of all writing is to discern God's master plan in the life of our Christian nations, regardless of the greed or brutality of our fellow humans beings. It is alright to describe the customs of your people, even as they appear in your own life, Dieguillo, but see these events in the context of our Christian faith. The Devil himself runs your pen otherwise. That same devil that is in the lust of your male blood."

He shocks me much, as I remember the teachings of our *behikes*, how they spoke of our being as men, to accept the wish for the *yuán's* release. I mostly remember their words were true and gentle. Their words are still so much more clear to me than what the good friar reclaims.

Thankfully, Las Casas changed the subject.

He wanted to know about Guacanagari, the noble. "In thinking about the life of the admiral," he said, "the noble *cacique* Guacanagari appears to be a worthy counterpart from the Taíno culture..."

"Guacanagari was a pompous kid," I said. "He was not a man of the stature of real ni-Taíno *caciques*, like Guarionex or Behechio."

"Was he cowardly?"

"Not cowardly so much as very ambitious but weak as a chief," I said.

"Well, that is the level of discussion I could use from you."

"Guacanagari is next," I said. "As I describe how we made our way from Cuba here to La Isla Española, how we met Guacanagari, and why the admiral founded his first colony at Fort Navidad."

"Good," he said. "Tell me about the *caciques* of that time, how Columbus met them, and their first relations."

I promised I would. We were still talking when the call came to board ship. He said this: "One thing to keep in mind. As we know, the Carib were moving north onto the big islands with their raids. Had the Spanish not come, it is possible they would have eaten all of you by now."

I laughed at that one, though bitterly. "No, Father," I said, as he walked the plank, basket of fruits in hand. "We Taínos were incorporating both Macorixe and Ciguayo—and even the fierce ones that you call Carib—we were marrying them into our people, our women were teaching them our ways, we were defeating them with love."

I got a nervous laugh out of him then, as the plank was pulled up, though I was serious: we Taíno had our diplomacy and our strategy; by our law we lived and let others live.

September 22, 1532

FIFTY-SEVEN. *BREEDING MY MARE.*

It has been five days since I have written. With the good friar at sea on his way to Spain, my life is much quieter. I took time to catch up with my gardens and to have my mare bred, as she gives good young *potros*, which are always useful and a source of revenue. The good mare that I have and received from my famous namesake, Don Diego Colón is a fourteen-hand roan of Andalusian stock. I got lucky to breed her with an Arabian stallion owned by Don Federico Castellanos, a local hidalgo who has extensive cattle ranches. Antoncito, a half brother of Silverio, provided the entry, early last sunday, after I noticed Cariblanca dripping. I walked her over two pastures, and the Arabian paced excitedly with her smell in the air. Antoncito dropped the gate and walked away to hoe a field of yams. The horses pawed and sniffed and didn't take long to consummate the act. The Arabian was still on Cariblanca when a huge swarm of bees, thousands and thousands, flew buzzing overhead. We were happy they missed us. Had they swarmed closer to the ground and bumped into us, they would have been quite dangerous.

FIFTY-EIGHT. *SURVIVAL IN HUMILITY.*

Soon, I will go to the Bahuruku. Enriquillo will have *cohoba* ready. I will go there and we will mix it together. Then, according to his *behike*, we will snort and smoke right then or wait for a more propitious moment. I prepare now, fasting and concentrating. A route to peace must be found for the baby boy and his camps on the Bahuruku. Enriquillo's people are the last of our free people on this island. Valiant they have been but are yet a small cay in a sea of Castilians. Growing Spanish numbers we face now that will not abate; they are stronger with each passing year. In Cuba, we are more than a dozen strong communities still, scattered here and there in mountain valleys. In Borikén, too, we hide camps in the mountains and in remote coasts. Of course, on my little islands, I hear, we are almost none left. And here in La Española, after thirteen years of war, we must find ways for the Castilian (or Spanish, as they call themselves more and more) to allow a community, a peaceful camp of Indians. This we cannot do by proposing such direct political opposition as Las Casas suggests. We suffer greatly still their dreaded coughs, as much as their furious swords. They surround us everywhere, and not only Castilians, but of the covered kind. French and English have I met, Christians also, talking differently but looking the same, doing the same. We Taíno, ni-Taíno, or *guaxeri* will survive meekly, I fear, or not at all.

FIFTY-NINE. *OUR WAYS WERE RESPECTFUL OF REPRODUCTIVE POWERS.*

I find it comical listening to the good friar's preponderance of words about the lust, invoking the Devil, even his cryptic references about our Taíno naturalness. I think today on my early *cohoba* teachings, and I recall the instruction, even before my own manhood. They would tell me to concentrate on the use of my eyes, my spirit, to control and amass the urge of the loins. This, we were told as young-sters, you do by identifying the lustful urge whenever it surfaces and putting it consciously at your side, like in a hanging bag. The man can do that, and it should not be a very difficult thing to do. At least, such was the teaching of my elders.

Our people used our mind a lot, not like the covered men, so forcefully, but subtly, in delicate ways. And, truthfully, I never saw a passion act among my people that was not intended by all concerned. And, unlike the covered men, too, it was not for its sup-posed evil that we controlled human passion, but for its power to communicate and create. Our own people went naked, it is true, but this did not throw off a tidal wave of lust coupling. People concen-trated on their many productive activities rather well.

Even as a little boy, I heard the grown-ups talking of the cou-pling act as the energy of connection with the Spirit World of our ancestors. In the moment of human intimacy, if everything lines up, they said, our ancestors on the other side will feed us the spirit of the child to be, the one that will form from the seed in the womb. They said the coupling act itself releases the connective waters between our living world and the Spirit World and can create life (and much grief). But, they also taught, and strictly, that the urge of the loins and its act is disrespectful during preparation for prayer ceremonies. Coupling is not a good thing to do when trying to set up ceremonies to communicate with the Spirit World.

During the special times of ceremonial *areitos*, and in the *cohoba*, the *behike* and *caciques*, the housemothers and midwives all advised the men and women to abstain; and they did, everyone, without any resistance, as all the people wanted to help out and make sure the ceremonies would go well. Our people understood that the spiritual connection brought on by the coupling act must be carefully guarded at ceremonial times, when the worlds line up and the ancestors visit us formally. In our discipline, the men were more directly charged than the women and were instructed as to stages of control. Taíno men were taught to control the desire, when proper, and could do this for life. The men in fact took pride in doing that, so as not to be led by the *yúan* but by the eyes in life.

I repeat, the discipline of abstinence was much appreciated in our important activities—in the fishing and the sea, in the facing of the elements or enemies. The urge of the loins, as enjoyable as it is, was not the thing to look for in life. In fact, it is a very poor concentration, as the dead who protect us and breathe us life are made uncomfortable with the life heat of lust. There is for instance a great bent for the act of masturbation among the covered men. They do it, they laugh about it, they hide it, and they punish it. But as boys, we Taíno were taught not to abuse ourselves but to use the energy to connect, to let our urges and emotions well up, and then on an evening especially tender, to imagine a love for our life before sleep. And this was an appellation to the Good Water herself, Attabei, to allow a human spirit *opía* visit our living hammock, to join our imagination in the dream-world and thus naturally release the pent-up love of our loins.

For Taíno, as you controlled your loins, so you gained spirit as a man and power to communicate with the spirits and *cemis*. In the home relations you followed their course, but in pursuit of spiritual power, you were not to let the passions dominate, and neither was strength meant to do violence. This was an understood agreement among our *cacique* and ni-Taíno families. Gentle treatment of the people by the *caciques* and by each other was a dominant idea for our people. I believe the discipline that Taíno men were taught about our "men's wishes" was very important in making us see more clearly the larger things in life and to keep down the wish to do violence.

Women's disciplines were very different. Even their language was different. In sexual adventure, they had more permission, particularly the young girls, who were guided in these matters by their old ladies, all mandated to increase the babies of their households and some of them quite lecherously given to the task. In one special ceremony, we even coupled the *opías*, or dead spirits, with our living *goeizs*, or souls, and even with our living bodies. (You can always tell an *opía* because the dead have no belly button.) Yet, even for this one ceremony, fasts from food and coupling were held in preparation, and *areitos* were dedicated. Pulp of *guayava* was fed to the spirits on those occasions and it was on those nights dream couplings and other experiences were reported by many people. YaYa, Vital Principle, marrow of life, was called forth by the women elders at that ceremony.

At regular times, the old people would say, it doesn't really matter what people do. When the spirits rest in their *Coaybay*, when we the living are left to our own fortune, then permission to copulate was assumed, sometimes very openly, though I must say, among our men, the lure was the pleasure of the woman. This was pointed out by the old men as a man's best reward, as they said, "to make a woman cackle." Angry violations of our women I never saw and never heard of among my people prior to the arrival of the covered men.

Father Las Casas would call these notions vehement, but I noticed the Castilians, particularly the early ones without women, were often driven wild by desire when they saw our naked people. Hot loins, they had, lusting for the coupling act, a lust of possession itself that easily turned to blood. They put a lot of words to it, which the good friar repeats, but it defined them nonetheless. The Castilians, being dressed not naked, could not control their minds about it. They saw our women's nakedness and had to have them, mostly by violence. And in their killing, they enjoyed the brutal sexual joke, cutting testicles and breasts and laughing about it. Constantly they needed enforcers for their laws to control their people. Even among their priests, who are supposed to abstain, very few do. Most fully dressed of Spaniards, many of the priests go for boys.

SIXTY. *I DO NOT REALLY FEEL SHAME.*

I am glad to write about all things. Shame I felt when the good friar recalled my words about my night of puberty but it was mostly surprise. I realize now it is he who was shamed, maybe for his own memories or actions. The Castilians are different from our men the way they wish so much to hide their nature from each other and even from themselves. I still call them covered men, though I am now also covered, and I, too, would be shamed of my nudity.

I will be extra careful to select the good friar's readings from these pages. I will not show him in writing anything that I could not tell him in person. I find the writing hard. It is so much easier to know what to say face-to-face. The moment guides our use of words. I tell a thought in the mood and the climate and the uniqueness of a moment, how it carries our heart's secret meanings, to the eyes, to the body, and to the *goeiz*, to the trees and to the winds that record them.

September 26, 1532

SIXTY-ONE. *INDIANS TELL COLUMBUS TO LOOK ELSEWHERE FOR WOMEN AND GOLD.*

I write now about early December 1492, during the first voyage, just seven weeks after leaving my home of Guanahaní with the first Admiral Columbus.

For days we scouted the coast of Bohío, having crossed over from Cuba. In Cuba, after losing several of their own people as captives, the local Taíno had raised the admiral's expectation for gold. "*Caona*," they said, pointing to Bohío, this Taíno homeland that would become this luckless Española. "That way, too," they said. "You will find an island inhabited by only women. Matininó it is called. Women and gold, women and gold to make your heart glad."

Columbus was intense as we left the Cuban coast at Maisí Point to cross the windward channel. I could say all the Castilians on ship were intense, very serious, talking only of gold. They believed it inevitable they would find a large mine. At vespers, as the admiral led the singing he would invoke a prayer, "Oh, please the Lord, lead me to the source of the gold mines."

The good friar pointed out that Pinzón, captain of the *Pinta*, split off with a good wind and sailed part of Bohío's coast on his own. I believe, (or, I should say, the admiral believed, since I formed this opinion from his) that Pinzón wanted to be first to sight the land with the gold. But Pinzón is not important. He rejoined us in due time with nothing of consequence to tell. (This Pinzón made it safely back to Spain. However, he died within days of his arrival, while the admiral lived to enjoy the glory of his deed.)

SIXTY-TWO. *DIVING FOR YELLOWTAIL WITH RODRIGO AND CARÉY.*

To continue: On the *Santa Maria* and the *Niña*, sailing the coast of Bohío, the days took a happy turn. One morning, drifting east along the coast, the admiral announced to our people that after exploring Bohío, he would return us to our homes, in Cuba and Guanahaní. Suddenly, the *caniba* tales were a lot less threatening and even the women relaxed. Suddenly, a red snapper run was all around our ships, the sea red with fish running by the tens of thousands.

I remember Caréy, Rodrigo, and I diving off the stern of the *Santa Maria* into a school of red snappers and yellowtails, how

Caréy surprised everyone by catching a red snapper with his hand. Caréy held his fingers stiff like the head of a spear and, swimming with the fish, suddenly thrust his hand behind the gill of a snapper passing by. He held it up. Several sailors saw him do it and called to others. We were off the coast of what is now Cape Elephant, not far from the *cacique* Guacanagari's village.

Sixty-three. *Cibanakán faces the hammerhead, impressing the sailors.*

In the water, hunting in the school of red snapper, which ran by us for hours, two sharks appeared, a small blue and a large hammerhead. Caréy and the rest of us left the water. Cibanakán reproached us. "Taíno men don't leave the water because a shark appears."

It was afternoon and the admiral napped. Two sailors were fishing on orders from Captain Juan Niño. Twice in a row, as they hooked and pulled on snappers, the hammerhead swooped in and sliced off a bite that left only the head on the hook. A crossbowman was summoned, and he shot several arrows at the beasts, hit the blue shark once but superficially. The blue disappeared, but the hammerhead persisted. A small crowd gathered.

Cibanakán pulled on my arm and I followed him to the captain. Cibanakán wanted to borrow the captain's dagger. With hand signals and the Spanish words for *fight* and *shark*, Cibanakán indicated he would take care of the beast. I was very impressed by this; the captain was intrigued and gave us the dagger. Cibanakán faced the east, lit and smoked his cigar a few minutes, and watched as the hammerhead circled the caravel. Occasionally the shark would disappear underwater to come up moments later on an opposite side, swimming fast in a circle that widened and tightened as the fishing men hooked new fish. Cibanakán waited for the shark to go by and slipped into the water, swimming out as the shark circled wide then came around the ship toward him. He held the dagger in one hand (my father had done it with a coral knife) and I knew from the way he treaded water he was intent on a maneuver of our fishermen, flipping backward in the water as a shark rushed to bite, then coming up from underneath to stab its soft belly. It was not easily done and highly dangerous, and he took my breath away because it was one of the four great deeds for which my father was honored.

All the men awake on shift and all of our own people watched intently as the large hammerhead came around and Cibanakán swam calmly in place, dagger in hand. The ugly crab-headed beast was round as a horse, dorsal fin slicing the sea toward my uncle; suddenly, it darted like a swallow in midflight, going out wide on a circle away from the ship, staying on the surface and circling back, and Cibanakán in the water waiting. On the second encounter, the hammerhead came in strong and again suddenly darted, a sharp turn away from the large human form half in, half out of the water, turning and darting away in that great speed of sharks in a panic, sounding to the deep, away from the ship, away from the coast and out to the ocean free. The sailors and all our people cheered. Cibanakán climbed on board nimbly, though I could detect a slight shaking, and gave Captain Niño his dagger back. The sailors continued fishing.

It was already the next night when Caréy, lying in a hammock on one side of me, sang out loud enough for Cibanakán, on my other side, to hear: "Cibanakán had a dagger. He was brave. But he didn't have to use it. The shark bolted in fright just to see his face!"

Cibanakán was our elder but not by so much that we couldn't tease him. Even so, the teasing was also a way of honoring the deed. Tired as I was, I giggled over Caréy's jokes half the night. Caréy was funny, going on about the hammerhead, how he would report to his spouse about the giant frog that suddenly appeared and what a fright it had given him.

SIXTY-FOUR. *A GENEROSITY OF PARROTS.*

On December 12, 1492, a Wednesday, one of those dates I still remember from my day-keeping duties on the *ampolleta*, a young woman wearing a ball of gold encrusted in her nose was captured. Immediately the admiral was summoned. He ordered her clothed and fed. He gave her many presents and had several of us accompany her inland. "Make friends of her people," he told me, this time sending Rodrigo along, as he was learning our language faster than any other sailor.

The young woman, whose name I remember was Tinima (though I never saw her again), was the daughter of a village *cacique*. We went with her to a village of a thousand houses, but everyone fled. She went on ahead of us and we got close enough to tell her people that we had come with men of the skyworld, who had presents for all that they met. As they listened and lost their fear, they asked what the spirit men wanted and for lack of an answer I told them parrots. Within a day, two thousand people had come, bringing great quantities of food and hundreds and hundreds of parrots. It was near there, on December 16, that we first saw Guacanagari, the young chief of the Marien, who they said was also fond of gold. Guacanagari was brought to the beach on a large hammock, carried by four of his *naboria*, or assistants, and he was surrounded by more than five hundred other men. At his sides, as always, his four elder uncles constanly whispered in his ear. Among his principal people, many wore gold in their ears and noses, in pendants and arm and calf clips, and in necklaces.

SIXTY-FIVE. *GUACANAGARI, FIRST TAÍNO SACHEM TO MEET COLUMBUS.*

The admiral was overjoyed to meet Guacanagari. "But for going naked, he could be a king anywhere in the world," he declared. In fact, Guacanagari was a rare *cacique*, upon whom several lineages converged. By virtue of his generations, Guacanagari was related to more principal families in the Marien region of Española than any other man. In Taíno ways, this made him a most important person, to whom all would give great care and tenderness, for such a man could be trusted to the greatest impartiality in resolving disputes among his many relatives.

They say much nonsense about Guacanagari these days. Some call him the noble *cacique*, but Las Casas insists he was a coward who sold his own people out. Oviedo praises him for his friendship with the admiral. I will say that he was a man in love with his own person. I talked with him myself many times, during that first trip and later, upon our return from the land of España. Guacanagari had no peer among his own people, even though he had done little to deserve his standing. When he met the admiral, he exuded an immediate love and excitement that touched the admiral, making him very happy, and, I am ashamed to admit, making me very jealous.

SIXTY-SIX. *COLUMBUS'S SHIP* SANTA MARIA *SINKS ON CHRISTMAS NIGHT.*

On the night of December 25, 1492, we were set to in a small bay on Guacanagari's coast. Rodrigo and I had fished all afternoon. Schools of yellowtails, mixed in with mullet, sole, salmon, hake, pompano, all feeding on large beds of shrimp and eel. We hung from ropes at the bow, tied by chest and legs, and speared fish as they went by. Seeing the catch, the admiral summoned Juan Ruiz de la Peña, a Biscayan and his best cook on board, who boiled up a large fish soup, complete with rice and lentils and seasoned with salt and chili peppers supplied by Guacanagari's people. All the officers ate together with the admiral, a rare occasion, and many prayers were said and toasts utttered. Twelve bottles of wine, of sixteen the admiral had stored, were drunk that night.

After the Mass for the Eve of Christ, Columbus sat on a folded sail and talked to all the men, arguing some with Captain Pinzón's brother about the fate of the *Pinta*, but mostly declaiming on the pattern of his own life and his devotion to God's master plan for men on earth. I could understand enough Castilian by then to follow the admiral's discussion and remember him using the Latin words *spiritualis intellectus*, by which, I have come to know, he meant the understanding of the world and of the seas, which he believed was his God-given gift, the intellect of the Holy Spirit working through him. "I prayed to the most merciful Lord concerning my desire, and he gave me the spirit and intelligence for it," he said to his sailing men and particularly to his captains.

Captain Niño had posed the question of divine providence. "How does it come to be that the plan of our Lord, Jesus Christ, now on the 1,492nd year of his divine birth, is fulfilled on earth?" Juan Niño was the admiral's favorite captain, even during that first voyage. Later he traveled with us throughout Spain. For his question about the fates, the admiral praised him. The admiral responded to Juan Niño's question late into the night, drinking much wine. Some of his sentences I have reconstructed from later conversations, but the sense I have of his meanings and topics of that night is more exact thanks to my conversations with Father Las Casas in recent years. It is Las Casas who has given me the Bible to read, as well as many documents from Oviedo, the admiral, and others, all of which have helped me, more and more, understand the thinking of the covered men.

The admiral said to Niño and the other officers that night: "I believe that the Holy Spirit works among the Christians, Jews, and Moslems, and among all men of every faith, not merely among the learned, but also among the uneducated. In my own experience, I have met many times simple villagers who could explain the sky and stars and their movements better than those who paid their money to learn these things." He pointed to Cibanakán and Caréy, who had guided him expertly through the islands and cays many days already.

I remember being mesmerized by the tone of his words and what I could understand about what he was saying. Among the white men I have known, only the admiral ever spoke this way so movingly about himself.

"The Lord proposed that there should be a miracle in this voyage you have taken with me. I tell you that this too is the fulfillment of prophecy," he went on. "I tell you that it was the Holy Spirit whose marvelous illumination gave me abundant skill in the mariner's art and whose concern gave me the mental capacity and the manual skill to draft maps and to draw the cities, rivers, mountains, islands, and ports, all in their proper places. For thirty years, I searched out and studied all kinds of texts: geographies, histories, chronologies, philosophies, and other subjects. With a hand that could be felt, the Lord opened my mind to the fact that it would be possible to sail here from Spain and he opened my will to desire to accomplish this project. This is the fire that has burned within me."

All the men were astounded by Columbus that fateful night. The admiral spoke into the late evening, and most of the officers stayed the whole time. But he drank a great amount and grew weary and slurred his words. "I also believe that the Holy Spirit reveals future events not only in rational beings, but also discloses them to us in signs in the sky, in the atmosphere and in animals, wherever it pleases him, as was the case with the ox that spoke in Rome in the days of Julius Ceasar, and in many other ways too…"

I listened very intently, trying to catch the words about the skyworld. I had a running argument with Caréy about the spiritual nature of the Castilians, for which idea I had become a main spokesman as we traveled. "I have seen them cut themselves," Caréy argued. "They need water, same as us; they eat like humans, they piss, and they drop their leavings. They need their sleep. They lie with our women…"

"A god can lie with a living woman…"

"Guaikán—you are hard-headed for them!"

Wrapped up in a cotton hammock on the deck next to me, Caréy had turned over to sleep when, suddenly, Columbus stood up, catching himself in his indulgence with the wine. "But I will retire now as it is late," he said. He shouted an order for Juan de la Cosa to take over the watch then went below. In a few minutes, it was very quiet. As he heard the admiral snore, de la Cosa ordered a young page to take over the wheel and went to sleep himself. I laid down to sleep myself, thinking that the night was deadly quiet as we floated on a thick sea that swelled without waves. About four a.m., all the good officers asleep, the page also asleep, the *Santa Maria* crashed on the reef, tearing a hole in her underside that sank her.

SIXTY-SEVEN. *GUACANAGARI SAVES THE DAY AND PROVIDES THE FIRST GOLD.*

The admiral was despondent for only a morning. By midday, Guacanagari had more than sixty canoes ferrying cargo, including cannon and anchors, from the wreck, and, as is the custom of our people, everything was kept meticulously. The *cacique*, who wept with Columbus at the sight of the broken *Santa Maria*, assigned several large *bohíos* used for fishing gear and his own canoes to all the cargo and had many men available to transport the posts and planks from the ship to be stacked on the beach. Guacanagari had arrived in full court and soon promised the admiral he would dress him in a suit of gold. Just days before, he had gifted the admiral with a mask made of gold. When he gave it to the admiral, he had asked him to look through the eyes of the mask, to look through the mask of gold. The admiral did so, looking all around. "I wish I would see only gold through these eyes," he said. Which in Taíno translates as "My eyes see or look only for gold." This made Guacanagari very happy, as he thought he had a great deal of gold to give the admiral and thus felt power coming into his court from the covered men. On the 28th, he brought the admiral several chest plates made of thin gold, and he restated his promise to build a full gold suit for the Grand Mariner.

In turn, the admiral looked more positively on the loss of his ship. "The Lord helps in mysterious ways," he said, "destroying one of my vessels precisely where gold and a natural ally have been found." He decided a fort must be built there, and a group of men were chosen to remain. Because the *Santa Maria* had crashed on Christmas Eve, he named the fort The Nativity. When we left for Spain, thirty-nine Castilian men stayed behind at the fort, the first colony of the covered men to settle in the Taíno islands. The admiral's final instructions to these men were to search for the source of the gold and to try to get along with the natives. "Everything that has happened was for this purpose," he told them, "that this beginning may be made."

SIXTY-EIGHT. *THE WHITE MAN'S INDUSTRY IS AS IMPRESSIVE AS HIS HUNGER FOR GOLD IS IMMENSE.*

Those days, I was impressed with the white men's industry. The way they built the fort, mostly of planks and posts from the stranded vessel, was a new wonder for me. I saw another part of the Castilians—how they worked together, how they hammered with nails, sizing up wood with rulers and serrating the wood with an iron that cut right through the widest posts and trunks. So far, I had seen them on ship, tending to sails and directions, ballast and cleaning of the vessels. This they did well, and they fished and they explored the lands, here and there. But the building was something different. Columbus directed all of it and prayed a great deal, and before our eyes, in days, two large, very strong houses appeared, surrounded by a small stockade.

Those days, the admiral walked the woods with Guacanagari's old men. He took note of everything, listing the types of woods and plants he saw, calculating distances, rivers, and the populations of the many villages. The old men, more than the youngsters like me, had noticed that the Castilians ate a great deal and pursued our women indiscriminately. Through Guacanagari, and using me as interpreter, they offered young women of various *bohíos* in marriage to the young men of Columbus. The Castilian men scoffed at the idea, which for some reason at the moment did not bother me, although I knew it would the old *caciques*, and I did not pass it on to them in my translation.

I cannot now explain it, even to myself, but I felt at the time it might be right that gods or spirit men from heaven would not take wives among our people on earth. The old counselors of Guacanagari were quicker than me. They did not mind the couplings of hospitality but got suspicious when not one offer of marriage was accepted. So, they told the admiral about a great island, three hundred miles southeast, that was totally covered in gold. Near this island was another island named Matininó, they said, full of women only, who mate with men but do not tie them down to marriage. The admiral was very impressed. You should go there, they told him. This part I relayed to him, and he wrote it down. He wrote many things down in his journal and he talked of plans and of places that made little sense to me at the time. "With this gold, I swear our sovereign kings will take back the citadel from the infidel. Jerusalem will belong to Christendom once again."

Later I will write how in Spain, at banquets in Barcelona and Seville and even in the new siege-camp town of Santa Fe, near Granada, Columbus, with me at his side, would expound on all the wonders of the Indies, this New World. The great *señores* would sit me with them and ask the questions often raised by the "discoverer." Is there really much gold? they would ask. Yes, I would respond. Some islands are full of it. They liked me and fed me well in Spain, but that was later, after the first trip back and the horrible storms of snow and ice on the Azores, where Cibanakán and so many others were lost.

SIXTY-NINE. *THEY GET MORE GOLD FROM US.*

It has been more than forty years since those first days with Don Christopherens, my adopted covered-man father, who pulled me from a home to which I never returned, although it lives in my heart and memory, even today. The good friar will forgive me if my memory jumps from here to there. It is true that I want to follow the sequence of these episodes, but sometimes things make more sense if pulled together. Like the thing of the gold, how the Castilians reckoned the worth of this metal in its weight and purity, how it manifested things in their governments and markets. This thing of the gold was of utmost curiosity to us, the Taíno people. We could understand that the Castilians were intent on obtaining gold, but we wondered why they were so very absorbed in its quest. Why, when just a little gold is a great treasure to be cherished in ceremony? Why, when the earth and the sky and the sea provide so well for our peoples? Why, when it is only in the sharing of the bounties that we learn not to fight, that we learn to do our tasks together and appreciate how lucky we are to breathe the same air and feel the same heat?

Guacanagari gave more gold to Columbus than had any other *cacique*. The admiral was very happy, and the happier he got, the more gold Guacanagari brought to him. It was the *cacique*'s natural Taíno instict to supply the admiral's happiness. Back in the cities of Spain, the admiral would tell all who listened about the great gold mines, the docile people who would serve the Spanish, their fertile valleys, full of gardens and orchards, the cities of gold of the Great Khan, whom we would find in time, offering a wealth of possibilities in mining, agriculture, and trade.

SEVENTY. *SPIRIT MEN REMAIN BEHIND AS WE SAIL OFF FROM FORT NAVIDAD.*

Craftily, as he had noticed the admiral's fondness for me, Guaca-nagari asked me to stay, but the admiral would not allow it. The *cacique* had good reason, as his elder uncles were more and more concerned with the Castilians' penchant for our women, which, even before we left for Spain, had begun to irritate our people. Guacanagari suggested that both Rodrigo and I stay behind to help with the interpreting and, I am sure, to help calm the impulses of the Castilian men. I am glad now the admiral refused, for I don't think we would be alive today if we had stayed. But at the time, I was saddened, as the admiral made it clear we would first go to the Castilian country before returning us to our homes, and from my friend Rodrigo's explanation, I could see that the admiral's destina-tion was completely away from my home island, first east along the coast (where we found the *Pinta* and Captain Pinzón), then west and north and finally across the big water, going east. And this is the course I sailed with the admiral on the *Niña*, the *Pinta* follow-ing, on January 9, 1493.

One afternoon before we left, the admiral ordered a lombard shot fired at the remaining carcass of the *Santa Maria*. The explosion made Guacanagari's people all drop to the ground; they later mar-veled at the hole left by the iron ball. The effect was to make Gua-canagari more fearful of the Castilians and more impressed with his new friends, over whom he was quite jealous. Though the admiral inquired after other great *caciques*, Guacanagari insisted they were minor people compared to his court, which was the "grandfather of all grandfathers." Once, several canoes full of important elders approached from the nearby island of La Tortuga, wanting to meet the spirit men, but Guacanagari shooed them away, shoving water at them in our customary signal not to land their canoes. What-ever Columbus gave Guacanagari, simple things like a coin, some pointy red shoes, or a flask of orange rosewater, the *cacique* had his principal men carry on a bed of cotton in their arms, parading the trails and beaches to show off the gifts. His people put up enormous amounts of food for the Castilian men, who impressed everyone with their great appetites.

The admiral always saw what was before him but seldom clearly. He thought of Guacanagari as the main king of this Espa-ñola island, this great *bohío* of Haiti or Santo Domingo, where I now live out my days. Yet, I myself told him of my conversations with Guacanagari's mother, who asserted to me that the Great *Bohío* land was comprised of six large *cacicasgos*, or courts, belonging to at least five established *cacique* lines. Guacanagari was one of them, and his territory was called the Marién. However, she insisted, her son lacked volition and several of the other *caciques* were stronger and had more territories. I heard from her lips for the first time the names of Guarionex, Caonabó, Guatiguaná, Mayobanex, and Bohekio. She asked me to tell the admiral a story about the marriage of Caonabó and Anacaona, sister of Bohekio. Anacaona had been destined for Guacanagari. However, on arrangement by Guarionex, she refused him and married Caonabó, a very tough Ciguayo chieftain frequently in fights with the Taíno *caciques*. The marriage to Anacaona of a very strong Taíno line would bring Caonabó into the Taíno fold. "Of all of them, Guarionex is the thinker," she said. "He straightens up the fights." Guacanagari's elderly mother was an alert woman and had much to teach us. But it was a complicated story with too many names, and the admiral lost interest.

As for Guacanagari, since the fort was in his territory and he had offered to feed them, he persisted in his effort to marry the covered men formally to his young women. He was impressed with their industriousness, too, as well as their weapons, although the Castilians who stayed behind held themselves above Guacanagari and our people. Yet, they ate together every day while we were there, and this, to us Taíno, is a sign of good intentions. Sailing away, even as I dreaded the journey across the great water, I was impressed that spirit men were staying among our people. I felt something good would come from it.

SEVENTY-ONE. ESCARMIENTO—*THE FIGHT TO LEAVE A WARNING.*

The first fight happened on the way out. I did not see it but heard the details from the men who fought it. We headed west on the northern coast of the island looking to sail for the open sea when the admiral decided to put in on a calm beach and caulk the *Niña*. It was Ciguayo country, and it was not long before we encountered the long-haired, black-faced bow-and-arrow warriors of Mayobanex.

One old man with very long hair was captured in his canoe. I helped the admiral interrogate him. At that time, the Ciguayo to me were as enemies, maybe the dreaded Caniba of our most horrible tales. Later, I would know them differently. The old man's language was strange to me; I could understand only a few of his words. The admiral was harsh. He also believed them to be the Caniba of our Taíno nightmares. These Ciguayo, I would learn in time, were partly assimilated into our people. Their fierce appearance and war abilities resulted from their fights with mainland raiding parties. These realities, however, were not the concern of Don Christopherens.

The admiral released the old man but the next morning, spotting a group of warriors on the beach, he sent a boat with seven armed soldiers to produce what he called *un escarmiento*, a sort of warning. "This one is for our comrades left behind," he told the men as they boarded. "Show your fighting skills. Leave a memory here of the bite of our steel."

Pretending to trade for the Ciguayo's bows and arrows, the soldiers tried to slowly disarm the group on the beach, but the Ciguayo warriors suspected the ruse and became agitated. They hid their weapons and approached with ropes to trade for the hawk's bells that intrigued them. Then the soldiers attacked, one man slashing at the two nearest warriors with a broadsword. With one blow he cut the buttocks off of one man and with another, half of an arm. A crossbowman quickly fired two arrows, one through a man's chest and the other through a runner's leg. The Ciguayo retreated to shoot their arrows, but the two crossbowmen continued to wound them in their bodies from much greater distance. Nor did any more Ciguayos dare the sharp steel of the three experienced swordsmen who preceded the crossbowmen, swords slicing menacingly through the air. Recognizing they were up against deadly foe, they took flight into the forest.

Seventy-two. *Sailing out to the great water.*

Just days later, we sailed for the great distance, beginning the monotony of the open ocean. That is the way we left the sea of our reptile islands and thus that ends the narrative of the first voyage of the admiral, Don Christopherens Columbus, to this world he called the Indies. Such are my notes as requested by the good friar, Don Bartolomé de Las Casas, at the Monastery of Santo Domingo, about my memories of those early sailing trips and what they meant to me.

Folio III

To Go Forth and to Return

So much to tell... Storms at sea and the loss of my father-uncle, among others... The traveling priest... Columbus and the chickpeas... King João's bean maps of the Caribbean... Palm fronds and one less Indian... First sight of Spain with Caréy... Laugh and cry—"La cabra" of the Inquisition... How Las Casas remembered me... The admiral requests my words... Rodrigo Gallego becomes our servant... Meeting Queen Isabel, who requests my adoption by the admiral... A dinner party in our honor, Rodrigo meets Matilda... Out with Aragonese girls in Catalonia... I find the fair-haired woman of my dream... Caréy's bout of drinking... The admiral is titled and granted... Something about Oviedo: he lies about my people... With Rodrigo's Gallegos at Otero del Rey, his mother's offering to the duendes *of the water spring... A run with bulls for San Fermín... Rodrigo's home village... Good-bye to Atoya, and Castile... A country where many are poor and destitute and a few are very rich... The romance of Cúneo's mares... Captain Alonso de Hojeda, the perfect soldier... Meeting the "man-eating" Kwaib, how tales get started... Discoverers are saved by Indian grandmother... Perfect proof of Carib perfidy: a castrated boy... Hojeda draws first blood, Cúneo in on first fight... Cúneo's treatment of a Kwaib warrior woman... Caréy responds to Cúneo... The news on Fort Navidad... The story of how Fort Navidad was overrun by* Cacique *Caonabó... The story denied... Isabela is built, the first metropolis... My loss of innocence... A devilish bout with the grape... In need of punishment... Las Casas reports mixed news... I must get to the Bahuruku... Flogged out of my guilty stupor...*

October 10, 1532

SEVENTY-THREE. *So much to tell.*

I have much to tell and a good stack of paper left over from the good friar's contribution, so I will continue to write. Rather than disturb the narrative, as I await word from both Enriquillo and Father Las Casas, I will write on about the voyage to Spain, what I saw there, and how the admiral prepared his return trip.

October 12, 1532

SEVENTY-FOUR. *STORMS AT SEA AND THE LOSS OF MY FATHER-UNCLE, AMONG OTHERS.*

Yesterday afternoon, a late summer storm came up, bringing a rare coolness in the evening vapor. In the early morning I had dreams of Cibanakán, old father-uncle of mine. I felt him again hunched over behind me, nearly curled around me as I crawl out from his grasp of death.

On ship, going to Spain with the admiral, at the onset there were almost a dozen of us Taíno and four Ciguayo, a third as many as Castilians had remained at the fort named Navidad. None survived of their colony, and that is a story I will detail later in these pages. While of ours, of the Indians on ship, I can say that only seven survived the voyage. Maybe half died on the way there. Others died in Spain.

What got my Taíno were two terrible ice storms that caught our ship, the *Niña*, as we entered Portuguese waters. The whole length of that great ocean we had sailed, and pleasantly, to tell the truth. When snow and ice as we had never experienced took our destiny, with winds that ripped the sails and clashing waves tossing our ship in midair, lightning and cold, incredible cold where leather and sail froze, most of us Indians had no clothing. I am certain to have died but for my great father-uncle, Cibanakán.

The storms followed each other by two weeks, February 12–16 and March 2 and 3, 1493. The first one started in the early morning with heavy winds, and by afternoon, as the sun lowered, it turned to pure ice, first a blizzard of snow, then sheets of ice that froze your feet and fingers. Our people found their best, most secure places onboard but died by the threes and fours as the night progressed. The Spanish, even those few who were so inclined, had little time to tend our needs. They shared little of their clothing, particularly the water-waxed items, and even our own Taíno cotton, gathered from the many islands to show their monarchs, remained under lock and key. I secured a blanket from the admiral and called to my uncle, who gathered two more young men under it. I caught the chills badly within minutes of my first soaking, ice forming on my bare skin, and came out of that first storm coughing and shaking badly. Somehow, Cibanakán survived alright that night.

After the first storm passed, Cibanakán nursed me, and

Rodrigo strove to secure us food, mostly soggy *cassabe* and dried fish but a great thing to suck on when you are sick. I never felt so loved as by Cibanakán during those few days. He took on the appearance of my own father, caressing my skull gently and singing quietly to me. My illness lasted for more than a week, during which the admiral put in at a port on the island of Santa Maria of the Azores, and I was lucky for the gift of a chicken, which I ate in a broth. The admiral departed hurriedly from the small island on February 23, as the Portuguese authorities tried to hold ten of his sailors who had gone ashore to pray. I was too sick to take notice of those events before the ships removed again to the open sea, but I was almost recovered as the tempest picked up again on February 27 and 28.

The second ice storm descended fully on March 2, so violently that two experienced sailors were washed overboard by giant waves. Ice storms were all around us, and the decks glistened, slippery with ice. Under a ship's boat, Cibanakán curled around me from behind, wrapped in our blanket. He held on to me all night like that, breathing his warm breath on the back of my neck, all night and a day and another night doing that for me, my father-uncle, holding me, keeping my back warm.

On the third day, the sun came out first thing in the morning, a hot ball and wide beam on the water facing from the east and I was still in the arms of Cibanakán, though as I gained consciousness, I felt the stiffness of his embrace. I was cold as the deepest of mountain streams, colder than that, as cold as ice, my feet and hands, my nose and ears. My ears hurt so much, so stiff and cold I could not touch them, though my neck and back had still some warmth. Awakening, I wriggled out of Cibanakán's stiff arms and only a bit of warmth could I feel in him, around the area of his heart. But despite that warm spot, he was stiff from cold, his neck and shoulders, which he had surrendered to the elements, frozen hard as ironwood.

He was not dead, quite, but there was nothing left in Cibanakán's eyes, his breath was cold vapor. And that next cold night, though I held him all day and evening, and Rodrigo tried to feed him broth, Cibanakán died. The next day, morning was sunny again and without meaning as we surrendered my noble Cibanakán to the waves.

October 15, 1532

SEVENTY-FIVE. *THE TRAVELING PRIEST.*

Las Casas must be now arriving at Spain. I like it that he is heading in precisely the direction of my narrative, on a ship sailing to Spain, now nearly forty years later.

That priest is an indefatigable traveler. The ocean he has crossed at least a dozen times. He has mountains of energy, and in his campaigns at court he causes quite a ruckus. I pray he will be calm and help to soften the king's heart—maybe through the queen. I hope and pray that he arrives well.

SEVENTY-SIX. *COLUMBUS AND THE CHICKPEAS.*

For the *Niña*, that first time, the landfall was Portugal; I remember how the admiral tacked on the coast, I remember the certainty of command he had over his ship and how in the worst of the first storm, while the *Niña* took each wave in its own angle, he offered a vow to make pilgrimage and give his thankful prayers at the altar of his favorite virgin at Santa Maria de Guadalupe, in Estremadura. One chickpea among many was marked with a cross and put in a sack. Whoever drew it would undertake the fulfillment of the vow, upon return to land, as promised to the Lord in common prayer. And it was Columbus who drew the pea, not once but three out of four times. And it was in the wake of his final vow that the storms abated and we sighted the Portuguese coast.

I was good, by then, at the afternoon ditties and could understand most of what the Castilians said. I even sang high the Salve Regina for the admiral, *"Dulcis Virgo Maria,"* loving and respecting him who had shared his blanket with me during the storms and who had hugged me to him as one after another of my kinsmen had been slipped overboard.

SEVENTY-SEVEN. *KING JOÃO'S BEAN MAPS OF THE CARIBBEAN.*

In Portugal, we were questioned by the monarch himself, King João, who disbelieved the admiral his news of the discovery of our lands. There was fear he might imprison the admiral or even have him killed. Finally, the king took Caréy aside and had him draw out with beans a map of our islands. As Caréy finished, using several beans for the larger islands and single ones for the smaller ones, the king studied it carefully then disturbed it. Then he called me over to do the same, which I did, in much the same form as Caréy's. This convinced King João, and we went on our way, sailing into the harbor on the Rio Tinto, at Palos, Spain, on the fifteenth of March, Year of Our Lord, 1493.

SEVENTY-EIGHT. *PALM FRONDS AND ONE LESS INDIAN.*

The admiral led us into Seville on Palm Sunday (March 31), where a large crowd was gathered. The local people put palm fronds on the road. Having procured a burro, he rode into town surrounded by us seven remaining Indians. Hundreds and hundreds came out to see us, and they sang for him and asked him to speak at every turn. "The man who discovered the Indies" is what they called him in Seville. In Seville, too, we lost another *lucayo*, named Bexuco, who, like myself and Caréy, had met the admiral early on. Shaken still by the voyage and unable to swallow the Spanish food, he walked away in his dream. The sleeping death Bexuco chose one overnight in Seville.

SEVENTY-NINE. *FIRST SIGHT OF SPAIN WITH CARÉY.*

The admiral left Caréy and me at a family *pensión* in Seville during our stay in that city. It was a four-story house by the Gate of the Imagenes, near the Cathedral Square. Our room was on the third floor and had a window facing the street, and you could see other stone and wooden houses, next to each other so they always shared a wall, and you could hear horse carriages going by on the street below. The room had one small bed that Caréy and I shared. The bed came with two warm woolen blankets, which we learned to appreciate.

I remember that room in the *pensión* house in Seville, and here at the convent it feels like I am in it again. Caréy was all I had left from my world by that time, and I feel him with me tonight. That night we laid together and huddled to make our bed warm, and for the first time I cried. I cried so hard that Caréy started crying, too. It was a night of recovery for us, a convalescence. We talked about our time on board, the death of our people who had died in the storm. By morning, the shock and fright had subsided, but the pain was still with us, and the strangeness.

Everything in the Castilian country was a great marvel to us those strange first days. We saw how people moved in horse-drawn carriages and barges and canal boats, how they lived in houses made of rock and wood, with iron doors, and some with windows of many colorful crystals. We saw barley fields and valleys of wheat, groves of squat olive trees, evenly spaced and all the same height, and leagues and leagues of sheep grazing in the plains and meadows. We made our first acquaintance with the wheelbarrow, a marvel of a tool, and of course we were surprised by the covered people's many uses for oxen and horses and mules. Often Rodrigo or Captain Niño or Luis de Torres explained things to us, how to eat, where to walk on the street, when to stand and when to sit in church. What nothing could have prepared us for is what we saw near the cathedral in Seville, the use they had for the goat. This, a Christian scene, we witnessed some days later, after Holy Week had passed.

EIGHTY. *LAUGH AND CRY—"LA CABRA" OF THE INQUISITION.*

Luis de Torres, the converted Jew with whom we had journeyed to Baigua's village in northern Cuba, was assigned to keep company with Caréy and me in Seville, where his parents lived. We felt alright with young Torres since sharing his peculiar experience with the eager village women of Baigua.

That morning he led us to breakfast down the street from our *pensión*, to an inn run by his parents, where he stayed. We ate a meal of lentil soup, bread, and a piece of sausage. I remember his parents were darker than most Castilians, and they were very quiet.

After eating, Torres led us through a maze of very thin streets, in and out of rows and rows of houses. "I am to show you the cathedral today," he said. I remember thinking that without him leading the way, I would easily lose my way in those streets. That area of the city was La Judera, the Jewish people's quarters in Seville, where families kept indoors and hung crucifixes near every window.

The fear held by Jews for the Spanish authorities I had already seen when a group of church inquisitors inspected the *Niña* at the port of Palos. Palos was especially harsh on unconverted Jews, as many had been recently deported from Christendom through that coastal town. I remember Torres, how he volunteered to pump the filthy ship's hold just as he saw the group of priests board the *Niña*. "Don't let them talk to you," he advised me as he disappeared below.

"Pretend you don't know the Castilian." I did as he warned and stood mute near the admiral as he told the group about his mission on behalf of the Catholic sovereigns and showed them one of the gold masks Guacanagari had given him. With a knife and iron block, he tapped off pieces of the gold to give them. "This gold of the Indies," he said as they left, happily clutching the gold pieces, "will finance our Christian armies. With its wealth, Their Highnesses will retake Jerusalem."

In Seville, both Caréy and I would see more of the Inquisition. Trailing Torres, we passed an arched gateway out of La Judera and out onto a bit broader street, where we turned left and walked two blocks, the street opening into a plaza surrounding the biggest of buildings, a construction of stone that went up into the sky. This was the Cathedral of Seville, a century old and not quite finished when I saw her.

Torres stopped. At one corner of the square, around the side from the main entrance to the church, a crowd gathered. "We'll see what the attraction is today," he said, as others ran past us, and I heard someone else say, "Hurry, they're bringing out the goat!"

At the edges of the crowd, Caréy and I pressed behind Torres, and in brief glimpses I could see a man tied by the arms sitting down on the ground, his legs pulled apart, straddling a post. A stick went under the knees and secured them with rope. Through the crowd I could see the man's very white bare feet and legs on the stone floor. At the entrance to the cathedral, only a hundred feet away, several monks and an archbishop stood solemnly. They wore pointed white and purple hoods over their heads and faces, status of the Grand Inquisitors, defenders of the Holy Catholic religion.

I had seen several lashings aboard ship and thus I thought this might be occurring. From the look on the man's face, he seemed unbeaten but very frightened. A guard next to the man nodded, and a peasant leading a billy goat by a neck leash made his way through the crowd. He handed the leash to the guard. Then, he unwrapped a cake of honey paste and smeared the condemned man's toes and feet. I sensed something very bad was going to happen but could not fathom what. Then he tied the goat within reach of the man's feet and stood back. "Suffer, blasphemer!" he yelled and stepped aside. "Laugh and cry."

"Laugh and cry, blasphemer!" one and two more yelled back from the crowd.

Forty years later, I still fear the memory of this event. I have seen even worse happen to my own people, death accosting us on all sides, but nothing had ever prepared me at that age for watching that goat lick the man's toes, tongue lapping the arches of his feet, and the man stretching himself taut, a forced smile breaking his anguished lips as the goat licked and licked, and a giggle broke out of his throat. The crowd laughed heartily at the man's giggle.

In my throat I could taste the heavy sausage of my meal, and it is that sensation I remember most of that moment. Because the very next thing, the honey was licked clean and the goat, after licking his lips and looking around, bent down and siezed upon a large toe, ripping strips of flesh as the poor devil's shriek in that cathedral square put the shock of ice on my spine. The goat chewed for a hour, taking his time and looking around.

That was *la lengua de cabra*, "the goat's tongue," a favorite punishment, among many, meted out in Spain by Inquisitors. It was one of many tools of torture. That luckless peasant, while drunk on wine after a Saturday market, had cursed the Virgin Mary, describing her genitals in a lewd bar song. Several people heard him and reported him to the office of the Grand Inquisitor, who promptly had him arrested. As the peasant did not deny his song, he was sentenced to laugh and cry with the *cabra*, who might teach him the difference between solemnity and frivolity. Others, such as heretics and witches, would be burned to death, much as I have described in Jiqui's execution. I saw two of those in Granada, where a man and a woman, she a Moor, were immolated for having raised a question on the identity of Jesus Christ as prophet rather than as Lord or God. They were flogged and burned, both of them, and before that she had the nipples of her breasts yanked off by a special instrument. The torture session was private, but they announced the torture and the executioner held high the actual iron instrument, and I myself saw the blood on her garment as they went to burn her. I know the institution of the Inquisition well and have discussed it with Father Las Casas and others of the monks many times. They are of various minds about it now, but at that time in Seville and Granada, all the religious backed the Inquisition as the main defense of the Christian faith.

"Laugh and cry!" I remember people in the crowd yelled as the goat ate the man's toes on both feet and licked at the blood for a full hour. "Laugh and cry for all blasphemers! Laugh and cry for all Jews and Moors!!"

Remembering *la cabra* makes my leg twitch even now. I can still see Torres taking our hands and leading us away, and I could tell he was shamed and worried for us to have heard the taunts at the *judíos*.

He took us into the church of the cathedral, a huge cavern but built by human workers, big as a small mountain, a door like the entrance to our largest caves. Inside it was dark and cool, and the tap of a boot resounded deeply into the huge space. Every surface of the wall seemed to be handworked, and looking up and up, craning the neck to follow huge columns as thick around as three ancient *ceyba* trees and three or four times as high, all polished stone, it had a clean look but smelled of musk and incense and oils and dead people.

Entering the large central hall, where Mass is celebrated, Torres pointed to the altar. "Go kneel and make your prayers," he said to us. "Remember the storm we survived together." Caréy and I both prayed, kneeling by that altar. As prayers help me respond to my pained spirit, I asked for the man outside the huge cavern church, whose feet were eaten by a goat and who would undoubtedly die. (Actually, he did not, I now know. He survived the ordeal to join more than two dozen other such men in Seville—the *cabra* men of the Inquisition.) I was very intense in my prayer and have sometimes since wished I had not been so intense about this man, as I have dreamed the event numerous times throughout my life, and I have always awakened from those dreams in ice-cold horror.

October 20, 1532

EIGHTY-ONE. *HOW LAS CASAS REMEMBERED ME.*

Father Las Casas has told me he saw us, *los indios*, that time with the admiral in Seville. I don't remember him then. My earliest memory of the good friar is from the time he first came to Española, in 1502. Of course, I believe he did see me, as he has described me correctly, at the admiral's side, a skinny, long-haired young boy handling four cages of parrots. "A boy," Las Casas has told me, "who had an eye for everything."

EIGHTY-TWO. *THE ADMIRAL REQUESTS MY WORDS.*

In Seville, at a luncheon sponsored by the Duke Medina Sidonia, the admiral requested some words from Caréy, as the elder Indian left from Guanahaní and also from an even older uncle of Guacanagari's. But my fellow Guanahaní-ti proved shy in front of an audience, words failing him, and the older uncle, quite frail and having suffered tremendously during the ice storms, said little that was understandable. After Seville, the admiral had Caréy handle the parrots and freed me up to speak as he might request. He told me to stay close to him at public appearances and banquets.

EIGHTY-THREE. *RODRIGO GALLEGO BECOMES OUR SERVANT.*

In Barcelona, where Queen Isabel of Castile and King Ferdinand of Aragon, the Catholic monarchs, held court that season, the crowd was no less excited. We were traveling by royal wagon train now, and even us six Indians had servants. Torres remained with his parents in Seville, but Rodrigo Gallego was still in our party and was assigned by the admiral to cater Caréy's needs and mine.

"They treat you like kings, and me, a boy of the country, no less a hero, I am your servant," he complained, but mostly in jest. Rodrigo was unlike most of the white men I ever met. He never minded anything he had to do and was always helpful. Rodrigo was humble by nature, smart, and kindly disposed. He was also sixteen years old and, we were finding out, had an itch for adventuresome ladies.

EIGHTY-FOUR. *MEETING QUEEN ISABEL, WHO REQUESTS MY ADOPTION BY THE ADMIRAL.*

We spent the night in a royal farm on the outskirts of the central city of Catalonia, and the next afternoon, the twentieth of April, 1493, flanking the admiral, who rode horseback with his officers, we entered the Plaza of the Cathedral, crowded with townspeople. King's guards opened the way for us as trumpets sounded. It was sunny but cold, and the admiral had requested us Indians strip to the minimum, wear our feathers, and hold high our parrots, spices, *cassabe*, and several large jars in which fruits from our islands were preserved. I remember that someone suggested the Indians wear a *bozal*, or muzzle, as they would put on wild animals, and we even tried some on, which, to our relief, did not fit us. I wondered about this idea, seeing that the cathedral was carved on the outside with beasts, *gárgolas*, that seemed to leap out from the dark stone.

King Ferdinand and Queen Isabel received us in a small plaza, seated up at one end of a platform that had stone steps leading to it. As the monarchs rose for him and the crowd gasped, Don Christopherens hurried forward to kiss their hands. They blessed him and his whole enterprise, welcomed him, and requested he seat himself with them, whereupon the crowd gasped once again. They sat thus a few minutes only, as a wind picked up the cool of the afternoon and the queen requested the reception be moved into her royal chamber.

Caréy and I were quite happy to go into the large stone room and placed ourselves near two large fireplaces that were burning warm. Before even all the seating had been arranged, I noticed the queen's eye on me and perceived her kind smile. I felt a great deal of love for her at that moment. Later, after all greetings and reports were heard and new honors were bestowed, her page found his way to me, grabbed my arm, and pulled me to the edge of her court. "*Veníd*," she signaled with her hand. "Come."

"And this one," the queen said to Columbus, as I stood before her.

"He's the one who speaks our language," he said.

"What are you called?" she asked me.

"Guaikán is my name," I said, adding as instructed, "Your Majesty."

She smiled, but I could tell she was curious about the name. "It means a kind of fish," I said. She nodded, raising an eyebrow at me.

"You're very smart," she said, and I looked down.

"And your home is the Antilles?" she went on.

"Yes, Your Majesty, the islands."

"Then tell me, what is the most beautiful thing in your homeland?"

"The ocean," I said, "and the face of my mother."

The queen almost cried. She pulled a silk cloth to daub her eyes, and a lady-in-waiting behind her grimaced, clicking her tongue at me. But the next moment the queen hugged me, and the same lady-in-waiting immediately smiled.

"What a darling child," said the queen. "You should adopt this boy, Columbus, give him a Christian name. Name him Diego, for your younger brother who accompanies you."

Don Christopherens nodded and put his arm around my shoulders as all rose to sing the Te Deum in thanks to God for the successful voyage. The next Sunday, I was baptized Diego Colón, and the queen had several of her ladies attend. Caréy was also baptized and the rest of my Indians. One was named Fernando de Aragon, after the king, and given to the monarch's young son, who was chosen as godfather to all of us. This Indian Fernando, whom we knew as Atoya but whose child's name was Ximon, was most unfortunate of all. Years later, when I was enslaved in Cuba during the time of Velazquez, I came to know that the young man was from the region of Bayamo and Macaca, who had cursed the admiral. Atoya, although from the opposite coast of Cuba, was in fact one of the ones taken captive by Columbus in Guamax's area, where the young man was visiting relatives to attend an *areito* and a ball game ceremony. The time that old man Guamax came to curse Columbus from the water at the stern of the *Santa Maria*, he was complaining about the taking of several captives but primarily about Atoya, a son of the sister of Macaca and a very sensitive young boy, destined by his people to become *cacique* someday. Poor Atoya. He was taken from us right away by the prince, Don Juan, who wanted him instructed in the Christian faith.

October 23, 1532

EIGHTY-FIVE. *A DINNER PARTY IN OUR HONOR, RODRIGO MEETS MATILDA.*

There was actually a dinner party in honor of our baptism later that week, a large one, at the house of a Catalonian duke, whose name I forget. Of course, our baptism was a miniscule occurrence, a pre-text, I believe, for the duke's lavish display of public support as the Catholic sovereigns presented their new hero of the ocean sea. The queen was in those days nursing the king, who was under rest orders. Only months before, King Ferdinand was stabbed in the neck by a madman, saved, so the legend went, by a thick chain of gold he wore as a collar. The monarchs did not attend, but sent several of their ladies and gentlemen, plus many royal dishes, to this great party attended by local royalty and landed barons. While the grandees ate in the fancy salons, Rodrigo, Caréy, and I explored the kitchens and the many side salons where various parties had settled themselves to enjoy the feast. Among the younger ladies-in-waiting, a young Matilda Cuesta de Peralta was quite brazen. She and Rodrigo got along quite well, and she teased him that many of the girls talked about Rodrigo "and his Indians." We were the novelty of the season in Barcelona that spring.

Matilda was no noble but a *muchacha* from one of the families of fancy courtesans kept by high men in King Ferdinand's side of the court. She had many relatives in Barcelona, and it appeared that other women in her family were also courtesans. They were not prostitutes, as I have come to understand the term, and did not have a brothel, such as the one in our docks here in Santo Domingo, but their whole house seemed to ply the trade of entertaining men discreetly.

EIGHTY-SIX. *OUT WITH ARAGONESE GIRLS IN CATALONIA.*

The girls, who liked to have fun, invited the three of us to drink wine with them at their home, on the boardwalk near the municipal docks. As we had our own quarters at the Royal Pensión in the city, no one to report to, and nothing in particular to do the next day, we accepted. Everyone else in town that we knew was also celebrating that evening, and some were quite drunk, talking and talking, and some of the women tipsy with wine were dancing. Both Caréy and I were quite happy to follow Rodrigo (and a fourth comrade), as they walked down the dusty shoreline streets of Barcelona looking for the fiesta house.

Rodrigo himself had a bottle of wine, and his friend Mateo, a local boy who spoke the Catalan language, had two. Caréy and I had none, but we were quite willing to drink. "These two Indians are good boys," Rodrigo kept telling Mateo, who understood Spanish. "You should have known their uncle; he faced down a shark in midsea."

Matilda and three "cousins" were home and let us in quickly. Two older women were also home and, after greeting us, made us stand still to be looked at. "So this is what Matilda drags in," one said. "Who's the captain?"

Rodrigo nodded. She looked him in the eye up close. "You can cover these boys?"

"I can," Rodrigo said. "But these boys are faraway guests of our king and queen's court. It would honor our grandees to gift them at least once."

"They're a bit dark and swarthy," she said. "But do they got a pecker like any old boy?"

Rodrigo laughed and pulled out a bag with a thousand *maravedí* in it. I am sure he did not have much more, but this impressed the older woman, who immediately leaned up against him, fondling his butt in jest. "I'll send you kids up some wine," she said.

EIGHTY-SEVEN. *I FIND THE FAIR-HAIRED WOMAN OF MY DREAM.*

It was quite a party. The older woman sent a mandolin player along with the wine. I drank a good bit of wine, but Caréy drank even more. He was really funny for quite a while and danced with Matilda and her cousins and Rodrigo and Mateo. That night I met and talked for a long time with Maria del Carmen, who was very sweet and curious about me. She drank wine, too, and we both drank together, and I talked to her for quite a while about our islands, the storms on the trip, and the king and queen. She was well impressed and did not hesitate to touch me, and very affectionately. I fell in love with her and we retired early, and I am not ashamed to say it— we spent a night of much comfort in each other's embrace, humid and passionate, with a natural timing in our passions that not only overwhelmed me, the first-timer, but even impressed her, who had considerably more experience. We took to each other like honey and wax. Maria del Carmen was exceedingly exciting to me, and I went back to her house several times during our stay in Barcelona.

Eighty-eight. *Caréy's bout of drinking.*

The next evening I was off with Don Christopherens to a round table of town burghers, men who would invest in the mining enterprise that the admiral envisioned for the Indies. It was our first in a round of important meetings, where Don Christopherens formally introduced me to give testimony on the gold, pearls, and precious woods in our "Indian" lands. We went to several dozen like that over the next few weeks while the admiral arranged the credits and provisions of our return trip to the "Antilles," as everyone was calling the Taíno islands.

My cousin Caréy, however, continued the party through the next day. He and Mateo had become friends while Rodrigo was off in love with Matilda. Through the day, the two young men found a sailors' whorehouse and through that evening and subsequent days drank many bottles of wine. They became a famous duo on brothel row, and the whores celebrated Caréy from one end of their street to the other. On the fifth day, Rodrigo came running to get me. Caréy is very sick, he informed me, and is vomiting blood. I found him at Matilda's house, on a cot, facing up. There was blood on his shirt, and every few minutes he was wracked with dry heaves. His eyes were wild and far inward. "He can't stop vomiting," one of the older women informed me. "Leave us, please," I said.

Alone with Caréy, I talked to him sweetly, in our language. Instinctively I wet a rag and held it to his lips, as we do for the elders at the end of a night of *cohoba*. I stayed with him all day, gave him lots of water, held him, and rubbed his lungs from behind. He coughed up horrible things and then fasted on only water. That night, as he was breathing calmly and sleeping soundly, I went to the admiral about the need to employ Caréy in something, and it was decided he would be sent to Seville as a second Indian page for the queen's prince Juan during our time in Spain.

Eighty-nine. *The admiral is titled and granted.*

On May 28, 1493, in a large ceremony, the Catholic sovereigns granted Don Christopher Columbus full perpetual nobility and his own seal. His brother Don Bartolomé was titled *adelantado*, a type of forward commander. This was a great day for the Columbus family, and everyone acclaimed the act. The admiral kept me close to him all that day. I was very proud and felt the genial delirium of our great Guamíquina, and I was quite conscious that a large fleet was getting together for our return to the islands and men of the highest ranks in Spain were pressing the admiral to go along. Father Las Casas's own father was among those who went on that second trip. Friends of the admiral arrived from Genoa and Portugal and Flanders. All of the Spanish court, including many destitute noble families, glued their attention to the admiral's tales of the islands' wealth. That other Spanish historian, Gonzalo Fernández de Oviedo, who is presently here in Santo Domingo, has told me he was there in Barcelona and saw me with the admiral as we walked and rode carriages around the city. Several times that I have seen him here in Española, Oviedo has declared this knowledge.

NINETY. *SOMETHING ABOUT OVIEDO: HE LIES ABOUT MY PEOPLE.*

I will say something here about Oviedo, who was and is a gold counter and *encomendero* who has become a historian. Oviedo is not a friend to us Indians; truly he has put forth many peculiar lies about our Taíno life and mocked our religion many times. It is true that Father Las Casas dismisses our Taíno religion, but at least he defends our capacity to become Christians. Oviedo scoffs at that very idea, accusing us of "wanton heathenism" for having ignored the preaching of the apostles, whom he says must have come among the Taínos at the time of Jesus Christ. This opinion he bases in the writings of Saint Gregory, who claimed the church had predicated all over the world the doctrine of redemption. "Indians can't pretend to be ignorant of the Christian faith, as they had news of the evangelical truth," Oviedo says now, and he justifies the *encomienda* as our fair punishment. He also says that we Indians have rock skulls so thick the Spanish used to break their swords on our foreheads. That is another of his lies. However, it is true that he was in Barcelona at that time, and the words he remembers me saying ring true to me now. "You talked about rivers of gold and men walking about wearing large plates of gold, who would trade gold for many of our things. You, Diego," he has mocked me several times, "brought more of our people from Castile to this island than anyone I know."

As I think about it now, this despicable man who predicates the enslavement and inferiority of my people is right to taunt me. And I do take responsibility that I seconded the admiral his claims during my stay on the Castilian lands. I got so used to talking up the good things, telling everyone what the admiral wanted them to hear, that I myself elaborated how much my people would love them, treat them graciously, and feed them, and I know that already in these claims the elements were being gathered for our destruction.

Why did I not see that earlier? Why was I so trusting to continue to believe that the Castilians had our best interests at heart? Why did I not see that as I bragged up my people's gentility, the men of those cities saw not friendly tradesmen and neighbors but easy servants and slaves; as they heard of gold in our hills, they thought not to go themselves to gather it but of how to force my people—men, women, children—to dig the gold and take it out for them. Oh, what my people have endured, what suffering and physical reduction for that mining of the gold! I hate to think of how I helped open that door, and even now I feel the need to atone for that and to do what I can to see that our people, however reduced, survive.

November 2, 1532

NINETY-ONE. *WITH RODRIGO'S GALLEGOS AT OTERO DEL REY, HIS MOTHER'S OFFERING TO THE DUENDES OF THE WATER SPRING.*

Rodrigo Gallego, our faithful friend, was going home and invited me to go along. He was from Galicia, from the village called Otero del Rey, near Lugo, west of Catalonia across the Basque country to the northwesternmost part of Iberia, north even of Portugal, where his own Gallego people lived. The admiral was done recruiting investors and granted me permission to go for the more than four months of the journey. That was my good-bye to Barcelona, as I would head south to Seville from Galicia. Rodrigo was not to go on the second voyage, but, as he was granted a royal appointment for the Academy of Guards at the court in Seville, after our visit to his parents he would accompany me to the Andalusian city, where I was to meet the admiral, Caréy, and the other travelers.

Leaving Maria del Carmen was difficult. I had little realized how deeply in love I had become. She was my first love, and, for days, as we rode away from Barcelona, lonely as a baby possum, I longed for her and cried. I thought of my elders in Guanahaní, and I remembered the dream of my puberty night and it was certainly her, Maria del Carmen, waiting there in my destined path, coming toward me across the *batéy*, old Ayragüex laughing at how he had seen it and it was all true.

The trip with Rodrigo had many weeks. He had bought all sorts of provisions for his family, including ax and hoe heads for his father and needles, cloth, and iron pots and pans for his mother. We traveled on two horses and led two pack mules, one with our provisions and the other loaded with gifts. We also carried the queen's seal in a letter of free passage, which proved useful while crossing the country of the Basques, through the low southern hills of the Pyrenees.

NINETY-TWO. *A RUN WITH BULLS FOR SAN FERMÍN.*

One of our stops, about halfway to Galicia, found us among the Basques, in a town called Pampeluna. I do remember we arrived there on July 6 of that year, 1493. I remember the day because the admiral had instructed me to keep a count of my days. He gifted me a pen, which I kept for many years, and two long-scroll rolls of paper. Every day of every week and month I made a mark. I did not yet know how to write or read (my Jewish friend Torres would begin me in that stead later in Seville), but nonetheless, I dutifully made my daily mark. This is why, often, long-distant dates jump before these written memories in the eye inside my mind, certain as the convent calendar.

Pampeluna was a crazy place, as cattlemen had driven in their cattle and their *vaqueros* had money for wine. A ceremonial time it apparently was, too, and a god of the Pamplones, a spirit man they called San Fermín, was on everyone's lips that day. In the early morning, an explosion of cannon or rocket awakened me to see Rodrigo already dressed and hanging out the window.

It was a cool summer morning, crisp as baked *cassabe*, but everything was confusing for me. The streets of the large village were crowded with people yelling and dancing with their arms around each other's shoulders. Before I could ask who San Fermín might be, so that I might greet him, too, Rodrigo joined in with the crowd, squirting wine out of bags into everyone's mouths. Then the crowd was yelling, "*Encierro, encierro*," meaning "enclosure," which I also wondered at, and then we were all moving down a very dusty street, the dust so thick I could hardly breathe. Down the street I could make out two big wooden corrals on the edge of an enclosed field, both full of ornery, horny bulls, big and thick as a fat *manatí*, thicker even, and with pointed stakes coming out of their heads and big sacks of balls dangling under the hind legs.

I was carried by the crowd at times, as everyone pressed together, jumping and crowding around the corrals. There was a priest, and some of the cattlemen stood by the gate of the corrals and they, too, were drinking wine. The crowd, all men, was hooting and laughing, and the bulls pranced around wild-eyed inside the corrals. Then the priest blessed the bulls with holy water. The crowd quieted and he was very solemn, speaking not Castilian but the old Basque language, and it made sense suddenly for me that they lived off the balls and production of these great bulls, and they were appreciating their food in a way we do also our *yucca* and our *hutía*, our doves and parrots, our iguana and our many fish and turtles, especially the turtles, which are so very useful and sacred to us.

What happened next was craziest of all. As the priest ended his blessing, cries of "*Viva San Fermín!*" filled the air, and the jumping and hollering all began again. I wondered about this San Fermín, that he might be a bull spirit, and was thus daydreaming when the crowd began running past me, and I found myself facing four bulls sniffing an open gate briefly before charging on me like a pack of sharks.

I folded myself into a ball on the hot sand. I pretended to be a turtle, just as I'd been thinking, and the bulls stopped short of me, again sniffing, and then there was Rodrigo actually hitting one on the snout and running, and the whole crowd running, and the bulls jumping past me. One stepped on my hand as he charged away.

I always remember that afternoon, nursing my hand and climbing on a fence to watch the bulls running with the crowd from one end of the field to another, and how the men touched the bulls' horns and jumped over them, and finally a bull charged into a group of men who fell back on each other, hooking his horn with a snap of the neck that sent men flying, one torn entirely across the gut so his entrails spilled out.

It was that bull that was left behind in the field as the others were coaxed and herded, with the aid of several steer, back into the corrals. The violent part happened then. A dozen men holding knives and sabers came out. Without hesitation, they charged the bull, who faced them, a bit winded but still defiant. Then they were all over him, cursing and stabbing and cutting at him as he humped and ran with men hanging from his legs and neck, stabbing into him and making him bleed.

Finally the bull stopped moving. He tried to hook under his own belly as a man gutted at him from underneath. Then the bull's entrails dropped on the man and he still stood as the man crawled away. Then all the men stabbed at him again and succeeded in pushing him over. A great cry went up from the crowd.

Rodrigo and I watched it together. I thought it way too bloody a ceremony. I wondered about the need of the men to kill the bull so violently, so bloodily. If they love the bulls so much, live off of them and even bless them, why do they fight them in a fury like that?

"It is just a custom," Rodrigo said when I asked him that as we rode west. "All over Spain they fight bulls."

He told me too that San Fermín is not a bull spirit, but a man saint, which confused me about it all over again. So I don't know even now what connection they were trying to make, but, truly it was repugnant to me. In our way, killing was done quickly, not excitedly if at all possible, and always apologizing, not cursing the being that will feed us.

NINETY-THREE. *RODRIGO'S HOME VILLAGE.*

Otero del Rey, Rodrigo's home village, sat on a knoll overlooking a tree-dotted plain. The whole valley plain was covered by small and large gardens and scattered sod huts. I saw men and women walking behind ox carts and leading pack burros down dusty roads. I saw the valley spread before me and it looked pretty.

As we rounded a hill, across the bottomlands from Rodrigo's family home, the news of our arrival preceded us. Descending a spiraling road opposite from us, a group of people was walking toward us. They met us halfway through the valley, shouting for Rodrigo and thanking out loud the Virgin Mary, Blessed Mother of God.

Those days were my best in Spain, quiet, listening to Rodrigo telling tales of his travels with Columbus, about whom they had not heard the news yet in Otero del Rey. Of course, the people marveled at me, touched me and pinched me, felt my long hair, fed me many soups and breads, even slaughtered a big pig for me on our second week, which they roasted and we fed on for days.

Rodrigo had four sisters and three brothers, all at home or living in nearby plots. They spoke a language called Gallego, different from the Castilian of Seville, the Basque of Euskera, and the Catalan of Barcelona. The brothers, their father, and two uncles worked the farms together, planting wheat, lentils, garlic, and large fields of cabbage. They also kept pigs, one cow with calf, and a flock of chickens. They all worked all day, every day, but, like in our own villages, Rodrigo's people had enough food and water for their families. On Saturday they drove a two-wheel wagon to market, and on Sunday they gathered at the same plaza to hear Mass.

One day I especially remember. Rodrigo helped his father fix a wagon wheel while his mother, Josefa, asked me to carry wide buckets of water for her. She was a small woman, rather wiry, and she was very kind to me, always ready with a broth or the herbal tea they called *cocimiento*. I walked with her and one sister up a mountain trail and then down to drop into a thicket of trees, where the air was suddenly moist.

"Wait," the mother of Rodrigo said. She had a small bundle of flowers in a bag and pulled it out. I watched as she knelt down and made a cross on the ground with a stick and then circled it. Then she lay down the flower bundle, thanking *dragas* for keeping the tree cover of the spring lush and maintaining the water flow. It impressed me that she used that very image, our own circle bisected, cut into the four directions. Her offering for the *dragas*, their "little people" guardians of the water spring. On the way back, Josefa said, "Don't tell anyone about my offering to the *dragas*, but if you must talk about it, talk about it with Rodrigo."

I never did ask Rodrigo about their *dragas*. It was something private for me, shared by his mother, who reminded me of my own mother and her own stories of the *higüe*, our ancient little beings that live under trees on the shores of our Guanahaní lake. My mother, too, offered gifts to the *higüe*, sometimes tobacco seeds, sometimes food. Often, she would crack open a *guayaba* and other fruits and leave them out for them.

I was sorry to leave Otero del Rey, where I met my friend Rodrigo's family, his mother Josefa and his father Manuél, a countryfolk who treated me like one more brother in the family, but at least Rodrigo would ride with me as far as Seville, and from that point on I would be on ship to return to our islands. The fervent hope of my heart during the long days on our way to Andalusia, as we crossed the interminable plains and mountains on horseback, was to open my eyes and see our little cove in Guanahaní, see our fishermen paddling their canoes. I would jump overboard and swim, swim to my shore, run to my village and my mother, my uncles and their many *bohíos*. My urgent need, I remember, was to see them once more and to tell them of my trip and of what happened to the women and our other people who had left on ship and tell them, too, of the strange and astonishing things I had seen in the Castilian land and how Cibanakán died.

Ninety-four. *Good-bye to Atoya, and Castile.*

Once on board at the Port of Cadiz, it was thirty-four days before we sighted Caribbean islands. Caréy was with me, and we missed Rodrigo dearly. Three of our Taíno compatriots returned with us, all except poor Atoya, who was given to young Prince Juan, Queen Isabel's son. Atoya, whom Caréy got to know quite well, was that nephew of Bayamo's. He appealed that we both go to the admiral directly with his wish to take the voyage home with us. He cried with us several times as we readied to leave Seville, but the admiral admonished us not to raise the question. "Inform Don Juan," as Atoya had been baptized, the admiral said, "that he now belongs to the prince of Castile, whom he serves. Tell him he will be educated in Christian ways by the prince's own majordomo and will forever reside in the court of the prince, who someday might be king." Poor, sad Atoya lasted less than a year in Spain, where he died of heartbreak at his lonely fate. Years later, when I heard that Prince Don Juan died after a hunting accident, breaking the heart of the king and queen, I felt Atoya and his people working their power from the other side.

November 8, 1532

NINETY -FIVE. *A COUNTRY WHERE MANY ARE POOR AND DESTITUTE AND A FEW ARE VERY RICH.*

That second voyage to our islands opened my eyes and taught me what I had not yet learned about the covered men. I met Cúneo on that trip, and Alonso de Hojeda, Doctor Alvarez Chanca, Father Buil, Pedro Margarit, and many others. Only a very few were kind or generous people in that lot. The majority were nobility, but of the impoverished variety, and there was nothing noble about them. One sailor made up a ditty: "Poor in Seville gets rich in Antille—and always regal in the eye of the Lord." They liked it so much, it was sung aboard many of the ships, over and over as we crossed the ocean.

The royal nobility, or the Hidalgos, as they called themselves, laughed among themselves and often derided the crew and low-caste artisans and laborers on board. They ordered them around rudely and imposed so many punishments the ships' captains had to intervene to quell rising hostilities. On one thing, however, all the Castilians were agreeable: all desired the gold of the islands, all dreamed of striking it rich and returning to Castile as *gran señores*, a goal for which they were willing to take amazing risks and inflict the most horrendous of punishments, particularly on us Indians.

I had a better idea now what the Castilians meant by *rich* and *poor*. I had seen it in their cities and even in their villages. Among some families, you saw some very large houses, with walls around them, called castles, surrounded by stables and barns and fields of herds and crops. These big families mostly raised sheep. They employed or held some peasants, who are their poor people, but don't feed them much. It happens these poor people don't have enough to eat, yet they are not allowed to use the land freely, even if it is abandoned. All the land belongs to the king or the barons, or the church, and these vast expanses are not open to the common people.

This I had noticed as we traveled south from Galicia across Extremadura to Seville. Their poor people were everywhere, and there was hunger everywhere. In the country villages, those who had land of their own survived better, raised crops, and kept their people together. But most of the people had no land of their own or land that they could work and inhabit. In the cities, they had next to nothing, not even food sometimes, and begged in the streets.

The poor Castilian huts in the cities were crowded together, most often with pigs and chickens, even cows. While walking through those parts of their towns, I often found their stench unbearable, and I was always affected by the wild look in the eyes of so many children, who were scabby and sickly and kept begging and begging from anyone who walked by.

November 9, 1532

NINETY-SIX. *THE ROMANCE OF CÚNEO'S MARES.*

I have written earlier about Michele de Cúneo, when I told about Bayamo's curse on the admiral during our later trip to Cuba. Indeed, of that second and, for me, final crossing of the great waters, I remember most indeed the deeds of this great crony of the admiral's. Of great interest, too, is Captain Hojeda, a powerful, brutal man. But first, I will write about Cúneo's mares.

Cúneo, that Genoese dandy, had a great eye for opportunity, and I believe he was the first of the colonists to make a profit on that journey. During the voyage, as an investment for settling in the islands, Cúneo transported two mares on board our ship. By the third week of warm, calm seas, many men on board felt desperate with lust. Cúneo perceived the opportunity and organized matters to make gains on his two mares, initiating a quiet affair that went on for several weeks. I was full of wonder that many of the men on board were comfortable with the use of the mares to pacify themselves, but it appeared to be so, as even of those that did not participate, none questioned the arrangement. And Cúneo took in thirty *maravedí* per session.

A close friend of the admiral's, Cúneo was the only man I knew who could tell raunchy stories to the Great Mariner. No one else would have dared, but Cúneo had a way of speaking Genoese that Don Christopherens appreciated and made him laugh. Even Don Christopherens knew about the romance of the mares, as Cúneo called it. Many evenings while they dined together in the admiral's cabin, I heard Don Christopherens laugh as Cúneo regaled him with jokes and his tales of the "romance."

November 14, 1552

Ninety-seven. *Captain Alonso de Hojeda, the perfect soldier.*

We came upon the southern islands, those that guide our way from the mainland, early in November 1493. The people of those islands were not Taínos, Siboney, or Ciguayo, but tribes of the Kwaib, the island warriors who raided against us in the northern Caribbean islands.

The admiral delighted in sighting the new islands and went about naming one after another in his language. He named one after our ship, the *Marie Galante*, another one Dominica, after his own father, Doménico, and so on. He insisted on doing this, even though I always told him our word for each place, words always more exacting than the Castilian he provided.

Among the men on board who quickly distinguished themselves, Alonso de Hojeda stood out. He was a short man among the Spaniards, but everyone commented on his perfect physical being. I remember in Seville, during an afternoon when Queen Isabel invited local entertainment, it was Hojeda who impressed her. First, he won a ball-throwing contest, throwing a rubber ball higher than anyone else. Then he walked on his hands for a full hour, straight as a tree. Then he amazed the court by stringing a rope high from one building to another and walking upon it, back and forth. The queen gave him special mention and inducted him into the second voyage herself.

On ship, though not a sailor by profession, Hojeda could climb the mast faster than all the seamen. And he could haul sail, pull rope, take fathom, and load anchor in superlative fashion. He was also quick to fight and to draw blood. Hojeda saw combat as a captain in the Moorish wars. Cúneo, who had also been a soldier, befriended Hojeda at that time, and Hojeda reciprocated, though his obsessive devotion to the Virgin Mary and his severity of character did not allow him to approve of Cúneo's horse enterprise.

Ninety-eight. *Meeting the "man-eating" Kwaib, how tales get started.*

We were anchored in a small cove. Several men had gone ashore days ago without return. Hojeda went with forty men to hunt the lost party down but returned without them. The men had vanished in the dense foliage. For days, the admiral tacked along the shore of the island. Hojeda made several forays. He reported sighting villages and brought back baskets full of bones.

On board, he showed them to the admiral, who said, "Man-eaters," and had Dr. Chanca examine the bones. Dr. Chanca found scrapes and notches on the bones and declared them to be tooth marks. "These bones have been chewed," he said. On another occasion, human bones were also found boiling in a pot. This time it was Cúneo who declared the island inhabited by man-eaters. "Write it in your journal," the admiral told him. "I will write it, too," Dr. Chanca said.

On both of these occasions, I remarked to the admiral that the boiling and the preservation of bones in baskets was more a funerary practice than it was about man-eating, as these were both customs of our own Taíno people as well, and we certainly were not man-eaters. We dried our dead in the sun and the rain, then used shell tools to scrape the remaining flesh from the bones. The flesh is buried near where the belly button of the person was originally buried, and the bones are either buried or accommodated in baskets which are kept in the *bohíos* of those families. These things are considered sacred among our people.

"You are wrong," the admiral snapped at me. "Guacanagari told me about these people. And your own women cried about them, and your uncle Cibanakán commented on their raids. These are the Carib man-eaters!"

I withdrew my observations, but I was not convinced. I always felt that these were mostly old stories and beliefs of our people. Even though some of these practices occurred, the extent of the man-eating was aggrandized. It is true that my own Guanahaní island was quite far for such raids, and thus we had less contact with those legendary enemies of the Taíno. But it is also true that I have heard stories told in the ancient *areitos*, both among my Guanahaní people and the people from Haiti-Bohío, of the ancient blood feuds and how warriors would expect the right to eat a dead enemy's thigh and heart.

It was later, from the elder *caciques* of Bohío, especially Guarionex, that I heard the other stories, the ones that told about the "change of heart" ceremony. These were tales made up of episodes, each detailing, one by one, how the old warriors who lived to make war and eat their enemies were convinced to love the gentle peace ways, how, as the years went by, they would become Taíno, lovers of sea breeze, lovers of the gentle waves and the clean running waters.

I have seen also a canoe of Ciguayo warriors who paddled back from a fight with an enemy's thigh hanging at the bow of their canoe. They would let the meat dry and harden in the sea salt and sun, and then, at special times, those men who had been in the fight would taste of the jerky from the thighbone, at once honoring the warrior and consuming his flesh, spiritually defeating him.

What I never, ever heard of was anyone cooking up human meat as a daily food, as basic meals for their people and children. Yet this was the talk among the important Castilians on board the admiral's ship, some even claiming that the man-eaters would castrate their own boys and fatten them up for the *barbacoa*. The soldiering men on board began to take out their weapons, sharpening swords, stringing crossbows, and cleaning harquebuses.

November 16, 1532

NINETY-NINE. *DISCOVERERS ARE SAVED BY INDIAN GRANDMOTHER.*

An old Kwaib woman whose name I never learned guided our lost party to a promontory from where she estimated nightime fire and daytime smoke signals could be seen by the ships. Those men could easily have been ambushed and eaten by the Kwaib at that time, but they were not. Instead, they were fed, and on the second day a sailor on the high mast spotted the smoke signals from shore. Hojeda was dispatched on rowboats to fetch the group.

ONE HUNDRED. *PERFECT PROOF OF CARIB PERFIDY: A CASTRATED BOY.*

A conversation I heard some days later between Cúneo and the admiral and some officers and hidalgos about the rules of war during the early crusades and even back in their old-time memory to the Greek and Roman wars. Again the topic of man-eating was discussed, with Columbus and Cúneo explaining that such men were judged among the most abominable of heathens and were legitimately considered slaves. The people now encountered were opposed to my own Taíno people, whom the admiral said to be peaceable and potential converts to the true faith. But the Kwaib, or Carib, eat people and thus are enemies that should be taken as slaves, he said. There was much concurrence about the disgusting nature of the practice of the Caniba and even our own Taíno on board thanked the admiral for making the distinction between us, Taíno, men of the good, and the horrible Kwaib who would eat people. I must admit, I felt some relief and even pride at that moment that we had such a standing with the admiral, even though I did not believe and have never seen where people would eat the meat of humans as a regular meal.

At one island, I forget which one, several young men and women were captured. A young man was wounded and sore in his crotch, causing him great pain. To my eye, the wound was infectious. He had scabs on his thighs and on the edges of his lips and it was my impression that our dreaded genital illness, the one that is passed through coupling, had taken hold in him. I could not make out his language fully, but he was able to tell me that a Kwaib healer tried to remove one if his swollen testicles, and that had caused him greater pain. The admiral had Dr. Chanca inspect the boy, and he noted the partial amputation. "The young man has been castrated," Dr. Chanca declared.

"Why would they do so, I do not know."

"I would assume the purpose was to fatten him up and soften his flesh for the pot," Cúneo said as the admiral nodded. But they were all unfamiliar yet with diseases of our hotlands.

Everyone nodded and grimaced, and word spread like fire through the seventeen ships of the armada. Several officers requested permission to inspect the young man in the days ahead. Dr. Chanca insisted at first that the analysis of the castration was speculation, but Cúneo and the admiral were convinced of its accuracy. Cúneo became a guide to the young man's corner. "They not only castrate these youngsters," he would lecture, "but they eat their own off-spring that they engender in the captured women." He would laugh loudly and wink. "They say the flesh of the young boys tastes better than the young girls!"

ONE HUNDRED ONE. *HOJEDA DRAWS FIRST BLOOD, CÚNEO IN ON FIRST FIGHT.*

We were anchored in a cove at the island of Ayay, which the admiral renamed Holy Cross. Cúneo and Hojeda organized a party to explore inland. They were already in the large rowboats when a canoe full of Kwaib rounded the point of the cove and came to a complete standstill in the water, mesmerized by the sight of seventeen Spanish ships and caravels.

"At them, by Santiago!" Hojeda and then Cúneo both shouted. "Get the Caribs!"

They were four men and two women, and they showed no particular fear as our men in two rowboats, filled with twelve soldiers each, plus the two captains and four rowers, started toward them. As the boats neared, one older warrior in the canoe notched an arrow and shouted at the rowboats to stop and hold their distance. But the oarsmen kept rowing hard, and the captains steered at the canoe.

The Kwaib paddled to the side, avoiding the first pass. Two crossbowmen let lose with arrows, wounding one warrior as three men and one woman among the Kwaib also let lose with arrows. The older warrior this time spiked an arrow through one of the Castilian men, who fell to the bottom of the boat. Another soldier caught an arrow in the stomach, but it didn't penetrate far beyond his leather vest.

The Kwaib might have paddled away rapidly as their canoes are faster at paddling than ship's boats, but it didn't seem to cross their minds. I watched from the ship, thinking how our own Taíno people would have taken flight, given the opportunity to survive. Victory for us was many times as simple as surviving to continue pursuing our way of life. Rather than fight head-on, Taínos preferred to retire from the field of action, if at all possible, and let the ires pass.

Not the Kwaib. They liked a good fight. These ones never paddled again, but rather let their canoe drift, lapped toward shore by the waves. Cúneo's rowboat stayed near, menacing and firing arrows at the canoe, but with small effect. As the Kwaib drifted toward a sandbank, still some distance from the shore, Hojeda's rowboat, which had unfurled a sail and was maneuvering quite rapidly in the cove, managed to ram their canoe, spilling them all in the water. The fight took place within view of many of us at the stern of the *Santa Maria*.

Treading water, the Kwaib, all except the wounded man, raised themselves out of the water and fired their arrows. The woman warrior was exceptional, a long-legged swimmer, with strong, long arms. As Cúneo's boat approached dead on to hit her in the water, she swam to the side and let go an arrow that traversed an oarsman, doubling him over as the boat passed. But steering the boat, Cúneo turned his stern into her, knocking her over in the water, circling rapidly around to pull her in.

Not far away, Hojeda's crossbowmen fired volley after volley of arrows into two other Kwaib, including another woman; they looked like spiny fish in the water after a while. The first wounded man Hojeda himself decapitated just under the ears as he passed him on the water. However, an old Kwaib warrior, a good shooter and fast swimmer, reached the sandbank. He managed to wound another one of Hojeda's men and was wounded himself with arrows to the legs as the boat approached him. The old warrior jumped into the waves just as Hojeda spiked him through with a lance. Hojeda bore down on the lance with the old man under water for a couple minutes then yanked it back forcefully. The Kwaib went limp, but as Hojeda began to turn the boat around, slowly, the old warrior, using only one arm, started swimming away toward shore.

This time, Hojeda overtook the Kwaib easily, using a gaff to hook him and pull him in. Then he had a soldier yank the warrior's head over the edge of the boat while he brandished his sharp cutlass, hacking the neck clean through in two sharp blows.

"Watch the man-eater swim now," I remember the priest, Father Buil, saying on board as Hojeda held up the head for us to see.

November 20, 1532

ONE HUNDRED TWO. *CÚNEO'S TREATMENT OF A KWAIB WARRIOR WOMAN.*

One more thing on Cúneo. He showed his woman warrior to the admiral, who granted her to him as his personal captive. Cúneo pulled the woman to his cabin and tied her down. He came out to urinate and went back in. Immediately we heard him yell. Then, we could hear thrashing going on inside the room and the high-pitched, nearly inaudible screams of the warrior woman. Many men crowded around outside as the sounds of struggle gave way to the dull pounding of the admiral's great friend into her Kwaib flesh.

Cúneo emerged triumphant and smiling. The men cheered him and envied him. "Better than a mare, boys," he said. "Much better."

ONE HUNDRED THREE. *CARÉY RESPONDS TO CÚNEO.*

Caréy and I hated him. I would meet crueler men, more gross and more violent than Cúneo, but for some reason I hate him nearly most of all. I hate even the memory of his handsome, arrogant face.

In a fortnight, Cúneo was offering his woman slave out for lease at one hundred *marivedís* a session. Caréy objected. I cautioned him against it, but he insisted on saying something. "The woman is brave," he told Cúneo, in front of several men. "Allow her to recover and not be used by so many men."

Without warning, Cúneo delivered a great blow to Caréy's face, which felled him against a net. Cúneo, his face very red, put a knife to my countryman's throat. "Don't ever question me, dog," he said. "Or I'll sell you to these men. You might be better than a mare yourself."

He didn't rape Caréy but struck him another hard blow, this time to the chest, with the handle of his knife. Caréy doubled over in pain.

The rest of the voyage was day-by-day misery for Caréy, constantly taunted, struck, and threatened, not only by Cúneo but by several other braggarts on board, including two who really wanted to bugger my poor cousin. Father Buil was another one of them who had that inclination. I kept Caréy near me as I served the admiral and even inducted him into the *ampolleta* shifts, but he had become a desperate being, suffocating in the tension of the threats.

I lost him in Borikén, which we reached on November 19, 1493.

One night, while we drifted a mile from the coast, he loaded up on hawk's bells ("For gifts on the way home"), wrapped up a knife he had pilfered from a sailor, and announced to me he would swim to shore and take his chances from there. Three women from a group rescued from a Kwaib camp were from Borikén, having been taken by Kwaib weeks before. They had decided to go overboard and swim in to shore. Caréy was to help them by cutting their ropes, while they promised to speak well for him among their people. I asked him to consider our better opportunity to get home from Bohío, as the admiral had promised we would round the Maisí Point of Cuba later and go out to our little islands. But Caréy was decided, and in the dark of a night without moon, he and the three women slipped overboard. I heard them swim away, my heart praying for love among our Boricua brothers to help get my cousin home. I don't know if he ever made it, and I never saw or heard of Caréy again.

November 2e, 1532

ONE HUNDRED FOUR. *THE NEWS ON FORT NAVIDAD.*

The admiral was terribly excited as we sailed on to Española's coasts, which we hugged in search of Fort Navidad, the admiral's first colony on our lands. Aboard all vessels there was great anticipation. The sea voyage had been difficult on the passengers, the majority of whom had no sailing experience. The talk was of buildings and the uses of woods and how much gold would be secured. I remember hearing long discussions on the carrying capacity of the various vessels, how much gold each of them could safely hold. "Gold makes great ballast," was an often-repeated ditty, though it never made it into song.

None had thoughts of farming at that moment, and I certainly don't believe anymore that even one of them had the Christian mission in mind. Father Buil, the ranking cleric, was an ornery, gnarled man. Nothing kind or inspired came out of him, though he talked incessantly, particularly at the admiral, who heard him out with absent mind. Buil, the buzzard, we called him, talked a lot about the Grand Khan and dreamed of establishing relations for his order of the Benedictines.

It was late November 1493 when we came upon the Navidad coast. As always, canoes from small fishing villages came out to greet us. The admiral meant to press on, but for several days the winds strongly disfavored us. One canoe that circled the admiral's ship I recognized. It had the three-line mark of Guacanagari's *caciquedom*. Two of the men seated in it were uncles of the young *cacique*.

"Taíno-ti, uncles of our great *cacique* friend," I greeted them as they came within earshot. "Can you see that the covered men from Heaven have returned?"

They nodded at me and paddled close to where I stood on deck. "We are glad to see the double tongue," they said and fell silent. They asked not for the Guamíquina, and their silence was ominous. I threw them a line of rope that they could hold. The older subchief stood in the canoe. "We would speak with the young Taíno two-tongue," he said. "Quietly, let us converse a day ourselves."

I sat in the low hold, the rope in my hand. "A horrible fight has taken place," the elder said, beginning a story that lasted all afternoon and ended with the words: "The covered men left by the Guamíquina are all dead."

ONE HUNDRED FIVE. *HOW FORT NAVIDAD WAS OVERRUN BY* CACIQUE *CAONABÓ.*

Here I will relate the story as told by Guacanagari's subchief, whose name was Guababo and who stood in his canoe as he said these words that are still clear in my memory. Guababo talked all afternoon. Several times he cried. I will write his own words as much as I remember them.

"As we promised the Guamíquina: after you left in the giant canoes, the people of our two villages nearby to Navidad supplied the covered men with food. We had agreed in my village that every day, men and women of my *guaxeri* would go to the covered men's houses carrying pack-baskets of fruit and our *ñames*, stacks of fresh *cassabe* bread, and at least two hand counts of fish or lobster caught that very morning. My village was one of two compromised to feed half of the men, which was the count of my fingers twice. This we performed for fourteen days without incident and were quite willing to continue, and more than that, it was a happiness for us to perform this task for our cacique, *Guacanagari.*

"My *guaxeri* group of ten assigned to this task started with the sun, sang *areitos* to bless the food gathered, and even paraded formally through my *yukaieke*, walking in the four directions of our sacred ritual, which is the design of our villages, before taking the trail to Navidad.

"I say to you now, a ceremony we established to feed the guests of our *cacique*, and this would have lasted right to today. I say happy we were to take this distinction for our beloved young *cacique* and our council, on which I, too, have a seat.

"Now, give me your ears, my relative. On the night of the fifth day, two loud thunders from the camp at Navidad we heard. Scouts were sent and much shouting they reported among the covered men.

"On the fifteenth day, our *guaxeri* their foods delivered to the Castilian camp. A man had been killed, they reported back to us. It was the young one we knew as Jácome. His body was layed out in a hut, showing blood and stab wounds, and the covered men had gathered at two ends of the camp. One group called themselves Biscayans while the others said they were true Castilian.

"On the seventh day, precisely while our *guaxeri* were at the camp, two men fought suddenly with sharp sabers, and one was cut badly in the arm and retreated. The victor, whose name was Pedro Gutiérrez, said: 'Now I do as I please.'

"Among our *guaxeri* food suppliers were a mother and a daughter, both healthy women. The father in that family was a fisherman who was one of the suppliers of the food, though he was not a carrier to the camp. The soldier Gutiérrez took both women and had his men hold them. Pointing to the women, he said, '*Daca, daca,*' meaning "I am" in our language, but by which he meant "you are mine." That done, the women cried out, and all my *guaxeri* ran for home.

"On the eigth day, the woman's husband and his brother went to the camp. Behind them, our *guaxeri* feeders, still carrying their baskets of food, hid in the forest as the two men entered the Castilian camp. To demand his wife and daughter, the husband went to Gutiérrez and pleaded. Without speaking, Gutiérrez stabbed him. The brother another Castilian cut. The brother ran but our *guaxeri* husband dropped and bled and died."

This was the beginning of many horrors, according to the subchief. Every one of the covered men then took women—sisters, daughters, and mothers together—and they used them in coitus, and harshly. The men hoarded three or four, even five women each. Husbands and brothers who demanded their families were cut and stabbed at will in the weeks that followed, and the people were angered.

"No more would we feed the Castilians, and a council was called with Guacanagari," said Guababo, who stood in the canoe, straight as a pole, despite the roll of waves, but trembling slightly all the time. "Our *cacique* attended. He heard the stories of the killing and cried with us. Then he and all his wise ones reminded us of our promise to the Guamíquina. 'They are men from Heaven,' he insisted to us. 'Let us continue as before until the Guamíquina returns.'

"In all truth, we tried. Our ways you know, young two-tongue. We ni-Taíno tried to forget the atrocity, but none of our people would go near the covered men. The Castilians fought among themselves, again and again, until finally they broke up in three groups, two of which left, one to the Magua of our uncle, *Cacique* Guarionex, and the other to Maguana, the region of *Cacique* Caonabó, titled by Taíno but a Ciguayo warrior man nonetheless, not to be disturbed."

Guababo related that both groups took women and food along the way and cut down any man that objected. Thus, the word spread of their marauding, and the chiefs admonished all to stay away from them.

"Their comings and goings we tracked with scouts and runners," Guababo continued. "They were two small groups and they moved fast. Our people are very good at disappearing in the trees, and some were still surprised in their daily chores. Without warning, then, more and more, the covered men attacked and killed the Taíno men, took the women, and chased off the children. We heard the stories as our runners returned, telling of each incident. Caught with gold on his neck, an old man they tortured, gouging his eyes when he could not turn up more gold.

"Three moons passed and our *cacique* received a messenger from the Ciguayo *cacique*, Caonabó, anouncing a visit. Caonabó, who I say is a Ciguayo and only by marriage a Taíno, only now learning our ways, soon himself arrived at our own *cacique*'s village. He demanded to know who these men were that were doing such terrible things to his people. Soon, he said, his many warriors would destroy these men.

"Our beloved Guacanagari argued with Caonabó against attacking the Castilians. Caonabó told him: 'Cousin: if you are host to these people, why are they so mean to my own? As for you, man-boy, you are a little thing. Cousin: understand, the deed is for me to do.'

"Two more moons passed. It is known that one group of the Castilians went through the country of Guarionex, then in time it passed as well into Caonabó's villages. We did not hear from Guarionex, our revered grandfather, until much later, but then we learned that he had gone in retreat over the news of the Castilians and that, like Guacanagari, he ordered his warriors to avoid contact with the roamers. Over these news of covered men, seven days twice, Guarionex fasted, and many times at his runners' descriptions of the covered men he cried."

At that point, standing in his canoe, the old subchief cried, too. And as I write now, I, too, cry, remembering the jolt of his tale upon my eager ears. It was the most horrible thing he was telling me—not the many abuses Guababo's people had suffered, which already in my mind I felt would be remedied by the admiral's presence, but I feared I was about to hear of a retaliation, of an ill deed committed against Castilian men by our island people, and that shook me to the bone.

"By his *cacique* permission, Caonabó's fighters took down the Castilian covered men," the subchief said. "By ones and by twos, arrows they shot into them, and from behind trees they clubbed them. When most had suffered wounds and other Castilians panicked, our warriors rushed them and finished them off."

"Killed all were they?" I asked in our common tongue.

"Every one, yes. Then to Navidad Caonabó came, and the fort he burned. To the sea the Castilians rushed, swinging swords, as foolishly they fled into the waters, where no match were they for Caonabó's men."

ONE HUNDRED SIX. *THE STORY DENIED.*

At the end of the tale, the elders would not stay. They would come back later, they said, with presents for the admiral.

That evening (November 27) they did return and the admiral they greeted by candlelight, seeking out his face in the dark. They talked a long time as I waited anxiously for the story of the killings to emerge, but it did not. Instead, the admiral was told by the uncles that the Navidad fort was still well, reporting a few deaths due to illness and nothing else. A gift of gold they gave Don Christopherens, two gold masks of beautiful workmanship, for which they took back, and happily, a dozen hawk's bells.

Out of sight were they in their canoes when I told the admiral the truth of the situation, how Caonabó and others had killed off all thirty-nine Castilians left behind. He yelled at me. "Liar!" And he was much angered, calling me a dog and a braggart, loudly, and I believe he might have struck me, but the shriek in his own voice stopped him. He was already fatigued of mind in a long season that would take him into the next September, the first full cycle of Castilian inhabitation in our islands.

Earfuls he got now daily from the large number of men onboard the ships, crowded and indisposed these many weeks. The heady boasting of great wealth to come, easy servants, and nubile maidens, bragging lies of Barcelona and Seville would now catch up with him (and me). Complaints there were and already accusations. They were quiet yet, murmurs, but they were constant.

I slept outside Don Christopherens's cabin door that evening. I heard him cry, and that's when I knew that he knew. Next morning, we came upon the site of Fort Navidad. Bodies were found, first two, then eleven, even more later. The fort was burned to the ground, no notes or messages of any kind left behind.

Numbly, over the charred ground, the admiral walked, then he directed a search for gold, digging out the well now covered with stones and turning over other likely sites as well. But no gold was found. "Damned barbarians!" was a favorite expression, spat often from those days.

I remember Father Buil. All were angry at the deed of violence, but Father Buil was maniacal. Face contorted, he walked to and fro. "They should hang for killing Christians. They should burn," he demanded, although he officiated not even one burial of his people, a strange act I never understood.

The admiral led us away, to a place up the coast where he would found a new town, which he called Isabela, in honor of the queen. For eight days we fought contrary winds before landing the armada (a word I would come to understand) at his chosen site.

ONE HUNDRED SEVEN. *ISABELA IS BUILT, THE FIRST METROPOLIS.*

I remember now the building of Isabela, where I learned to pound nails and size up planks. I remember Columbus talking again with Guacanagari, how his people still helped the Castilians build and how they marveled at the cows and pigs, chickens, sheep, and horses that came off the ships. I remember Father Buil crying for blood, Hojeda angered, and how everybody in that first town seemed irritated all the time. They were angry at our ni-Taíno, whom they were, for the moment, obliged to respect; they insulted our *guaxeri* their lack of building skills; they quickly abused our *naboria*, assuming a complete superiority toward our simpler cousins; they were angry at our trees, which were so big and hard to cut. They prayed to the Virgin Mary and the Holy Infant, Jesus; they prayed to the Holy Trinity; they prayed to the pope and the queen and the king. But right from that moment, as they fixed their corrals and their mills, as they planted new seeds brought over from their world, they cursed everything ours. They cursed at our insects, they cursed at our foods, they blasphemed our spirits and *cemis*, they even cursed at the mother sea.

A deep sadness settled over my spirit as we built Isabela, one I had held at bay, I realize now, even since the intimations of my father-uncles that first night at Guanahaní, what the *cohoba* had shown them. All we Indians could see, for one thing, the Castilians were building Isabela on a pestilent swamp, where no good water was to be had. For all their mountains of knowledge, we were learning that the covered men are often blind to the simplest, most obvious things. Any simple *naboria* can tell you a village must be built near good water.

My elders' words came back to me often at that time, and I so much wanted to see them and my mother again. I had already a terrible agitation in my belly, and then our heat made the Castilians' wine go sour. As the covered men built their houses, our *guaxeri*, by order of Guacanagari, brought them gourds full of juices from dozens of fruit trees that grew all around, wonderful juices not to be found anywhere in Spain. But the Castilians cursed them nonetheless, and many sipped obstinately on their rancid wine. The darkest of clouds was gathering, I could tell, a temper of ire in the back of the eyes, the *cassabe*-colored men were so hard. Such was my feeling in that first season of colony, as their first houses were built and the plans were drawn, right at the admiral's table, for the settling of Castilian towns on our Taíno lands.

January 6, 1533

ONE HUNDRED EIGHT. *MY LOSS OF INNOCENCE.*

It has been three weeks and I pick up this pen. This pen I hold that opens forth so much hurt, arousing memories of a more innocent time, of my own elders and what happened to them. I sit to write and the mere act provides picture after picture, as in those painted *cuadros* that I saw at the Cathedral of Seville, Christ being flogged, Christ being stabbed, Christ bleeding in the agony of crucifixion. I remember real crucifixions; I remember beheadings upon beheadings; I remember wanton injuries to child and mother, wanton, wanton, the boot of the soldier applied to the neck, the torch of the Inquisition to the pyre of Taíno. But of all that my mind can hold, I most dread the memory of my own innocence, my Taíno goodwill upon which I have gathered so much hatred.

ONE HUNDRED NINE. *A DEVILISH BOUT WITH THE GRAPE.*

The result of memories brought on by this task of writing, plus a touch of devilry, an incident occurred on New Year's Eve. It has cost me dearly with the monks and even puts in jeopardy how much I can do in the Enriquillo negotiations. I am so bothered with myself, I will write it here, as confession.

In agony had I finished writing on Carey and my elders when Fray Remigio offered a bottle, an error in judgment for both he and I. A bottle of wine we passed back and forth, the young monk and I, as we weeded my patch of onions and peas. The wine we drank in the late afternoon as the sun cooked my brain. By dinnertime, a holiday affair that day, I was deep in my spine, or, I should say, my spleen. For one thing, I sat at the abbot's table without care, waiting as the younger monks served me. Usually, I would serve some part of the table. As wine was passed, I drank a glass and then another. His Eminence, abbot Enrique Mendoza, sat at the head chair. He is a calm man, old and a bit frail for his many duties, though he walks steadily through his day, and his sharp eye misses little.

"Master Diego has had his pleasure in the wine today," he said, with a glance at Fray Remigio, who immediately felt the scrutiny.

"My mind is clear, Your Eminence" I said. "Fear not unreason from this humble *guaxeri*." It was true: I had just entered that place that wine can bring you where everything gets starkly clear. It had been a long time, nearly five years since the last time I succumbed, though I admit I have had my long days of inebriation.

"I fear not," the abbot said. "Tonight is the eve of the new year. We shall eat well and enjoy good company. Among others, Judge Suazo himself will soon join us, and I believe he brings along that noted intellect Don Gonzalo, who I am sure will prove highly entertaining."

A worse combination could not have been joined by the devil himself. Don Gonzalo, of course, was Oviedo. I felt my whole body stiffen—anticipation and loathing quickly stirring my senses.

"Fernández de Oviedo y Valdés," I said with loose tongue, pronouncing fully the Castilian sounds I have learned too well. "It is a good thing Don Bartolomé is not present."

Several monks laughed a bit too heartily and the abbot smiled, mischievously, knowing Don Bartolomé and Oviedo are bitter enemies. Abbot Mendoza has a sense of strategy. He supports the positions of Don Bartolomé, but the two men are often at odds on daily matters. The good friar's reputation and authority can at times suffocate all other volition, and the old abbot is often overshadowed by Las Casas. So, in his absence, the abbot courts the same high office holders of Santo Domingo, including Suazo, who have approached the good friar.

Minutes later, *Oidor* Suazo and Oviedo were the first guests to arrive. Oviedo recognized me at once. I remained in my chair as he took his seat, and in his face I could see some wonderment at my presence at the table. "Our great admiral's Dieguillo-boy has grown into quite the personage," he said. "Now he sits as a guest of abbots."

"Properly, sir," I responded. "It is you who are my guests, as the islands are my natural home."

Food and wine were presented promptly by monks who hurried in the silence following my remark. But I was feeling good. Besides, custom was on my side. Governor Diego Columbus himself it was, legitimate son of the admiral and former governor of the Española island, who in his father's own memory granted me the right to join a Castilian table, sitting me near him many times at official gatherings in the final weeks before leaving his governorship.

"The Indian is a notable one," Suazo joined in, as always speaking of Indians only in the third person. "Truly, he can say he was with the first admiral, may his grand soul rest in eternal peace."

"Thank you, sir," I replied, reminding them: "It was by order of the Columbus family that I have this privilege—"

"Very well, Dieguillo," the abbot interrupted me. But I continued.

"—to sit in the company of such esteemed intellect and authority as the present company."

The meal began quietly at that juncture, and I was silent as the young monks serving plates of fish, fowl and pork, rice and beans, scurried about. I knew a reproach was likely from the abbot if I persisted, and though my nerve to push the conversation was taut, I naturally backed off. In my mind I have been contemplating the work ahead with Enriquillo and the good friar and have wanted to avoid, now most of all times, any public altercation whatsoever.

In my silence, as always with a *guaxeri* like me, I was totally ignored. Perhaps I am that good at dissimulation by now, after years of surviving by blending into my own trance. But it was not hard, really, as the company quite readily ceased to see me altogether, even the abbot (thus I continued sipping).

As they do on this island on New Year's Eve, other gentlemen dropped by, and the table grew to more than ten important men. Only I and young Silverio, who was helping to serve dinner, were Indians in the room. The convent cook had prepared four large *brazos gitanos*, a common sweet cake of Valencia, and the abbot turned over the wine cellar key to the serving monks, who kept pouring it. The company conversed about many subjects, from the preparations for planting new sugarcane to the variety of accommodation and experience of the ocean passage, but finally, as always, their conversation ranged to the life of the people who had been encountered on our islands, how they did this or that, subjects acutely painful to me.

Of course, Oviedo dominated in this regard. He liked speaking about my people, as he is also writing a history of the Indies, talking of Indios and ni-Taínos, this *cacique* and that one, about villages of the large islands and of the *lucayas*, speaking even of my long-lost home of Guanahaní. I sipped as he explained who we were and how we acted in the times before the Castilians. For nearly two hours, the wine, rather than excite me to violence, distanced me from Oviedo's words.

At one point, while drinking steadily, Oviedo talked about the marriages of my people and how they were accustomed to making love. He went on and on, as I had heard him years before (and precisely at the table of Don Diego Columbus, the second admiral), about the *caciques* having many wives and how upon a *cacique*'s death, sometimes one or more wives would be buried with him.

Everyone laughed. "A hard lot on wives," said an *ascendado* sitting to my left. "Of course, the Indians did many barbaric things."

I twisted inside myself, not because what he said about *cacique*'s wives was totally untrue, but because in my mind it was not cause for such ridicule. In my mind, the Castilians did much more barbaric things. "It is of interest," I said, "that more often than not, a wife's devotion and love compelled her voluntary journey to the spirit island, what we call Coaybay."

"Even so, a barbaric custom it is," Oviedo answered quickly.

"Yet, I wonder if a Christian lady would ever consider doing so, that is, out of devotion?"

I got a laugh out of most of the men, including *Oidor* Suazo.

"The Indian is clever," said the *oidor*.

"So observed the most revered Queen Isabel, the Catholic, at Barcelona, when she met me in 1493," I said.

I realized I was being boorish to speak so much, interjecting myself like this, but as I sat in my chair and looked upon their persons, they all became smaller and smaller, and I felt the superiority of my knowledge.

"The Dieguillo is clever," said the abbot, "but tonight his tongue rides the nectar of the vine. He forgets our Spanish ladies, whole convents of nuns, are devoted to the one true Lord."

I raised my glass to him with a nod, both in deference and mockery. But it was a table gesture I had seen in the nobility, and it ingratiated me somewhat (or so I thought) to the group.

Oviedo continued, more calmly now, about our abilities. "It is true that here and there a clever Indian is found. Witness our natural companion this evening. But overall the Indians were a sorry lot before our coming. Most were imbeciles, made by nature to serve."

About our holy people, he said: "Blindly, the Indians believed their witch-men, *brujos* they called *behikes*, who fooled everyone by babbling with their little *cemi* idols. Of course, our priests discovered immediately an assistant of the *brujo* who would hide behind the altar of *cemi* and emit sounds, so as to frighten the people."

Oviedo lifted his wine glass and pretended to hide behind it, making phantasmal sounds, then feigning a witch's voice: "I am your master. Give me your tribute!"

He might have gotten applause for his drama, but at that very moment I interceded. "We never had tribute; it was always exchange, trade."

It was my mistake. He had had enough of me. Quietly, a blotchy redness flushed Oviedo's oval face. "Idolaters!" he spat. "The true Indians from those days worshipped images of the Devil himself!"

"Never mind this *diablillo* know-it-all," the abbot interfered, to calm him down. He looked at me sternly, then turned with a smile to Oviedo.

"I understand from Don Bartolomé that they were an abstinent people about coitus," the abbot goaded him deftly, by way of deviating his anger.

Oviedo snapped forward. "Nonsense. They did as snakes, wrapped up under the leg, men with women, men with men. Anti-*natura*, in the wrong hole!"

I gestured to speak and spilled my glass of wine.

"Diego might consider a retreat," the abbot said quietly.

I shook my head, and he did not insist. "Father Las Casas is a truthful man," I said. "Of all Castilians, he understands our people best."

"Only in going after gold did they abstain," Oviedo said loudly, talking over me as if to ignore me. He glanced around the table and laughed loudly at the group. "Did you know that? Before going to gather gold, the Indians abstained from coitus. It was the only time. Every other time they plugged everything in sight, mothers excluded." He laughed again. "But they abstained when they went after gold. Ha, and Las Casas the Great Defender says the Indians didn't put value on gold!"

Of course, he was all wrong, but for the moment my head swirled and my heart raced. Twice, my elbow slipped on the table as I tried to keep a silent composure. The love I do feel for the good friar was suddenly high in my breast, mixing in with the many emotions.

Oviedo spoke on of sodomy now, in a torrent of words that pierced me deeply, though he ignored my face. "Repulsion and shame," he kept repeating, calling our people "irredeemable liars, lazy, dumb, a people who would rather kill themselves than work hard. The pestilence," he said, "was only to be thanked for wiping nine out of ten Indians off of the Caribbean islands.

"It was divine intervention directly worked to deny a place on the earth to such savage and bestial peoples, abominable and vicious. It fits them well and it is most convenient the frightful sentence carried out against them by an eternal and sovereign God!"

My head in a fog, his words pierced my breast, again and again. It was another half hour before my mind calmed enough to formulate words. This is where the wine lifts all caution.

"Only the blacks of Africa are more bestial than were our own natives," Oviedo was claiming, recalling Governor Diego Columbus's acts of swift violence in 1522 while suppressing a slave rebellion in his own sugar mill. Then he made a mistake as he wound down to stop. "Your own benefactor, Dieguillo," he said, pointing at me. "He hanged them by the dozen, including many Indians who joined in."

"The second admiral, who saved my life twice, was only a man," I retorted. "And a Castilian."

I saw young Silverio jump in a corner.

The abbot sized me up. As I only held him in check with the potential for greater scandal, I continued quickly, by way of explanation.

"In the case of the Negro rebellion, exactly ten years ago, the second admiral acted swiftly and brutally, it is true. More than twenty blacks had gotten away, and word was spreading to other sugar mills. He sought to—"

"Everyone knows he feared a general rebellion," Oviedo had caught my challenge. "But why do you say, a Castilian—by what meaning?"

"The way of your punishment has been to hang and burn our elders," I said. "Or is this strange to your learned ears?"

"Only rebellious ones," *Oidor* Suazo intervened. I think he tried to change the conversation. "What say you, Don Gonzalo, of the efforts to deal with Enriquillo?"

"If done properly, he would be hanged," Oviedo replied quickly, looking at me, and then spoke slowly. "He is a brigand, Indian or not, and has committed acts of theft and cruel violence."

"He fights only for a justice denied him," I said.

"He is an outlaw, a rebel and a murderer, regardless of—"

"He is a man of conviction," I interrupted, "not a fingery gold-counter!"

Oviedo stood, making as if to reach for his dagger. "This Indian must go," he yelled. "Insult I will not tolerate."

Oviedo, now turned historian, came to these islands to count the king's gold. Everyone knows that, and there are many stories on the depths of his pockets. Two monks stepped behind him, I think to prevent violence, as he stood erectly facing me, hand on the hilt of his dagger.

"Las Casas knows these things," I said with deadly calm. "He writes the truth about us."

The abbot stood. "Dieguillo must retire," he said, as Oviedo, facing me, yelled: "Las Casas is another lying fool!"

I stood, too, wanting to insult him again, but more words were not forthcoming. I was ready to kill that Oviedo, to yank out his lying tongue. Leaning on the table, my hand clasped a serving knife, a gesture noticed by the abbot. "Go at once, Dieguillo," he commanded. "You are dangerously close to illegality. Do not threaten an officer of the king."

Thus did I retire to my cloistered cell, in the early hours of this new year, marking now 1,533 since the birth of the Christ.

January 10, 1533
ONE HUNDRED TEN. *IN NEED OF PUNISHMENT.*

Two days my body felt a wretch after contention with the bottle. Only Fray Remigio, the Franciscan, and young Silverio visited my room, and then briefly, after meals. I ate steadily from their offerings to stabilize my corpus, but as my body recovered, my mind and heart bemoaned my thoughtless indiscretion.

Now I am ashamed, not because of the insult to Oviedo, who is an old whore full of calumnies, but because my own stupidity allowed such a scandal. How I think of Enriquillo I gave away and precisely to the wrong people. Nothing did I hear from *Oidor* Suazo nor, of course, from "the intellect" about the need for peace with Enriquillo, though they pronounce such thoughts in their more public gestures. It is not a good moment to lose my anonymity.

With the knotted rope the convent keeps for such a purpose, I will ask Fray Remigio to flagellate me. I will ask him to strike me hard, make me bleed from the shoulders and suffer. I am such a fool, and I have always been such a fool. And how can I change now, but through more pain? I must concentrate my mind on the task before me, which is to ensure that Enriquillo lives, that his movement is not crushed just as he would make a peace.

January 12, 1533

ONE HUNDRED ELEVEN. *LAS CASAS REPORTS MIXED NEWS.*

As if to torment my agitation, a letter arrives from Las Casas, but full of troublesome news—all the more reason provided me for the painful remedy I have dictated for my soul.

The good friar met with the empress, as King Charles was not yet back in his Iberian court. Long dialogues he reports, though the empress was not well disposed. As of July, 1532, she commissioned a captain to press the war on Enriquillo, annihilate him once and for all. His name is Barrionuevo, and according to the friar, he and more than two hundred soldiers will have left for our island by my receipt of the letter. The friar will also return now.

He writes: "I demanded from the Empress Isabel of Portugal, wife of King Carlos I, an adequate plan for a peace in Española based on the principle of just treatment." "She called me a meddler and referred to more than a dozen documents of complaint against my person, several authored or seconded by the *oidor* Suazo, of late so endearing with me.

"What to make of all this I am not sure, except that a strong position at the court is that Enriquillo should be invited to come here on an embassy from which he will not return. I am more worried than always now, noting the empress's response. I believe the king is more disposed to establish a peace, but he is tending to his German dominions and is not expected for several more weeks."

One bit of good news: my old friend Rodrigo Gallego is to make the voyage as an officer of the guard. He is now a captain and well regarded. His application to join the mission was easily accepted. The good friar reports long conversations with Rodrigo, who professed himself a sympathizer these many years to the plight of our Taíno people. I am very happy about this news that I will see my friend, missing from my life since our tearful farewell in Seville, in 1493.

"Seize the initiative to negotiate on our own with Enriquillo," writes Las Casas. "The island hidalgos have the stealth for a devious assassination, but I don't believe they have the courage for more campaigns in the Bahuruku, which describes the empress's plan. Assist the baby boy [here he employs my code] to design a careful negotiation. A captain and a soldier, Barrionuevo nevertheless carries secondary instructions to recognize Enriquillo's original complaints. I expect, if our efforts are rewarded, that he will go empowered to grant pardons if peace can be achieved.

"As you receive this letter, I will be on board a returning ship. Please be very careful and strategic as the moment comes for definitive action to make gains at the end this fourteen-year-old affair. I have raised the *encomienda* as a point of discussion. Yes, it angers everyone anew to discuss this sin we all share, but it must be raised, again and again, until justice is done.

"My friend, I remember seeing you those many years ago, not far from where I now write these words, your skinny young frame and quick smile and the wonderful parrots you handled. I hope you are well and commend you to keep writing, keep writing. What you have to say about those early days is I believe of great importance."

ONE HUNDRED TWELVE. *I MUST GET TO THE BAHURUKU.*

Now I sit and ponder, hoping my lunatic indiscretion with Oviedo and the *oidor* will have minor repercussion. The monks, I know, are watching me more carefully. Most are sympathizers of the good friar's mission, but I fear their constant curiosity for my expressions on the *cacique*. So they watch me, wondering, and I wonder, too, is there a traitor among them? And how can I leave here without notice? How can I get to the Bahuruku to talk to Enriquillo, which I clearly must do, and not give him away? I am such a magnus fool for what I have done, and at such a wrongful moment!

ONE HUNDRED THIRTEEN. *FLOGGED OUT OF MY GUILTY STUPOR.*

Finally I am flogged. Fray Remigio understood my request and gracefully backed me up without word, administering my torture faithfully and quietly, assisting me to my cot as on the fortieth stroke I crumbled from the pain. A prayer I intoned when I awakened, and for two days I have forced movement on my arms and shoulders, a dismay through my neck and head that has made me wretch anew. Such is the power, though, even in my stupidity, that one day later an opportunity arises. I feel the strength of the spirits in this, a prayer returned. The sugar mill near San Juan de la Maguana constructs a new *trapiche* building and has called for carpenters. I will go there and set a message out for the baby boy.

Folio IV

A Visit to the Rebel Camps

Francisco Pedro, Yoruba friend... Two weeks later, sugar mill story... A new day begins... In the free Taíno territory... Greetings by Enriquillo and Doña Mencia, council of captains... Younger captains' proposals for raids to procure arms and munitions and tools... Touring the camp, the young men... The capture of Caonabó... Lessons for the boy-warriors... Castilians dance for gold... Caonabó serves notice on Fuerte Tomás... Blood not spilled, but a chopped hand... Discussions in the evening... Caonabó's deception by Hojeda... Nobody liked the story... San Miguel's deception... Seeking a path to peace, Enriquillo... Looking for the behike... Early cohobas with Guarionex... Fasting and old stories of Taínos... Peace-pact ways of Guarionex... Friar Pané, el terco, the busybody priest who got many good people killed... A Castilian army readies for battle... Maniocatex riles up a war... Pané riles up a cacique's yukaieke... The Battle of Christendom over the Heathens... Guarionex is prisoner... Guarionex is released, Guacanagari disappears... A Taíno offer on the land... The first Castilian rebellion: Roldán attacks the admiral... I take a bride, Ceiba... Making a family, home days... Enriquillo's camp is like the old yukaiekes... The old man knew so much... Death Spirits that open sores in our faces... Roldán and the first Indian repartimiento... Guarionex retreats to the mountains... Guarionex falls, and Mayobanex... Castilians swarm the island... Surrounded by young Taíno, education for peace... A song comes to me... Going to meet the medicine...

One hundred fourteen. *Francisco Pedro, Yoruba friend.*

I write tonight from a small *bohío* near San Juan de la Maguana, where I have come with young Silverio. The *bohío* belongs to a free Negro named Francisco Pedro, who served with me in the *encomienda* of Pero Lopez before that singular son of a she-dog lost his Maguana holdings, during the time of the admiral Diego, and returned to Santo Domingo. Francisco Pedro is a good friend who, like myself, has benefited greatly from the friendship of the second admiral and that of Father Las Casas. He is a lucky African just as I am a lucky Indian to come out alive from inside the nightmare of the past forty years. He was one of the first Yoruba men brought over by Antonio de Torres, before the time of Nicolás de Ovando in 1502.

When I was *encomended* in 1514, along with Enriquillo and his father, already Francisco Pedro, whom I call by his common nickname of Yoruba, was an older man. Today he fixed us herbal tea and cooked a hen in onions and rice and boiled *yucca* for us, and he seems as agile as in those days. "*Muchacho,*" he still calls me, though I am certainly not a boy anymore. "You better rest a day and be ready to work when you go over to that Solana's sugar mill. You are now used to that soft life of the convent, dusting *maguacokío* altars and cooking for priests. But the mill—they work you, even a freeman, sixteen straight hours, with a one-hour stop after midday."

He is right, of course. The life of the sugar mill is the worst now. And what he is too polite to say: Indians don't work the cane or sugar-grind anymore. All that has gone to Negroes in the last ten years, the strongest arms for *macheteros*, and the biggest ones to work the grinding *trapiche*. Wielding the machete in a field of cane, spiny slivers by the millions falling on your face and sweaty neck, burning sun of the harvest torching your head, is about the hardest work a man can do on this island, now that the gold mines are nearly exhausted. Almost all *macheteros* (canecutters) are Negroes now, while Indians are harvesting *yucca* and herding cattle. Many Negroes are like us in build, but many more than us are big and muscled heftily, and those are put to work inside the mill, where the machinery is huge and heavy and everything is hot to the touch. "The Castilians treated Indians as if you were wild game," Francisco Pedro told me today, "but they treat us Negroes like beasts of burden."

Tomorrow I will ride into the Spanish village of Vera Paz, what used to be the main *yukaieke* of old *Cacique* Bohekio, here in the province of Xaraguá. I am to go to the sugar mill and cattle ranches of Don Diego Solana and his wife, Doña Maria de Arana, where a new *trapiche* building for squeeze-grinding sugar cane is to be constructed. Solana is probably the biggest cattleman on this side of the island, with more than twenty thousand head of cattle, thirty Spanish foremen, three dozen Indian peons, and more than one hundred African slaves. Most of the plain from Santo Domingo to the foothills of Bahuruku is crowded already with cattle, sheep, and sugar cane. It is hard to believe how much everything has changed. I count forty years since the first Castilian settlement on these parts, and it is amazing how the sugar cane sea of deep green has spread. Sugar cane tastes sweet enough, but it burns the land and feeds nothing but ships going to Castile. Not even animals or birds does the sugar cane feed; no animal does it feed except for the plague rat that came over in their own ships. And that one not even the *mahá* snake eats. The sugar feeds not even the men of the sugar boilers. At the refineries, the Negroes near the boilers are forced to wear *bozales* (muzzles) so they cannot open their mouths to swallow even a bit of its product.

Silverio rides a yellow gelding I rented from the abbot, who was pleased to see me off. "The work will do you good, Dieguillo," he said, though he warned me not to go near Oviedo's cattle ranch near San Juan de la Maguana. Of course, I intend doing no such thing, as my mission here is to work two weeks at carpentry on Solana's *trapiche*, while Silverio rides on to the Bahuruku. I am trusting young Silverio, who is mostly a resourceful lad, precisely from the people of Guarionex, with this delicate mission. Interestingly, he worries not the danger presented by the governor's *cuadrillas* but wonders if Enriquillo's warriors might not lynch him, which deed they have carried out at various times against suspected *mánso* informers. "I can avoid the Castilians, Don Diego," he assures me. "But I fear the *guaxeri* of the *cacique*."

I prepare for him tonight a note, waxed over and wrapped inside the sheath of his machete, that will deliver him and be delivered to the baby boy. Meanwhile, I will write not during my stay at Solana's sugar mill but instead will hide my writing things away here with Yoruba, whom nobody bothers, while I fulfill my obligation in that stifling atmosphere. When I find myself at the Taíno camps, at our free places on the Bahuruku, where my people are still maintaining themselves, there I will write again.

One hundred fifteen. *Two weeks later, sugar mill story.*

Once again tonight at Francisco Pedro's *bohío* I take up the pen. Two weeks exactly have passed, and later this morning I will ride my whiteface mare to the old Camin River, where it enters the plain. Word from Silverio already awaited me here, delivered two days ago by a mounted *guaxeri* of Enriquillo's. It indicated the place of my entrance to the free country.

I make only two quick notes before departure. One is how excited I am to be near the baby boy. The daring ride of his messenger, who was chased by two Spanish squads before slipping free, warms my heart.

The second note is this: at Solana's hacienda, which is on the foothills of this plain, I saw the remains of the irrigation canals used years ago by Bohekio's gardens. This dry plain, rich in soil but poor in water, required an intricate plan from that thoughtful *cacique*'s forebears, who turned out large quantities of *yucca*, yams, corn, and beans.

At the hacienda, a foreman from Asturias berated an African man. "Negro *etúpido!*" he yelled as the Negro man led a wagon of water pulled by an ox. The trail was rough and the African, who led the ox by way of a nose ring, kept tripping, jerking on the ox's nose so that it bled. The foreman let fly the whip, three, four times, at the poor Negro man's shoulders. Their activity was to transport a huge barrel of water, carried by ox wagon, to moisten the soil of the vegetable gardens. As the blows stopped, the African recovered his composure to lead the ox, but then the wagon wheel itself became stuck as the road's edge collapsed. I was walking by with two planks of wood, keeping my head low. That's when I saw the old canal, under the dry-cracked lode. It was the old irrigation canal my good Taíno brethren used forty years ago to water all of this beautiful plain, turning a dry valley, year by year, into mountains of food. Typical *maguacokío*, I thought, beating someone else in frustration when the solution to his problem is right under his feet!

One hundred sixteen. *A new day begins.*

Tired I am tonight, exhausted and agonized by my cramping leg, after a journey through iguana trails, down rivers, and up buttes. But I am found, I say, and I write this in the bright night of a circle moon. I am here, I say. I am lying up in a hammock, in the *yukaieke* of the *Cacique* Guarocuya (my baby boy Enriquillo), surrounded by the constant din of the forest.

I saw him already; he was there at the water's edge to greet me, Doña Mencia, as always, at his side. They are so young and yet their manner so grave, so beautifully calm. I am entirely content to see them, to be here, to write these words—incredibly, wonderfully—by moonlight. Now the *coquí*, our tree frog, barks in his quick rasp and the whole forest chirps back. I note it happily. Near me, also on a hammock, young Silverio sleeps, breathing in tandem with the night.

Silverio helped guide me here. He came in the company of a young warrior from this camp, a tall thin man named Cao, after the black crow of our islands. He claims descendancy from Hatuey's people, on the old Guahaba province, just north of here. I could see they were good friends already. In only three weeks with Enriquillo's men, young Silverio has lost the nervousness that has characterized him for me. I met the two by a huge *ceiba* tree that grows in a place of large boulders, where the river turns west and enters the plain. We rode upriver a while, then it got thick and they let their horses go.

I left the whiteface in a meadow. With the help of the *guaxeris*, I made a corral surrounding a heavy salt stone. The corral is closed off by the river on one end and thick brush and a post fence hidden behind trees. I expect she will be alright there. We then walked for six days, the going so rough at times I wondered if we would crisscross the Bahuruku's thirty leagues of length along the coast and twenty-five leagues of width inland before getting somewhere. We followed the river up rugged peaks and through brush so thick we had to crawl on hands and knees. Then slowly we made our way down the valley called Cayobani to the shores of the big lake called Aybaguanex. Cao located his canoe, hidden in the brush, and we paddled off, trailing a line and a wide basket weighed down to scrape bottom, which caught about three dozen hand-sized *xaiba* crabs. The line caught one large fish I did not recognize but which Cao said was good eating.

Enriquillo and Mencia waited at the waters' edge. It brought tears to my eyes to see them in white cotton garments surrounded by captains and *guaxeri* and to hear the sweet words of our language, "*Caraya tao, cacique Guaikán,* welcome to our home."

It was late afternoon. We drank a pineapple drink, ate *guayabas* and small sweet plantain—a food of the Africans that traveled quickly into our *conucos*—but no hot meal, as there were yet another four hours to walk. It was this walk, brisk and totally uphill to a plateau, that cramped my leg and lay me out.

ONE HUNDRED SEVENTEEN. *IN THE FREE TAÍNO TERRITORY.*

I now see part of their *yukaieke*, eight wide *bohíos* set back on the open plateau, saluted by moon's shadows. I smell the smoke of the braziers, where fish and pig and crab are barbecuing, and I can hear the soft murmuring of *guaxeris* as they prepare the food and they greet and feed the outposted warriors coming in from their guard. Tomorrow I will see the place by sunlight and the enchantment will, I am sure, dissipate, a war camp it is, after all. But now as I struggle with my tired eyes and fight the pain of my caimán-bitten leg, I feel with certainty the reason for my being alive. Thanks it be to the Yucahuguama Bagua Maórocoti, first powers, Lord Spirit of the Yuca Beings, Spirit of the Sea, Male Spirit without grandfathers of Woman Only Born; it is in you, the Three Combined Into One, who still breathe life into our Taíno nostrils; thanks it be to your mother, Atabei, Mother of Waters; thanks it be to Itiba Cahobaba, Ancient Bleeding Mother, mother of Deminán, leader of the Four Brothers, remembered creators of our Taíno world: please be with us, all the greatnesses; thanks be to all the *cemis* you have empowered, Xán-Xán, please be with us, yes, all, and thanks to you, yes, again, yes, and again and again, yes. Xán, Xán Katú, Xán Xán Katú.

ONE HUNDRED EIGHTEEN. *GREETINGS BY ENRIQUILLO AND DOÑA MENCIA, COUNCIL OF CAPTAINS.*

Three days have passed since I touched this pen, three days full of life I have spent with the men and women of this place. Now, on a clear day, I will make notes.

The morning after my last entry, I awoke with the sun already midsky. A boy watched over me as I opened my eyes. He peered to make certain I was awake then ran to tell. I was up and stretching when Enriquillo and Doña Mencia walked up. He brought water in a bowl and she a white cloth. I washed and then we went to where they had food for me. Enriquillo was immediately busy with two men, and Doña Mencia indicated a meeting was starting that morning. As I ate, nine captains arrived, one by one. They all took a drink and sat around the fire.

None of them I recognized. Five were clearly of Taíno or Ciguayo stock, three were mixed Indian with Castilian, and one Indian mixed with African. They all dressed like Enriquillo, in grayish white cotton pants to just below the knee, no shirt, their *corazas* (suits and vests made by rows of thick, tightly woven chord) spread out at their sides. All nine captains carried sword and lance, three held crossbows, and two were armed with harquebus. One by one, they all bowed their heads to be touched by Enriquillo or Mencia before taking their seats.

I will tell first about the young *cacique*. Barely over thirty years old and already a fighting leader for fifteen years, Enriquillo has the old Taíno look, with a long, hawk nose, long black hair, lean body with a broad chest and taut calves. Enriquillo is taller than most Indians. He wears wrapped leather sandals made of *manatí* hide and braids his hair in one lone strand down the center of his bare back. He too protects himself with *coraza* and has two pages who carry extra swords for him. His eyes are stone black and deep, with a brightness in their gaze that touches the soul. He seldom smiles, never laughs, but speaks in a low tone, gentle but firm, a concentrated mindfulness I have seldom seen before in any of our people. It has been ten years or more since I saw Enriquillo. Once was in the second year of his struggle, when I carried to him a message. He looked more then like the guinea hen he had been nicknamed after as a boy. His eyes scurried and didn't fix. He spoke to me then, our first time together in several years, with great distance, openly but tersely, even haughtily. He had the attitude of the free stallion toward the tamed donkey. The haughtiness is totally gone now. The eyes fix intensely, and he is calm. All the captains hold him in great esteem and some revere him immensely. His two pages, thin young men, complain that he seldom sleeps but nightly leads them around his camp's perimeters and sometimes even out to other lookouts, weapons always at the ready. In the Indian Bahuruku, Enriquillo is *gavilán* (big hawk), the final judge. His word, trusted by all, often becomes law.

Doña Mencia is his reason for being, his open love, and his greatest ally. In our old saying, "The men are the jawbone; the women are the backbone." Thus with Doña Mencia, who takes care of everything. Never does Enriquillo's return find Doña Mencia asleep. This she would never allow. In her words: "He watches over all of us; I watch over him and what he does." Everything is ready, always, because of her. She runs the whole food line, organizing harvests and food preparation at the camp and at far-off *conucos*, where stashes of food are kept. Her stashes have saved many a cutoff Indian chased by Spanish *cuadrillas*, many a camp discovered and scattered via insufficient vigilance. Standing with her feet wide apart, legs straight, hand on a hip, usually with a baby or small child from one of her young women, the look of Doña Mencia penetrates. Regal is her demeanor as she points with her chin or lips for *guaxeri* to pick up or bring food, instructing messengers to other camps, crew leaders to their fields, a constant source of direction and information.

Doña Mencia wields a machete with total dexterity and one captain, Romero, told me yesterday that she has wiped blood from it after combat. She wears pants, too, cut at the knee. A cloth wrapped around her torso covers her breasts. She likes a shawl, too, in her evening repose, when the elders talk and smoke. There is nothing extravagant about Doña Mencia, but she commands naturally, clearly of ni-Taíno line. In her face Doña Mencia is slightly round, rather like her grandmother, the well-loved *cacica* Anacaona. She is well-rounded of breast and buttock, also, again, like the revered *cacica* of this old Xaraguá province, who was a most imposing woman.

The meeting of captains the morning of the day before yesterday was little about my visit, as they are all active warriors with many responsibilities and important points to discuss. Enriquillo introduced me briefly. "An uncle I have in my camp, whom you now see," he said. "He is one of our *caciques*, who saved my father's life and my own, many years ago. Though he lives with the friars, as I once did, he is Taíno." A small white pipe he lit with tobacco and had me smoke first, a sign of respect, then rolled tobaccos were passed around to the captains and to Doña Mencia and other principal women, who sat in the second circle backing their men.

Done with his smoke, Enriquillo spoke to everyone. "All of you are my nephews, your children are my grandchildren," he said. "Always treat each other well and help each other." "Xán, Xán Katú," the captains returned, in agreement. The warrior captains, with the women of their families, then greeted Enriquillo and called him grandfather. Everybody brought presents, which Enriquillo promptly offered to the visitor, baskets of fruit and *cassabe*, stacks of tobacco leaves, a good rope, a hammock, a cake of wax for light, a large clear conch full of live *cucuyos*, the lightning bug of our islands. These were all put at my feet, as guest of Enriquillo. Doña Mencia later bundled the gifts up in the hammock and had them carried here to my *bohío* across the clearing from her own. (The *cucuyos*, or lightning bugs, I let go a few each night in my *bohío*, where they cut back and forth, hunting mosquitoes by the hundreds.)

Of the captains, three are from other main camps and six run separate *conucos*, or garden camps. There are four main camp areas, spread out in the Bahuruku over several days' walking distance. They also have hidden gardens and fruit orchards. Warrior groups on raids emerge from the thick and rugged mountains in places far from the home camps. Usually a major action is preceded by the taking of several horses, somewhere in the vicinity, which are used in raiding haciendas or towns, holding up travelers and particularly in helping outrun Spanish squads, or *cuadrillas*, which take their toll.

ONE HUNDRED NINETEEN. *YOUNGER CAPTAINS' PROPOSALS FOR RAIDS TO PROCURE ARMS AND MUNITIONS AND TOOLS.*

The main purpose of that morning's meeting was a request by three of the captains to carry out expeditions near San Juan la Maguana. They spoke in favor of a "lightning" raid to a ranch in the nearby foothills, where they could apprehend ax handles, iron hoes, and saws for planking wood; they spoke of a place where they could gain more powder and shot for their harquebuses, maybe even a small piece of artillery.

The two younger captains spoke directly and stood together firmly, yet their manner was quiet and deferential to the *cacique*, who did not respond at first but invited more reasoning from the raid's proponents and the opinion of the others. As the captains discussed the proposals, groups of *guaxeri* walked by and stopped briefly, but this was clearly a captains' meeting and no one offered them seats, so they went about their business.

The wizened captain named Tamayo, who commands four dozen men, reasoned for the younger captains. "My *cacique*," he said. "Everything that makes us stronger in our fighting, I favor always, so my opinion will be obvious. In full sincerity, hear it then for what it is.

"The Castilians press on us with more and more frequency. There is talk of a big attack, from several sides, as they have done before. We need better fortifications, gun powder and I think a piece or two of artillery, for which they would respect us that much more."

This Tamayo is a tough fighter who has led most of the rebels' excursions into the plain and all recent raids on ranches. The Castilians fear him most of all, as he gives no quarter and expects none. Recently, after a skirmish, he captured two Spanish soldiers. One, an older man, cut the gut of his lieutenant, named Antonin, who later died from the wound. Tamayo ordered his men to hang the Spaniard. The other prisoner was a sixteen-year-old Castilian lad. Tamayo pitied him and spared his life, but he ordered the boy's sword-handling hand cut off. When the young man offered his left hand, the warrior who captured him complained, as he had seen him fight with the right. The young man begged and cried. "'Don't petition us, you lucky boy," Tamayo told him. "You are fortunate that, because of your age, I don't hang you."

Of the other captains, one more sided with Tamayo, while the rest nodded to Enriquillo to speak their mind for them. The young *cacique* stood to speak. He took in his hand a black, *caoba*-wood cane. These will be his exact words, translated into the Castilian.

"Tamayo, my captain," Enriquillo began; the use of a personal name indicated some tension within him. "I am very happy that you are with us. You are a strong warrior and a defender of our people, and I greet you. Remember our history in these mountains, which we entered separately and yet on similar grounds. I am very happy now two years that we have joined forces, as I have sought that for many years previous to our mutual pact, when you agreed to come under my *cacicasgo*.

"Now, hear my words. In all my time in the Bahuruku, since the year of 1519, I have been the advocate of our quiet withdrawal, fighting as we had to, but with constant vigilance. This, as you know, has been my strategy. Defensive vigilance, survival, and, always, retaliation. Not attack, but retaliation. Thus, my young men and women are trained early to run, fight, plant, and harvest, recognize the herbs, fish and catch birds and pigs and iguanas, all on their own. Thus, many times the Castilians have tired of hunting us, as we seem to them to live on air and feed on tree leaves and, as they say, on lizards. As they tire of hunting us and will run out of food and wind, I have sometimes punished them, and hard. Thus the time of the seventy we trapped in a cave, before you came to us; thus the time I punished the Castilian captain San Miguel, his malignant attack on our camp in 1528, when I followed him home and burned his ranch.

"Open wide your ears, my nephews. Only twice in thirteen years have they caught us unawares, and those only because of traitors, because careless warriors led them to us, giddy with the triumph of raids on the coast. Let me say, yes, I have gone out to take them in their own ground, to teach them their own homes will not be spared. But I seek not from them, I do not descend the mountain just to irritate them, just to steal from them.

"Since those first days, when we defeated Valenzuela and his men with sticks and short knives, killing two of his dreaded foremen, we have sought to disengage, to build our own small ranches in the hidden valleys of the Bahuruku. Never have the Castilians wished to fight us on our grounds, and as we have left the forefront of their memories, passing from their eyes unnoticed like soft winds, for years at a time, they forgot us, and so we built our lives.

"Nephews, continue to widen your ears.

"I am not saying they do not want us. They want us very much. Ten hard captains they have sent against us. Each and every one our warriors routed. We have fought like cats gone to the wild, which is what we are, cats and dogs gone to the *manigua*; and, yes, hawks— hawks who have grown claws and teeth and even talons; we have made carapaces for ourselves, see, like the turtle, and even the thunder stick we now use. I will fight to the death, and I sleep not my nights in my vigilance, but I will remind you, it is our quiet watch and, of course, our willingness to fight when pressed that keeps our peoples here alive. Raids only scare the Castilians into action, into wishing to murder us and press our families into slavery.

"Now, I repeat my observation: as we go about, quietly constructing our camps, we have what we need, and they do forget us for a time. But, as some of our captains continue to raid and kill, so do Castilian angers grow. They take up pesos and set squads actively against us. I remind you captains of this reality and ask you to temper your excursions. Think not just of your strongest arms, think of your weak ones, your children and old people, your women caring for your homes.

"You hang much with warriors, Tamayo. Spend more time with the women and the children, the old men. Listen to them. Let them tell you their fears and their hopes."

The captains listened carefully and even Tamayo nodded. After a time, all looked to Romero, Enriquillo's brother-cousin on his mother's side, a genial man who is their main spider or webmaker man. It was Romero who brought Tamayo into Enriquillo's circle. He is short and stocky with a face that cannot stop smiling.

"I love you all," he began to speak. "Taíno-ti, my fellow cousins. The words have been good and should not wound. Love each other, captains. Respect our *cacique*, who has guided our survival these many years. We have never defeated the Castilians but our mountains have. Their own thirst and exhaustion, their fear of our thick brush and darkened forests, these are the things that have defeated them. They cannot fight us if they must hunt us among these peaks. But they are many, many. And if enough of them came for us, they would find us, and they would kill us all.

"Relatives, where is our Ciguayo comrade? Where our great brother, Hernandillo, the One-eye, whose great singing we enjoyed so much?"

Romero never quit smiling though he shed a long tear before squatting back on his flat *duho*. The two captains he mentioned had been killed in recent raids. I had met the Ciguayo, that other time, and was touched to hear of his demise. The One-eye, Hernandillo, I knew only by reputation.

Next, I was called on by Enriquillo to express my thoughts. I did this by informing the captains of my message from the good friar that, indeed, if peace could not be struck, the king himself would order total war on the Bahuruku. The words of the young *cacique* had warmed me, confirming the veracity of my own instinct for preserving his hard-won jurisdiction. I told the captains they had good friends among the friars and that the important men of Santo Domingo were tired of the war, so it was possible they could make a peace while keeping their freedom. "Some want to hang and burn you all; others would bring an end to the hostility and let you settle once and for all," I told the group. The rest of my words I gave to Tamayo: "The cutoff hand of the young man has been much seen in Santo Domingo and has stirred up hornets," I said to him. "But, since there was cruelty in the kindness and kindness in the cruelty, it has them confused."

Tamayo, whose face carries three large scars and one ear cut by half, smiled uneasily at my words, and Enrique invited them to smoke again, closing the circle with these words. "I seek the trail that allows us our survival. War is not the trail itself but only the horse we have been forced to ride. My captains, I am still on that horse, but I prefer to walk. Our people have been walkers, and we will live by walking, even if, for now, we must ride the horse."

ONE HUNDRED TWENTY. *TOURING THE CAMP, THE YOUNG MEN.*

We eat well. There is plenty of corn, peppers, and tomatoes, lots of *cassabe* and many fruits, always a bit of meat. The *yucca* plots, I have learned, must be protected by young boys against packs of wild pigs, which have multiplied all over the island. A good job for the boys, they learn to shoot a straight arrow and bring in extra meat.

Enriquillo has liked my words. Yesterday again, as I was writing, he honored me with a visit. "Come, uncle," he said. "Let's walk."

I quickly finished my last entry, where I write about Tamayo's request. Enrique asked what I was writing so intently.

"I write the early stories of Columbus," I said. "And also some of what happens as I go every day."

He was leading me down a thin trail through a dark woods and suddenly stopped.

"Do you write about me?" he asked.

"I have," I admitted. He cleared his throat and looked away, giving a moment of thought to this information then continued walking.

We came upon a clearing where groups of boys were jousting. Enriquillo hurried. "Come see the boys," he said.

Some thirty boys and young men practiced with various arms in the open area, under instructions of two older *guaxeri*. The boys used sticks as lances and swords, pairing off in twos and fours, sparring and thrusting, feigning, and swinging at each other with more than enough ferocity. As we watched, one boy caught a stick behind the ear and nearly passed out. "Take a rest," Enriquillo told them. Then he had a lesson for them, showing the boys how to take out a man on horseback bearing down on them. He asked me to put a young boy on my shoulders and charge him as he stood his ground with a long stick.

"Squat down into a ball, and as the horse approaches, spring up. This will make him rear back," he said. "Then jab at the face, first of the horse, then of the rider. One-two, one-two. If you face him and fight him, you are faster on your feet by jumping to and fro, jabbing, jabbing with your lance. But never turn your back on a horse unless you can make the bush. In open savanna, he will ride you down and lance your back."

The boys listened attentively. Enriquillo is incredibly agile, rolling on his back to land on his feet, back and forth as he demonstrated in front of me, jabbing his stick nearly into my face but never touching me. The demonstration over, he had the boys sit. He queried them on their dexterity with the crossbow, the spear throw, and their force and accuracy with rocks. "Always be alert," he reminded them. "Walk our trails, go on watch to the coast. Learn to see and smell the Castilian and his *mánso* Indians and Negroes. Spot his track and sign. Never trust that Castilian man. He feigns friendship then captures you."

The young men were quite enraptured. Enrique described torture for them. The yanking of the fingernails, the slow burning of the feet and underarms—what the Castilians will do to make them tell where the camps are located. "Can you resist such a torture? Would such a pain make you betray your grandparents?"

The young men all agreed they would die before betraying anything. "Live it then, boys," Enriquillo said. "Be alert, but don't go looking for trouble. Defend us. Help your mothers and grandmothers. Always help the women. Listen to these old *guaxeri* who would teach you, and never forget you are Taíno."

What I loved were the faces on the boys, who smiled so hopefully, so lovingly, even as they trained for war. They are still Taíno, young men of noble sentiment, who can be aroused by the love of grandparents. And I could see Enriquillo's strength, its origin, in that same feeling, that warm, loving attitude that was foundation and center pole of our Taíno hearts, our strength in spirit. My people have been so beautiful and their reduction so brutal. What joy in my heart to be in this camp! What joy to see our survival yet in the light of our boy-men's deep black eyes. Now I feel we are not dead men walking, like so many of our people *encomended* to the haciendas; no, not here in the Bahuruku, where the Taíno still walks alive and free.

Enriquillo asked me to tell them a story. Of course, I wanted to back him up with his people, to have my own words serve the cause of his dignity and his survival. I thought of Caonabó and I thought of Guarionex, two of the grand *caciques* of the early conquest, who they were, what they tried to do, how they fell. I settled on the story of Caonabó, to illustrate both our valor and the deviousness of the Castilians, whom we then called the covered men.

ONE HUNDRED TWENTY-ONE. *THE CAPTURE OF CAONABÓ.*

Not far from where I write, just down the mountains some five leagues, near where that so-called savant Gonzalo Fernández de Oviedo now owns a large sugar estate with more than sixty *encomended* Indians and many more enslaved Negroes, Caonabó, our first warrior against the Castilians, was deviously captured. He was taken in his own village by Alonzo de Hojeda, that captain of the admiral of whom I have written in earlier pages when telling of his attack on the Carib canoe as we sailed on the return voyage from Castilian lands. It was precisely that Hojeda, a great devotee of the Virgin Maria, who drew first blood on both Carib and Taíno. And it was he who captured Caonabó.

On this island, the first cut Hojeda made was in a village of Guarionex's territory, where the noses of two *caciques* he himself left hanging on their faces like the split breast of our mountain dove. Not only that, their ears then he ordered cut, top half sliced completely off, again on both *caciques*. These wounds I witnessed myself later, and so I told the Taíno boy-men, whose eyes focused beyond my person to imagine the scene.

What I told them happened in 1494, even as the town of Isabela was constructed. Remember in my story how we landed at Navidad, the first fort left here by the admiral. We found all Castilians here dead, punished by Caonabó, *cacique* of Maguana, of whom I am sure some of you, I told the young men, are descended.

The young people's faces were a wonder of curiosity, and I pledged to instruct them on their history as much as my memory allowed. To my bigger joy, four of the young men, two of the young women, two of the older women, and three of the captains can read, and they approached me last night and asked me to write it so they can read it to the others after I am gone.

These stories in my memory, of Caonabó and the admiral and the first season of the Castilians, I told them over several days and nights, starting with the young men in the clearing and continuing later in the evenings, the circle growing each night.

Today, my mind and imagination are strong and I feel charged in my heart with my people's mandate to do this for them, their spoken request that makes me shiver in my determination to write these truths, as I pledged before, so that no matter what is forgotten, our inheritors, our people of the stones, like my young men and women of the *xiba* mountain, will remember.

March 6, 1533

One hundred twenty-two. *Lessons for the boy-warriors.*

The young people knew parts of the history after the fall of Xaraguá to Ovando, in the year of 1503, more or less. They knew a lot about Ovando—Nicolás de Ovando, not to be confused with Gonzalo Fernández de Oviedo, with whom I quarreled on New Year's Eve. Ovando was a knight commander and a priest who came to the islands with twenty-five hundred men. A cold and mean man, he conducted the worst of all massacres, the one against our queen of peace, Anacaona. Many of Enriquillo's people are from her line, so the young people knew more of their Xaraguá region, here in the southwestern side of the island and of the fate of their revered *cacica* grandmother.

But of Caonabó, who was her first husband, of Guacanagari, of Guarionex, of the Ciguayo Mayobanex, and the other old *caciques* from other parts of the island, they knew virtually nothing. Of our sister island, Borikén, they knew nothing. Of the largest of our islands, Cuba, they knew very little, only the story of Hatuey. Of the admiral and the first conquistadors, two boys believed still they had been spirits (my own lie persisting these many years).

When I goaded the group for their ideas, nearly all the young men believed we had started the first wars, that we Taínos had first attacked the Castilians. About Caonabó one said he had heard that he had desired to eat Castilian meat. This bothered me very much, even though the boys laughed heartily at the image of Caonabó chewing on a Castilian thigh.

Caonabó, I told them, whose name means "Lord of the gold," was a very special man, a Ciguayo, part Kwaib, yes, from Guadalupe, but one who had come to Bohío as a boy and settled with three older brothers in the land of the Ciguayo *cacique*, Mayobanex. No, Caonabó, as I see it clearly, was a great man of our people, a defender who saw quickly, much before I did, the darkness hidden in the covered people's desperation for the shiny light of gold. "It was really about the gold," I told the boys. "This is what commands their thoughts."

And I told them, too. "Xán, Xán, yes. Believe, yes, that your ancestors fought over the women in our families, our mothers and grandmothers, sisters and wives and daughters. But it was not jealousy. We were not that way. It was because of what I saw with my own eyes, how they raped our mothers and sisters and butchered the grandmothers."

I could see the boys all stir, realizing what they had not yet learned.

This Española, our Bohío, this Quisqueya island was a central point of the Taíno people, I told the boys. Here our people came to parley, here is where the great *caciques* talked and sang for days. They came from Borikén, from Cuba, from Xamayca, even from my little islands farther to the east, seamen chiefs of Taíno, the ni-Taíno and their relations met and knew each other and shared the knowledge of their ancestors. Here in the great Bohío, our great and first house is found, in the caves at Cacibajagua and at Amayauna, where the ancestors, good and bad, guided by the wish to bathe in the streams, emerged from the earth, from the long tunnel of our mother.

We Taíno were a large people, with many learned ones among us, I told the boys. Our people knew how to do everything we needed to live well and happy. We were on these big islands a long time and knew our places of respect and prayer, where we gathered to remember our ancient stories. The Cuban *caciques* were the best traders, in ropes and in good conch; in Borikén, they held the best ball games; in Xamayca, where many Macorixe settled before our Taíno, they knew archery and there was interest about the bow and arrow among our other Taínos in how they did that. "Remember that your peoples had possession of these lands at one time. Just that will make your thinking stronger," I told them.

To the east, I told the boys, past Borikén, the Kwaib raiders still inhabit the little islands. Before Castilians arrived, only Kwaib raiders came to our shores to bother us. Truly they were fearsome, but they hurt us not that much, compared to what would come. Raids came and went for a very long time, generations upon generations, and yet our Taíno multiplied and grew stronger. And of the Kwaib, many also settled on the northwest coast of this island. These were the Ciguayo territories, which were a kind of defense and entry point for Kwaib people who tired of raiding and intermarried with our people, especially through Guarionex, who formed the most clever alliances.

The young boy who became Caonabó was one of those, and he proved an able defender against Kwaib raids from other islands. In time he became well known not only among the Ciguayos, who were mixed descendants of Taíno and Kwaib, but also among the pure-line Taíno *caciques*, like Guarionex, Guacanagari (who greeted Columbus), and Bohekio, the brother of Anacaona.

Caonabó was fearless and feared. For years he warred on all sides, yes, on many sides, as he not only defended our island shores against Kwaib raids, but as often he disputed over land with the villages of Guarionex and Guacanagari, giving battle fiercely against them and raising the level of turbulence.

Here in Bohío, when I arrived with the admiral, there were five chieftainship lines, each with many village and village cluster chiefs. They knew each other, spoke a common language, and shared many common memories of the clear lineages of careful intermarriages. On the other side were the Cuban *cacicasgos*, Taíno as well, and their simpler, older relatives, the Siboney. In Borikén, under one main *cacique*, Agueybana, they were the people of the ball game, of which I remember tales, even in my home islands, of how Borikén's large valleys were framed with ball courts, where *caciques* in grand ways hosted dozens of competing villages and clans, and some of my own people had gone, in years past, to the Borikén ball games. Then we had people of our own talk in Xamayca, too, and they were quite belligerent, even against each other. And, of course, there were the smaller outer islands like my own Guanahaní, and we were the same people. But the origin island was always this one of Bohío, our home, where the origin caves remain, where our Taíno gold veins were born.

The old *caciques* of that time, Bohekio and Guarionex, together held ceremonies and put through many doings for their peoples. These oldest *areitos* of the Taínos, kept among the grandmother-guided lineal-breeding sachem families and among the *behikes* and some of the learned *guaxeri* of the clans of the ni-Taíno lines, were the laws by which our villages were sustained, so that fighting could be kept to a minimum and never wars to destroy the mother lines. Mutual recognition there was among all the main *caciques*, both Taíno and Ciguayo, including Guacanagari, Bohekio, Guarionex, Caonabó, Cotubanamax, and Mayobanex—respect they had for each other's place in our island world, and it was balanced.

Yes, of course, sometimes they fought, but these were men who considered it a victory when the big shark could be diverted while the canoe paddles away without notice. So a fight might be decided most of the time by one combat, a good whack might sprawl a man on the ground, and the old men throw up their hands and call a halt to the fight, call for the peace-pacting talks. Inevitably, despite their mutual irritations, the *guaxeri* groups peace-pacted. This was a common custom, to call in the old *caciques* who valued harmonious relations. Of these, Guarionex was the grand old man. Others, like Bohekio, whose line was quite strong, had the prestige but not the art. Guacanagari, first friend and ally of the admiral, was much younger. He was gifted with the most clear genealogies and was about equally considered with Bohekio, but Guacanagari, the bosom friend of Columbus, was a mere child compared to Guarionex.

I told the boys: the two prominent *caciques* here in Bohío were Guarionex, who was the *cacique* of peace, using the laws of reason about safety and sustenance of the *yukaieke* and using also the art of the gift in provoking peace offerings; and Caonabó, who was decisive in war and excelled at leading warriors in fighting.

What made Caonabó and his brothers fierce was training by a Kwaib father who prepared them for war, even as they learned to walk. From two years of age, the boy is made to run, endure hits, eat raw fish and meat, and swim long distances, and always he is urged to fight fiercely. Caonabó endured the Kwaib boyhood discipline. But he was named and taught also by his mother, a woman of Taíno line through Guarionex, and she, before her death, saw him named Caonabó, Lord of the Living Ancestor, the Place of Gold.

Guarionex was a holder of the most ancient *areitos* of our people and, through them, a great strategic thinker. The peace-pact *areitos* were central to his knowledge. Guarionex's power, even more than that of Bohekio and Guacanagari, was based on the refinement of the *areitos*, he and his men and women societies could sing. Guarionex was a gifted singer whose sweet, lilting song could melt any Indian heart.

Guarionex's *areitos* came from the second cycle of Deminán stories, in the original tellings, which Guarionex's people remembered in disciplined fashion. At the time that the admiral reached our shores, Guarionex was fashioning the system of alliances that were to ensure the Taíno people's life in the whole of Bohío. The success of his life's vision, he professed in his *areitos*, could guarantee generations of peaceful existence for our island peoples. As his vision of prolonged survival required not only strategy, but also the best defenses against the raiding Kwaib that he could secure, Guarionex had engaged Caonabó, channeling the fierceness of the warrior chief to protect the Taíno future.

It happened some ten years before the coming of Castilians. Bohekio's sister Anacaona inherited the *caciquedom* of Maguana, with its main village in the valley of the gold, Bonao, ancestral entrail of our island. Gold, as you must know (but the young people didn't quite know it, I realized), is the residue of the spirits of our ancestors. It is not to be disturbed. In those days, Bonao was a territory guarded and respected as a most spiritual place.

Guarionex planned it all. It culminated his vision and life's work. Anacaona, "flower of the gold," he offered the young Caonabó ("keeper of the gold") in marriage. Anacaona, who was a trained peace queen, royal in all her lines as her brother Bohekio, gifted in the poetry that calms hearts, and leader in the carving and spinning arts, was a lovely woman and would make Taíno out of the Ciguayo's children. Thus it was done, a marriage peace pact. Thus Caonabó was brought in to the sister *caciquedoms* by the old peace pact maker, Guarionex, who taught him the *areitos* of the ancestors and assigned him to guard with his fierceness the sanctity of the Bonao. All this, I told the boys, is part of your old history, of the time before their coming, when our world could be understood in our own minds, when the currents of our own migrations, settlements, wars, and alliances had their own dictates and interpretations. The Taíno were a people who thought of peace. Among them, of the generation of *caciques* when the Castilians arrived, Guarionex sought peace the most. He was a true Taíno. And among them was the fighting defender, too, Caonabó the Ciguayo, who supported their peaceful, respectful ways with his truculent character and his ironwood arm.

ONE HUNDRED TWENTY-THREE. *CASTILIANS DANCE FOR GOLD.*

Caonabó acted quickly, I told them, when the Castilians imposed their presence on our people. It was he who first said, enough, when the forty covered men left behind here from the wreck of the *Santa Maria* took to killing and raping and stealing. Not one of our women did a Castilian ask for in marriage, not one mother or father was consulted, no one's recognition sought, but by rape their relations began. Not once, after months, did any honoring of the Taíno families take place. So it was Caonabó, as I have written before, our first defender, who told his men to arm for battle and led the parties that hunted down and killed all the left-behinds.

The boys hollered in delight, and I waited for them to quiet down.

But the admiral returned, and I with him, and of Castile came another many, I continued. They settled a town, Isabela, the first one. And immediately the clamor among the Castilians was for the death of Caonabó. Occupied with pressing matters, the admiral did not hurry to vengeance. I helped in this by reminding him of the many misdeeds against our people committed by the left-behinds, and I believe my words helped tame the admiral's potential for revenge, which, in any case, was overshadowed by his organizing the first gold-mining expedition. For this purpose, he ordered Hojeda and others of his trusted captains out into the territories, admonishing them with strict instructions (as he had left with the forty of Navidad) to "treat well the Natives," taking nothing but food and gold and giving many presents.

Thus in January 1494, I was sent by the admiral to translate for Hojeda as he crossed over the coastal cordillera and south into the Magua plain, later called the Royal Plain, this territory of Guarionex was famous for its leagues and leagues of *conuco* gardens. With Hojeda, we came to the foothills of the sierra of Cibao, on the edge of Caonabó's territory of Maguana. There, reverently, shyly, our own people pointed out to the Castilians gold dust and slivers in the rocky crevices of rivers.

This is where for the first time I saw the Castilians dance for the gold. And, yes, dance they did, laughing and splashing each other and hopping around, screeching like parrots and several even linking arms on shoulders and hopping together in what they call a *jota*, a dance of King Ferdinand's country, which looked to many of us Taíno then something like our own *areíto* and confused us that maybe a thanksgiving was offered. And it was, but it was not a thanksgiving for the gold. It was giving thanks for finding the gold, for being led to the gold that they meant to take out of there and trade it for other things. Not for our *caona* but their *oro*, which could transform their lives, they danced and sang.

Even this behavior on their part no longer surprised me, I said to the boys.

I remember the report from Hojeda to Columbus at Isabela days later. The hidalgos present did not quite dance but paced and spoke in high glee, and joyfully a column was organized, commanded by the admiral himself, that would take formal possession of the gold streams and build a fort. This was truly the beginning of the end, I feel now, for by this action was announced the taking of all that is precious to us. I must confess, too, at that time I understood enough of the covered men's passion for the yellow metal (the vibrating of our ancient souls, our people said, could be felt in the streams and places of gold) that I accepted the admiral's decisions as inevitable and questioned them not.

I remember the cinching of horses and porters, the dressing of the soldiers, banners unfurled, the admiral and troops anointed to the field of battle by Father Buil, armor on all shoulders and chests. But there was no war that time, only the long, fatiguing march through thin trails in the heat of our Caribbean month of first rains. Coming fully into the villages of the Magua, the admiral had lombards fired and scrolled pronouncements read in Latin and all our people were once more astounded by the covered men and offered them great quantities of food, which they hardly touched at first, and helped them cross rivers and carried their packs and even sang for them. Thus was a fort built, called Santo Tomás, beginning on March 15, 1494, and some twenty of the best miners, guarded by a squadron of more than thirty soldiers with harquebuses, were left behind to commence mining operations under Captain Pedro Margaritte, whose report I later heard.

Twelve suns passed, and I returned with the admiral to Isabela to witness, incredibly, a little town manifesting, more than a hundred houses and *bohíos* for more than a thousand Castilians and several hundred Indians. Only twelve suns and I was horrified to witness the creation of a little piece of Seville or Barcelona or any Castilian town, without the cathedral, yet, but with cows and pigs and men living with each other inside houses, slop all over the place and the men stinking so violently the new town was already pestilent.

There was insult and accusation in the air. What Castilian men were not sick with fevers and vomit or famine were in active opposition to the admiral. These included the priest, Buil, and most of the so-called nobility, who resented the forced labor imposed by the admiral on all able-bodied men, regardless of nobility or rank. Father Buil, whose shouts and insults against the admiral I heard again and again, was the leader of the disrespect. Perturbed and agitated was Don Christopherens by all this, and only by the invocation against mutiny and rebellion and the imposition of lashings for the mildest insubordination was his command maintained.

ONE HUNDRED TWENTY-FOUR. *CAONABÓ SERVES NOTICE ON FUERTE TOMÁS.*

The *cacique* Caonabó, aware that the covered men were walking his territory again, requested to know if they were accompanied by women this time. Informed they were men alone, he inquired as to their treatment of the local people, which, at first, was not abusive. (Pedro Margaritte was one of those few Castilians that were touched by the message in our natural kindness and was adamant that his men not impose upon our people.)

For a few days, Caonabó watched as the covered men built the fort. Then, on the fourth day, a crew of miners went to the richest river and began to extract gold. This the *cacique* found intriguing, as the very activity was meaningful and sacred to our people.

Remember, I told the gathered group, the *caona* for us was the bright light of the sun made matter through us, the humans; remember what the old people said, in those places, even without *cohoba*, you can feel the emanations of the earth; there, the breath of our ancestors mixes with ours. They stayed with us our ancestors and would not be dissipated if the places were prayed over and often resin smoked.

I must note my surprise to see how many of the young people awakened to my words. Even Enriquillo, who was, after all, educated by priests, grew up at a distance from that knowledge. Thus, over the past few days I have been talking now, the group has grown, including more and more young women.

I have told them a teaching of our old *behikes*, who believed that the best of ancestor spirits rested and were reflected in the gold. Blessed with much light in life, these "good-minded ones," these most Taíno of our people, do not fully depart the earth at death, but deposit their spirit in the gold, adding ever so slightly to its creation in the rocky crevices of brooks, there to keep cool and to be gathered and fashioned to our likeness and to reflect our ancestors in the light of the *areito* fire at all-night ceremonies. We go to the sun when we die, the old people said. The spirit that is in us in death, travels to the bright yellow father of the cloudless sky. As our flesh dries in the wind, our spirit is released and returns to the sun. Thus the shiny metal was respected and loved, and what was made of it—masks and chest (to reflect the heart) pieces and belts and ankle braces—all had a purpose and a connection. The gathering of gold was reserved for the most serious of ni-Taíno among our people, and always they abstained from sexual relations twenty days before going to gather it.

The gold taking bothered Caonabó enough, but then on the seventh day, a walking group of five miners came upon two of our girls bathing and captured them, making use of them repeatedly and with desperation. This Caonabó was told by one of the girls who could do so, as the other one was sick with vomit almost immediately and later bled from her insides and died. Caonabó gathered warriors and descended on the miners, demanding that they leave and threatening to burn the fort and kill everyone. Margaritte sent out three men who half-ran to Isabela and were pushed around by the warriors but, as they were leaving, were not killed.

Thus started the second war between Castilians and our people, just as the admiral prepared to sail on to Cuba and his encounter with Bayamo, who cursed him with the *guanguayo*. Those were indeed dark days; dozens and dozens died. The Castilians, at first, would not eat our foods, refusing even our offers of fish. Everyone complained at Columbus. "Where is the gold that washes like rocks on the beaches?" Father Buil taunted him. "Where are the friendly native servants that will do all our bidding?"

The admiral wanted to escape the tumult. He was a man of the ocean and thrived in long silences. The future of his enterprise, he felt, lay in Cuba, which he intended to prove a mainland, the outreaches of Oriental empires. Discovery of a mainland on this second and misbegotten voyage would indeed make the trip worthwhile, at once achieving hegemony of the promising mainland and rekindling support for his explorations. Thus, the admiral entrusted Hojeda and Captain Margaritte with orders to pacify the island, organize for war of conquest, terrorize and warn—*escarmiento*—using terror first of all, and while he did that, I must admit, I happily loaded his three new caravels.

That was the time I thought I would go home. It mattered little to me that moment here in Española; truly a lonely thirteen-year-old I was, and I was going home. War was next. I knew it. Caonabó would be attacked. Caonabó, whom I feared as much then as I have come to respect and love his memory. Truthfully, I wanted to miss it, I wanted to go home. At that time, my fervent anxiety was to return to my home island of Guanahaní, the first of our lands to be touched by Columbus, to see my kinsmen, my mother, be again in my *bohío*.

I remember Hojeda organizing three hundred infantry and thirty mounted Castilians and twenty-eight mastiffs and eight hundred men of Guacanagari. Guacanagari always allied with the admiral. Hojeda lined up the troops and marched them, ran them in phalanxes and squared them into squadrons. Do you know phalanxes? I asked the growing group of youngsters and adults. Phalanxe is the pointed attack formation of the Castilians, also called the wedge. From Hojeda, it was, I first heard those terms, as the Castilians he organized for war. He requested me from the admiral, as translator, but was refused. Thus busy with preparations for sailing, I was happily spared the bloody campaign of *requerimiento*, a conquest by announcement and massacre, which, after all, required little interpreting.

"Understand," I told the circle of young people and the many *guaxeri* and captains who had joined in. "I have lived in this Española island longer than your *cacique* has years, but I am not from here. I had my home on the Guanahaní, one of the cays. I was a fisherman with my father and uncles when Columbus took me" (Here I fibbed to simplify the story).

"Did you ever return home?" A young man asked impolitely.

"No, I never did arrive at my *bohío*, not ever again," I said.

Maybe now, in the passage to Spain of some ship, by paying a captain plenty, I could go to my old island. I care not to. No one is there anymore. All my own people were hunted down for slaves, sold into *encomiendas*, a few here, most in San Juan de Puerto Rico or in Cuba. No one lives anymore in my old island or my old village; all is empty.

I had not done with my tale that first afternoon before the boys were needed in other activities. I was thanked by them formally and made to promise to continue my story in the evenings, for which Enriquillo offered his *bohío*. Here and there, over these past weeks, I have responded to requests for my interpretation of events, and in this vein, I find the words to write it down.

ONE HUNDRED TWENTY-FIVE. *BLOOD NOT SPILLED, BUT A CHOPPED HAND.*

Thus it continues.

Armed groups went out against Caonabó. But even Captain Hojeda, who hunted and killed well, could not locate him, neither in ambush nor in frontal assault. Nevertheless, Hojeda moved his troops around the country looking for the first incident as the "pacification" had begun.

On the Vega, Hojeda encountered Indian humor, which he rewarded with blood. Two Castilians had requested rides across a river on Indian shoulders, trusting their clothes to porters. Halfway in the river, they were dumped by their young carriers and left naked. Watching the naked *cassabe*-butts swim and hop to the other side delighted the young Taíno men, and for days the village laughed itself to sleep on the vision of the hairy Castilians enjoying a river bath.

Hojeda stormed the village and took two minor *caciques*. This is where the noses were slit down the middle and the ears of the two *caciques* were sliced in half, a deed of which Indian runners informed me within a day of its occurrence. Oh, the blood, one said in my ear, and scurried. Others arrived on their heels, *caciques* tied about the neck and pulled as they pull now the Negro people coming off the African ships. Two of these *caciques* and one their *guaxeri* the admiral studied glumly and ordered: "Decapitate them. In two days."

But we were ready with our voyage to Cuba, and I had not the need to look. In my mind every day and night, I hugged my mother and lay in my hammock, hearing her songs. Many came to beg the Guamíquina, as they called the admiral, relatives of the doomed who pleaded. "Please, don't kill our fathers, please don't kill my *cacique*."

They spoke in my ear, too, and the night before the execution, as the admiral readied for bed, I brought him fruit.

"The people here would cooperate more if their women were not violated and the cruelties would stop."

"The men are sentenced, Dieguillo."

"Consider the sentence, my admiral. Noses have been slit for the mere dumping of a pompous ass." I knew the admiral enough to intuit he did not like the dumped hidalgos and got the slightest smile out of him, though he answered: "I cannot underestimate the element of respect. An Indian must not challenge the dignity of an hidalgo."

"Even so, my *señor*, consider the balance. A well-deserved bath against two with slit noses and ears. Their warriors, even now, they want to make peace. They want no war with you. They fear, they even love you."

Finally, he released the two men, after all their *subcaciques* and ni-Taínos pledged perpetual tribute to his jurisdiction.

Those days, we were ready to sail but going nowhere as the winds proved contrary. The admiral ordained a round of Masses. These were about finished and the prevailing winds shifting in our favor, when a "thief" was caught with great excitement. A young Taíno man had stolen a cutlass. He was brought in tied by the hands. The admiral, impatient to go, was petitioned to grant the maximum sentence against the thief, that is, the chopping off of his hand.

I remember the young boy. He was about my same age. They tied him to a post at the docks. "Why do they do this?" he asked me as I brought on board the last of the fresh *cassabe* torts. "I took the blade only to cut a few vines. Before, they took my pendant, and this man whose big knife I took even gave me a name. Why can't they just let me go?"

I wondered what response to give him when I heard the admiral. "Dieguillo, get away!" he shouted. "Leave the thief alone."

The admiral of the Ocean Sea was busy with instructions for everyone. There were ships to be dispatched for Spain; final instructions to his war captains ("Reduce all resistance to the king's dominion"); instructions on what to build and what crops to put in. The boy sat in the sun and cried, knowing what his punishment would be. "We are not a thieving people," he said a few times. "Like all my people, a simple reed I will respect."

The ax came down as we pulled away, the admiral witnessing from the poop deck. I meant to miss the moment, working below deck and burying my gaze for minutes at a time. It was fate itself forced me to look out a small hole, precisely to see the arcing blade and hear it hit, the boy crying like a caught seagull as tears popped into my eyes to join his running blood.

ONE HUNDRED TWENTY-SIX. *DISCUSSIONS IN THE EVENING.*

"What makes them that mean?" It was Enriquillo speaking. "So many things like that they have done to our people."

This meeting was on an evening, at the *cacique*'s *bohío*. For three straight nights I have told stories, many more even than I can write. Most of the captains, including Tamayo, and many *guaxeri* come to listen. Cao, my first guide of the trip, was there and, I noticed, seated behind Tamayo. I spoke of the chopped hand because of Tamayo, to help put him at ease with my words over his recent deed. I want to be closer to this warrior captain. It is important that Tamayo accept Enriquillo's orders to stop raiding. Ill-timed violence could destroy all chance at negotiation. I looked to Tamayo and nodded the palaver over to him, which he recognized.

"I believe the gold makes them crazy," Tamayo spoke after a few minutes. "That is truly their god. Gold is more important to them than their own people."

"That is what Hatuey said when he fled over to the Cubans,"

Romero said. "'The Castilians worship only one God, and his name is Gold,' he told them."

"I heard that story as a child," Enriquillo added in. "How Hatuey was burned at the stake."

"Yes," Tamayo continued. "That story was also in my ears. Everybody told that story some years ago, even the priests. It impressed me very much how he knew that about the gold. I was told he even put together a new ceremony, which he introduced at villages in Cuba. He would lead them to the top of the mountains overlooking the sea, carrying their baskets with all their things made of gold. The *behikes* would sing death and farewell songs, offering their spirits back to the waters, a way of refuge. Hatuey would sing an *areito*, asking the winds to hold the Castilians back, and they would throw all the gold into the deep waters."

"Hatuey was caught by mastiff dogs," Enriquillo said. "They say he killed two hands of Spaniards."

"I was there when he was burned," I told them. "At the place called Yara, near Bayamo, Cuba. But we are getting ahead of my story. Hatuey's death was in 1512 or so. I was telling you about things that happened at the very beginning, the war against Caonabó, in the year of 1494."

"And Guarionex," Enriquillo added. "They were the old *caciques* then. Big men. Because Hatuey was a lesser *cacique* here on this island. He was respected, but he was not as important as Caonabó, Bohekio, or Guarionex. And, it is true, his story comes later, when he fled from here a year after Anacaona's massacre," Enriquillo said.

"Yes, maybe about five years after the massacre, around 1507 to '08, maybe later," I said, noticing Doña Mencia, who looked away at the mention of Anacaona, her own mother's mother, and the memory of her sad demise. "But what I was referring to, in the very early wars, happens against Caonabó and Guarionex."

Enriquillo stood. There were upward of sixty or more people surrounding the elders' circle, where my stories were being heard. He looked over the group. "Tonight many have come, our people," he said. "It is a risk of assemblage I do not often allow. We are nevertheless well guarded by warriors at all corners.

"My elder, Guaikán, sitting here with us, gifts us with his memory. He makes me very proud to be Taíno tonight. You, our younger ears, hear his tale, as he would tell it to you. He knows your four generations. He speaks of the generation before our own, the generation of Caonabó and Guarionex, Guacanagarí and Bohekio, and Anacaona, those first ones to meet the Castilians. And before it is over we will hear of Caiçiju, who was of a generation before that. Guaikán knows that story, too. His own generation comes next, and then ours, of Mencia and myself, and Tamayo. Then comes you. So, these stories are your stories. You will do well to remember them and listen to what your elder says."

Finally, in truly regal manner, Enriquillo turned to me. "Ni-Taíno Guaikán, our questions have taken you away from your story path. But since it is late and some must travel before they sleep, perhaps you could finish with the story of Caonabó, how he was betrayed and caught by gold and of his final moment. Of course, the next time, we would like to continue with the story of Guarionex and even hear about Hatuey."

So, I finished that evening's round of stories with the capture of Caonabó, a memory I dedicated to my young guide, Cao, who had been true and ensured my safety into camp.

ONE HUNDRED TWENTY-SEVEN. *CAONABÓ'S DECEPTION BY HOJEDA.*

Caonabó was a warrior's warrior. His own father was a Carib war leader and his father's own grandfather was the first in his line to settle on this Bohío island. I was gone on our trip to Cuba when his capture happened, but I heard the story from him.

Caonabó was caught by gold, treacherously. Hojeda chased him several times after raids near to Isabela but had not dared battle the old *cacique* into his own territory.

Hojeda was on his own and he was clever. He did the one thing Caonabó did not expect: he lied to him. Hojeda sent Caonabó a message that the admiral wanted peace with him, and would the *cacique* come to visit? He wanted to give him the bell at the church of Isabela, he told him, the bell that rang so loudly and that, he said, was heard directly by the Great Spirit. Caonabó would not come but, wondering on the bell and its meanings, instead invited Hojeda to visit him. The intrepid Hojeda took nine men on horseback to see the *cacique*, knowing he would be received in peace. Caonabó said he was suddenly encouraged by the Castilian's friendly approach.

Over the next few days, the *cacique* took a genuine liking to Hojeda, who was quite the diplomat and full of acrobatic and jug-gling tricks and whose men were on their best behavior and pretended to respect Caonabó's court. They talked about customs and visions, and, mostly, they talked about gold. They both respected the gold, though for very different reasons. Hojeda had brought a set of handcuffs made of a shiny bronze, the metal we call *guanin*. These shiny handcuffs were not *caona* but a fine metal that is also cherished by our people. "They are very special," Hojeda told the *cacique*, "meant only for a great king." A few times, Hojeda let Caonabó handle the intriguing contraption, even locking one handcuff onto the *cacique*'s wrist and using the other side to hold around the forearm, but always releasing the *cacique* before suspicion could arise. Caonabó wondered as to the shape of the cuffs, but did not connect their purpose. He was reassured by Hojeda's references to their sacred nature and assumed that no one would invoke the spirits deceitfully. For another thing, Hojeda, at that time, was still quite a correct man and forbade his men from abusing the women. This was very encouraging to the *cacique*, that such a value could be established with the Castilians.

One day, the Castilian captain solemnly proffered to gift the *cacique* with the golden handcuffs. A dream he had the night before, Hojeda said, that prescribed a ritual bath in the Taíno custom. The *cacique*, at ease deep in his own territory, agreed. Hojeda led the *cacique* to a stream where the ni-Taíno liked to bathe. Both men entered the water and conversed through an interpreter. Hojeda by then had learned some of our Taíno protocol. He spoke of cleanliness of body and spirit, the sacredness of the *digo*, our own Taíno sudsy herb. Then he spoke of a horse ceremony that would properly honor Caonabó, who agreed to let Hojeda honor him after the bath, when the Castilian captain seated the *cacique* behind him on his horse then ceremoniously placed the handcuffs on him. The *cacique*, happy and very confident about his Castilian friend, complied with all the requests. Suddenly, the golden handcuffs secured his second wrist, the Castilians were all mounted around him, two lances held to his neck, and quickly they rode away with Caonabó a prisoner in his own land, in chains and on his way to Isabela.

One hundred twenty-eight. *Nobody liked the story.*

Neither young nor old liked this story, how it ended for Caonabó. It was easy. He was too fierce to fall so easily. Even some complained about the evil of pretending friendship in the *cacique*'s home *bohío*, only to betray him.

"Learn," Enriquillo told the group, after I sat down. "In such a maneuver fell our fiercest *cacique*, Caonabó, the guardian of our ancestors' gold. Think how easily we can fall ourselves if we trust the white man."

ONE HUNDRED TWENTY-NINE. *SAN MIGUEL'S DECEPTION.*

Tamayo felt compelled to speak up. "We are clever now in ways our fathers were not," he said. "Like the time with San Miguel, when his troops went for the gold."

San Miguel was the captain who pressed Enriquillo into moving his camps deeper in the Bahuruku. San Miguel's Indian trackers uncovered Enriquillo's main camps one time, in 1527. The Castilians attacked constantly and overran Enriquillo's *estancias*. "Do you know of that episode?" Tamayo asked me.

A little, I indicated by showing half a finger. I was unclear about the sequence of events, except that substantial bullion of gold, worth more than twenty thousand pesos, was recovered by the Castilans at the time.

"San Miguel was hurting us," Tamayo told me. "We were hard-pressed to fight off so many well-directed attacks. They were hurting us to the gut. At one moment I remember our fighters were scattered wide, and we did not know who was lost and who survived. So, they had us by the throat—the only time ever. It was then, when I believed all was lost, our *cacique* thought to request a parley and began negotiations. You should have seen it, elder. He met San Miguel on the twin peaks, which are only twenty feet across from each other but separated by a deep abyss." Tamayo turned to Enriquillo. "But please tell us yourself," he said.

Enriquillo smiled thinly. Tamayo and everyone's mood suddenly lightened, even at this slightest signal from the revered *cacique*.

"We fooled San Miguel," Enriquillo said. "As we talked, for two and then four weeks, our camps moved farther up the mountains. Still, San Miguel massed his troops to bear down on our trails, and he had good guides. He negotiated harshly and mandated a date for my capitulation. So, we hurried to move our camps, and we searched for a way to break his strength."

I could hear loud whispers in the group. "The gold," a captain said.

"Yes, the gold," Enriquillo repeated loudly. "We had gold from a raid years before, bullion taken in 1519 from a Castilian convoy traveling by trail to Santo Domingo. It was gold from the mainland, not from here. I always kept that gold, never spent any of it. In truth, I did not want it and even punished the captain who led that raid. Yet, the gold saved us, for on the morning of August 4, 1528, when San Miguel came to take me in, his guides found instead five piles of gold, neatly stacked.

"We were already in retreat, moving fast to cover our trails and disappear. The gold gave them pause. Three captains San Miguel ordered to follow us, but they found ways to discuss the orders and never chased us. They quarreled about how to distribute the bullion, to which, I heard, San Miguel immediately proclaimed his own captaincy's 10 percent. That claim, plus the king's 20 percent and other formal claims, kept the troops near the gold. Not one squad chased after us. They watched each other closely as they transported the bullion down the mountain. For two years, I later heard, San Miguel's captains sued each other over their claims to shares in the gold."

There was a lot of nodding, and the cacique *was* silent.

"Our *cacique* fooled them," Tamayo spoke. "And later we punished them, even San Miguel. We burned his ranch house, we killed all his bulls; we beheaded every one of his stallion studs, every one of his boars and his rams. And we hanged or strangled every *mánso* guide that ever trailed us. Every one."

ONE HUNDRED THIRTY. *SEEKING A PATH TO PEACE, ENRIQUILLO.*

Enriquillo knows he can't win in the long run. Yesterday morning we walked his perimeter, and he was very measured and determined. He started twice to talk but ran out of words. "It happens like that," he said. "My thoughts of the future stop coming. My ears and eyes I have fortified over the years. I do not think so much but feel for danger. I am the hawk in the tree, watching. I am the *cagüayo* lizard, scouting the outer trees, spotting for the flocks of shiny blackbirds that would eat the egg of my young…"

He had started by saying that he thought it best to settle for a peace now, that it was better not to push the Castilians if the king actually sought peace. "I consider that I would bring my men in," he said. "I tell my warriors that the reason we are here is not to make war but to ensure the survival of our people. My warriors, you see, are trained for war. I demand a vigilance from them that is complete. We have put up a world here, in these mountains. Our hunters and guards are instructed, as in our Taíno times, to take seed pouches into the woods, to propagate the *guayaba*, the *anón*, the *caimitu*, and the *mamey*; thus we have orchards in the forest whose location only we know. Preparation for survival from battle, the assurance that we will be attacked in our villages, has been our constant idea, so we have plantations deep in the forest."

We walked in silence for a very long time, his two pages trailing behind us. Again later, as we circled back, he tried to talk. He complained that he still must teach constant vigilance to his people. "Our Taíno are still too trusting of the white man. Our men sometimes will walk the savanna and run into woodcutters, or cattle boys, white, Indian, and Negro, gift them with foods, and establish talk. This happened so often I have been forced to threaten with execution any such act," he said. "Survival this way, I know. Making war I know. But I see not how we go if peace is possible. I just don't know…"

No more words came to him, and he walked rapidly a long time. Suddenly, Enriquillo froze. A pig could be heard in the forest. I watched him stalk the pig with only a short, thick stick in his hand. As the pig fed, so Enrique moved in. As the pig froze to listen, he, too, froze. Truly he is very keen, his face and eyes have the quality of a hawk, though his movements were those of the *mahá* snake, his body blending in smooth motion, positioning to fix on the feeding pig. Suddenly Enriquillo darted and threw the stick, the pig yelping loudly as he circled butt first around a broken front leg. The pages made the kill, gutted him quickly, wrapping the tripe around a stick. Tucking the carcass into a *macoutí* backpack, they carried him to camp.

ONE HUNDRED THIRTY-ONE. *LOOKING FOR THE* BEHIKE.

Seeking talk of the future, then, we circled back to Enrique's *bohío*, where we found Doña Mencia directing four helpers, two of them full African men, in the structuring of a new cookhouse. "We should convene our *behike*, Baiguanex, and see what we can do," Enrique told her, after they had kissed. The men also greeted us cordially, and Enriquillo gave them his kill for their evening meal.

Doña Mencia accompanied us around the camp. She and Enrique held hands, and then she also held my hand as we walked. I was curious about the *behike* Baiguanex, whom I had not met.

Nearing the hut of Baiguanex, some distance from the main camp, Enrique cooed like the mourning dove and without stopping for an answer walked up a slope to the *bohío*.

"Enter my home, which is your home, *cacique*," a voice said from inside the circular, thatch-roofed *bohío*.

We entered to the left and sat down in a circle as he instructed. The *behike* was younger than me, but I felt seriousness in the way of his deep composure. From the rafters of his *bohío*, he had various herbs drying, and he had a small white pipe that he loaded with tobacco and lit, passing it to Enrique, Doña Mencia, and myself. He took his pipe back when we had smoked, reloaded it, and smoked long and hard by himself, filling the hut with spiraling fumes.

"I know I will hear questions today," he said. "I know, too, that the words carried to my *cacique*'s ear by the elder Guaikán will change our world."

I had met the *behike*. On an earlier evening, after one of my talks, I spotted him among the listeners, his eyes looking a bit beyond me. I noticed that all the young men requested his blessing, touching their foreheads with his hand, and that he conducted himself simply. What he said about my words changing their world touched me, as it described my history with the Castilians and their entrance into our world.

"A change is certainly coming," Enriquillo said. "What we have protected here, with our vigilance and our lives, would now accommodate itself in their Castilian laws."

The *behike* looked past me then focused on me in a cross-eyed look. "Guaikán has much story," he said. "But where does his trail lead us, *cacique*? That is one question."

"I think of our survival, *behike*," I said quickly. I accept my own pain at the fate of my people, and I am aware of my own particular failures these past forty years, but I accept no other man's impugnation about them. "I am at calm with my grandparents," I told him. "The earth of this island is now mine. I have buried love here, and blood. This young *cacique* of ours," I said. "His life I held in my arms."

Enriquillo confirmed it. "He pulled me from the massacre at our great clan mother's," he said, and Doña Mencia held my hand and began to cry quietly.

The *behike* lost all reservation. He looked me straight in the eyes, and I had confirmation myself that he was very old inside and that he had been trained properly.

"I apologize to my elder," he said. "I am not worthy to run ceremony for you but should wait for yours."

"I am pleased to accept your guidance, *behike*," I said. "You have the hand, I am sure, for what needs to be done."

Baiguanex had no Castilian name and knew only a few of their words. He had lived with his grandparents in the Bahuruku from before the rebellion, hiding in a deep valley and living the old way. He was alone by the time Enriquillo left for the mountains and tracked Enriquillo's people for weeks before making contact.

"My parents died in the famine of Guarionex," he has told me since. "They sent me ahead with my father's father and his two wives into these hills. My grandfather was a *cohobero*, who left me two *cemis*, the Sleeper, which is a warrior spirit, and the Baibrama, which is center of my altar, the *yucca*-maker who can can reach Yucahuguama Bagua Maócoroti, the one who can thus give answers to our human questions."

"My father, too, was *cohobero*," I said.

"I can tell," he said.

"Guaikán worked the peace pacts with Guarionex," Enriquillo said to the young *behike*. "He knew the generation we missed."

"They all died," the *behike* said. "But they still can help us."

"We are going to talk to the Castilians," Doña Mencia said. "We are going to make the peace."

"Then their help we need very much," the *behike* said, reaching behind to touch his *cohoba* bundle and gazing deep into my eyes.

ONE HUNDRED THIRTY-TWO. *EARLY* COHOBAS *WITH GUARIONEX.*

Twice during my years with Guarionex I partook of the *cohoba*. Once, it was early on, shortly after the Battle of la Vega, when he sent runners to get me. This was months after my return with the admiral from the Cuban voyage. With Caonabó in chains, a calm of sorts had been worked out, but it was not peace. Guarionex was troubled. Early understandings he had assumed from the Castilians were not forthcoming. Instead, a great battle had taken place, not directly against his villages, but many of his people, including his own son and hundreds more, had been slain or taken prisoner. Many lesser *caciques* were beheaded. He himself had been taken and nearly executed before his brothers petitioned the admiral and his soldier brother, Bartolomé, with great offers of tribute.

One hundred thirty-three. *Fasting and old stories of Taínos.*

Fasting I am for four days, while the *behike* prepares *cohoba* snuff for me, making his prayers and burning for me. This is the outcome of our meeting with him. I am to snuff *cohoba* on behalf of Enrique, whose keen senses are too protected to partake of *cohoba*'s dream world.

Cohoba I know will be a difficult ordeal for me. It has been a long time, and I carry too much life, too many convoluted thoughts. *Cohoba* respects not the twists of a mind but attaches to the cool-headed, sincere intent, for it cannot avoid opening the trails of memory, leading the sight spirit into your dream world of blended time, where so much is possible. Already, the memories of earlier ceremonies remind me of the deepest pain, make me cry just to think about her. I think of *cohoba* and Guarionex and I think of her, my Ceiba, mother of my twins. Of all my loves and relatives, I have had her memory buried from my sight, a pain so deep it makes me sleep.

"I am your relative by marriage," I told the young *behike* today. "Guarionex and his principal wife, Ainaicua, became my second family; his young sister, Ceiba, was my wife. We joined together in 1497."

"I remember my grandfather's mention of them but vaguely," Baiguanex said. "When I was very young, a little boy, he talked of *areitos* at Guarionex's main village. He said there was always a lot of food and a lot of singing."

"Yes, Guarionex handled both food and *areito* with mastery," I said. "His ni-Taínos held the oldest of our songs and dances. They were truly beautiful ceremonies, and the Ciguayos and even Caribs themselves coveted those songs and teachings. Guarionex was best at using the teachings as exchanges to develop his permanent relationships between Taíno and Ciguayo villages. But when he tried his mastery with the Castilians, it all went the wrong way."

"With the sand-faced men everything is contrary," the *behike* said. Since he is of Guarionex's line, I am glad to tell him this story, though I never met him or his family in those days.

Guarionex was tall among our people and quite stately. He was already an elder when I met him, and he moved slowly. His hair was very long, and his wives would braid it for him so that it reached his knees. They said that as a young man he had wrapped an enemy's neck in that braid, holding the man for capture. Even then, they said, Guarionex sang peace songs to the Kwaib raider as he held him.

Today, his great-nephew *behike* worked the fire for me, he puri-
fied me with smoke (I gave him the tobacco leaves Catalina gifted
me) and heard my dreams. The *behike* is quick to grasp the way to go
with a thing. He told me: "In the humility of your hunger, consider
this: What makes them do what they do? Why are they the way
they are?" He said then: "Remember well and tell your stories of
Guarionex, and later we will call him and see what he can tell us."

ONE HUNDRED THIRTY-FOUR. *PEACE-PACT WAYS OF GUARIONEX.*

Tonight, on the third full day of fast (only water am I allowed), I
close my eyes and think of Guarionex and his times. I think of the
peace pacts, how they were working. I think of the love and respect
my people were instructed to carry for each other.

The main value of the peace pacts was to share the soil, share
the bounties of the *yucca* and *maize* and other harvest cycles. This
was the basis of our law. The world had so much for our people
in those days, in the way we made our lives. We had great fishing, much fowl, iguana, *manatí*, and *hutía*, great tubers, great fruits,
grasses and herbs, and, always, the wish for peace.

I state without hesitation: our Taíno ways sought peace. We
did fight sometimes but briefly and with small consequence. Our
people simply had not the wish to war. This is why I say: prior to the
Castilians, Guarionex was defeating the Kwaib raiders with love—
with food, and with our oldest of ceremonies, which they loved to
receive, and, most of all, through the marriage of our sister-women,
making marriages that would bind.

The Kwaib raiders, Carib or Caniba, as they might be called
by the Castilians, and sometimes the Ciguayos, the mixed people,
and even the migrating Macorixes, who were great archers—they
could be mean and hard but, truly, they admired, many of them,
admired the peaceful, prosperous way of the Taíno. Many a Kwaib
captured among our people and married in found himself intrigued
by our name for ourselves, Taíno, "those of the good," and by our
elders' argument for happy human existence based on good heart
and dutiful mind. Honesty and generosity, amongst a clan or a village, and even with strangers, were greatly valued by our old ones.
Thieves and liars were quickly purged among our people. Truly, a
skinny reed across the door of a *bohío* was all the fortification needed
against theft. Not all of us always lived up to those ancient ways,

but it is true that these beliefs caressed our people's minds from childhood, and most of our people accepted the truth that good treatment begot good treatment. It was disrespectful and impolite to deny or to offend other people. The Kwaib could see the thinking in that, whenever they were broken out of their predatory track, and Guarionex, following the prophesy of his own grandfather, Caiçiju, made it his life's vision to interrelate them with the main *cacicasgos* of the Bohío island. Guarionex was a great man, I say.

It was Guarionex who, over the objections of the timid Guacanagari, worked through the marriage of Caonabó, the Ciguayo, with Anacaona, a queen of exemplary Taíno line. It was Guarionex who gifted the other Ciguayo *cacique*, Mayobanex, with two important *areitos*, something the Ciguayo treasured and never forgot. It was Guarionex who was working intermarriages between that same Mayobanex and Cotubanamá, the Taíno *cacique* of Higuey. It was Guarionex who offered Columbus to take in a simpleton friar named Ramon Pané, who was assigned, as the admiral put it, "to gather Taíno idolatries and to impart the true Christian beliefs."

One hundred thirty-five. *Friar Pané*, el terco, *the busybody priest who got many good people killed.*

I would tell here about the *cohoba* ritual, how Guarionex ran them, but it does not feel right to do so yet.

Yesterday afternoon they accosted me, many young men who gathered from several camps. "We respect you are fasting, but your stories we would gladly hear." So I told them about Pané and how he introduced the gospel of the Holy Trinity on our lands, the Christian evangelism Friar Las Casas talks about in such great affirmation.

Father Pané came to the islands with the toughest Columbus brother, Bartolomé, the *adelantado* (forward commander), who arrived in Española shortly after our departure for Cuba. A man of action and well titled, Bartolomé Columbus imposed rigid controls on behalf of the admiral. He fixed on Guarionex's obvious prestige among all *caciques* on the island and was equally preoccupied by the open rebellion of a Castilian captain named Francisco Roldán, Don Christopheren's earlier choice for mayor of the Isabela town and a thoroughly soured man. While pursuing the truculent Roldán, who confiscated many horses and cattle from the royal ranch, it was the *adelantado*'s own idea to place the little friar, Pané, in the village of *cacique* Guarionex to see what he could find out.

Pané had an obvious facility for learning our language and so commanded the ear of the *adelantado* much the same as did I the admiral's ear. He was a real pouter, though, always silently angry and vindictive about something or other. Both Don Christopherens and the *adelantado* gave Pané instructions. The admiral asked him to gather stories of our ancients, and he did write a small book that Las Casas has shown me. However, for the *adelantado*, Pané reported on the movements of warrior groups and the general opinions of the *caciques*, particularly Guarionex, about the Castilians.

As we were just now back from the trip to the southern coast of Cuba, during which the admiral's health deteriorated, I was still close to him. For weeks after the curse of Bayamo and Macaca, as we sailed the many cays and bays of southern Cuba, he caught not a good sleep, reaching points of exhaustion and a clairvoyance truly astounding. At times I saw him stand on deck in bedclothes, slight from lack of food, a constant vomit in his condition, red hair flaming up like fire. More than once, as blackened clouds of the Caribbean came out of nowhere at him, snapping their thunders, I saw the head of our giant reptile mother, Iguanaboina, wide as a storm cloud and as blackish gray, its eyes flashing on Columbus's neck and shoulders, hissing and hissing, and I knew he would never recover from our old men's curses. He did slowly get his health back, but his spirit never returned to him, and he was increasingly a vacant man even as his intellect continued to command him. For five months, while I helped nurse the admiral's bouts of delirium after our return to Isabela, Pané was assigned to live with Guarionex.

Monthly, Pané returned to inform his patrons. Often these sessions occurred at the admiral's bedside. Guarionex had installed the friar in his own *bohío*, where he learned some Taíno language, conversed with elders, both men and women, and wrote down some things he was told about our *areitos* and old stories. When he would come back to report to the Columbus brothers, he complained about having to live in dirt "with Indians," who were all miserable beings, except for his own servant, who fiercely accepted the Word of God.

I remember Pané's reports, how he mocked everything. Pané particularly vilified the mother of Guarionex, an old clan woman who could see into his eyes and disliked him intensely, as he constantly denigrated the Taíno food (when she fed him iguana soup, he spit it out) and scoffed at her reverence for the *cemís* in her home.

I state further here that it was Pané who was responsible, out of his own vindictiveness, for starting the first war on Guarionex.

ONE HUNDRED THIRTY-SIX. *A CASTILIAN ARMY READIES FOR BATTLE.*

Truly, Guarionex's subchiefs all wanted war on the Castilians, but the old *cacique* held out for his peace pacting, accommodating Pané and accepting the imposition of the gold tribute, even though its terms were brutal. Caonabó's old villages were fully under tribute at that time. Guacanagari, as principal ally of the admiral, provided food from his villages and more than a thousand healthy men to the *adelantado*, who immediately set them to train for war. Under Hojeda and others, these Indian troops of Guacanagari quickly learned the use of the phalanx as tactic of attack; they learned to wield cutlass and sword and were goaded and trained to attack a body of enemies fiercely, with full anger and intent to kill. "Blood is good," they were told. "Cut deep and leave no life." The captains had under them now a well-organized force of four to seven hundred seasoned Castilian troops, including several mobile pieces of field artillery, eighty men with harquebus, eighty mounted cavalry, and about twenty mastiffs commanded by a troupe of eight efficient handlers. The Indian troops were trained to follow Castilian squads in frontal attacks.

Guarionex worked to keep the peace, but Caonabó's three brothers gathered an army, intent on freeing their powerful sibling, who was in chains. The prominent question among Indians that season was: Why do the Castilians continue to stay? Will they ever return to their lands? For long months, no ships entered or departed from the harbor at Isabela, a place of continual pestilence, and the injuries to Indians continued to mount.

It was during this time that a young man named Diaz, who fled punishment after stabbing a sailor in a knife fight, was taken in by Doña Catalina's people from the southern coast. They had a large, well-fed settlement on the banks of the wide Ozama River, which flowed into a beautiful and calm bay on the most protected coast of the island. Diaz and three companions married sisters of a local *cacique* and learned to appreciate the qualities of the site for a true Castilian city. It turned out that the stabbed sailor recovered, so Diaz went to the *adelantado*, Don Bartolomé Columbus, who forgave them their transgression, as they had found him, he proclaimed, the perfect site for a prosperous city. Thus did the *adelantado* set out to establish the port and city of Santo Domingo, the present capital of this Española island. This was terrible news to the central island *caciques*, who for the first time fully appreciated the permanency of the Castilians on the Bohío island.

ONE HUNDRED THIRTY-SEVEN. *MANIOCATEX RILES UP A WAR.*

Maniocatex, second brother of Caonabó, called together representatives of the *mayor caciques* of the island, both Ciguayo and Taíno. Bohekio sent several ni-Taínos, as did Cotubanama. Guarionex came in person, in the company of Mayobanex, a Ciguayo. More than three hundred lesser *caciques* also attended.

Maniocatex called the *caciques* to support him in a major battle against the Castilians. "Give me men, let your men come to my army, and we will march on them and together push them to the sea. They have taken my brother, they have taken our mothers and daughters, they are killing our people and abusing us without respite."

Guarionex asked for time. "The Castilians have many desires. Let us try to satisfy them, as we have all our enemies. There are only so many of them. Remember, too, they are very good at killing and will do us much harm if unleashed against us."

Maniocatex formed an army of nearly ten thousand men. Many *caciques* who joined him brought whole villages to camp on the Vega. Guarionex was impressed, but he cautioned against a frontal war.

ONE HUNDRED THIRTY-EIGHT. *PANÉ RILES UP THE* CACIQUE'S YUKAIEKE.

In those days, Pané was all the time in Guarionex's village, living in the *cacique*'s own *bohío*. He had the disgusting habit of asking for the old stories, taking notes as the storyteller humored him, and afterward arguing with the elder storyteller, declaring the stories nonsense and devil stories and always invoking the biblical story of Jesus for the listeners.

It was these dialogues with Pané that most bothered Guaironex, for Pané never deviated from his opinion about our most sacred tales. One day, insulted, Guarionex left a session abruptly and spoke harshly to a gathered group against the Christian efforts to indoctrinate his people. "They are thick-headed," he said. Next day, several of his young men took the message to heart and brought down a large Castilian cross that had overlooked his village.

Friar Pané was incensed. He went to the old chief and demanded to know how Guarionex could reconcile such an action with the fact that he himself had invited the catechism of his children and grandchildren. "We learn from you, but you care not to learn from us," Guarionex told him. As Guarionex was increasingly called out to the growing camp of fighters, Pané attempted to organize against him in his own village. He was challenged in this by the *cacique*'s mother and nephews, who finally ran the nitwit priest out.

The admiral heard Pané's angry report and, despite his slowly recovering corpus, implored his brother to let him lead the troops into the imminent engagement. On March 25, 1495, they dressed the troops for battle, which the admiral named The Battle of Christendom over Heathenism.

"Crosses have been dumped to the ground," the admiral himself exhorted the war captains. "We have just cause to battle and, by Santiago, the Lord is on our side." He ordered the marshal of troops to read the law on war slaves. This was another of the Torres brothers, from the *converso* family in Seville. The queen's law stipulated that natives of these Antillean islands, like others in Africa and elsewhere, could be enslaved if taken as a result of war or to prohibit cannibalism and other abominable heathen practices.

The Castilian army marched in two formations toward the Vega, where, upon reaching a plain they called The Hope, the admiral ordered a fort built that he called Magdalena. "Crusaders are we in these far lands," the admiral told the captains. "The infidel has declared his devilry. It is not just ignorance, my fierce captains. The savages now repulse our savior and a lesson must stamped on the land."

Maniocatex organized the battle for the Taínos, but nevertheless it was up to Guarionex, as senior *cacique*, to confront the enemy first. Ritually, Guarionex deployed his men in one long row, and behind them Maniocatex and other *caciques* led their own men. They were all there but had made no real plan and assumed their superior numbers would suffice to convince the Castilians to sue for peace. I was told that Guarionex said to his ni-Taínos as he watched the Castilian troops approach: "If they agree to a peace, blood may be unnecessary," just as the harquebus units and the artillery pieces fired all at once in a wide pattern, some eighty detonations of the shouldered weapons plus the two midget cannons that spewed forth all manner of shrapnel. Nearly one hundred Indians fell dead or wounded. The carnage amazed and froze everyone. Guarionex would later tell me he saw the eyes of death in a cloud behind the Castilians and that he was left without thought at the sight of the totally severed torso of his own second son. The cavalry and mastiff handlers waited nearly two minutes for a second volley, which dropped another hundred Indians and panicked everyone else, *caciques* and everybody running this way and that as the mastiffs and the cavalry charged among them at will, in complete killing discipline.

I stood at the admiral's side, holding the handle on a dagger but surrounded by his private guard of twelve men, while the *adelantado* and eighty others on horseback charged the mass of running Indians, hacking and stabbing with swords and short, sturdy spikes propped against their saddles, piercing back after fleeing back.

Not all Taínos ran. Many were fearless, watching and trying to grapple with the soldier formations, trying to wound them with our spears and *macanas*, but the Castilians and, yes, their Indian troops, advanced swinging heavy, sharp swords of steel. Three, four, five, I think as many as twenty major discharges were directed against the Indian mass, now divided in two or three groups, with the crossbows shooting volley after volley and the dogs chasing and tearing at the many trying to escape. I saw how it was done. Truly we were chased in place, denied the opportunity to regroup and kept moving by sheer terror so that large groups ran and ran into each other and in circles while the Castilians cut large swathes into them.

"Our idea is different now. We don't attack but chop at them little by little," a young *guaxeri* man said, when I told this story.

"Vigilance," the *cacique* responded. "That's what we have learned."

ONE HUNDRED THIRTY-NINE. *THE BATTLE OF CHRISTENDOM OVER THE HEATHENS.*

The Battle of Christendom turned into a long afternoon of gore. More than a thousand bodies were counted when the killing was done. Two dozen Castilians were wounded seriously and twelve died in the battle and for that dozens of prisoners were made to run gauntlets and other revenges. Two expert swordsmen delighted the company for a while in a contest to see who could cut the most prisoners completely in half with a single blow. The champion at this sport sliced eight men in half before having to repeat a stroke. The women seized were all raped, some repeatedly and very violently, then herded together with the children.

As the fight subsided, the admiral was still worked up. "Punish the heathen!" he charged, several times, not once flinching from the inflicted punishments. A dagger I saw him use twice, both times on badly wounded Indians, severing the spinal cord at the base of the neck, waiting the second time for his brother to witness the act. "I shall put him out of his misery," Don Christopherens said. "A Christian crusader can take pride in the painful spilling of heathen flood," Bartolomé replied.

Seven hundred sixty Taíno people were made prisoner that day, of which five hundred were later sent for sale at the slave market of Seville. A second large battle was fought weeks later as the Castilian troops cornered Maniocatex, who was captured and his villages scourged. The admiral delighted in the combats against our mesmerized *caciques*. As infidels taken in war can be sold into slavery by law, a cargo he now had, and legally, that he could send to market.

ONE HUNDRED FORTY. *GUARIONEX IS PRISONER.*

Guarionex was made prisoner. I went to see him with the admiral. "Why did you force us to kill your people," the admiral asked and I translated.

"It wasn't my idea," Guarionex said truthfully.

"You ordered the dumping of a Holy Cross."

"No, that wasn't my idea, either."

"Pané informs me you spoke against our Christ."

"I only wondered why you don't listen to what we have to say. I felt you disrespected us. My young men were angered and dumped the cross."

"Which ones?"

"All four died yesterday."

"You forced us to attack," the admiral said.

"I have seen your arms before. I wanted not this war," Guarionex said. "But even I did not expect you could kill so much so fast. It was frightful, seeing so much blood at once."

"Our Father in Heaven makes us strong," the admiral told him.

ONE HUNDRED FORTY-ONE. *GUARIONEX IS RELEASED, GUACANAGARI DISAPPEARS.*

Many came to request the freedom of Guarionex, and finally the admiral gave in, but he imposed a large gold tribute upon the *cacique*, on his own person and his people. For the wise *cacique* it was to be a full calabash of gold dust per month. Most everyone else was charged with amounts of half an ounce to one ounce every three months. That first tribute system for gold was very rigid, not only with Guarionex but with Maniocatex and Caonabó's people, and, more and more, even Guacanagari's villages were called upon to provide tribute, not escaping the harsh punishments imposed upon failure to provide. The tribute for gold worked like this: you brought in your assigned quota of gold and received a wooden pendant on a string, to be worn about the neck. Any Castilian could check any Indian under tribute. Any Indian caught without the proper pendant could be punished, either by whip or by the cutting of fingers, hands, or ears.

Now even Guacanagari, the admiral's "noble *cacique*," who saved him in his time of trouble, was pushed about and called dog. His own *guaxeri*, now trained as soldiers of Castile, imposed upon him his gold tribute, which they themselves would collect, fiercely aggressive toward him. During those days it was that Guacanagari walked into the forest one morning and was never seen again.

ONE HUNDRED FORTY-TWO. *A TAÍNO OFFER ON THE LAND.*

Guarionex was astonished that so many of his people were maimed. He had so much gold to gather that his *guaxeri* would give their portions to him to turn in and took the punishment meant for him. Guarionex decided to take *cohoba* at that time and an instruction received, which he followed.

Guarionex was to organize all of his planting *guaxeri*, a very impressive group that involved some of the best Taíno farmers. The *guaxeris* of the Yuca, of the Maize, of the *axí* (peppers) and the fruit orchards he brought together. A pilgrimage they would make, Guarionex informed them, to the *adelantado*'s farm. I was in camp with the *adelantado* when a runner came in from Guarionex, manifesting the peaceful intentions of the gathered group. The admiral came at once with his own troop. I remember thinking there might be another battle and was horrified, but indeed a quiet parley was the occasion.

Guarionex lined up his best gardeners, his orchard keepers, and thousands who came behind them, planting sticks in hand and seed pouches around their necks. The whole group sat on its haunches as the parley began, and Guarionex beseeched the admiral and the *adelantado* to consider his offer, which was to plant a huge sea of *conucos*, with *yucca*, *buniato*, and other tubers with *ajis* and *maize* and beans. He would work plantations that would run the width of the island from northern to southern coast, the *cacique* said, more than eighty leagues by thirty leagues square. "Never will you want from hunger," he promised. "You and your children we will feed, here and in your Castilian lands. So much food we will grow that you may never feel a threat to your existence. Happy, like us, you will be. Make the villages, keep your animals, cut the trees and build huge boats, bring your women. Yes, we will feed them all, as we have done before, but plentifully, and we will plant and plant and make *cassabe* for you, and fish for you, and present it to the Castilians with good heart and with consistency."

Guarionex's own words this day mixed in with a well-known speech among our *areitos*, one orated during the establishment of a new fire or village. It is called the speech of the *naboria*, and it was designed, in our own protocols, to invite a newcomer tribe to settle peacefully, as was happening with the Ciguayo in Española. For enticement, the *naboria* speech offered agricultural assistance, even labor. This was the oldest of *areitos*, used even by the earliest people we knew in in western Cuba, the Guanahatabey, when greeting with fruits and roots and conch meat the first Taíno to come on their beaches, in their eastern shores, many generations ago. It is the gentle way of the *naboria*, our ancient serving cousin, which was our own human way to cope with power and the migrations of warrior groups.

The Columbus brothers, including Diego Columbus, the other sibling, who came along with Don Christopherens on the second trip, listened to the great *cacique*'s offer, spoken in grand gestures and meant to cover the needs of generations. For a few minutes, they were entranced. "He is a smart old man," Don Bartolomé whispered. Guarionex finished by assuring the brothers that his men were most enthusiastic about the offer, and he looked at the admiral directly.

The admiral laughed. "But what could he want," he said, "in return for his food."

"There is something," the *cacique* responded. "Stop the gold tribute, which is maiming my people. We cannot meet it in any case and it seems without sense to cause so much injury and death of people. We are trying, *señores*," said the grizzled *cacique*, "but there is not that much gold to be gathered."

I translated Guarionex's offer as generously as possible. It made sense to me, as the Castilian colonies were in fact suffering from constant hunger, and making food is what Taíno could do best. Relief provisions had not arrived from the motherland for them, and production in our own villages was greatly diminished by the comings and goings and incessant terror of Castilian squads. Famine had materialized in the areas most affected by violence. I could see that Guarionex's gesture spoke to our ancient Taíno idea to always offer food and gifts as a way to peaceful relations.

With sneers and short laughs, the Columbus brothers dismissed Guarionex's idea. I knew their mood and expected as much, as all afternoon I had heard them discuss the operations of gold mines (a bigger sifting pan seemed a good idea) and the upcoming trip by Don Christopherens to represent the long-term reality to the monarchs. "Thank the great *cacique* for his generous offer, Dieguillo," he said. "Tell him we will certainly receive his men to work many *conucos*. However, as to the mines we offer a better idea."

Bartolomé explained: "This is our wish: the great *cacique* is to redouble his efforts to mine for the gold. Identify new streams and mines to work on. By all means, plant more and more, but bring the gold without manufacture of fanciful excuses. Failure to do so will be to force harsher punishments on his people." For good measure, the *adelantado* demanded the *cacique* take back Friar Pané into his village and continue his work of conversion.

"The *cacique* will not be heard," I told Guarionex in our language, when I was certain his offer was not considered. "I am sorry, for it makes sense to provide for the food supply." I even told him how honored I felt to spend time with him and to help him make the offer.

Guarionex left in full dejection but looked at me warmly as he left. I approached him, and he put his hand on my arm. "I appreciate your attempts to help us. Come and see me; I will tell you my stories."

Later, the *caciques*, with Guarionex conducting them, refused for two seasons to plant extra *yucca*, thinking thus they would starve out the covered men. Just when the plan might have succeeded, a convoy of provisions arrived from Spain, the Castilians were replenished, and the *guaxeri* of Guarionex faced famine and much sickness on their second season without a *yucca* crop.

One hundred forty-three. *The first Castilian rebellion: Roldán attacks the admiral.*

By this time, 1496 or '97, Francisco Roldán, the former mayor of Isabela, was in open rebellion against the *adelantado*. With a hundred Castilians under him, this *fascineroso*, or torrid one, as Columbus called him, moved constantly from the Vega Real to the Xaraguá region, making excursions into Bonao to commandeer gold and to Isabela to steal horses and cattle. Roldán made pacts, after his own manner, with several *caciques*, camping out with them, marrying himself and his men into several *cacicasgos*. The *caciques* listened with interest to his call for ending the tribute system and his threat to kill the Columbus brothers, but then recoiled at the treatment received from his own desperadoes.

During one of these runs, Roldán himself and another captain took over Guarionex's village and twice raped his younger wife, Bema. As Guarionex pondered starting a second war on all Castilians, his mother's helpers once again ran the persistent Pané off and took hold of all the church items left in a small chapel the friar had built. For lack of a better approach, they buried the religious items in a recently planted field of *yucca*, a field assigned to the ceremony of the three-cornered *cemi*, the Yucahuguama, planted thus with the new tuber field, prayed for and watered by urine to call forth early germination.

Pané was mortified and cried for the admiral the news of the great sacrilege. Demanding swift punishment for the perpetrators, he identified six men who took part in the act, all nephews of Guarionex.

The *adelantado* ordered the six men captured. Then he burned them at the stake.

I visited Guarionex during that time. He cried in fury and agony at the punishment of the young men, having also lost his own son at the Battle of la Vega. Even though I was in the service of the admiral and the *adelantado*, Guarionex and I talked a great deal. I commiserated with him about his poor young men, and he accepted me without hesitation as a fellow Taíno seeking also for a way out of the horror that had befallen us. It was then he asked me to stay with him a while, calling me a nephew and introducing me to his youngest sister, Ceiba, in consideration of marriage.

One hundred forty-four. *I take a bride, Ceiba.*

I had met Ceiba twice, we had even spoken, and neither of us had qualms about meeting again during a couples' dance arranged by the *cacique*. The *adelantado* Columbus was in the vicinity, chasing after Roldán, when Guarionex's offer to me was made public. For his own reasons, the *adelantado* encouraged me to stick close to the old *cacique*, whom he still considered potentially dangerous. With our route opened by Guarionex and Ceiba in agreement, I quickly began the arrangement for a marriage ceremony by moving a hammock into my new wife's *bohío*.

This was the beginning of the best part of my miserable life. For nearly a year, the Castilians busied themselves with the building of new forts, starting new mines and moving the main metropolis of Española to the new site of Santo Domingo, on the southern coast. The *adelantado* chased Roldán and his two hundred men around the Xaraguá area (not far from where I write), while the admiral embarked for Castile to combat accusations by the rebel's friends, including Father Buil and Captain Margaritte, that the "Genoese tyrants" were committing atrocities against Castilian and Indian alike. A respite of sorts, short but sweet, was the gift of those days for me.

One hundred forty-five. *Making a family, home days.*

It is only now, experiencing as I am the freedom of this rebel camp, that I fully appreciate those days with Ceiba, in the old court of Guarionex, those blissful few months of a season of relative peace, when Guarionex put through *areito* after *areito*, singing from his great repertoire of hundreds and hundreds of story songs and ceremonial chants, recalling the ancient prophesies and teachings with me.

Ceiba and I liked each other. She was a mature woman, slightly older than me. In our second month, a full wedding ceremony was arranged, and Guarionex had a new *bohío* built to house the new couple. In our custom, a nuptial *bohío* like this must be built all in one day, with many people working. That day was a great celebration, with many joyful elements, all the more heartfelt as the times were certainly harsh and the people had already much to mourn. But the people of her *yukaieke* loved Ceiba a great deal, and they accepted me as a possible factor in relieving the great burdens imposed upon them. And it did happen, once, that I turned away a band of four Castilians who wounded a *guaxeri* of Guarionex and were intent on settling forcefully in the village. The *adelantado*, I lied to them in perfect Castilian, had given strict orders, under penalty of death, that Castilian soldiers stay out of Guarionex's village.

Ceiba and Catalina's people were friendly and frequent visitors. Thus a large group came with Catalina to the wedding. Catalina, a cousin of Anacaona's and older by ten years than Ceiba, led her young cousins in singing moon songs. In the early evening, she gifted us a fortune telling, looking to our destiny as a couple, a fertility search with *manatí* bone games that always came out two. Everyone nodded as this was considered good fortune, and the elders all reminded me of it months later when our twin boys were born. Catalina, bless her heart, came to help with the birth.

ONE HUNDRED FORTY-SIX. *ENRIQUILLO'S CAMP IS LIKE THE OLD* YUKAIEKES.

I am glad to be here. This camp reminds me of those days, when we went for months not seeing even one Castilian and we could take the time, every day, to be Taíno. Ceiba and I put in a *conuco* all our own, even tobacco and herbs we planted. We worked together every day, bathed at the stream twice a day, and coupled excessively, day after day, wherever and whenever we wanted. She was wide of shoulder and hip, a strong woman who could work and work in the sun and who made love with certainty, grabbing a man firmly and opening herself in full trust, and she was so easy and so wonderful to love. For those months, as her belly grew and we continued to sneak around like mice in the corn, I became a poet in the style of old Guarionex and my grandfathers of childhood, full of thoughts for our little family and for our village and formulating thoughts of peace and words of love for Ceiba and words of reason and harmony for the Castilians, feeling in love strong enough to carry impacts of importance.

ONE HUNDRED FORTY-SEVEN. *THE OLD MAN KNEW SO MUCH.*

I sat with Guarionex and I heard him many times ponder the future. I grew to love the old man and through him was once again touched with the beauty and the reason of our Taíno customs. Guarionex knew it all. He was one of the very few, even in the best of times, who could remember the songs for all the *areitos*, all of the origin stories, the traditions and safekeeping practices for each and all of our *cemi* helpers. About the medicines, he knew their ceremonies and could check and instruct *behikes* and medicine women who regulated such things. But his interest was the peace pact, for which he could draw on a great repertoire of memories.

Peace-pacting was a strong tradition in Guarionex's court, and he was often drawn to help resolve fights between *caciques*. With me he talked much about these things, and together we wondered the motivations of Castile, why they settled on Taíno lands and what accommodations might yet be made with them so that our people could survive.

ONE HUNDRED FORTY-EIGHT. *DEATH SPIRITS THAT OPEN SORES IN OUR FACES.*

It happened, too, that with the spread of Castilian settlements new illnesses grew among our people. There were constant deaths in villages where once the occasion was relatively rare. Every day now many people were dying and many others laid up on hammocks, very hot and retching and unable to eat, ears and noses running liquid and in many cases, open sores formed on our peoples' faces and bodies.

Guarionex pondered out loud on all this. Through the *cohoba* I experienced with him then, I did see my elders (though I could not talk to them), and I remember that they gestured for me to not come near them, but to stay where I was and open my ears and eyes wide. I saw my old men of Guanahaní and my father's mother, who waved at me, clasping her hands with two thumbs raised. I had not experienced the *cohoba* long enough to know what to do within my trance, nor how to move about, nor how to bring forth sound. I had no real skills, though I felt at ease with it, and in the morning my body felt clean and my mind clear.

Guarionex was powerful in *cohoba* and could communicate with his grandparents and especially with his great-grandfather, Caiçiju, a *behike* of renowned power whose *cohoba* vision of three generations before Guarionex shared with me.

"Caiçiju fasted six days," Guarionex told me. "Every night he took *cohoba* and dreamed. Three nights he received sorrowful messages for one or another of his relatives. Then, even animals reported to him stories of future hardships. One night, Vital Force Supreme Spirit, Yucahuguama Bagua Maórocoti, the one without grandfather, of grandmother born, He who is Creator of our sea and islands, creator of all fish and of our Taíno people, Ancient Waves of our Ocean, spoke to him. He took Caiçiju out of himself and into the bright day sky past a thin cloud cover. Caiçiju told later that he reentered our world through the clouds to see our crablike island. On the ground, he moved through his known haunts. A man spirit, not Yucahu, he said, showed him his third generation on this earth, not free, as was his own, but enslaved, chained and lashed, dying of hunger. He saw covered men, he said, who came from the east and rode four-legged beasts full of fury.

"Caiçiju asked himself, how can this be? Who could do such a thing? He thought of the Carib, their pesky raids, but that didn't make sense, as they seldom settled for long and even then, more often than not, were taken in by our people.

"Of course, whom it was I know now," Guarionex told me. "The Castilians it is whom he was shown by Yucahu Bagua Maórocoti; the covered men were carried to us in his own Great Spirit vision, on the waves of his own mother sea."

ONE HUNDRED FORTY-NINE. *ROLDÁN AND THE FIRST INDIAN* REPARTIMIENTO.

One day in early spring 1498, some six months after our twins were born, Guarionex came to our *bohío*, which was nearly a mile from his main village and a quieter place. He was distraught. His men had been severely punished in recent weeks. "So much blood I cannot sleep."

And now something worse he had heard. The *adelantado* sent an offer to Roldán. The rebellious mayor and his men would receive land grants from Columbus, including whole villages of peaceful Indians. Roldán and his men would be installed as captains over *caciques*. Guarionex asked me to check this information for him and I did by spending some days in the *adelantado*'s company (I took a wide cape of parrot feathers to him from Guarionex).

ONE HUNDRED FIFTY. *GUARIONEX RETREATS TO THE MOUNTAINS.*

Don Bartolomé confirmed the offer to Roldán. It was true, the *yukaiekes* were to be split off, and Roldán would receive land and many Indians. Francisco Roldán, who led the first rebellion against the Columbus brothers' central authority on the islands, was a troubled man, quarrelsome. At times, he took up the Indian cause, demanding an end to the tribute system. And this way, here and there, Roldán enlisted *caciques* in plots against the admiral. Thus, at one moment, Guarionex himself threw his lot into a battle at Concepción, where his warriors wiped out nearly a whole garrison.

The problem was Roldán's men had no morals. They relied on the *guaxeri* for food but constantly abused the women. Roldán sought our alliance against the admiral but just the same demanded complete subservience from us. After one such campaign, I have written, Roldán raped Guarionex's second wife. Now, the admiral, whom Roldán insulted a hundred times, was to give him as gifts our lands and people. It was the final act for Guarionex.

"I see Castile fight, son against father." (He meant Roldán versus the admiral). "They would kill each other. And in that fight, each of them seduce us to be of each their ally. But no matter with whom we elect to stand, they each, in the end, despise us and disdain our place. Our friendship ceremonies, our *guatiaos*, the change of faces and exchange, our *areitos* we have sung them, it all amounts to nothing. They are a people who live in constant shame."

Guarionex would start to speak slowly, but the words soon pounded out of his mouth in stark blows. "I know his weapons can blow men apart. The fury hurricane he commands, and it does horrify. But beyond the horror of death, what truly frightens is the way they are. How certain of their destiny are these covered men, and yet how willingly they have lied to our *caciques*. This covered man sees not my eyes. He sees not this world. He is not a god, that is certain, but he is not a human like our people are human."

Guarionex was agitated by his growing perception. "I will withdraw from my territories," Guarionex said. "My people the admiral cannot just give away like so many fish in a canoe."

That day, Guarionex asked Ceiba and I to take his mother's clan house under our care, hoping they could avoid direct persecution as he went to war. Ceiba and I agreed to make a village for more than one hundred people, and Guarionex asked the people to accept me as *cacique*. As his sister's husband, I could take this place, according to our ancient tradition, since she held the actual *cacique* line and not him. Of course, in calmer times, she and her sisters would raise one of their boys to be *cacique* rather than choose one of their own husbands. As the *adelantado* had granted me, with Don Christopherens's permission, a tract of land, my new relatives I settled then into a formal *cacicasgo*.

Days later, the old man moved his main villages into *Cacique* Mayobanex's territory, who had offered to protect him from Castilian attack. Mayobanex was Ciguayo, a strong warrior and elder. He greatly esteemed Guarionex's superior knowledge of our ceremonies and stories. Weeks passed and then a war Guarionex started that raged for several months. Guarionex and Mayobanex both led warriors and raided with impunity. Many ambushes of Castilians took place during that time, and it wasn't always clear who had the upper hand. Divided as he was by the attacks from Roldán's men and the various Indian skirmishes, *Adelantado* Bartolomé Columbus strung out his forces, until accommodations with Roldán allowed him time to pursue the Indian chiefs.

ONE HUNDRED FIFTY-ONE. *GUARIONEX FALLS, AND MAYOBANEX.*

The story I told last night to the young men (and captains) in Enriquillo's circle, of how Guarionex and Mayobanex, a Ciguayo and a Taíno, stood together and were destroyed together. I told them of the character of the *adelantado*, who chased them mercilessly, finally cornering each of the old men in turn and alienating their jurisdictions. Poor Guarionex was chained and placed in isolation in Santo Domingo. Nearly three years he languished before being sold into slavery. His only luck was to die en route, no longer a *cacique* but not yet a slave.

ONE HUNDRED FIFTY-TWO. *CASTILIANS SWARM THE ISLAND.*

The Castilians were beginning to swarm the island by then. The central plain was nearly pacified. Santo Domingo and the other Castilian forts grew. I hear Las Casas tell that some three hundred *repartimientos*, or early *encomiendas*, were already granted by the year 1500, including many ranches and mines and large fincas. I do remember that they cleared roads for their oxen wagons and horses, and they traveled in groups between towns. At that time, I did all I could to hold Ceiba's *yukaieke* together, feeding and protecting her old people and our growing twin boys. We had settled into the valley granted to me by Don Christopherens, a remote *conuco*, away from the traveled roads, and we went nearly undetected for five years.

Many of our people did what they could during that time to hide away in remote places. Three of the five main *cacicasgos*, the

Taíno bighouses, and one Ciguayo, had been annexed or destroyed by the Castilians. Guacanagari was absorbed, then lost. Caonabó, Guarionex, and Mayobanex were taken down. Only two provinces, Higüey and Xaraguá, on the eastern and western ends of the island, retained their own territories. Neither had gold to offer, yet each paid substantial tribute, in *cassabe* and fish, in woven cotton and the labor of artisans. Only later did I travel to Higüey, so I never met its *cacique*, Cotubanamá, though I often met people from their region in Santo Domingo, when they came to deliver their goods. I had more contact during this time with Bohekio and his sister Anacaona, widow of Caonabó, who maintained their Taíno *cacicasgo* intact, this in the province of Xaraguá, which surrounds these Bahuruku mountains. They were very calm people, just as my own little village was calm, and it seemed for a few short seasons that peace might return and a common ground could be reached with the Castilian towns. Of course, Ovando, the knight commander, had yet to come.

ONE HUNDRED FIFTY-THREE. *SURROUNDED BY YOUNG TAÍNO, EDUCATION FOR PEACE.*

Speaking for their young Taíno minds last night, surrounded by friendly forces, I felt incredibly light. I am light anyway from my fast, and my mind is light, too, like dew on a spider's web. I move in a flow and the warriors notice. The *behike*, whom they greatly respect, is constantly with me, and Enriquillo signals approval at every turn. He likes my stories and attitude, and I am conscious of returning his new message to his fighting people. I must educate them at every turn, prepare them for a possible peace. For fifteen years Enriquillo has taught them to abhor and kill Castilians, to kill especially *mánso* Indians like me, who have always been the greater threat. Now he needs them to appreciate an end to hostilities, if such should come. For this, he even interrupts his vigilance; he produces me as his voice. Sometimes, as I speak, I feel his face on my own, the weight and the tension of his brow in my eyes.

ONE HUNDRED FIFTY-FOUR. *A SONG COMES TO ME.*

This afternoon, on the last day of my fast, I write. Tonight we snort *cohoba*. Day by day, the *behike*, often with Enriquillo in attendance, sits me facing west, looking away from the sun, a circle of *yucca* and conch shell dust drawn around me. At dawn and dusk, a small *hicara* (gourd) of water. Each morning, with my back to the morning sun, he whispers, "Shoulder his power." I thank this mountain site, thanking, too, the ancestors who pay attention. When the sun hits directly my face from above, my circle of protection the *behike* opens by brushing aside a line of the *yucca* and shell dust, inviting my hand and step.

"Maybe you cannot sing," he said before, as he noticed my silence. "Make the noise, hum it, if you remember it."

This morning, as the dew steamed away, a song came to me. The mist was still around us. The *behike* burned the lightest bit of *tabanacu* incense, and the smoke rose in little puffs that dissipated before reaching the forest canopy. It was the puffs of smoke as I watched them that recalled the touch of that old wooden drum of Guarionex, which he beat many times singing *cohoba* songs for me. Suddenly in my ears I picked up a song that went on and on, repeating itself and branching out, and I could hear in it voices that had not lived for many years. What a good sound it was, how pleasing and warm to the memory!

One hundred fifty-five. *Going to meet the medicine.*

I make final notes and prepare my mind. Afterward, I will not write but prepare my return to the convent in Santo Domingo. There I will write more. For now I can say that my mind is very calm and that I feel as complete as I have in years. I am convinced of the life that exists beyond our awakened earth, the resounding mind that accompanies our walking days, and the many spaces and folds in its world. My father is there, I can tell. My father is with me. Nearly every day, here and there, I sense him. I see him in my dream, and I smell the sweat of his back on first awakening.

Today, walking through the woods from the *behike*'s, I felt the ground rise and fall in waves beneath my steps, soft earth supporting my body with her heat. Everything smelled green. The world was green smelling as I walked lightly, so lightly over the earth.

It was then I felt them all around. I felt warm winds embrace me, even dance around me in the woods, walking so lightly, walking in the weakness of no food, of hunger denied and then ignored, removed. So light I was I felt the water as I drink it travel through me in clean rushes, a coolness in my thighs. So light I feel I could see them already, even in the light, knowing as they do that the *cohoba* is being prepared, greeting me in their shy way as I walked. For them, the earth said to me: Remembered son, I clean your feet with my dew as with your step you caress my back.

My father told me: Never rush the first medicine. Even your certain medicine, don't greet it personally on the first pass. So, I asked the earth, Sacred Guakeya, I intoned: On you, beautiful land, why is there so much suffering for my people? I asked, too: And, will there be survival for the good Taíno?

Folio V

COHOBA DREAMS

Two weeks later, at the convent in Santo Domingo... Journey with cohoba, *a returning memory... The* cohoba *journey... Message of the* cohoba, *a way to guard the survival... I conduct a strange ceremony... At the convent, Las Casas returns... I ask Catalina to help me... In the woods with Catalina... At my old* yukaieke *in the lower Magua country... With* cohoba *again, with Ceiba... Finding love with Catalina... Barrionuevo has arrived... Tempering the good friar... I hate telling a lie, but... The good friar confesses a deed of his youth... Las Casas goes again... In the memory: Velazquez presses me into service... The route to Xaraguá, with Velazquez... The Massacre of Anacaona's Banquet... The killing begins, Enriquillo in my arms... Encounter with Manasas at the stream... Suspected in the killing... My village is encomended...*

ONE HUNDRED FIFTY-SIX. *TWO WEEKS LATER, AT THE CONVENT IN SANTO DOMINGO.*

Quietly I have returned to the friars' cloister. No one questions my long delay at the sugar mill, though I know that there are whispers about me. They wonder about young Silverio, who decided to stay, who decided to be a warrior *guaxeri* among his people. About him, I have said that he stayed to work in carpentry on a second Maguana sugar mill.

No one has raised any question about the way I look and act. I have decided to speak to no one, directing but very brief words to Fray Remigio, who took up the care of my poor, mangy mare and announced my deep *retirum* to silent prayer the morning of my return.

Truly they think of me as another monk. And though I have never taken vows of any kind, I could run a high Mass, a baptism, a confirmation, a marriage, and even the extreme unction. Now I protect myself by retiring into prayerful sacrifice, and they must respect it. No one speaks to me directly, and I put on their hooded mantle, and I emerge only in the quiet moments and spend much time in the chapel, kneeling for my faith.

ONE HUNDRED FIFTY-SEVEN. *JOURNEY WITH* COHOBA, *A RETURNING MEMORY.*

I entered the Coaybay in my trance. I saw my elders again. Smitten I am by the *cohoba* messengers, and I walk every day, all day and all night, in the company of that recent memory.

Baiguanex and Enriquillo assisted me. Light already from my long fast, I was led by them to the fire. Behind a western peak, the day's sun splayed its final signals. Light I was of body but not weak inside, not in my heart nor in my mind. The moment was alive as in my childhood days. Nor were my eyes weak that could see with precise clarity. A long, low *duho* seat Baiguanex had out for me. I sat in the recline of its curve. "Close your eyes, uncle," the *behike* instructed, and I did.

Baiguanex said: "Prepare to leave our world of human senses. Prepare in darkness now as the *cacique* and I will smoke you with sacred tobacco, as Doña Mencia prepares your tea and cleans your spatula. Prepare in the darkness of your own mind, human being. Share the darkness, little *guaxeri*, as we clear the spirits of animal and tree, shrub and herb, and we open the very place where we are sitting. Yes, our little uncle, keep your eyes closed. Here, drink from this *güira* the juice that will fully cleanse you. But don't open your eyes while the snuff of *cohoba* I prepare in your bowl; stay in the darkness from which you will travel, yes, yes."

I sat in darkness and remembered the words of Guanahabax, our old man of my home island. "Remember all your days that *cohoba* loves you," he said. "It will always welcome you. Xán, Xán Katú."

All these years later and I still have my own spatula. I lost the feather fans, the two-pronged sniffer, I lost the rattle and broke my gourd, all years and years ago. Somehow, the spatula I never lost. It was my father's spatula, made of hard, smooth coral, and I always managed to keep it. I drank freely from the cleansing tea, filled my belly to its bursting, then asked to face the woods. Eyes closed, I was guided by my assistants. The tea caused my belly to expand. Situated, then, I heard, "Give it back, now, uncle," and I used the spatula to cause a sudden torrent of vomit, long and dark, to flow out of my body. I staggered, and my assistants held me up then guided me back to my reclining seat.

"Prepare to travel," Baiguanex said, approaching me. "I will now load my *cacimba*," he said. "It has two blowholes that I will place at your nostrils. Then, as I was taught, I will blow the *cohoba* dust into your head. And you will be released."

I heard him stand up then. He offered the loaded *cacimba* to the four directions. He sang the song of Deminán and the four Cara-caracoles, the skywalkers, the ones without fathers. He sang the *areito* of Attabei, the Ancient Bleeding Mother. Then he invoked his two *cemis*, Baibrama, to guide me, and the Jumper, a helper who would instruct Opiyelguobirán—canine guardian of the Coaybay—to not accost me but to receive me and, later, release me. In a few moments the *behike* said, "Are you ready, uncle?" I nodded, then felt the *cacimba* lean into my nostrils. "Blow," I whispered to my guide. "Push off gently from this shore my slippery canoe."

ONE HUNDRED FIFTY-EIGHT. *THE* COHOBA *JOURNEY.*

There was light, and transference was immediate. I held the sneeze, felt my body give, then succumb. Then it was midday, clear as sun-light, and I sat on a dock made of two long tree trunks, tied together with *bejucos*, that jutted out into a cove. The cove was on the mouth of a river, and many canoes paddled out to sea. In the cove, some canoes were latched to each other as people talked. Two men in a canoe glided up the dock. They were old and naked, brown wrinkled skin hanging from thin arms and faces with missing teeth and alert eyes. "Boy," one said to me. "We have a full canoe, but you can't come with us." I looked and saw that their canoe was not full but actually upside down. And now they paddled away, chuckling to themselves at my surprise.

Now I was chopping wood. I was by myself. I had a Spanish ax and I had a log against which to chop. I was cooking *leña* for Ceiba. I was in my woodlot, near the *bohío* we kept in the valley of Guarionex. I was chopping wood by myself, and I could hear the twins calling to each other. I could not see them, but I could hear their voices nearby. "Good Wind," said Heart of Earth, "come see my worms. I have many of them in a pool." And Good Wind replied, in that high, pretty voice he had as a little boy. "Let's go fish the river, my *himagua*."

Then I was alone again in the same place, but there was no sound at all. I felt a group of men approach through the woods, eight or ten of them, Taíno *guaxeri* of the old generation, all hardy and straight standing. Without sound I could tell they meant for me to drop the ax and go with them. They walked, and I fell in line as they moved fast through the woods. They half-ran in the old manner, single file, at a half-trot, for hours. This is the way the men liked to travel in the old days. Form a line, put a singer at its head, and trot to the next destination. And there I was for hours, it seemed, trotting behind a pair of calves and hairtail spinning in the wind and running. Once the singing started, it went on and on. Among many voices I heard Baiguanex, and I knew, briefly, he was working with me from the living world.

Then we were at the bottom of a rocky mountain. The man before me pointed out a small trail, and I was alone again, walking that trail up the hill, which suddenly opened to a plateau. I heard a snarl behind me, turned quickly, and saw only a rustle in the grass. Then he was ahead of me, the *cemi* Opiyelguobirán, guardian and master of Coaybay. I could do nothing suddenly, could not move as his mere gaze captured my movement. Opiyelguobirán sat just as his *cemi* depicted, on his haunches, with front arms extended like legs. The friar, Pané, called him a dog spirit and having known the Spanish dogs I can see why. Opiyelguobirán was small and he was big, so big at moments I felt just his nostril could take me up in a breath. Suddenly the songs caught up with me, the sweet running songs and then the ones of Guarionex and the ones of my father and even the death song of Cibanakán, long imbedded in my ear from the time of his freezing. Hearing Cibanakán's song, Opiyelguiobirán began to diminish in size. Then, quite small, he wagged his tail, tended his head for me to pat, and darted away.

Sunshine appeared. In a wide field I saw multitudes. There were Taíno people all over the plateau, and I could hear talking and I could smell roasting *cassabe* bread and roasting corn. An old man I did not recognize came up beside me. "We can smell the food," he said wistfully. "But we cannot eat it."

He moved on, and then Guarionex was there and my father behind him, and the other old men of our *cohoba* circle in Guanahaní. It was all men, and they circled around me then began to walk me up the hill.

"We welcome you, beloved," old Guanabanex said, and I heard my father singing softly behind him. I could see ahead of us the entrance to a cave, a dark hole in the side of the mountain, maybe three feet wide.

"This is the way we come," the old man said, crawling in. "Now, let's enter."

Inside we could stand. Sabananiobabo, lord of the *jobos* (dead men turned to wood), guarded the entrance from inside. He is an old man with grave eyes. He greeted us and walked next to me. Suddenly, from above, large swarms of bats dislodged and flew around us. Sabananiobabo waved them away. The last flier of the swarm was not a bat but an owl, who circled once over me and flew off. Sabananiobabo sat the others in a circle but took me aside. "Come look at the owl's reminder," he said. "You have something here that he retrieved for you."

Then in front of us, near a stream, there was a hut. He pointed through the door. A long log bench I saw inside, with two men sitting on it. One was the soldier Manasas, a hefty Extremaduran man; the other was the foreman Moises, thin and slight. They didn't look up, neither of them, their necks hanging low. I recognized their bodies and faces. They are the two men I have killed.

"I can do nothing with them, so they will wait, until you meet them at your proper time," Sabananiobabo said.

The cave was large and open, very old and musty, humid, almost cold. Now, both women and men walked through as I sat in the men's circle. The *cohoba* twins—the twins in everything—I saw float by, crying, yet watching everything and reminding me of the meaning of *cohoba*, the opening to the other self. Reminding me, too, of my own boys, gone from me now these many years.

My father now sat to my left in the circle. "They still live, both of them," he answered my silent question. I was totally happy and dared not inquire further about them.

"And your mother," he said. "She is alright, here, in the Coaybay."

Happy to know that much, I inquired no more about her either. He said nothing more but sang his canoeing song for me. "Glide in this cloud of a sea," he sang. "Carry my son ahead of me, carry my son ahead of me..." And for a long while, in his celestial canoe, I leaned into my father's back, smelling the sweat of his neck, listening to his favorite song. Suddenly from our right side, out of the endless sky, Opiyelguobirán and his twin brother, Corocote—one guardian of the House of Death (and felicity), the other always harbinger of life (and love heat)—flew past us, crossing our path.

Then I was in the circle of men, and I was very young, a boy in a circle of elders. I knew I was receiving instructions. "Protect the baby boy," one man said. It was Caiçiju, father-uncle of Guarionex, prophet of our people's doom. There was also my second father, Cibanakán, and my grandmother, and my uncle Jiqui, and my brother-cousin, Caréy, all among the many faces in the circle of *cohoba*. I had no need to greet them directly, but they had come and I had come, so we were all now here together again. Guarionex sat next to me, real as anything, and now as I write in this Christian convent I close my eyes and see him next to me still, as in a waking dream.

My *cohoba* memory comes and goes. I remember most the talking, the sound, darkness in my eyes but all from sitting in that circle, between the songs. Guarionex was much there. He whispered in my ear. "The Castilians need us no more," he said. "That I know."

Someone else said: "Between the Castilians and their gains of gold, the baby boy now stands. They would make a peace, finally, and leave him more or less alone."

Guarionex said: "A warrior of the Castilians who has killed must be opened again. Sing a song of words in his ears. Clean his eyes, his ears. He must hear if he would give the baby boy respite..."

This was repeated. I remember clearly, he said: "Those who would kill him: put gold in their path. Even revenge they will ignore for gold." He repeated, several times: "Gold in their path."

They talked about our people and continuing to be.

"Our own warrior man-killers, they too must be cleansed. Taíno they all must be again."

"Guaikán of the living sea," I heard, and it was Caiçiju, our prophet of doom. "Taíno they must be!" I could see him, how skinny he still was, even in spirit. But he was the most adamant, crying at me from his *duho* seat while the others stood to dance. "Torrent waters of white and black faces will wash the mountain current of our blood. But Taíno they must be, even if all that remains of our generation is the depth of our black eyes and the love in our living bones."

ONE HUNDRED FIFTY-NINE. *MESSAGE OF THE* COHOBA, *A WAY TO GUARD THE SURVIVAL.*

I sat with Enriquillo and the *behike* for two days. I fed on bits of *cassabe* and dried fish and drank the juice of *guayaba* and other fruits of our trees. Everything of my *cohoba* they would know and interpret, and I told them everything I could.

"The ones who would murder you," I said to Enriquillo, after hearing Guarionex's message. "We should guide them to the gold. A few bars of the bullion that you have left we can put in their path, with which to knock them into our trap."

This was agreeable as the method has worked before, though the details remained shadowy. I mentioned Valenzuela and Pero Lopez as likely culprits, among others. And I prepared a written message for Lopez, an invitation for him and Valenzuela, the offer to meet and exchange gold bullion for a pardon and good terms for Enriquillo. I suggested the use of the good friar as a go-between, to confirm the gold exchange and the manner of the pardon. This, too, was agreeable.

The message I wrote with the point of a fishing hook on leaves of the *copei* tree. This broad leaf will maintain such an inscription forever. I saw it used by Captain Hojeda early on in the conquest, and he would fool our people often by sending messages to others in ways that appeared divination to us.

With Doña Mencia I talked about Catalina Diaz and her daughter Julia, who work on the Valenzuela estate. If the would-be murderers can be diverted and a real peace is possible, I promised that it would be Julia who would deliver the message.

Enriquillo himself took me to my horse, crossing the lake accompanied by eight canoes. I felt very connected to the young *cacique* and loved everything about him. We found my poor mare, Cariblanca, quite molested by red ants during my absence. She was a bit wild, and it took me an hour to calm her down. "The good friar gets full of ants like that," Enriquillo commented. Then he instructed me with great certainty: "I do not want him near the peace negotiations. Later, to guarantee the safe passage to our new community, yes. Then he would be useful. But not now, not for this mission of peace pact, when calm must be at the center of our discussions."

I took this as an order from him.

Cacique that he is, Enriquillo then listed for me the core of his negotiating conditions: "I must have these four things: One, the embassy must come from the king himself. No one from the island will I speak through. Two, the king must guarantee full pardons and freemen status for all our people here. Three, he must guarantee land and our own community. And lastly, the law should deputize my captains to guard the peace and manage the arrest of future runaways. Thus we will keep our weapons and our power to travel the roads."

ONE HUNDRED SIXTY. *I CONDUCT A STRANGE CEREMONY.*

I did the old peace-pact orations with the captains during my final days at Enriquillo's camp. I offered this to follow the instructions in the *cohoba*, to cleanse the warriors of so much violence. Our pine tree resin the *behike* had shaped in candles for me, and the altar I set up as Guarionex had shown me. Then I called on the fiercest warriors to come into my discipline that I carry from those times.

Tamayo was the hardest, but even he believed in me when I knelt him down facing the fire of the resin and its smoke and I asked him to feel it in his chest. I implored him then to open up the throat, the ears, try to use the eyes, deliciously, to love the world again, what he might see or sense of being alive.

Tamayo's mother had been disemboweled, his father burned alive. In reprisal, these past few years, he had killed much. "I have liked it," he said, his voice quavering. I asked him to cry if he must and he did. He cried vigorously. Tamayo has been very hurt. "You've made me cry, uncle," he said after the ceremony. "I hope peace is truly our new way. Because war will be harder now."

I worked on young Cao, who, to my dismay, had killed almost a dozen times. Of all of them it was young Cao surprised me the most, as he truly had killed without bother and had no remorse to clear away.

Astin the Lucumí, a veteran from the rebellion of enslaved Africans at Don Diego Columbus's sugar mills in 1522, was another hard one. He helped hang many whites during that rebellion, even one or two who were friends. "Ever since, I have killed Castilians," he said. "By myself, more than twenty men."

So much hatred came quickly out of the men that I became concerned lest they surrender their fighting spirit too soon. One plan I could not get out of my mind: the capture and just punishment of Valenzuela and the monster Pero Lopez. Tamayo it was, I felt, that must set the trap for Valenzuela and Pero Lopez. In the midst of my doings with them, I was suddenly certain, in a darkening of heart, that I wanted Tamayo and his most experienced killers to do that job. Tamayo and Cao and the Lucumí, I knew, would kill Valenzuela, would kill Pero Lopez, if given the chance.

I enlisted Tamayo for the ambush of Valenzuela and Lopez then, and on his own he picked Cao and Astin and three others to go along. I would lure the men to their trap, where they expected gold. The rest was left open, though Tamayo hated Valenzuela immensely, and I knew, in my revengeful heart, survival was not likely for our former masters. A strange ending such talk provided to a cleansing ceremony, and Enriquillo avoided having to approve the plan. I did feel twisted, behind my eyes, and I noticed later the *behike* disappeared to the woods without saying good-bye.

ONE HUNDRED SIXTY-ONE. *AT THE CONVENT, LAS CASAS RETURNS.*

Las Casas is back. He returned quietly, day before yesterday, on a busy morning when four other ships came in. From my high window, I saw him enter the convent, hiding under a cape. The next evening, Fray Remigio came for me. "The good friar wants to see you."

In his main room we met, Fray Remigio quietly withdrawing after ushering me in. Las Casas sat in darkness by the window. "Do not look upon me," he said. "I may or may not be here yet."

He would go out this evening, and he intended the next day to come in overland, as if from La Plata, he said, to dissimulate his comings and goings. "That way, maybe I was in Spain, maybe I was not, but on the mainland or in Cuba."

"I am happy not to see you again," I said, following his logic. The logic was not strange considering that assassins have tried to kill the good friar. He ignored my remark.

"I have had your letter," I informed him. "The news of Barrionuevo has reached the baby boy, who is willing to entertain a real peace."

"Excellent," Las Casas said. "It is of great importance that I carry word of the rebellious *cacique* myself. I must have an exact idea of his demands when Captain Barrionuevo arrives."

"Enriquillo has formulated his own plan on this," I said, feeling guarded about the priest's willingness to command the negotiations with Enriquillo.

"The final crisis for Enriquillo is upon us," he pressed on. "Barrionuevo arrives in days. I have things set up so that the results of Enriquillo's treaty with Barrionuevo will be taken immediately to Spain, where several orders are ready to carry our demand."

"What demand, Father?"

"The abolishment of the *encomienda*, of course."

I was quiet and decided not to oppose him. The good friar is like that; once a goal enters his mind, he does not deviate. I was glad for the clarity of Enriquillo's final instruction to me. I love the good friar, but at that moment I decided myself how to deviate him, by subterfuge, from attending the negotiations. This I write with some shame: at that moment I decided to enlist him in the trap set for Valenzuela and Pero Lopez. In the midst of a peace-pact mission, I cannot get out of my mind and heart the face of Pero Lopez the day he took my son and sold him, and I cannot get out of my mind my joy at the sight of his face when Tamayo corners him. I thirst for the justice coming toward me in this arrangement.

"Enriquillo has communicated this to me," I said. "Two negotiations he would conduct, good friar. One is with the king's ambassador, Captain Barrionuevo. The other one is with Valenzuela, his former *encomendero*. The second one is the dangerous one."

"Valenzuela will have to adapt to the king's capitulation, of course."

"There is danger he would destroy the negotiations, by killing or capturing Enriquillo himself. Such an occurrence, remember, would save the king the embarrassment of making a treaty with the Indian bandit, as Oviedo calls the *cacique*."

Las Casas said immediately, "How can we shield the *cacique*?"

"A message must be carried to Valenzuela, from Enriquillo, just as Enriquillo makes contact with Barrionuevo. The message will call Valenzuela and his men in a deviant chase, away from the real negotiations."

"At any time, whatever Enriquillo needs, I will do," Las Casas offered. "This message I will deliver, if need be, before I leave for the negotiations."

"I am certain it will soon be time to do so," I said. Then I cleared my throat, taking my time.

"I have some notes for you," I said, still clearing my throat. I gave him a stack of written pages. "They are about the early days of Bartolomé Columbus and Guarionex."

"The Battle of la Vega?"

"It's in there."

"And Pané?"

"He, too, is in there, how he went to live with Guarionex."

"I have his little book," the friar said. "I got it in Seville. Martyr de Angleria had a copy made by Pané himself. It is a wonderful recollection of your people's old tales. I am certainly glad he noted all that."

"He didn't learn that much," I said. "Though he always had his nose in somebody's armpit."

The good friar laughed. He was happy to be back and to get the pages. I slipped away before he could deliver me with instructions. I know for certain now he would attempt to represent Enriquillo and believes he is empowered to do so. That could wreck everything. I need time to lay out my plan and have things ready for when Barrionuevo arrives.

ONE HUNDRED SIXTY-TWO. *I ask Catalina to help me.*

Today I sought Catalina. For the fourth day, on awakening, she was in my mind's eye. A message I sent her to meet at the back of the church. I reached from the bench behind her and put a bundle next to her. It was *cohoba* and tobacco. "The baby boy is well," I whispered. She grunted lightly.

"I must visit the old place where the Ceiba is resting. I must talk with her, in the *cohoba*."

"I can help you," Catalina answered. "I will say a birth has come up."

"I am afraid I would stay in the other side if there's no one to remind me."

"Yes, I will excuse myself and go with you."

One hundred sixty-three. *In the woods with Catalina...*

We went by way of deep woods, walking north for four days. We wanted to see no one, and we talked little. Mostly she walked ahead of me and set a brisk pace. At night she rubbed my thigh forcefully for a long time with her liniment and strong, thin fingers. Then, in silence, she made her own sleep in her own hammock. Twice I hunted *hutía*, which we roasted at night and ate with *cassabe* torts carried in *macoutís* looped to our foreheads. On the way, we gathered fruit and other things to eat. In 1533, I can write that it is still possible to find the old orchards and even old *conucos* where the herbs and nut crops planted by Taíno farmers forty and fifty years ago still come up and can be harvested.

One hundred sixty-four. *At my old* yukaieke *in the lower Magua country.*

Our third morning out I stood in the place where once I chopped wood with a Spanish ax. It was my first time back. The clearing was mostly overgrown, but I did find my old ax handle, and I found the center post to our old *bohío*. Catalina found things, too, which she bundled and put away without showing me.

I propped the old post up between two low, parted branches on a huge *ceiba* tree then lay my back against it. Catalina prepared the *cohoba* and made fire. In this ceremony she would also take the *cohoba* snuff, but only to thank her spirit helpers and Attabei, Great Birthing Mother of Waters, with whom, as a midwife, she is particularly related. Catalina had a double *cacimba*, which she loaded. It went both ways, placing the snuffers into both of our nostrils at once, so we could blow each other's load at the same time. "I have not much powder in mine, so I will come out first," she said. "Do what you must and return—set your mind to return. Listen for my song, and I will bring you out."

One hundred sixty-five. *With* cohoba *again, with* Ceiba.

That is how we did it, two days ago. And it worked for me just as I hoped. We sat in darkness a good while. The night was early, warm, and dry. We blew together, then separated. Once again I took the trail, only this time I got there on my own. This time, too, the dog-like *cemi* walked at my side. "Beloved son," he told me with his mind as he trotted. "This will not be hard."

We came to a plateau again. Then it was not a plateau but my old little valley, and I was walking near the brook. Near the water, on a rock I remembered, Ceiba was sitting. She looked only at the water but her body was happy to see me. We had no need for greetings.

"I was told they are alive, both of them," I told her without speaking.

The light of her spirit body emanated, and I could see it. She turned my way so I could see her face but still she did not look upon me. "One went south and one went north," I said. "They are both well, and there are children."

"You are a good *guaxeri*, my husband, to come to me this way."

"I want you to rest. Go home to Coaybay, where the elders will surround you."

"I should not have left you, but I could not live without my Good Wind."

"They are still on earth; I cannot know more."

"Thank you, my husband. I will go join my parents. As for you, accompany yourself, make a nest for your days ahead."

Ceiba walked away, following the current of the brook. I felt very complete and greatly satisfied. I felt tremendous peace, even in her lonely walk. I felt all my pain suddenly lift, and tears began to pour from my eyes, purging my heart and lifting the pressure from my shoulders. Then suddenly my right leg, crocodile-bitten all these years, felt strong and had bounce, and I began to run as I turned from the stream to the flat field of the plateau, jumping and hopping and with each step bouncing higher and higher. And there I was, jumping about my old little valley, bouncing from clearing to clearing, and suddenly, below me, seeing my curled up body, a shiver in my lightning spirit, and I began to bounce higher and higher, and I was going away and I wanted to go away and I could feel the tremendous harmony of my breath and of all Taíno memory, all Taíno goodness, all the ancestors, all of our beautiful knowledge, all of the seas and valleys of our spirit domains and I heard her singing.

In the path of flesh and blood you walk,
Come and join me, man alive, come and join me.
Your mission is done, your celestial steps complete,
Come and see me, man alive, come and chew and come and swallow.
Come and join me in the light, man alive, come and sleep.

Over and over I heard the song, and I didn't resist it. I let it call me down and lull me, and I followed it back until I felt the heat of the fire, and I remembered that I was alive.

One hundred sixty-six. *Finding love with Catalina.*

Catalina had fixed our hammocks. I slept until midmorning and she was already up and had prepared a tea and a plate of fruit for me. After I ate, she led me to the stream. "Bathe," she said, handing me a crunched up ball of *digo* root to lather with.

I entered the stream and bathed. Then I swam against the current a good while. Catalina sat by and watched me. "Work your leg against the water," she said. She, too, had bathed and now wore a skirt but nothing over her breasts. Neither her nakedness nor mine bothered us. We bathed naked for several hours, occasionally walking along the shore and picking fruits and nuts for the journey. The nuts made a good paste, which Catalina put in a gourd. I found a tree full of honeycombs, and we sweetened the nut paste, and it was very good. It was like the old days. Ceiba and I would do this, too, gather foods with her aunts and uncles, all of us naked in the old way, without a care about it.

That evening, we slept again, and in the false light of dawn I caught sight of Catalina's eyes gazing on me. I motioned her to come, and she came to lie in the crook of my arm in my hammock. We felt easy with each other and soon she lifted her leg over my thigh, and, lizardly, I hooked myself into her hold. I felt her slightest tremor and didn't move at all. She hugged me with her deepest love, and I was ironwood for her, holding fast. Catalina sighed softly and leaned down. She leaned down hard and held on so tightly it hurt. Then she caught, as we say, the rhythm of the hammock, and we took the long ride together.

We walked back in silence but full of love. Now she walked behind me, watching me. That night we stopped to rest, and again, in the night, she came over. In the morning she cooked for us as I greeted the sun and the four directions. Then we walked again, and she followed me, and I could feel the warmth of her eyes. I could feel her woman's heart envelop me, and it had been many years, and it was as obvious as frogs croaking at the clouds before rain that Catalina's was the love I needed to call warriors to peace.

ONE HUNDRED SIXTY-SEVEN. *BARRIONUEVO HAS ARRIVED.*

Barrionuevo has arrived, the king's ambassador. Yesterday morning, as I sat down to write, this was the shout of the town. Still, at that very moment, full of words and tears of joy, I was ready to pour my heart upon the page. Four days I have been back, four days without Catalina, and I am as lonesome as a *manatí* pup; I, sour man with a hide like leather and a heart full of scars, I love a woman again.

But Barrionuevo has arrived. Time speeds up. The town has gone crazy with criers and rumors, the cathedral's bell rings, and the archbishop and mayor have invited the town's *señores* to a public meeting tomorrow. Las Casas himself has been summoned twice this afternoon, and official discussions have begun.

Barrionuevo brings two hundred men, including Captain Rodrigo Gallego, my old friend. I saw Rodrigo, though I will wait to visit, as he is posted across town in the house of a *señor* named Quesada. This Quesada is quick to see deviousness in little acts and might suspect my motives. Rodrigo looked portly and quite tall. His face jowls down but still it is kind, as it was when I knew him. Rodrigo commands a troop of seventy-five men, and he is second captain under Barrionuevo. I saw him line up his men and lead them to Quesada's *posada* and horse stables, where they will bivouac. Something warmed inside me to see old Rodrigo, a friendship reawakened from those old days.

ONE HUNDRED SIXTY-EIGHT. *TEMPERING THE GOOD FRIAR.*

Barrionuevo is housed in special rooms at the House of Contracts, where *Oidor* Suazo is providing grandly for him. Las Casas goes back and forth from the convent to the House. He went for a late lunch, then returned to rest and ponder. Later, he was invited to a late dinner, where he is now. After his nap, he summoned me, and I put his clothes out as he bathed. He has a small tub and a sponge, with which he wipes himself off, stepping in and out of the small tub.

"They now know I am their best mediator to Enriquillo," he said. "The hook is in."

"I am glad they listen to you, Father."

"The *oidores* know I am the one who can talk to Enriquillo. So, they are attuned to my every word," he replied. "You can be sure we will gain wide concessions."

I cannot tell the good father, I cannot even intimate to him that his argument for the negotiations centering on the abolishment of *encomienda* has already been dismissed and that he himself is not desired at the treaty-making. I must not confront him but divert his mind and his feet from the path of the Bahuruku parley.

"You will remember this Barrionuevo," the good friar told me as I helped him into his robes. "He was a soldier under Velazquez in the war against Guahaba and Xaraguá, around 1504, 1506."

I remember not Barrionuevo, but I remember Diego Velazquez, conquistador and first governor of Cuba. I remember him and I remember the campaigns against Anacaona of Xaraguá and Hatuey of Guahaba very well. Eight years before his mandate to conquer Cuba, in 1511, Diego Velazquez commanded troops under that master of assassins, Knight Commander Ovando, here in Santo Domingo. It was Velazquez who actually ordered the torching of Anacaona's eighty *caciques* at the banquet massacre, in 1503. The same Velazquez hunted down our people afterward and caused the enslavement of my own family. In 1511, Velazquez took me to Cuba, where he again gave me into servitude. I can say I remember Velazquez, and I know what the soldiers did under Velazquez.

"Before the Massacre of Anacaona and the war against Xaraguá," Las Casas went on, "Barrionuevo commanded troops against *cacique* Cotubanamá, in Higuey. Afterward, around 1508, he went on to the conquest of San Juan Bautista de Puerto Rico [Borikén], with Ponce de León."

"Many took part and were brutal at that time, Father," I said.

"He is a much older man now," the good friar responded, staring directly at my eyes. "Barrionuevo is forthright about his mission."

Las Casas said this curtly, staring at my eyes until, out of respect, I looked away. My remark, we both knew, recalled his own involvement in the slaving wars back then. He himself committed acts against Taínos at that time that now make him suffer with remorse. Knowing the good friar for many years, I know that spiking his heart is the only way to keep his attention. I very much want to keep his attention.

"Forgive my opinion, Father?"

"Be kind, Dieguillo."

"I would stress to Barrionuevo that a pardon with dignity for Enriquillo and his people would be an acceptable route. Enriquillo desires peace with freedom most of all."

"The king instructed Barrionuevo to make a quick peace or a total war."

"Total war would be disastrous," I said. "And a quick peace is possible, if we don't press for too much."

"I think Enriquillo's position is stronger than you think," he responded. "I tell Barrionuevo that a new military campaign would be costly. If it were to fail, and if Enriquillo appears victorious and multiplies his forces with Indians and Africans, the Spanish could very well lose the island."

"A war would be disastrous for us, Father," I insisted. "According to Enriquillo, there is not much area left to retreat to. They could not sustain multiple attacks…"

"Well, but Barrionuevo, as the king's special envoy, can agree on principle to abolish the *encomienda*."

"One thing at a time. The *encomienda* as a main negotiating point could delay the impulse too long. It could raise opposition and lead to the war."

"The moment is ripe now, and such a pronouncement, from right here in the Indies, would mean much more. At this moment, Dieguillo, if we plan this right, Barrionuevo will accept this. A royal decree just now, on the eve of a major peace—think of it Dieguillo, it is the only justice possible for the Indian people."

The good father being resolute, I took the route of diversion.

"As you say, Father, the strategy is all. 'Everything in its time.' So I would add: Please let Enriquillo make that demand; let him demand the end of the *encomienda* himself. And if Barrionuevo balks at it, then you step up, for you must know you will be right there at Enriquillo's side. He asked me himself to tell you. At his side."

Las Casas looked relieved and alert. I smiled upon him, making my lie complete. For the first time in the twenty years I have known him, I have control over his volition, and it takes a lie. The good friar wants very much to be at the center of this event. I thought as we spoke: I truly have his attention now.

"Let Enriquillo lead the discussion," I pressed on, pulling now on the priest's heartfelt wish to help our people. "Let him approach as the sovereign *cacique* that he is. He deserves this moment."

"Absolutely," Las Casas said. "I will sit at his side as a supporter, but he will lead the talking. Barrionuevo must see him as his equal."

"Excellent," I said.

"When he mentions the *encomienda* and demands a royal decree, I will be there to support him, to throw the weight of my church behind him."

"At the parley, Father, please. At the right moment. This is very important to Enriquillo."

"Yes, of course. I will wait for his demand, then support it."

ONE HUNDRED SIXTY-NINE. *I HATE TELLING A LIE, BUT...*

I hate telling a lie. But the father, Blessed Protector, would endanger our lives with his love of our cause. No, he is too agitated and too controversial here on the islands to represent Enriquillo's interest. In fact, he will not get there. The baby boy himself spoke about the need to maintain the peaceful mind, keep humble so as not to block the path of peace.

I will ask Las Casas to certify the existence of more gold bullion and Enriquillo's offer to have a special gesture with Valenzuela. This will happen soon. He will carry the word to Valenzuela for us, I am certain, in order to divert them from the negotiations. Then to Las Casas I will assign a *guaxeri* guide who will pretend to lose his way *and* keep the good friar himself from the parley site. I do this now without hesitation, though I know it can confuse my living spirit, my *goeiz*, to be this way. Valenzuela and Pero Lopez I thus send one wrong way. And the good friar, too, will follow another wrong trail. With this I hope to keep clear our thin path to peace.

ONE HUNDRED SEVENTY. *THE GOOD FRIAR CONFESSES A DEED OF HIS YOUTH.*

Again I saw him tonight. It was a long, difficult day for both him and me. I write here again how sorry I am to lie to him. I do hate to lie to this great man that trusts my word.

Las Casas paced slowly several times around his room. He was puff-eyed like an owl from lack of sleep. I prepared his cot. Finally, he sat down. "We spoke much about Ovando," he said. "Gonzalo Fernández ... Oviedo was there. He knows it all, as usual. The gold counter is writing a book about the Indies, and he read some parts to Barrionuevo and the assembled gentlemen. It was all I could do not to fight him. He speaks of Knight Commander Nicolás de Ovando and his times as the 'years of civility' on the island. He claims Ovando established good government and stimulated a true economy here. Ovando is his big hero."

"What did you say, Father?"

"I held my tongue, the bastards."

"I thank you for your silent indignation."

"Ovando massacred coldly," he said. "He calculated everything about his ways of terror."

The friar was deeply upset. He breathed heavily and rubbed his temples.

"Ovando watched it with arithmetic," I said. "He counted the dead, like logger captains count felled trees."

"That violence we have shown your people," he said harshly. "I retch at the thought of it."

"You have done your best, Don Bartolomé. No one…"

"I, too, have killed men of your race. Dieguillo, I even took slaves, several times, and sold them, I accepted an *encomienda*…"

"You don't have to confess to me, Father," I said. "I am pitiful before you."

"Tonight you are my confessor, Dieguillo," he said. "You who remember those days."

He had fought as a soldier, and once led a cannon crew, during the roundup of *caciques* after Anacaona's massacre. During a skirmish, he held the igniting ember on the cannon when a Taíno group of about fifteen people approached. "We had fought all day," he said. "They had only wooden weapons and there was no fight left in them. There were men and women, and I knew they would not attack. Yet, the fury was part of me. I had the urge. I bade our crew prepare to fire. I looked at the group of poor Indians and lit the fuse. I remember the blast was of a furnace exploding toward them. Of fifteen, six fell dead, cut to pieces, and then everything was still. I can see the faces of the ones left standing, how surprised they looked."

"I know what carnage looks like," I said.

"Oh, Lord in Heaven, forgive me," he said and knelt. I touched his head. I felt mildly sick.

"On behalf of your people, Dieguillo, forgive me."

I could forgive him, too, even though it was precisely during those campaigns I lost my own free village and even my family. "You have saved more than a hundred times six of our people, Father, and many more, since that time. A devil's act in your youth does not define your destiny. You did not cause the wars, nor did you command your own place in the circumstances. As for the dead," I told him. "In our way, we believe they will be waiting for you when you pass on to the Spirit World. There you will have to explain yourself to them."

"Forgive me now, Dieguillo," he said. "So I may be absolved that horrible deed."

"I forgive you, Father," I said. "And I pray for you that they, too, will forgive you."

ONE HUNDRED SEVENTY-ONE. *LAS CASAS GOES AGAIN.*

Today early again, Las Casas went over for meetings. I caught him shortly after the seven o'clock Mass, as he left the convent by the big wooden doors. "Remember that Enriquillo is a peaceful man," I repeated to him. "His intentions Barrionuevo can trust to settle a community with his captains, to farm and raise cattle and be good neighbors." Las Casas nodded. "Friend and brother, we are in good accord," he said. "We will free many Indians with this one."

ONE HUNDRED SEVENTY-TWO. *IN THE MEMORY: VELAZQUEZ PRESSES ME INTO SERVICE.*

In the morning, I sent Father Remigio with a note for Rodrigo Gallego, inviting his visit to the convent tomorrow. I ate at midmorning and then took a nap, having stayed up writing last night. I dreamed vividly during my nap, and now I write my dream.

I saw Manasas in my dream, just as I saw him in the *cohoba*, sitting, looking away from me. Manasas was a big man, a soldier's soldier. He was Extremaduran, and he wore plated armor and carried two swords. I killed Manasas at the Massacre of Anacaona, in the late afternoon, after ten hours of mayhem and carnage, when the Taíno men had retreated and Ovando was counting the dead.

That was in 1504, or thereabouts. I say that truly because even though my duty on the ship's *ampolleta* fixed in me the breaks of daily time, those later years have blended for me one on another. Those were my seasons of peace, my only ones since I left home. That was when Ceiba ruled my world, my *cacique* queen who could run a *yukaieke* of 140 relatives with the precision of nature itself. That was when I saw my two boys, who are still alive, who are still alive, that was when I saw them grow and sprout, those two skinny reeds forming out calf and butt, strong little chests, running and jumping in the grass. That was the time when the Castilians forgot about me and my little village *estancia*, and for almost five years we tended our *conucos* and gathered our honey and fished in several abundant streams. We grew pigs even then, in those early years, and *hutía* was still abundant, and *yaguasa* and iguana and *mahá*, and as always in our lands, there was abundant fruit. Perhaps this is what Enriquillo's camp intimates for me most of all, of those peaceful seasons before I met Las Casas, between the time Guarionex left us, in 1498, and the time in 1503 when Captain Diego Velazquez and a hundred of his Castilian troops with more than three hundred Indian *mánsos* came into my little valley looking for me.

Velazquez carried a letter from the new admiral, Don Diego Columbus, pressing me into service as interpreter and guide. At the end of my service, which was mandatory in any case, I would receive a horse, the letter said.

I left with Velazquez within the hour, apprehensive anew for the many soldier's eyes that had gazed upon my valley. Avarice and *sinrazón* were the expression in those faces for the pretty gardens and layout of the streams and the able-bodied *guaxeris* that they saw there in my *yukaieke*. I remember Ceiba's eyes that would not cry in my presence. The twins played behind her in our *bohío*, and I saw only flashes of them as I walked away.

ONE HUNDRED SEVENTY-THREE. *THE ROUTE TO XARAGUÁ, WITH VELAZQUEZ.*

"We travel south and west to Xaraguá," Velazquez informed me as we camped for the evening. "Anacaona is to greet us. The knight commander, Nicolás de Ovando, and his army, are to visit her villages soon."

Of the major seats of Taíno authority on the islands, Xaraguá was the only one left. Bohekio, its distinguished old *cacique*, had died, but his sister, Anacaona, who held several clan lines in her own person and who was the highest ranking *nitaina*, commanded increasing respect. Anacaona, who was Doña Mencia's direct line grandmother, was quite a woman. Tall, beautiful, and regal, she was in her late thirties and had boundless energies for every sort of activity. With the demise of the great *cacicasgos* of Caonabó, Guarionex, and Guacanagari and the death of her brother, Bohekio, the court of Anacaona became, more and more, the gathering place for the island's younger *caciques* and elder *guaxeris*.

Of the island's *sachem* women and their families, from which the *caciques* were chosen, Anacaona was queen. Beyond holding nearly all hereditary lines, Anacaona herself sponsored many *areitos* and organized societies of singers and dancers. She had been an intimate of Guarionex and had married Caonabó, and she had been the forbidden love of Guacanagari. She was Taita Grandmother, and all of our Taíno people gave her great respect. Moreover, adept agriculturalists were her *guaxeri*. They had an ingenious system of irrigation that distributed large volumes of water from the verdant hills to their much-drier plains. In Xaraguá, they brought up huge quantities of *yucca* and produced mountains of *cassabe* torts, also much corn and peppers and beans of several types and tomatoes of several types. For their feasts, Anacaona's *guaxeri* produced many combinations of foods, recited poetry, and put up jousting contests, huge ball games, acrobatics, and other things.

Along the way to Xaraguá, Velazquez, who rode a red Andalusian gelding, spoke to me in ways that inspired some hope for a positive meeting with Anacaona. Velazquez had already forty years by then, but he was lean and tough and very vigorous. "Xaraguá is well-organized," he said. "The people are productive and Anacaona wants peace, it would seem."

"My captain," I said, always repeating a Castilian's words back to him. "This Taíno queen would make peace with the Castilians, and her people produce many beautiful things."

"I have seen her gifts to the *adelantado*, Don Bartolomé Columbus."

"The Xaraguáns have paid much tribute," I said.

"They have no gold," he said. "But I am told they are fine artisans, that they can build good boats and homes, and they can feed a mighty number of people."

Then, without another word, he rode off. That was on our way to Anacaona's main *batéy*, her court of Xaraguá.

Later, as we approached her villages and the Xaraguá men spotted us and began to trail us, I hoped some friendship could be maintained. Maybe, I thought, the Castilians will the see productivity of the Xaraguáns and allow them to continue with their own *conucos* and villages.

ONE HUNDRED SEVENTY-FOUR. *THE MASSACRE OF ANACAONA'S BANQUET.*

I will write about the massacre here, because, of course, I was wrong to hope. The knight commander joined forces with our troop at the Yaqui River, just at the entrance to the Xaraguá province. More than three hundred Castilian soldiers and some seven hundred Indians, more than a thousand combined troops, formed companies and marched into Xaraguá. I should have known the knight commander planned a wicked thing, but at that moment only the officers knew. The Indians were not told until just before the deed.

Anacaona's main village was squarely set, following the four directions. In the center, a large *batéy* opened quite wide. The visit began with song and ceremony, with a feast and a dance, and with the highest of expectations among our people that the Castilians might still learn, after all. Anacaona feasted everyone. She had foods prepared for weeks of feasting and some eighty *caciques* gathered to celebrate *areitos* with her and to see what the Castilians might plan for them. Our thousand men she distributed, ten or twenty to each *bohío*, for the *cacique* families to feed and host. Our herd of seventy horses she assigned a large pasture with water that Castilian soldiers secured and guarded.

The knight commander was an austere man of the church, lean and cold, with a very big face and head. He wore long robes, even on horseback, and he forgot nothing, ever. When two years before Bobadilla took the three Columbus brothers, including the admiral himself, to Spain, in chains, accused of excessive violence, corruption, and other abuses of power, it was Ovando, a count, who was the king's selection to clean up the mess. Ovando was a man of great authority and inquisitorial character.

The fateful morning, I sat with Commander Ovando and his captains as they met with Anacaona and several of her *caciques* in front of Ovando's *caney*. This was a large palm structure given to him by the *cacica*, where I myself had hung my hammock at the commander's instruction. At a second *caney*, almost as large, built across a corridor, the commander ordered a cross put up.

I knew I needn't interpret for Anacaona, since she spoke more than a bit of Castilian by then, but she intimated not her capacity, and I did not either. However, I felt a great tension, though all the talk was diplomatic and many gifts were exchanged. Anacaona sat next to Ovando, her voluptous breasts barely covered by a black Spanish shawl, a gift of *Adelantado* Bartolomé Columbus in earlier years. The commander looked away as he spoke to her and even as he gave her gifts of combs, mirrors, and small looms, but Anacaona was wonderful to look at. Not only was her body radiant; a woman of proportion, she was endowed with a masterful energy, a vibrant, continuous motion. The urge to hold and envelop hung around Anacaona like a warm mist.

Anacaona's diplomacy, I could tell, agitated the knight commander. A natural consequence of her energy was that she approached principal men with both her mind and her body and had thus known several of the commanders that had come her way. Thus she had tempered the excesses of both the *adelantado*, Don Bartolomé Columbus, and of his mortal enemy, Francisco Roldán. Don Bartolomé was honest with her, but Roldán it was, precisely, who denounced her to Ovando as treacherous and rebellious.

On Ovando's his first night in, after a late meal and some wine, enveloped in her fog, Anacaona led him across the yard nearly to her hammock, where suddenly the commander declined her invitation curtly, walking rapidly away, eyes widened and red streaked. Everyone saw the move, *caciques* and officers, and Ovando made his blood-furious plan. I heard him say in the late evening: "A rebellion is in the offing here. The filthy slut won't let things be."

"Her people will follow her, Commander," Velazquez, who was nearby, said.

"She is in need of a Christian example," Ovando replied.

ONE HUNDRED SEVENTY-FIVE. *THE KILLING BEGINS, ENRIQUILLO IN MY ARMS.*

When, after lunch the next day, he told her he would celebrate a Mass for her many chiefs, I interpreted Ovando's words to the *cacica* and thought to myself how simple and easy everything might turn out. First a parade of horses he would show them, then a Mass he would celebrate. He loved their souls, he said, and would endeavor to show them the way to everlasting life. Yes, I thought that maybe I was seeing Christian love for our people. Tribute would be exacted, no doubt, but possibly softened by the mission of the sacred sacraments.

Among the horses, a bay gelding was trained to dance on his hind legs, to bow and curtsy. He did this to sounds from a flute. It was quite gracious. Thus all seventy of Ovando's horsemen were mounted when Ovando requested the Indian chiefs of the region to join him inside his second *caney*. About eighty *caciques* went inside, and I was to follow, when Ovando held my arm back. "Stay with me," he said. He then grabbed a golden crucifix that hung from his neck.

Suddenly the captains jumped into action and the *caciques* were surrounded in the big *caney*. Velazquez seized Anacaona, looped a rope around her wrists behind her back, and brought her out. Led away by two soldiers, she stopped in her tracks where I stood with the commander. "What have we done to you?" she cried to him. "We received you with song. We have offered you all!"

"You are as soiled as a mudsnake," Commander Ovando said calmly to her. "By authority of Church and King, I will hang you for your sins against nature."

Holding lances and swords at the ready, a hundred soldiers and another hundred *mánso* Indians surrounded the captive *caciques*. "You are prisoners," a captain said, instructing ten men to tie up the *caciques*. "Submit, or we will burn your queen," he told them. A dozen other soldiers held flaming torches, and many others piled dry branches around the palm-and-thatch building. When most of the *caciques* had been tied up inside, the soldiers exited and tightened up around the building. "Fire to the devils," Velazquez cried, on a nod from the knight commander. All around, the *caney* was lit and a fire roared in minutes. There was much groaning and coughing. A few men tried to break through the cane walls, but the soldiers sliced and poked at them as they did, then pushed them back on the burning pyre.

Guaxeris and the few remaining *caciques* not at the banquet but around the *yukaieke* began to come over, inquiring on the fire and commotion. They met a quadrant with lines of horses, bowmen, and harquebus shooters. Then four companies of swordsmen were signaled to rampage. Great mayhem broke loose, hundreds of people running then circling back and attacking with rocks and lances, *macanas* and daggers.

I stood by the commander, frozen. He had ordered a crossbow and, after several shots, spiked an arrow into an Indian's neck. Ovando had a guard of twenty around him, half mounted, half on the ground. Suddenly he mounted his own horse. "Commander," I said, fearing for my life to be left alone, battle raging all around me. He looked at me and took off his red shoulder cape, then hollered to the troops all around us. "Do not harm Diego Colón, who is protected by my cape." Several captains and soldiers repeated the order, and many Castilians looked my way in midfight. Then Ovando was gone, mounted and with his lance set to his stirrup, out to run Indians through.

Back and forth the running went. The *guaxeri* of Anacaona fought well. They attacked fearlessly, trying to get to their burning *caciques*, and more than once the Spanish horsemen had to retreat. Many horses were killed and more than fifty Castilian soldiers. I moved little from Ovando's assigned *caney*, as the Castilians in battle often went berserk, killing even *mánso* Indians like me.

Once, after several hours, I was suddenly alone, the battle having moved on to a field on the edge of the village. Venturing out, I turned and found myself facing a wounded Taíno, a minor *cacique* with a deep cut in his shoulder. I helped him back to the commander's *caney* and dressed his wound. This was Enriquillo's father, who died months later from his wounds. Suffering horribly, he told me about his two boys, who were hiding in a grove of fruit trees about a hundred yards away. The soldiers had almost found them, so he had jumped out to draw them away. He took a sword blow but distracted the soldiers and kept running. "Please get my boys, *guaxeri*," he said. "Bring them here before the *maguacokíos* kill them."

I could see the tree grove through the door of the *caney*. Small groups of Indians still confronted soldiers in the distance, but around the *bohíos* the fighting was dying down. I walked rapidly to the grove of trees, wearing the commander's red cape. "Come, boys," I whispered, as I came near. "Follow me to your Guarao, your father."

The boys came out and took my hands. Just then three Castilian swordsmen came around a corner of a *bohío*. "Who goes?" they challenged me. "Under orders of the knight commander," I lied, walking away. "I am to care for these boys."

"The knight commander has skewered half a dozen like that," a big soldier said. He had huge hands and forearms. Manasas (Big Hands) was his nickname. "Don't you know that nits make lice?"

He walked behind me, on my left, his sword in hand. The two boys and I hurried, but now the other two men ran around my right, to cut me off. They were mostly playing, those two, but I lost sight of Manasas, who was not. Then I heard the swoosh and the sword clearing by, and the boy on my left dropped, both legs cut off at the knee.

"And fuck the cunt of your mother to hell," Manasas said, threatening to strike me. I huddled down under the cape, pulling both boys under me, although the one struck was quickly dying.

"Enough, Manasas," one soldier said. "The commander ordered safe passage for this son of a dog."

Manasas put the point of his sword under my ear, then pulled away. "A turd on this guy," he said.

The boy was already dead as the four swordsmen walked away. The other one I picked up in my arms and held to my breast. I ran with him to the commander's *caney*, where his father hid behind bales of cotton.

That boy, then five years old, was Enriquillo. It was his older brother, Nicosa, whose legs Manasas sliced off.

In the late afternoon, the knight commander returned. He was weary and sore, having taken severe hits by stones and sticks on his body. One elbow was the size of a pineapple. As I helped him undress and hung his hammock, I explained to Ovando about the wounded father and his son, how they were good people and had volunteered to come under my command. "Let them rest in the corner," he said, as he lay down, "so they won't be counted among the slaves."

ONE HUNDRED SEVENTY-SIX. *ENCOUNTER WITH MANASAS AT THE STREAM.*

In the fainting sunlight, I noticed myself caked with blood and thought to wash in a nearby stream. On the way out, I spotted several daggers in the knight commander's sword case and, on impulse, pulled one out, tying it to a cord under my shirt and the commander's red cape, which I still wore.

Outside, some soldiers made small fires as others piled the dead in rows at the center plaza. Indians not captured had retreated across the wide savanna to a nearby forest. Captives were crammed into *bohíos*, threatened with death, and cut on the slightest pretext.

I carried a jug and told the guards, "The commander requires water." Then I walked down the maze of *bohíos* to a small hill circled by a brook. I followed the brook a few minutes into the grove of trees, in the darkening woods, to a small, deep pool. I took my cape and shirt off, folded the dagger into my clothes, and was about to enter the pool when I heard a crashing through the trees and retreated with my things behind a bush.

It was a Castilian soldier. I watched his big shadow as he took off his helmet and chain-link shirt and breeches. Then I could see quite clearly it was Manasas. He stood by a tree to piss, then took his pants off and boots. He was naked but for long socks, and then he was on his knees, leaning on the water's edge, splashing his face and scrubbing his hands and forearms, which glistened in the receding light. I was naked, too, and it was not even a thought but a silent command I felt in my chest and thighs, and in two bounces I was on his back and straddling his waist like a horse. I spiked the dagger deep into his lower back, right along the spine.

"*Cabrón,*" he jumped up, "*Indio e mierda,*" spinning around once and twice, but my legs were strong, and I held on to his hair and the hilt of the dagger that was deep in him. His hair smelled of rancid olive oil. I felt his hand came up behind me and grab my shoulder, and I twisted the dagger hard as I could and scraped it through the bony column and felt his back snap. He dropped to his knees and I fell off, rolling to the side. I could see him leaning on his elbows, trying to look up.

"Man of the Devil," I told him as his head drooped. "I have killed you."

And I had. His one elbow gave and then the other. I jumped on his back again, pulled the dagger, and carefully placed the point at the base of the neck, as I had seen the Spanish captains do. Then I drove it in. Manasas gurgled and vomited and defecated, and his body went totally limp on the edge of the pool.

I washed hurriedly, dressed, and came out of the woods with a full jug of water. The light of the sun made faint effort to guide my steps. I felt the cool of the woods recede, and I felt very good, and I felt very hurt, out of balance. I felt a great release in my breast, but a clog was coming up in my throat that I would cough up for days.

ONE HUNDRED SEVENTY-SEVEN. *SUSPECTED IN THE KILLING.*

Soldiers found Manasas's corpse early next morning. Some remembered my encounter with him, and others remembered my going for water the previous evening. I had put away the dagger unnoticed and stayed in the *caney* all day, but they came to accuse me. "Son of a dog," one of Manasas's squad told me. "Manasas should have killed you. You put the blade to our *capo* from behind."

"I am incapable of such a deed," I said to the knight commander, Nicolás de Ovando, whose side I dared not leave. "Besides, I carry no sword."

"It is true he is unarmed, and he has served me loyally," Ovando told the men, who desisted upon his word.

Captain Velazquez believed against me. He kept me in service until the main villages of Anacaona were secured then released me with these words. "Castilian blood stains your hand, Dieguillo. But for the knight commander's piety your eyes would be the shit of worms now. So take not glee in your freedom, a debt you owe my Lord and king."

ONE HUNDRED SEVENTY-EIGHT. *MY VILLAGE IS* ENCOMENDED.

That was, I think, late in 1503. I returned home, but within six months my little *yukaieke* was run over by new settlers and soldiers, veterans of the campaigns against Higuey and Guahaba granted their own lands. The next year, Queen Isabel called for hearings on the dreadful massacres, then died. Ovando held the requested hearing, where his own captains testified to the guilt of Anacaona in planning an insurrection. No one paid attention. New ships were arriving by the week. Before long, I heard say, twelve thousand Castilians populated the island, and some three hundred *hacendados* held very large estates of gold mines, sugar cane, and cattle. They had founded seventeen townships, and the great hunt for Indian servants and slaves was on. Those taken in war were to be slaves. But all were counted and tagged or branded and assigned to *encomiendas* large and small. Every soldier, every newcomer, brigand, or noble demanded his Indians to command and work.

In mid-1505, our whole *yukaieke* was *encomended* to Juan de Prastrana, a Christian man who died suddenly one night, having worked us for a horrible year that cost us forty-two people. Branded I was in the shoulder, yet I might have traded freedom for my early services, when, in 1506, the Admiral of the Ocean Sea, Don Christopherens Columbus, died in Spain. His brothers and sons still owned property and political office on Española, but they had many problems, not much real power, and no time for me. It was then Pero Lopez de Mesa bargained with Commander Ovando for the rest of us, and Ovando parceled us out to that son of a great whore. Our *encomienda* to Pero Lopez appears in the books, when such were formalized by Pasamonte in 1514. Although by then we were not even any longer under Pero Lopez, the book shows my assignment, with fifteen persons, and Ceiba's, under the name of Maria de Luna, with fifty-eight others. But truly, not six years later, even before it was recorded, I had not one of my village people, not

Ceiba, not my boys, not anybody, all dead or lost. But for that bastard, Pero Lopez, I might still have some family. Damn him to hell and to rot in the swamps for his wretched deeds!

Folio VI

THE FIRST GOOD TREATY

Death remains... Morning feeling... More gold for the Castilians... Rodrigo comes and hears my tale... I arrange with Rodrigo to guard Enriquillo's safety... On the king's vessel... Conversation with Barrionuevo, his campaign in Borikén... Barrionuevo has questions about Enriquillo... Picking at my wound... Hatuey, "Certainty of sun in the sky," our great hero... The spirits are all around us... Another conversation with Barrionuevo... Continuing to work with Barrionuevo... Opening the path... Making connection, the change of heart... Cruelties of Vasco Porcallo... Caimán-hunting days... One areito remembered... Another gold trap... Happiness to be in thick of events... Catalina becomes my wife... Going to the Bahuruku again... Deminán and the guanguayo turtle create the islands... Warriors who would be husbands... Catalina stays with Mencia... At the enchanted falls... More cohoba revelations... Details of contact... A hint of reversal... Guarocuya does a hawk dance, he takes me out... The behike explains... Tamayo's report... My paper runs short... Staying away from the peacemaking... Feeling the good friar... Last of the paper on the ship... Indians as dignitaries... All that I can fit...

One hundred seventy-nine. *Death remains.*

Today I woke up tired. I wrote late into the night and didn't dream but turned over and over. If I lay still my heart thumped brusquely in my chest, bringing a tremor to my limbs. I was not made for killing, and even the memory of my act, and of my second such act, later, in Cuba, when I killed "Skinny" Moisés, put shivers in my bones.

"Death stays with the man who kills," Guarionex used to say. I know what he meant. He did not mean the spirit of the dead will haunt you or that death itself will take you prematurely. He meant that the cold breath of death will be there to stunt the things that you give life to, to sour your human communion with the earth.

One hundred eighty. *Morning feeling.*

I reread last night's entry. This is true, too: writing these memories helps lift the weight of my spirit. More and more and more, I like what it does. Oh, but to have the time and paper to write it all, everything, now that my memory has fully awakened. I fear not the night, for I will never be alone. The little voices speak to me, the little souls of my dead people that say: remember it all, Guaikán.

One hundred eighty-one. *More gold for the Castilians.*

Time is now for the gold to be shown, according to our strategy. Fray Remigio I send today to Valenzuela. He will carry the message from Enriquillo, the one written in the broad leaves of the *copei* tree. I send with him also one of two small gold bars I obtained from Enriquillo.

At his mountain *yukaieke*, Enriquillo told me: "Use these gold bars, the last ones I have left. This is the gold they love that shines beautifully and is heavy."

"I see its light," I told him. "And it is beautiful."

"They will follow the gold," he said. "It is a certain thing."

The gold bar should convince the would-be assassins. The message tells them of the trail they will be shown. Valenzuela and Pero Lopez and one Vadillo cousin we will lead to the gold. Thus they will travel away from the place of negotiations. Thus we will protect the baby boy.

ONE HUNDRED EIGHTY-TWO. *RODRIGO COMES AND HEARS MY TALE.*

This afternoon Rodrigo came, my friend of the days of the *Santa Maria*. He has grown stout these past forty years and has a full beard, and his head is balding, but in his smile I could see the boy I knew.

"Guaikán," he said, embracing me. "My boyhood friend."

We sat near the garden, under a tall *guásima* tree.

"When Friar Las Casas delivered your letter, I was very happy," he said. "I knew that, if chosen, I would come."

"There are but few of us left, Rodrigo," I said. "You will remember the hundreds of villages, all over the islands?"

He nodded. "I forget not Guacanagari and the kindness of his people. I remember that time like a beautiful dream. Your people seemed so peaceful to me, the way they lived."

"We have nothing left of all that," I said. "But for the young man in the bush that you are here to pacify."

"I have heard the stories, through Las Casas and others," he said. "It saddens me what has occurred to the good Taíno."

Again, I think that Rodrigo is the only truly pure one I ever met among the Christians. There is an opening in him for me and my people because he himself is a man of pure motive. I have lived long enough to confirm that this is a rare thing among the covered men.

"Enriquillo, he is the only one we have left," I repeated, looking at Rodrigo's sincere eyes.

"Yes," he said. "And I believe we can settle with him. In fact, we have to resolve the hostilities. Total war will follow the failure of peace."

A young monk served us tea. Rodrigo was impressed and winked at me. "They treat me well," I said. "My place here is on a grant from the second admiral, Don Diego Columbus, who recognized my service to his father."

We talked of the first admiral, my adopted father, whom I had seen a final time in 1500, when Bobadilla accused him of corruption and took him back to Spain in chains.

"I saw him not much later, in Seville," Rodrigo said, "when the queen reinstated him and before he embarked on his fourth and final voyage."

"He stranded himself in Xamayca that time."

"Around 1504," he said.

"Yes," I said. "Knight Commander Ovando was governor then.

Ovando would not rescue him. He left the admiral stranded for
months. They say around here that voyage broke his health."

"I remember the news of his death, in 1506," Rodrigo said.
"Meager was his funeral." He shook his balding head. "Aye, Guaikán, it has been a whole lifetime for us since then. By 1506, I had
three children of my own."

"I had two," I said. "Twins."

"Boys?"

"Yes, boys," I said.

He wanted to know my story, everything about it, from the
time of our tearful farewell in Seville, in 1493, to the very present.
His own children were grown, he said, with their own families, and
he was a grandfather twelve times. I told him about my boys and
what happened to my wife, Ceiba.

"In 1509, just after first rain, they took one my boy. Good
Wind. He was eleven. They sold him to become a pearl diver. I
never saw him again."

My words quickly watered his eyes.

"Captain Hojeda set up an operation at Cumaná, on the mainland, where large beds of pearls were found. Pero Lopez, a man who
still lives, owned my *encomienda* then. My boy could dive well, and
Pero Lopez realized it. One afternoon, while I planted a field, he
took my Good Wind away."

"That presents a tremendous disgust," Rodrigo said. "Agh,
what horrible disgust!"

I told him about Ceiba, how she fainted, again and again.
Good Wind had understood immediately. This is what hurt her so
much. His mind was always so keen and clear. "Tell my father I am
gone," he told her. Then he put up both his thumbs next to each
other and told Heart of Earth, his brother, "This is us. At night I
will look at my thumbs and think of you."

Two weeks he was gone when Ceiba took the *hyen*, the poisonous juice of our *yucca*, and lived three days in mortal pain. "I am
sorry, my husband, my son," she said to me and to Heart of Earth.
"I can no longer live."

Rodrigo looked away from me. "She was heartbroken," he said.
"She died of a broken heart."

I thought of Ceiba in my *cohoba* dream, how lucky I was to
have seen her. But this is only mine to know.

"And the boy?" Rodrigo asked.

"I heard years later, from a sailor. Ten months my boy dived for pearls. Then once, he dived and never surfaced."

"I am sorry," he said.

"I believe he escaped," I said. " I don't know how, but I believe he escaped. He swam underwater somehow and escaped into the great forest."

"I pray that it is so," Rodrigo said. "And the other?"

I told him that story, too, how Heart of Earth and I went to Cuba with Velazquez in 1511, how we lived the conquest there, which was the very worst, how my boy left with Ponce de León on his voyage to explore the coast of La Florida, how he never returned.

"And his fate?"

"He lives. This I know, but nothing else."

"So he stayed in the Florida land?"

"Yes."

"And you believe he is alive?"

"With certainty."

I caught his eyes, which, without knowing how, understood the depth of my certainty.

"I am disgusted by my countrymen, old friend," Rodrigo stood up suddenly, going nowhere. "The thought of their deeds sickens my heart."

"*Dominus dedit, Dominus abstulit; sit nomen Domini benedictum,*" I said to calm his spirit. "The Lord giveth and the Lord taketh away. Blessed be the name of the Lord."

ONE HUNDRED EIGHTY-THREE. *I ARRANGE WITH RODRIGO TO GUARD ENRIQUILLO'S SAFETY.*

I am thankful for the presence of my friend. He stayed late into the night, and I told him many things. On our last few weeks together in Seville, after I had learned the Castilian thoroughly, it was the same. He liked to hear my stories then, too. I talked to him today about Ovando and the Massacre of Anacaona's Banquet and about how I carried the Enriquillo boy after his brother was killed.

"So you know the young man?"

"Like a son."

"Will he make peace?"

"If these monsters don't kill him first."

He promised to help in any way possible. I told him about the assassination attempt we expected and gave him the names to watch for among Valenzuela and Pero Lopez' henchmen, particularly that of Francisco Hernandez, Valenzuela's foreman, who will go along on Barrionuevo's ship.

"Barrionuevo is encouraged to go in search of Enriquillo," he said. "We are to sail along the southern coast. I can bring you along as an interpreter."

"I will go," I said, suddenly my heart racing. I know now this is the why of Rodrigo. That is the ship for me to be on at this moment.

"We take few troops as a true peace will be proposed, but enough to curtail the scabby rats that would kill the *cacique*. If the Enriquillo will react as you say, and everything goes alright, there should be no need for war."

Everything I have arranged via Rodrigo, including the use of Julia (Catalina's daughter, Inez), as intermediary to Enriquillo from Barrionuevo. The two women will meet me at Yaquimo. A loyal understanding Rodrigo and I achieve without need of promises. We leave in a week on board Commander Barrionuevo's ship. I also have made final arrangements for the misguidance of Friar Las Casas, who is to go the wrong way going north, and of the chief plotters against our baby boy, the heartless and the greedy triad, who will go the wrong way south, deep into the wrong peninsula. Remigio takes the good friar one way while Cao and Silverio make the rendezvous with Valenzuela and Pero Lopez. May the good father forgive me for my deceit; may the three walking murderers, especially that walking dead man, Pero Lopez de Mera, meet the fate they fully deserve.

May 8, 1533

ONE HUNDRED EIGHTY-FOUR. *ON THE KING'S VESSEL.*

I write today on board the ship *El Imperial*, which is the king's very own vessel. We sail west along the southern coast. Thirty-five soldiers Barrionuevo brings and sixteen Indians, including myself. A few sheets of paper I have brought to make these notes, though the bulk of my pages I have left in my room at the convent. I have grown fond of the pages I have written and read them over and over, despite the sadness they often bring me. Truly life has improved for me. Catalina is en route to meet me, and Rodrigo, my boyhood friend, is with me. We face the sea breeze together again. On the ocean now, we head toward Enriquillo's mountains, and my thoughts clear.

May 10, 1533

ONE HUNDRED EIGHTY-FIVE. *CONVERSATION WITH BARRIONUEVO, HIS CAM-PAIGN IN BORIKÉN.*

Knowing who I am and wanting to converse of the early days, Barrionuevo called for me today. We sat in his cabin, where the roll of the ship is little felt.

"I remember hearing of you during the campaign for Higuey, but I don't think I ever saw you."

"I was under Captain Velazquez then."

"And you served the first admiral in his first voyage."

"Yes, and in the second."

"And you were in Cuba, too, with Velazquez?"

"Yes," I told him.

"And San Juan de Puerto Rico, were you ever there?"

"Borikén, in our language," I said, and he nodded, recognizing the word. "Yes, I was there, but briefly, once, with Ponce de León. I was *encomended* to Pero Lopez de Mesa, here in Española, during that time, but he lent me out, first to Ponce and then to Velazquez."

"I fought in Puerto Rico," Barrionuevo said. "A difficult campaign, that one."

He spoke about Agueybanax, the main *cacique* of Borikén, who led a war against the Castilians.

"Our soldiers were real men in those days," Barrionuevo said. "Sleeping on the ground with rocks for pillows, swords at the ready, not like the dressed up darlings in Santo Domingo."

"Yes," I agreed. "They were very tough."

"Even so, Agueybanax gave us a good fight. He defeated Sotomayor and killed eighty of his men. And around the island, his warriors that time killed maybe seventy or eighty more of our men."

"I remember the dog, Becerrillo," I said. "He went on the same ship as I."

Barrionuevo laughed out loud. "Yes, the dog. I had forgotten that dog."

It was that awful dog, I believe, not the soldiers, that defeated Agueybanax. He was a war mastiff, big as a pony and with jaws that could snap a man's leg. In Borikén, when that war started, I saw two of our Indian men gutted out by Becerrillo in but a few seconds. This was the sport of Ponce, who favored that sort of spectacle. A great laugh he caused once, when the Becerrillo he let lose against an old Indian woman, made to run for the purpose of being torn to pieces. As the dog approached her, the old woman sat down. She said in our language: "Big dog, do not kill me, I mean you no harm." The Becerrillo sniffed at her but did not bite. Instead, he lifted his leg and pissed on her.

I told the story to Barrionuevo. I always tell that story to make the old Castilian captains laugh, and it always gets a rise out of them, how an old woman's terror ended in dog piss. Barrionuevo laughed. I knew he would.

"That dog was a wonder of nature," Barrionuevo said. "Never has there been such an animal again."

"He had not a chance to breed," I reminded him and he nodded. That was another story. Having gifted Barrionuevo his laugh at the expense of an old woman of my own kind, now I wanted to interject on our behalf. "The Becerrillo was executed by a poisoned arrow."

"A Carib war party murdered him," Barrionuevo offered.

A raid was mounted just to kill the awful beast and did succeed in putting a poison arrow into him. And they were not Carib but our own Taíno men from the lesser islands who killed him. But I let the error pass. The Castilians have always confused our different Indian peoples.

"Those were some grand days, eh, my friend?" Barrionuevo said as he walked away.

I am glad for his gesture of friendship, but I disagree. Those were horrible, confusing days. In Borikén, our Taíno still believed the Castilians to be spirit people, men who knew not death. Aguey-banax, a fearless *cacique*, could not get his men to fight such beings. One of his *caciques*, Urayoán, ordered his men to drown a young Castilian named Salcedo just to see if he could die. Three days Urayoán waited before declaring Salcedo dead. Then he went to war. That was on the Guarabo River, as I remember it.

One hundred eighty-six. *Barrionuevo has questions about Enriquillo.*

Barrionuevo listened out my story then commandeered the conversation. "But the *cacique* Enriquillo, he knows the Castilians can die."

I nodded. "There has been much killing, on all sides, to prove it."

"I quarrel none with that fact," Barrionuevo offered. "But I have a question for you: Enriquillo takes to the bush in 1519. I understand his reasons—the rape of his woman and the ill treatment at the *encomienda*. But why then, and why him? Such abuse was common, after all."

"Everything else failed for him," I said. "With your forgiveness, even the schemes of the good friar Las Casas, bringing the Hieronymite fathers to abolish the *encomienda*..."

"Those friars were bribed. They ended up owning Indians themselves."

"That is what I mean. Enriquillo could see no other recourse. He tried to bring his case to the court. He even understood the queen's laws protecting the family."

"I hear he carries himself with dignity."

"Yes, a very serious man."

"From Anacaona's people?"

"His father was a lesser ni-Taíno and a good man. He died of his wound later, but Enriquillo's *yukaieke* survived the massacre. On my own recommendation, Enriquillo himself went to the Franciscans, who instructed him in Christianity and the law."

Barrionuevo is short and rotund of belly. He has a wide, very white face that exudes determination.

"He sounds like a man of his word, from all I've heard. If he wants, he could make peace this time," he said. "His case is acceptable if he would seek a pardon and pacify his people."

I was gratified to hear Captain Barrionuevo express himself thus. Enriquillo has wanted no more. And he knows this is the last chance for peace.

"It is the general feeling right now to make a peace," Barrionuevo said. "The king has much to administrate already. Here, few of your Indians are left, but in Yucatán and Mexico, Nicaragua and Peru, they are many, many. And the Africans are expensive to bring over. The talk, even in Santo Domingo, is to secure a way that will not destroy the laborer or slave. What is sought is a long-term prosperity. After all, if Enriquillo can carry on such a war here, what might not happen on the mainland?"

"The young *cacique* is not a man of threats," I said. "A good approach by a man of your honesty..."

"Of course. If not by peace, the killing will be total when we press on. The queen herself said, 'No quarter for the treasonous...'"

"A man has only so much killing in him," I said, angling for his own sentiment.

"For me, it is so," Barrionuevo let on, opening his heart to me in a way that feeds my hope.

May 16, 1533

ONE HUNDRED EIGHTY-SEVEN. *PICKING AT MY WOUND.*

Today I write in Rodrigo's small room as our ship sails slowly against a strong current. We sail along the coast and soon will be at Yaquimo, a port near the foothills of the Bahuruku. There I will disembark and seek the baby boy to make proper arrangements for a parley. I feel totally engaged in this peacemaking now, my concentration deviates not, and it feels I have everything in motion.

I think of many things today. I think of my other son, Heart of Earth, who went with me under Velazquez. I think of Ponce de León, the conqueror of Borikén, who later went to Cuba. I think of Las Casas, who was there, too. I think, too, of that awful monster of nature, Vasco Porcallo de Figueroa, who settled Camagüey, in Cuba, as his own private kingdom, fornicating and killing our people at will.

Barrionuevo's casual reference to the lack of Indians left in these islands, referring directly to my own Taíno people, picks at my wound. Yes, it is true what he says, but I am deeply chagrined and would say this: Everywhere there has been death around me these past forty years, everywhere in my world. We had no pestilence here and we were healthy, healthy. The evil came with them; it did.

ONE HUNDRED EIGHTY-EIGHT. *HATUEY, "CERTAINTY OF SUN IN THE SKY," OUR GREAT HERO.*

There is so much to tell, and by this mist of sea that surrounds me right now I will leave as much of it as I can, speak the names and write the deeds of the dead, impolite though it may be to do so, jarring, in our Indian way as a badly sung *areito*.

The fight went to Cuba with Hatuey, a great hero of my race. Hatuey, who fought Velazquez in retreat after the Massacre of Anacaona, and who moved his people in canoes to Cuba. He settled near Maisí Point, and he warned his hosts: "The Christians have but one god, and that is the shiny metal they call gold. They must have it, and they will kill and maim anyone in the way of its possession."

Hatuey took the Cuban ni-Taínos to the top of a mountain that overlooked the ocean. He was greatly respected, even in Cuba, and when he asked them to bring all their gold ornaments, most people did so willingly. They had already heard the tales and felt the cruelty of the Castilians in Cuba. Boricuas had traveled to their island, and

Castilian slavers, beginning with the admiral himself, had many times taken captives away. Guamax, the elder, as I have written, and later Bayamo, cursed all covered men/floating cave dwellers during the first voyage days...

Hatuey, ni-Taíno and *cacique*, was a grave and valiant man. The Cuban *caciques*, as I heard it several times during my years in Cuba, gathered around him, and many old people touched his hand to their own heads. The substance of his words was still a fresh memory among our cousins there.

Hatuey told them: "Our people have things in common, but not so with the covered men, not so. They covet much and they are so small inside in their covetousness.

"They know many things, but they dismiss their dreams; they try not to think about them. Invited to *cohoba*, they hate it, then go on to kill our *behikes* and *cemis*." The gold he asked to be put in baskets. Together, many people, hundreds and hundreds of principal people, went up promontories by the ocean and over fast running rivers, sang, prayed, danced, and tossed their gold baskets to the waters.

Velazquez landed in Cuba in 1511, and within weeks his men engaged Hatuey several times. With much harquebus, they forced the *cacique*'s retreat over the coastal mountains. After one brief combat, two mastiffs cornered him on a rocky ledge. He was by then in the territory of old Bayamo, who had spoken so vigorously with the admiral twenty years earlier. At a place called Yara, the soldiers tied him to a stake and gathered dry brush, preparing to burn him alive. I tried to dissuade Velazquez from the deed by reminding him that Hatuey had a wide following, but he paid me no mind. "A lesson we will teach with this immolation," he said and ordered all captured Taíno to witness the act.

Hatuey looked gravely on, humming his death song. He begged not for his life, but a priest approached him and, with me interpreting, offered up words that recalled and continued that other dialogue, so many years ago. (I say we have places on these magical islands that make us repeat ourselves, places where time turns in a circle and the land reclaims its own intelligence from us humans, generation after generation.)

"You ought to seek the baptism from me, Hatuey," the young priest said to the grave *cacique*, "so that you may be saved."

Hatuey looked at him not but toward the sky, at the wide hot sun that dominated the day. Such was the meaning of his name,

Hatuey, "Certainty of sun in the sky."

"I offer you baptism, savage man," the priest repeated.

Hatuey answered loudly, so the other Indians could hear. "And what will it get me, your little water?"

All ears were glued to his words. Not only the Indians but also Velazquez leaned forward to hear what Hatuey might say.

"It will open for you the gates of Heaven and life everlasting," the priest responded. "Without it, you are condemned to the Hell of eternal fire."

Hatuey thought a while, looking at the sun and never at the priest. Finally, he asked, "And the Castilians. Upon death, where do they go?"

"If baptized and repentful, they go to Heaven," the priest replied.

"I want not to be with such mean people," said Hatuey loudly. "Baptize me not. I prefer to go to Hell."

The priest walked away, shaking his head. I watched the face of Velazquez, that queer man who later killed his own wife. I had to laugh to myself, he was so absolutely chagrined. Watching Hatuey, too, I saw the slightest trace of a grin on his face, which never wavered again. He burned alive for two hours and never cried out but stared at the sun while his strength held and then, as he drooped, gazed upon Velazquez and me, eyes open, even in death, that light grin still visible on his darkening lips.

May 19, 1533

One hundred eighty-nine. *The spirits are all around us.*

I am filled with longing for my boys today as we sail along these shores. Surrounded by Castilians am I, soldiers and sailors, but even with Rodrigo, as warm a friend as can be had and often at my side, I am alone with the little voices. On board, no action is required of me; I sit long hours looking back at the wake of our ship on the water, wondering. Visions I see in the foam of our waves, faces of our people in the fluff of clouds. Thousands upon tens of thousands were we, uncounted and replenished as the cloudy flocks of doves and parrots that fill our skies. And now we are but handfuls, here and there a group of huts, the rest in *encomiendas*, month by month replaced by Africans brought over by the shipful. We of the islands, we Taíno, now blend into the white and the black, and our language is little heard.

We were we not weak, truly, nor stupid. Our mothers taught us well. Taíno women bore children firmly, prepared sustenance, sang with the heart of the generations so our ancestors surrounded us, sharing the trance of the living. Remembered in the breeze, the spirits of our dead we breathed into our very bosoms. Adventurous and hardy, our men met the sea with full hearts. We feared not hurricane, we welcomed wind and rain.

Out of our very winds, Castilians have sucked the life, their very breath has made us die by the thousands. This have I seen: our people dropping one upon another, circling blindly like leaves in a storm. The worst was in 1519, just as the baby boy struck his blow for freedom. Though already cut by more than half, we were many even then. In 1519, we dropped and dropped. It is one thing to see the blood run and the body die; it is quite another to see the living spirit suddenly depart from dozens and dozens and hundreds and thousands of people at once and see no wound, no reason, no fault.

ONE HUNDRED NINETY. *ANOTHER CONVERSATION WITH BARRIONUEVO.*

I spent time with Barrionuevo again today. We talked about Cuba. It turns out Barrionuevo once knew Vasco Porcallo de Figueroa, the young cosquistador I was given to by Velazquez.

"We called Porcallo the ram," Barrionuevo laughed. "He was a small man, but so brusque and decisive in his actions, everybody feared him."

"He was another Hojeda," I said. "But without the physical grace."

"I did not know Captain Hojeda."

"Hojeda was quite good looking, in the Castilian manner. Fair-haired and perfectly proportioned in his chest and limbs."

"Vasco was not."

"He was a ram, a mounting ram," I said.

We both laughed. In fact, Vasco Porcallo did look like a ram, with irascible, curling sideburns and a compact head and neck. He even walked fast, with head lowered.

I was very happy that Barrionuevo liked me and could share a joke with me. He has his tender part, this Barrionuevo, but he is also an old soldier, one of the old guard, conquistador, capable of complete impunity.

Barrionuevo has said, in my presence: "I am instructed to make peace with Enriquillo, but lacking that, upon my word, the wrath of the monarch himself, ruler of the greatest power on this earth, will be mobilized against him, and then the two hundred or so men I bring, and the authorization that I also bring to enlist into my brigades two hundred more men right here, these numbers will only be as one-tenth the number that I can without reserve count upon from the royal guard, the best of our lion-hearted, whom I will deputize and enlist, and I will myself lead this war to this fugitive *cacique*, and I will burn all of the mountains if need be."

So today I told him stories all afternoon, and I laughed with Barrionuevo about the characters in the old days, the lion-hearted of whom he speaks that are as heroic and comical to him as they are despicable to me.

May 23, 1533

One hundred ninety-one. *Continuing to work with Barrionuevo.*

Rodrigo, too, helps me. He dines with the knight captain each evening, a function to which I am disallowed, as they discuss logistical and potential military needs. But I know he speaks of me to Barrionuevo and dissuades doubt the captain may carry yet about my sincerity. I had some thought of this most intimate of missions as I boarded on ship, but now it is obvious. Barrionuevo is the man to be near, and I am in the right place, by Rodrigo's grace, to feel his *goeiz*.

Today, in the afternoon, as Barrionuevo scanned the coast by long glass, I lay in a hammock and watched, face hidden behind the lace of the net. He searched the coast with his glass in a concentrated stance but saw nothing of what he sought—no sign of smoke or light or movement of any kind that could point to contact with the rebel camps. I watched and watched him then quit watching but felt my gut and chest move in his direction, taking measure of his time so I knew exactly when he was about to quit, anticipating the moment when he took down the long glass and looked my way. My head I lifted at that very second, looking to the coast in my own concentration. This brought him over.

"The search for this *cacique* of yours could be tedious," he said.

"He seeks not yet for us, my captain," I said. "After I disembark at Port Yaquimo, I will initiate various messages to Enriquillo's camp."

"I will find him on the coast, and I will deliver the queen's message to him," he said, and I was silent. Barrionuevo was not interested in my participation at the negotiations; he merely liked my information.

After a while, he said, "The thing of the ram made me laugh."

Barrionuevo likes joviality, which is the way to reach him. Barrionuevo was making obvious his enjoyment of my tongue. Vasco Porcallo, whom I served for nearly two years in the Camagüey region, was indeed a comical (and despicable) apparition.

"He was every bit a ram," I said "He even hopped rapidly about, from one place to the next." To humor his mood, I told Barrionuevo how Porcallo would take the Cuban girls, one after another, sometimes as many as eight or ten in a single day.

"Most often he did it from behind, like a ram," I teased. "And sometimes standing up against a post."

This got a boistorous laugh out of Barrionuevo, who said: "Dieguillo Colón, you nasty old-timer. You are a rascal to remember these things!"

ONE HUNDRED NINETY-TWO. *OPENING THE PATH.*

My tongue not only humors but measures Barrionuevo. Today, in his light-hearted nostalgia, I found a path to his mood and put in my pitch. Since in a few days I will leave him to travel ahead by land to the hills of the Bahuruku, I am glad to reach him.

ONE HUNDRED NINETY-THREE. *MAKING CONNECTION, THE CHANGE OF HEART.*

As he formally left me, Barrionuevo patted my back. "You have survived a great deal, Dieguillo," he said. Immediately, I sought and captured his eyes. "So have you, my captain," I responded, and he nodded. I said then: "And so has the Enriquillo, who is a decent and brave man, a man who wants nothing more than the peace of the land for his relatives and other Indians."

"Is this totally so?" he inquired, and, yes, I felt trust for my answer in his interrogation.

"Totally, my captain. Show this *cacique* but few soldiers, yet go to his lair. He is a fair man and will not attack an offer to parley. Then, do not threaten violence but show him the monarch's message and capitulate with him in clear language. Pardon issued, he would settle in a quiet farm somewhere, and your Indian war will be over forever on this island."

I looked into his eyes without fear or bashfulness, and I knew at that moment that peace was possible with this man, a real peace for our remaining free Taínos, with a settlement on land, pride, and authority, and even a community for Enriquillo and Mencia's people. "By the love of the baby Jesus, by the purity of the Holy Mother Mary," I ventured. "A great war captain could by an act of peace redeem the years of horror on this island with a measure of just finality."

"I will do my best," Barrionuevo said, and I believe he means it.

May 25, 1533

One hundred ninety-four. *Cruelties of Vasco Porcallo.*

This afternoon Barrionuevo and Rodrigo Gallego talk alone. I am very lucky to have Rodrigo here at this important moment.

I will write about my time with Vasco Porcallo, the man-ram of our joking, who put my remaining son and me to work mining gold at the swampy rivulets near the new town of Sancti Spiritus. Those days in Cuba repeated the events in Española but much more quickly. This time the Castilians arrived in larger numbers, always well stocked and with clear strategy to subjugate our people quickly. In their attacks and raids to take slaves, they chased them from their villages and *conucos* all over eastern Cuba, so that two and more planting seasons were entirely missed. Famine ensued among the Cuban Taíno.

Vasco, a young man of twenty then, but regal in his manner, was granted a huge estate, spawning cattle and sheep and pigs and many planted fields. His foremen organized gangs of gold pan-ners and rakers into regular squads, working long, long days with little food and the constant sting of the whip and the whap of the *planazo*, a blow with the flat of the cutlass or machete that easily turned bloody. Vasco ran his *encomienda* severely. As his raiders took many men prisoners, he would feed them not, but worked them for weeks until they dropped. Sometimes, a few were allowed to go after fruit, when in season. Once several men made a pact to assuage their desperate hunger pangs by copiously eating dirt. They knew, of course, that this would kill them. Vasco was personally insulted. He rescued the men by forcing large quantities of oil and water down their throats, then tied them to posts. If they could eat dirt, he said, perhaps they could eat something else. Then, he cut the testicles off three men and made each eat his own. The act was so horrifying to the people that suicides stopped. For actions such as that, Velazquez hailed Porcallo a "great *encomienda* administrator."

The obdurate Porcallo was among the most emulated of the conquistador class. And, yes, he was an untiring fornicator who day after day for thirty years passed over our women and spawned hun-dreds of mestizos. Porcallo was not without plan, however, as he conceived of peopling the region with his new race, the power from his own loins adapted to the land as the offspring of the indigenous woman. He had an accomplice and even a teacher in the old *cacique* of the savanna—Camagüeybax, who arranged many of these couplings and provided young maidens for the man-ram. Once, I tried to scold the old *cacique,* but he refused to be admonished. "War is useless against war-driven people. To pacify them with their own desires is our only protection and our only survival," he told me. Porcallo put up women who gave him children in their own *bohíos,* and he kept going back to them. Later, he went on to import artisan and even noble families from Spain to marry his first generations.

I hated it, all the fornicating and begetting without lineage, without any sort of guidance from the elder mothers. But having lived another twenty years, I know now that mere survival is our only possible victory. And wonder I do now that Camagüeybax maybe was right. The region of Camagüey is today peopled by our mixed race, and *guaxiro* is a term oft-employed to describe our survival in the loins of Taíno women, seeded by Castilian men. What matters, Camagüeybax would say, is that our old people's eyes and ears, our expressions survive in the generations and not just die away.

Some people say that every mestizo means one less Indian. I agree now with Camagüeybax that inside each mestizo an Indian survives to come through.

May 26, 1533

ONE HUNDRED NINETY-FIVE. CAIMÁN-*HUNTING DAYS.*

My boy and I were fortunate, saved from the killing hunger by the extra food provided through the meat of *caimán*, whose danger I was after some weeks assigned to eradicate by hunting. I was given an old harquebus, dagger, and lance and fashioned for myself several long *bejuco* ropes. Heart of Earth was not allowed to hunt with me but stayed in the gold panning. I fed him much *caimán* that year, and he lived on it. Oils from the *caimán* also I used on him, to rub his water-wrinkled skin that turned to blackened leather on his arms and shoulders. Thus I saved my boy from the open sores that killed many of our miners.

Las Casas I met also at that time. His own *encomienda* was not far away, on the Arimao River, and I was borrowed by his partner to eliminate a reptile on that waterway, a giant beast that had taken a servant boy as he filled casks with water.

I hunted that monster on canoe, by the light of the moon, and saw him one night leave the water to stalk a young calf. Knowing his hunting area, I cleared all animals away, but a young calf we tied in a field not far from the river. With eight men, I waited six nights, and then the giant *caimán* left the water. We surrounded the beast and a long pole we stuck into his snapping mouth. Killing him was easy after that. Las Casas was quite happy, and that night we conversed until the early hours. He was changing his mind about then on the keeping of our people as slaves and not much later gave up his own *encomienda* to take up the campaign for our freedom, a cause he has never relinquished.

I hunted large *caimán* by the dozen for nearly a year and was never hurt. Then, once, while bathing in a quiet little pool, clear as glass and with nothing in sight, a puny *caimán* not three feet long snuck in on me and bit my leg. He was so small, I walked out with him hanging from my thigh and ran him through with a knife, but the damage was done. His long tooth pierced me to the bone just above the knee, the wound festering to high fever until I lost track of all time. It was Las Casas who nursed me, upon hearing the case, and even in my sickness worried twice was I, as Heart of Earth took sick himself from the constant panning in cold, dirty water, and I was certain he would die.

I recovered first. Las Casas, who was still friendly with Velazquez, obtained my son for me. I nursed Heart of Earth myself, feeding him honey paste and fruits, rubbing him down with *caimán* oil and wet *digo* compresses and smoothing out the ridges in his now scaly skin.

Around that time, Ponce de León, who resided in Borikén, heard the tales of the Fountain of Youth, said to be found at Bimini or on the coast of La Florida. He would mount an expedition to find it. Word of this was heard all around, even in Cuba, where a group of volunteers agreed to join. A complex tradition among my people was this story of the Fountain of Youth, referring as it did to our own Taíno movement to the smaller islands (my own Guanahaní among them) and the settlement of new villages. Thus the youthfulness it promised referred to the founding of new communities and the rekindling of sacred *cemis*, not the rejuvenation of old men. But the Castilians took it as enchantment and set out to find an actual fountain.

Heart of Earth, who had recovered, thanks to the good friar, wanted to go along in Ponce's expedition. A young man of fourteen years, he would leave for the port of San German with the Castilian volunteers and reasoned thus to me: "Father of my days," he said. "Let us go, if allowed. No life is there for us here. I would go and see our days before us. With luck, we might see our people at Guanahaní and maybe find a spot of earth and a people of our copper color who will uphold us."

I myself applied to the expedition but Velazquez would not permit my going; the young man, yes, he said, after all, he offered everything I could, plus youth. Reluctant was I to see to see my son go, but no true argument against it came to me. Thus, he embarked with Ponce, and I know from later testimony he did land at Guanahaní, where he might have seen my people, and onward they sailed to Bimini and La Florida. On a Florida beach, Heart of Earth one day went out to chop a palm tree, I was later informed, and disappeared. I hope, I pray he walks among our own Taíno people, who previously settled in those parts.

May 27, 1533

ONE HUNDRED NINETY-SIX. *ONE* AREITO *REMEMBERED.*

I cannot help thinking at this moment about my twins, how they looked together laid out on the hammock just after birth. It turns my mind to the songs of the double twins in our origin stories: Deminán, first ancestor, and his three *ximagua* brothers. Many roundances were sung throughout the villages of the Taíno for these four beings. Episode after episode was sung, the cycle starting the evening after first rain and running, night after night, through the wet season.

Of woman born without male ancestor were these four brothers, who are the four winds, who gathered the powers from the world beyond the clouds; they who walked the rim of the sky. Said one *areito* song: "In the world where heat does not exist, the eyes can create." I think of it today, as I lie and write in a hammock that hangs low behind the captain's cabin. We are clipping fast toward Yaquimo, and this well-made ship, the king's own, has the grace of a giant dolphin. There is nothing like the swing of a hammock on a gentle ocean.

Our *areitos* said: this world of humans is of the heart, the belly, and the groin. Mind exists, and spirit, but in little proportion to the other three. In the world before ours that the dead endeavor to reach and are forever in, mind and spirit are nearly all. There is some heart, very little gut, and no groin, no link to the rudeness of procreation, no hope of the fleshful love, nor the command of touch necessary to its generation. Yet, in the mind is everything, in the spirit of the other self, the other me, the opposite, in that link is where movement originates and the spark of existence.

A pondering people were our Taíno on the measure and the breadth of our existence. Origins we had, and creators, generations of creators. Before ever I heard of Adam and Eve, ancestors of the Castilians, or of the Jesus from Nazareth, from a place beyond Iberia, in the Kingdom of Judea, whom all Christians venerate though his own people betrayed him—before all of that, we had Itiba Cahobaba and the Sky-walking Brothers, and before them Yucahu, and even before that, YaYa and Atabey and so much more…

Deminán was first among the brothers and many of our songs told the tales of his adventures, his intelligence, his beautiful looks. Deminán could swim in the wind, and while his three younger brothers were being born, his laboring mother told him: "Search out ways of creating a world where Taíno can live, a sea and a bracelet of islands, all manner of fish, the action and heart of man, the mind and love of woman, a language, and, best of all, the *cohoba* and the tobacco to make the link complete. All the forces necessary are in your path," his mother, Itiba Cahobaba, told Deminán. She, Ancient Bleeding Mother, said to him: "Spirit beings you will find in your path who hold the needed medicines and powers but know not how to use their gifts to spark the world into being. That is you. Your curiosity is the next creator," she told him.

Yucahuguama Bagua Maórocoti, first-force-*yucca*-giver-sea-provider-of-Woman-born-without-grandfathers, already existed and had accomplished his main labor on the heated earth. Birthed by Atabey, along with his brother, Guacar, they had been formed by their mother out of the invisible elements of space. Atabey, too, brought the life-giving powers to earth: she sucked the wind into herself, churned it into her spiritual waters, and birthed twin boys. They were the best and the worst, natural harmony and natural chaos. Yucahu, the harmony, continued to create the earth, and the sun and the moon he brought out of their origin caves. All this Yucahu accomplished. Beauty he had accomplished, on his mother's instructions. Guacar, his brother, in his own nature, sought disharmony. He liked ugliness; he created what his brother did not: all manner of disintegration, turbulent storm, pests, diseases, aggressive fish (shark), poison sea jellies, pain itself, and, of course, death.

But that was a time much before, and even then the world of human beings was already coming out of caves and forming out of trees and *manatí* and out of the heart of palm. Some paddled in the spirit waters, but blindly and lost and needed to be taught. All were guarded from the sun, who was fierce and unforgiving before he loved us. All this Deminán's mother, who died as the fourth brother emerged, told Deminán. Now, he must walk the clouds and follow his wishes, his curiosities, and all would be alright; he would accomplish the rest.

So, Deminán traveled, and his impulse was certain.

It so happened a spirit named YaYa was the ultimate existence, the weaving of time itself. He lived with his wife in a *bohío* that was the beginning and the end of the road. His own first son, who had a great gift, YaYa had killed. Yayael was the son. He was now bones in a basket hanging from the rafters in the westernmost corner of the *bohío*. One day his bones, caressed in his mother's hands, became fish, and both father and mother ate happily. Now with his wife, YaYa went to his *conuco*, where a patch of spirit corn needed cleaning.

Deminán, walking the rim of the sky, saw YaYa's empty *bohío*. He knew he should respect a strange *bohío* but on impulse approached and entered. His three brothers only waited at the door.

Deminán moved carelessly through YaYa's *bohío*. Spotting the basket, he climbed at the rafters without thinking. Suddenly the brothers whispered, "YaYa is coming." Deminán lunged for the basket and toppled it. Out came mountains of water, heavens of wet water; long, heavy fish tumbled out, all manner sea life, an immense volume of life-giving water world. YaYa approached his *bohío* angrily; he felt his son, whom he loved above all else, upset by a simpleton. Deminán fled, trailed by his brothers, and, the song says, all four were suddenly consumed by a hunger that craved *cassabe*, smelled *cassabe*—crisp-roasted tort of the *yucca* root, sustainer of Taíno life. This—smelling the heat of a cooking fire—just as the waters of the earth began to teem with life.

June 2, 1533

ONE HUNDRED NINETY-SEVEN. *ANOTHER GOLD TRAP.*

Soon, maybe by late this afternoon, we land. After a night of drifting in the open sea, a pilot who well knows the coast indicated a shadow like a darkened eye on the line of land. "That is Yaquimo," he said. "We can be there in half a day if the wind holds."

I talked again to Rodrigo, mentioning again the Valenzuela plotters. Barrionuevo approves the arrest of two guards on board, Valenzuela's men who mean to strike at Enriquillo at the earliest opportunity. They will be taken at the port of entry, handcuffed, and turned over to the local marshals in Yaquimo with six-month sentences. The charge, admittedly trumped up, will be: transactions in gold without authorization. This set up with the last piece of gold from the *cacique.*

ONE HUNDRED NINETY-EIGHT. *HAPPINESS TO BE IN THICK OF EVENTS.*

After so many cloistered years, I am living grandly these days, a purposeful happiness in my heart. I am relishing my intense participation in the effort for Enriquillo. Suddenly that old gift (or curse) of mine, to arrive at places of central action, to be in the mix between men who must converse, I feel it working for me. Something in my soul tells me I am the one to carry out this function, and I am enthused to join the two men and put them through an old-time, Taíno peace pact. Even the song of the *guatiao,* our exchange-of-names ceremony, I have been singing to these lonely waves. I feel I am ready to fulfill this destiny and through this work, if successful, to salvage from this life my shame that I carry to have introduced, so many times, the Castilians into our people. Shaking off the life of the monks, I feel more than ever my life is clear before me and I am my own man.

Catalina is to meet me at Yaquimo, and right at this moment, the wind in my ears whispers the music of another *areito,* also of the four brothers, about the time the men lost the women and how Deminán helped us. Why is it when I think of her the music of my childhood resounds in the wind? I long for Catalina so deeply right now, I want so much to be in her presence. And here I am again, after all these years, riding on the royal ship of the king of Spain, toward an Indian *cacicasgo,* a sovereign, and a people. The wind holds.

June 6, 1533

One hundred ninety-nine. *Catalina becomes my wife.*

Out again in the bush, down old trails and small *carreta* roads. Catalina is with me, and Silverio, both with good mounts. I have my Cariblanca. Today, the three of us rode the coastal savanna to these first foothills. We are resting tonight under the perfect canopy of two huge *ceiba* trees, where we made a small fire and hung our things. The horses we have tethered in a pasture of tall grass nearby.

Catalina met me at the dock, dressed like a white lady, Silverio acting the servant and holding the three horses at a distance. Her daughter, Inez, known to the Castilians as Julia, came along. I introduced the two women to Barrionuevo and Rodrigo. I used the phrase *my betrothed* when introducing Catalina, and both men bowed deeply to her. Her daughter stayed under the protection of both men, who vouched for her well-being. Julia will act as a guide to Enriquillo's camp when they spot sign to follow from the ship.

Catalina becomes my wife now, setting my hammock next to hers at night, prescribing my tea, and even tasting my food. I love to have it so. There is nothing I would not do for the Catalina now, nothing. As a teacher and midwife I have appreciated her and now, as my wife, her way I will make easier. Catalina is full of spark yet in the daytime but a bony bird she is at night, slight to settle in the curl of my arm and chest. I am complete once again in my time, called to the active life by this great occasion. Suddenly there is Catalina, again, the same and yet this time a different Catalina, ready to have me and give me life. Oh, I am full of happiness and optimism as we ride into the hills of Enriquillo's country.

(Difficult it will be to write long here. I've only ten sheets of paper left and little time. Nevertheless, I will continue to make notes.)

Two hundred. *Going to the Bahuruku again.*

Where the plain breaks into bush and begins to climb sharply, eight young *guaxeri* made rendezvous with us. I recognized only one man, but Silverio knew several by name and talked our old language to them without hesitation. They are severe about moving rapidly to meet with Enriquillo.

Two hundred one. *Deminán and the* guanguayo *turtle create the islands.*

At night, the warriors are polite but cautious. They are particularly impressed with Catalina, who shows them how to improve on a good balm for cuts and bites with the bark of the *jagua* tree. Now she hums *areito* music late into the Bahuruku night. The eight warriors crowd around her, listening.

I finish here the Deminán story, the one where he again accosts the *bohío* of a holy spirit man, requesting his cooked *cassabe* to eat. The irritated old man spirit spits a gob of *cohoba* on Deminán's back. A swollen hump forms on his back and he loses strength. Lying down on a sliver of sandy beach, in the middle of the vast ocean, Deminán takes deadly sick. Using a coral knife, one of his brothers lances the swollen hump. Out of his back comes the turtle. Where the first turtle grows, land surfaces, where a *bohío* can be built, where good people can make a home. Thus were our lands created.

Two hundred two. *Warriors who would be husbands.*

On the trail, I talk openly with Catalina and Silverio about our mission to Enriquillo. The young men warriors listen. I talk about our old Taíno peace pacts, and Catalina confirms my description. A leader of the warriors says: "Our *cacique* maintains we will marry, all, and settle down to farm with our wives. Is that possible? Do you think so?"

"Yes," I tell him. "If the peace can be arranged, it could be a very different life."

"I can help you boys get matched up with your own women," Catalina said. "When the peace is made, we will work on that problem."

The young men smiled all around. "Anything you need, great mother," one said, humorously but not in jest. "Only look my way."

Two hundred three. *Catalina stays with Mencía.*

Mencia recieved us at the water's edge. She led a troupe of twenty men and her three women assistants. Everybody is very tense.

Enriquillo is with the young *behike*. They are in *cohoba*. Tamayo is also gone, along with Cao and six other captains. Mencia is in charge of everything at the camp, which has been reduced. I do not discuss with her Tamayo's mission, which I put out of my mind.

"We prepare a great lot these past few weeks," she told me. "It is confusing because we build new hidden camps as precaution against sudden raids, yet I tell my young people a peace may take place, that we may get our own farms. It is confusing for the men who might now think of peace, yet still we prepare for war."

At their main camp, Mencia and her women received Catalina formally, singing an old *areito* about the creation of the moon for her. Catalina, who knew Mencia as a child, offered to stay with her while I go to Enriquillo. "I want to help my niece," she said. "You go see what you can do for the baby boy."

Two hundred four. *At the enchanted falls.*

Silverio brought me here. We arrived at midday. There are little falls just at the entrance to a cave facing the ocean. A gentle trail leads to it from the forest behind it, but facing out from the cave to the sea is jagged rock straight down to the hard-breaking waves. At the entrance, a pool is formed on clear white stone from a cascading spring of fresh water. The cascade flushes a mist that cools the day. We sat down a while, and Silverio cooed like a dove. Finally, Baiguanex came out.

"Guaikán, uncle, I see you again," he said, but heavily, not his usual light singsong greeting.

"*Behike*," I responded. "I find you in a place of beauty."

"We are in the enchantment now," he said, still serious.

"And how is our serene *cacique*?" I asked.

Baiguanex asked us into the cave, which smelled of *cohoba* mixture and old fires. At the rear of the cave, an opening from the top let the sun shine in. Enriquillo lay curled beneath a sheet, his lower body in the sunshine. The *cacique* slept with abandon, his breath pulling and blowing in long, rythmic aspirations. "Three nights he has been in *cohoba*," Baiguanex said.

Baiguanex led me to a ledge at the cave's entrance. This side of the cave is high on a steep promontory that juts out to sea.

"Seven days we have been here, four in fasting and three in *cohoba*. He has one more to go."

"So much *cohoba* for the *cacique*?"

"He requests it. As you see him sleep now, he has not rested in many years."

TWO HUNDRED FIVE. *MORE* COHOBA *REVELATIONS.*

I smoked with Baiguanex. He grew his own and rolled tobaccos like
an old Cuban. We faced the ocean, and he would not look at me.

"The *cacique* is tired. His young body has lived in perpetual
alertness."

"It is good to see him rest."

"*Cohoba* forced him. For two nights he saw nothing, heard
nothing. They filled his mind with night and collapsed him. On the
third day, I fed him. He ate a *cassabe* tort and drank fresh water from
this well. Then I gave him a piece of roasted iguana. He sprang to
life like a gray-tailed hawk. At noon, he danced for me, low on the
ground, swooping at the earth. That night, two evenings ago, they
talked to him. They thanked him for what he has done, and they
gave him permission on his new path."

Baiguanex scratched his back against the rock, watching the
ocean. "Then, last night, he saw the ocean and a Spanish ship coming toward him. It was coming from Spain, for him. The ship, they
told him, has the answer he desires."

"Barrionuevo's ship," I said.

Baiguanex looked up, but past me. "And then this morning,
this morning early, as he napped again, I saw the ship. Right out
there. The Spanish ship of his *cohoba* vision."

"A long one, with three main sails?"

"Yes. And a second one, a coastal launch with one sail."

"Exactly. Barrionuevo's ship. You actually saw it."

The *behike* nodded. "That much I think is good," he said.

TWO HUNDRED SIX. *DETAILS OF CONTACT.*

Enriquillo awakened an hour later. He called the *behike*, who
brought him water and a *cassabe* tort. Then he came out to the pool
and greeted me with eyes deep set, holding a dream.

"I am to meet the Castilian captain," he said. "Have you prepared a way?"

I gave him the details of the contact with Barrionuevo, how I
sailed with him, how Catalina's daughter, Julia, will be sent by Barrionuevo's guides.

"And is this captain from the king?" he asked.

"He is that," I said. "Even the ship he commands is the king's own."

"Can he enforce the king's law?"

"Yes, *cacique*, he can."

"Your path crosses with my *cohoba*, uncle," he said then. "I need your heart's eye on this man."

"Barrionuevo I felt in my being," I told him. "I believe he would be true to his word."

"We will guide him in then. Wherever he lands, we will have men chopping wood, calling attention to themselves. They will bring him to the edge of our lake. Julia can be sent for me from there. I will send Romero to set up the parley. Myself I will come down when this captain is settled on our lake."

TWO HUNDRED SEVEN. *A HINT OF REVERSAL.*

"I am ready to help with all that," I said. "The songs of Guarionex I have rehearsed. A peaceful moment we can make—"

But Enriquillo looked up, and I felt Baiguanex behind me.

Baiguanex touched my shoulder silently.

"I should tell you, Guaikán," Enriquillo said, for the first time ever calling my own name to me. "Many runners have come, from dozens of families, maybe hundreds, who want to join us if a peace is made. A very complex thing will peace be now for this *cacique*."

"Do you doubt that peace can be made, *cacique*?" I asked.

"No, but I know I won't live long enough to see it survive."

TWO HUNDRED EIGHT. *GUAROCUYA DOES A HAWK DANCE, HE TAKES ME OUT.*

The Guarocuya boy danced at noon again. He is a hawk when he dances, pure hawk spirit and motion. Baiguanex beat the drum, and Enriquillo twirled left and right, first one leg then the other, twirling and looking, swooping at the ground and pecking. I could see the hawk mind in his eyes that no longer would focus. Then, he slept.

When he awoke, he called me to him. "Uncle. Everything is set," he said. "This Barrionuevo I will meet. I am ready for peace if he is and if the king's word he carries. If so, I will make peace with the sovereigns and see what of our people can be settled, that at least a town of us could survive, a place we can gather our survivors."

"A town may be too big a project," I said. "But at least your band here could get a farm. There is talk of a farm at Azua."

"We will have a town," he said calmly and with total assurance. "The Indians on the island, the ones of us from here and the ones like you and so many others brought here from the islands and from the mainland, all will come to our free land."

"If the *cacique* says so," I said.

"Yes. And the Africans, the ones that came to us in '22, after the rebellion of the slaves on the second admiral's sugar mill. They must have a place in this town. So will you and Catalina."

"It is a dream of mine to live among Taíno again," I said, though in my heart, at that moment, I did not believe it. I have thought more in a pardon for Enriquillo. What the *cacique* now envisioned implied the end of the *encomienda* in Española.

"Possibly Barrionuevo is not authorized for suggesting a community scheme or a refuge for Indians. This is what Las Casas throws at them and arouses their anger."

"The good friar is accusatory and he angers everyone," Enriquillo said. "But he was right to push for abolishing the *encomienda*."

I nodded, thinking briefly of the good friar, where he might be at that very minute. I thought of Tamayo, too, and Valenzuela and Pero Lopez. There was agitation and cross-purposes in my mind suddenly where before I felt the medicine to make the peace pact.

"With careful words, I am sure, you opened my path to this new captain," Enriquillo said. "This means that twice you have saved me, uncle. I thank you. Our people thank you twice."

The words had a finality to them I did not like.

"There is more to be done," I said. "The negotiation is ahead, and the settlement—"

"My message is clear, uncle," he said, in that way of Enriquillo, that sense of knowing exactly the road to follow. "Your part of the task is done."

I felt very old suddenly. I felt his truth, that my part was done. I felt maybe my life was done.

"My *cacique*," I said feebly. "I know Barrionuevo now. Even his main guard is an old friend of mine, Rodrigo Gallego—"

"The *cohoba* says no. Your path is blocked now."

And I felt exactly that way, blocked. I had felt greatly needed, central, and now I am out of the events I have been fashioning. Over and over have I prepared for the pact, reflecting on the ways taught to me by Guarionex, thinking the words aloud.

"Forgive me, Enrique," I tried one more time. "I need to

continue in the making of this…"

"It cannot be," he said and walked back into the cave.

Two hundred nine. *The* behike *explains.*

I sat on the outside of the cave, looking out to ocean. Silverio readied our things to lead me back to Mencia's camp. Baiguanex came to say farewell, bringing two tobaccos for me.

"We follow the old ways here," he said. "The priests will never know it, not even the one they call good friar, but this great *cacique* of ours is guided by the *cohoba*. The time you came and were in *cohoba* with us you also helped us see the past and the future. You have brought much, Guaikán, but the spirits don't want you near it now. The *cohoba* says: take the edge now, not the point."

"I have done no wrong, *behike*," I said.

"No wrong," he said. "But you have worked too long in the devious mind of the covered men."

"I have learned to spin a web of scheme," I said. "I know that. But I do it for this purpose—"

"It is complicated, Guaikán, and we appreciate you. But you are not to come. Your heart is not right in this cycle. Now is time for you to smooth and comb your mind," Baiguanex said. "Pray for this peace and go home. The *cacique* will take the words from here."

I bowed, took his hand, and put it to my head. "Taíno-ti, Baiguanex," I said to this young man, then got up to leave.

"When you get back to her camp," he instructed. "Ask Mencia to send for Tamayo, who has been by here already. He has something to tell you."

(My supply of paper is running low. I have so much I want to write. And even back at the convent, I have but a few more sheets stashed away.)

Two hundred ten. *Tamayo's report.*

Mencia sent for Tamayo. Cao came with him. Both men were cordial but formal. Tamayo was sterner than usual.

"I thank you for your clever scheme, Guaikán," Tamayo began, and I understood completely why I could not be a peacemaker this season, why, as Baiguanex said, my "heart is not right."

"The piece of gold led the pale ones to us like the flower calls the hummingbird," Tamayo said.

I looked away. He would have to tell me his report, and I would have to hear it, just now. In my anticipation I felt deeply chagrined. I took Tamayo and Cao, and we walked up a nearby hill. The two tobaccos of Baiguanex we smoked.

Tamayo waited. When he told me, he relished the telling. He had killed for me, and he would have me hear it all. I will write this about it: Pero Lopez died quickly. He begged not for his life, and they were kind to him. They didn't stretch him up but put him on a horse. His neck snapped in the fall. (It is true, I could not resist feeling satisfaction when I heard it. The *behike* is right, I receive this death gladly in my heart.)

Valenzuela and his servant managed to break free, Tamayo said. They grabbed weapons and put up a strong fight. Cao himself was cut in the face before both men were run through with lances and daggers and Cao wrestled the servant down and cut his throat.

"Valenzuela lived the whole night," Tamayo said. "He cried for water all night."

The old war captain grinned at me. He has scars on both cheeks and an eyelid that dangles from an old wound. "The Castilian dog was gut wounded but didn't bleed much," he said. "He dried out quickly. You should have heard him cry for water."

The remark slightly sickened me. I have seen Valenzuela many times. I could see the scene before my eyes. Shameless he was and assassin he would have been, but I still could sense him and I could feel his *goeiz* on my neck and right shoulder.

"Like a bee to yellow petals, he came into our trap seeking the yellow nectar," Tamayo said, "the only one that can cure the malady in their hearts."

I saw Cao smile now behind him. Old Tamayo leaned forward, looking at me directly. "You saw everything before its time, Guaikán Columbus," he said. "I must grant you that. But you are not worth a crap as a *behike* man. You hurried my ceremony, put it through before its time, and my mind is very confused. Why did you open my heart only to set me up to kill?"

I could only look away. I knew, of course, he was right. I should have waited and seen the sequence better. In the midst of my peacemaking I doubted not my own revenge.

Tamayo continued. "I am not angry with you," he said. "I found my own way to make peace. I thought to myself: Tamayo, this Castilian might be the last one you get to kill. I wondered: what should I give a dying Castilian that he can take with him? And I had an idea. So we made a hot fire, found a large sun-caved stone and heated it red. And there I melted the gold bar. I melted it and melted it.

"Then, it was morning. Once more, Valenzuela cried for water. I opened his mouth and gave him the molten gold."

He saw me grimace and glared hard at me. He was right. I had no call to grimace, since he had done my bidding.

"And how did he like the golden water?" I asked, acknowledging his right to exalt in the cruelty.

"You know," Tamayo relished the moment. "He didn't like it much."

The warriors both laughed, and I joined them. I wasn't reluctant anymore but laughed sincerely at the perfect irony of Tamayo's torture. It is true: no peacemaker am I, not now, not anymore.

The two men told me the rest, too, how they disposed of the bodies and how they swore to secrecy their whole group, all the captains and Cao. I recognized their valor. "You have saved your *cacique*," I told them.

"In the next few days, we are to go prepare for the peace parley by the lake," Tamayo told me more directly, obviously feeling better for having reported the deed. "I think it may have been our last ambush."

As they walked away, I felt sad in my knowledge—about them and about me. I am not sorry about any of it, but I am glad it's over.

TWO HUNDRED ELEVEN. *MY PAPER RUNS SHORT.*

This is the last of my paper now. Tomorrow we travel back together, Catalina and I. We have camped by ourselves for two weeks on the outskirts of the action, gathering word. We kept to our own when Mencia's camp moved without us. It was late July. Barrionuevo's ship was spotted and signals of smoke went up. A launch landed days later, and *guaxeri* were soon available, cutting wood within earshot of Barrionuevo's soldiers, who then "captured" our woodsmen. From that point, everything functioned as planned. Two captains in canoes came up at the lake. Catalina's daughter, Julia, was sent out and contact was made. Enriquillo prepared his delegation of captains with more than half of their seasoned men, some seventy warriors, all ready for battle. Barrionuevo, I was told, came in with some fifteen men and few weapons.

It hurt me to have to hear of the parley secondhand. Silverio went back and forth for five days while Barrionuevo and Enriquillo made their peace. Silverio is a good boy but not the best relayer of words. I knew from his reports the parley was going well, but his lack of detail was frustrating. Tamayo himself came to see me. He had been sent by Enriquillo to tell me that pardons were granted all around, that six of his captains would be deputized, and that a tract of land big enough for a town with good fields would be allotted. "The Castilian captain gives his word for the queen. All Indians not slaves can live in our new lands."

TWO HUNDRED TWELVE. *STAYING AWAY FROM THE PEACEMAKING.*

Staying away as the peace between Enriquillo and Barrionuevo was made, for once I was satisfied not to be in the center of things. It is enough to know I have a place and to trust the mind of a true *cacique*.

I know that Enriquillo's decision to press for a territory of refuge for all Indians appears in the treaty, which will establish such a community. Barrionuevo is as generous as he was encouraged to be back in Santo Domingo. Of course, there are not so many Indians left now and more and more Africans. It is not so difficult to give up the Indian labor. It is in this way I see that Enriquillo gains more concessions without me, who have chastised Las Casas for the same opinion. Oh, and that poor friar, whom I have sent on a devious and misguided trail—God keep him, please. Truly my heart pays the price for my involvement in these affairs.

TWO HUNDRED THIRTEEN. *FEELING THE GOOD FRIAR.*

Silverio joined us, and with Catalina and Enriquillo's captain Romero we have started on our ride back to Yaquimo. We will take a barge out of Yaquimo and sail to Santo Domingo.

Today, I could feel the good friar. I walked down an open path for a distance, behind Romero and before Catalina, and it was the friar's legs and step that I could feel in my limbs, the length of his legs and of his neck, the way his neck stretches as he walks. I could feel his *goeiz* in the swing of my arms and my own step, and I was very nervous. He must be angry with me.

TWO HUNDRED FOURTEEN. *LAST OF THE PAPER ON THE SHIP.*

This is the last of my paper, this half a sheet. Catalina tells me of an *areito* Mencia sang for her, the one with the story of how the men fought with each other in the old days, became mean and lost the women, and how Deminán and his three brothers lulled the female again into humanity. She said this is everyone's topic in the camps. As in that *areito* there are many instructions of how men are to care for the women and women for the men. The men talk about what Enriquillo has said, about settling down, farming peacefully, finding wives. There are messages from many, many Indians, all over the island, who want to settle with Enriquillo.

TWO HUNDRED FIFTEEN. *INDIANS AS DIGNITARIES.*

Our horses we leave now with Silverio. Catalina and I go by barge to Santo Domingo and Captain Romero accompanies us. The citizens at Yaquimo came out to see him and even clap for him as for a dignitary. There is genuine happiness for a peace that every day seems more and more possible. We are well fed by the main citizens of Yaquimo.

TWO HUNDRED SIXTEEN. *ALL THAT I CAN FIT.*

I can squeeze but a few more lines into this sheet. The barge leaves today. The baby boy is safe. Our Taíno-ni-Taíno survives one more generation, and a place is marked, reserved for the future! And there are other worthy recognitions. I want to write but there is no more space for my mark. Xán, Xán Katú. This is all that I can fit. Greatful am I for the gift given and for the friendship of the courageous priest to whom I now return. Taíno-ti-carayá.

Folio VII

LAST TESTAMENTS

In the convent, news of Las Casas... In my room, a letter from the good friar... A year's wait... Preparing for marriage... I hear of Enriquillo... Journey to the new community... I see Enriquillo again, in his death-bed... At last in our bohío... *Final testament, 1539... A letter from Las Casas, the New Laws... A note for Las Casas... They will remember, my young generations...*

Two hundred seventeen. *In the convent, news of Las Casas.*

I write at the convent, on these few sheets I put away here. Thus I will write some pages more, though everything is doubly painful in this Castilian place and in this Castilian mind.

Catalina and I are separated once more. We have no place to be together and even our marriage is yet to be properly announced. Among our people it is so easy to just be, but here we must watch every move.

I long for Catalina immensely. I dread where I am and want to go.

For one thing, Abbot Mendoza is rude in his disappointment at my wanting to take a wife. "You were close to vows with our order," he said. "You have learned from us the Holy Sacraments. Consider the seriousness of your decision."

Like everyone else, of course, he knows about my problem with Father Las Casas. He mentions it not, but he watches me differently, all the monks do. Only Father Remigio is warm to me as usual.

Two hundred eighteen. *In my room, a letter from the good friar.*

In my room, on top of my papers, I found his letter. But the good friar is gone, refusing to even countenance me.

[Inserted letter from Las Casas.—Ed.]

June 10, 1533
To a Dieguillo who is a *diablillo*:

I have read all your papers. Thus I know of your deceit doubly, once on the trail, walking for nothing, and now again, from your own words that tell so many lies. Deceit I know I can find in these papers on your desk, as I leaf through them again, what I read before and the much I had not seen. So I see your calumnies against Cúneo, who was a gentle soul and I know could not have treated your cousin so badly. Your assertions of heathen curses destroying the mind of the admiral I must laugh at; then, to read of your inebriations with the *cohoba* vapors and of your infernal nightmares into the nether regions, oh, wonder that you are still the recalcitrant heathen; I lament the wastefulness of all your years of catechism, all that patient instruction, first from the great admiral himself, and then myself and so many others, all of us thinking you might take your vows someday, only to read right here in your room that you are a fornicator of old women (and in the past few weeks!), a frequenter of Barcelona girl whores, you who have walked through all that is holy of our sacraments, you who have taken the blood and corpus of our Christ and have assisted in all of our sacred rituals … how could you deceive me this way? How, how, how could you betray me in such a manner, Dieguillo? You are a true devil, chameleon, changing your colors with the shades around you. Was it vanity, lizard, fear that I might take your glory that made you betray my cause of unity with your people?

I credit you for this only: I know now with certainty the little trust of your pages. I see with ease how wrong you are about so many things. Is it perhaps your luciferous *cohoba*— is that what burns your head clean of sincere thought? Why, for instance, do you pick on Pané, that simple good friar who recorded so many things about your people? And why do you vilify Velazquez, claiming that he killed his wife, when he was one of the truly refined people to come to the islands? Of course, he was a conquistador—but his own wife? No, Diego… But you know what a great fibber you are.

I thought to destroy these pages, but I will leave them that you may read and reread your own profanities. I know not all your shenanigans, but you are securely beyond redemption and I would venture even less to consider what penance you might make for your brutish and odious twists of mind.

Consider, of course, that we are no longer friends. When you return, I shall be moved to another residence. I desire not to see you again. As for our shared ideas on Enriquillo's defense, feel released completely from any and all obligations. I certainly do. In fact, I shall visit the camps soon, bringing the sacraments and planning for their new settlement. In the event of our coincidental meeting, do not bother to recognize me. Consider it sufficient our years of convent life, and ponder the fate of our apparent friendship, a fetid swamp now where once ran a transparent stream.

Las Casas.

Looking at my papers, which are out of order still on my table, I can tell by the round ink stains where he sprinkled holy water on them. He opened my *cohoba* bundle, too, which I left behind, and he broke in half four green parrot feathers given to me by Baiguanex.

TWO HUNDRED NINETEEN. *A YEAR'S WAIT.*

Catalina and I are made to wait one year. Abbot Mendoza has agreed to seek her free-woman status but we are instructed to prepare for one year, save our pesos, and then set up our home. "If you are to be married, then let your Christian home be an example to your new generation," said the abbot.

I see Catalina in the market on Wednesdays and Saturdays and at Mass on Sundays. We sit together and chat, and we lock our ankles together under the benches.

TWO HUNDRED TWENTY. *PREPARING FOR MARRIAGE.*

I stay to myself, and thankfully, while in the convent. I go nowhere most days but dedicate my hours to latching together square pig traps, which Catalina sells for me at four pesos a cage. I make three or four pig traps a week, and they all sell. Pigs are everywhere in the woods, and they produce great damage against all tuber crops.

With forty pesos we put away per month, in a year we will have what we need. I want to put up a good *bohío* and get a few cows for beef steers and raise young horses. My *yucca* I will plant already this year, for the crop will take a full turn of the seasons and will be ready when we are. I can always keep making pig traps, and Catalina makes a fine hammock. We will live thus.

I look not for Enriquillo, nor for the camp at Boyá. Even that urge has left me and I am motionless in their relation. I ponder his words at our final meeting, and I hesitate not in seeing the meaning he dictated in my strategic actions. I know he is right. Once again I realize how the covered man continues to suck at my Taíno marrow.

I cannot write much more. I feel my urge in this activity leaving me, too. This play of words I have been at most of my life, as *interprete*, and now in this writing, tires me. Robbed am I of enough memories by this Castilian activity, images in words spilled to the page so that my inside mind can no longer see them.

Two hundred twenty-one. *I hear of Enriquillo.*

Ten months it is today, since our return from the Bahuruku, ten new moons. Silverio I saw today, my young helper. He has married and has his own *bohío* at Boyá. He looks quite firm and robust. I asked about Enriquillo.

"He is frail, cannot sleep, and is often irascible."

"Is he ill?"

"His lungs hurt him, and he doesn't sleep."

I asked about the *behike* Baiguanex.

"He never came in. We have not seen him anymore," he said.

Two hundred twenty-two. *Journey to the new community.*

I have decided to visit Enriquillo at Boyá. It is a bit of a journey from Santo Domingo, and I traveled with Silverio for nearly a month. This is truly the last that I will write.

Leaving Azua and entering the *cacique*'s community, we ran into a party of horse riders, six men in long capes and sabers. They stopped to greet us and a voice I don't forget said out loud, "The clever Dieguillo, I believe. What convenience."

It was Oviedo, the gold-counting historian. He went on, addressing a companion.

"My duke," he said, "this Indian right here will resolve our question."

"Dieguillo," he said, turning to me. "The duke wonders how the Indians of the first years saw us. Did you think we were human beings or angels?"

"I said many times you were angels, in those first days," I responded, to avoid conflict. "And many of my people believed me. I believed it myself for a while."

Oviedo laughed. Silverio was impatient but quick to realize they had us surrounded, outmanned and out-armed.

"And when did you start realizing that we were humans," asked the duke.

I saw my opening and responded.

"I once thought you might be angels, but, if the gentlemen will forgive an Indian's honest opinion, I never have thought you human at all."

Oviedo might have been angered, but he was jovial that day.

"Our *cacique* has quite the stamp," he said. "He likes his cups, too, duke. You ought to see him."

"Only with the Castilian wine," I replied. "My own *mabi* root beer I can drink and drink. It never gives me a headache."

"Saliva beer," Oviedo said, pulling on his horse and laughing loudly. "It's a wonder the Indians didn't drink piss."

The Castilian group, following Oviedo, reined their mounts away from us without another word, cantering away, the shod hooves of their powerful horses throwing clods of mud.

August 2e, 1535

TWO HUNDRED TWENTY-THREE. *I SEE ENRIQUILLO AGAIN, IN HIS DEATHBED.*

Doña Mencia is the same, perhaps a little heavier. Her hair is turned quickly gray.

She took and sat me by Enriquillo's hammock. He looked very old and thin and was coughing in great fits. But he greeted me warmly.

"Look how you find me," he said. "Uncle, I knew I would not last long."

"You are bound to get well," I said. "You were always strong."

"Its all spent, my wax."

"Rest and gain strength, you magnificent *cacique*," I said to my Enriquillo boy. "You have a long life ahead."

I felt foolish for not coming earlier, as he wanted to speak with me. But his comments were all about problems of the community. For one thing, the Castilians had promised twenty cattle and had delivered only six. Then, his deputized men, including Tamayo, helped track and recapture two escaped Africans. Many Indians in the community disliked Tamayo tracking runaways for the Castilians. "It's a big problem for everybody," Enriquillo said. "Even here they come talk to me about it. But I no longer see the workings of things. I only know that without our warrior discipline, everyone goes this way and that. On the other side, I know Tamayo's angers and they continue to grow. Tamayo is angry all the time. He doesn't think through his decisions."

Enriquillo caughed for a long stretch. A cloth he held was stained red. I felt so badly for him and for Doña Mencia, but such matters as the Castilians not keeping their promises to us or of Tamayo participating in the tracking and hunting of *cimarróns* I cannot contain.

"I liked the Bahuruku, our mountain trails," the *cacique* said. "The *behike* was right to stay away."

I wondered about Baiguanex but said nothing.

"I only hope he doesn't die alone," Enriquillo said, looking at Doña Mencia standing nearby. "At least I know I won't die alone. She will sing me to the Spirit World."

"Come back," Doña Mencia said, as we parted. "Tell us more of your stories."

I promised I would, though, truly, I lack the strength myself for such a trek again.

Two hundred twenty-four. *At last in our* bohío.

I have left the convent with Catalina, not toward the mountains but to the edge of the sea on the savanna, to an area apart, what Castilians now call vacant lands. We picked a place by a good stream, by a ridge she knows well, a place of fertile earth on her old people's lands.

Building our *bohío*, which we do alone, a rider came to see us, sent by Silverio. The young *cacique* died on September 27, nearly a week ago. Last night, when I complained to the fates about the young *cacique*, wracked with problems and now coughed to death, this after so many years of hard work for his people, Catalina shook her head at me. "My young husband," she said. "Remember our old saying, 'Expect nothing for your deeds.'"

May 5, 1539

Two hundred twenty-five. *Final testament, 1539.*

Fearing that I may pass on without assigning these matters, I am resolved here to put down a dispensation of my wordly goods.

I own:

— A *bohío*, which I share with my wife, Doña Catalina Diaz de Colon, and this *bohío*, of course, belongs to her person even more than mine, as the four directions of our *bohíos* always belonged to the female.
— A herd of ten horses, including five mares, two colts, two geldings, and one stallion. This herd belongs to Doña Catalina.
— A herd of six beef cattle. This herd also belongs to Doña Catalina. Of these two herds, I want Doña Mencia's people, on her behalf, to pick two mares and two cows for their community.
— Several pigs, all of whom will remain to Doña Catalina.
— All my *conucos*, in preparation or planted, belong to Doña Catalina.
— My personal belongings of correspondence tools, personal tools and clothing, one machete, three good lariats, two saddles and bridles, all of that I leave with Doña Catalina.
— Finally, these pages, which I have kept all these years, the early ones and the later ones, these items I leave to Father Remigio, of the Convent of Dominicans in the town of Santo Domingo. May he keep them for what they are, the incomplete record of my people's affairs in the years since the coming of the Castilianss to these islands of my heart. Maybe they will last, maybe they will burn. I only know this: from the sky of our beautiful seas, the stars they will not cause to fall.

Signed,

Guaikán

(Diego Colón, adopted son of the Great Admiral)

Two hundred twenty-six. *A letter from Las Casas, the New Laws.*

[Editor's note: Lastly, Diego Colón's papers included the following letter to Diego from Father Las Casas, some four years after his last testament. A partial reply was written by Diego on the backside of the same letter. Apparently, it was never sent.]

May 29, 1545

Dieguillo, old friend,

Last night I faced the evening breeze here on the coast of Barcelona. The coast and its smells reminded me of you, and I realized I have forgiven your actions toward me on the closing days of the Enriquillo war.

Furthermore, I want to apologize to you for my harsh words so many years ago. I have crossed the ocean time and again since then, and as they say, "Much water has passed." I remember those first days, too, when you were the first Indian I ever saw, there at Seville, you and your parrots. And that was more than fifty years ago! Certainly, I hope you still have your health and that your marriage to Doña Catalina Diaz has gone well.

Facing the ocean here in Barcelona, I realize also that I miss our conversations about the early days and about the Indian causes. It was precisely that breeze from the ocean, the one you always said spoke to you, that seemed to carry the memory of your face and words to me. I realize, too, how much your smile back then as a boy has stayed with me. In some hidden way, I believe the hand of God guided my eyes to that smile, which to this day represents the Taíno smile, the Taíno character to me. It was that quality in your island people that always tugged at me, eliciting finally from my heart a pledge to assist your race. This I have continued to do, since I have seen you last, and the urge is upon me to inform you about it. Again, I see the Lord's mysterious mind at work in my actions.

Since last I saw you I have traveled once to Panama and to Nicaragua, where I have seen the most dismal conditions endured by your mainland relatives. Thus the work on the mainland on behalf of the Indian communities is quite dramatic. I was engaged in attempting to curtail the wars of conquest on the tribes. There I did travel among the Maya Caxiqueles and Kekchies and developed a way of singing to them in order to obtain a peace without horror, without the war. This went well for a time, until certain conquistadors argued that it was not proper, as their rights of tribute and slavery they can obtain only through a war of conquest, thus peaceful conquest they considered high treason.

(The law they don't respect in its spirit but will twist at will, if allowed by its language and interpretation. But then, you always told me that!)

I was run out of Nicaragua, and in Guatemala, Pedro de Alvarado conspired to have me assassinated. The wheel repeats itself, dear Diego and the abuses and cruelties suffered by your people in the islands are continuing here. I abhor it all, my Dieguillo, as I have seen again the new slave markets of Panama and Nicaragua, where your copper people are herded by the hundreds, nay, by the thousands, branded, distributed, and sold, mother torn from infant, husband from wife. Pity the mainland Indians, Dieguillo. The conquest continues.

To Peru I tried to sail, but the winds would not carry me, though I certainly have all the needed testimony to condemn Pizarro and all his henchmen, how they have tortured and quartered those innocent towns of the mountains. To be sure, the methods of conquest used on the islands they have refined on the mainland, where everything is bigger and more abundant.

The war of Enriquillo, dear Diego, was one great mark. I see now how it set a standard for caution, for the option other than war. Men like Fuenleal (remember him?) have continued their magistries in Mexico, Yucatán, and Guatemala—men who knew the suffering of the island Taíno—and who could see that a second generation could still rebel and dangerously assail the Spanish cause. This is of some help now, as I campaign here at the court, petitioning the sovereigns and the Holy Pontiff himself, Pope Paul III, on behalf of the Indies.

Allow me to outline some recent changes that have me highly enthusiastic for a new chapter and many new verses with which to curtail abuses and protect the Indian.

In 1537, after much lobbying, the pope issued his Bulla Sublimis Deus, a bull upholding the rationality of Indians. It rebukes those who argue that the Indians are "beasts of burden that talk," by proclaiming, as we have so many times, "all the peoples of the world are men."

It was this bull allowed us to contain Pedro de Alvarado in Guatemala, finally. Pedro Alvarado, who was branding and selling Indians in a wide open slave trade, was opposed by

Bishop Francisco Marroquin, also a protector of the Indians. We petitioned also and the *oidores* agreed to let me attempt a peaceful conversion for five years.

Thus it happened, Diego. You should have been there to see it. We wrote songs of peace in the Indian languages, and our merchant friends, Indian, mestizo, and white, sang to the tribes along the rivers, telling of the One True Lord and his Gift of Redemption. *Cacique* after *cacique* came into the fold, Dieguillo, all happy to be baptized. Juan of Atitlan was first in July 1537, but by January 1538, most of the Kekchi *caciquedoms* were with us, what we named the Verapaces, the True Peaces.

This is where everything went bad and the *encomenderos* began attacking me in earnest. This is where they declared it their right to make war on the Indians, even if the innocents had come to offer peaceful tribute! But these new conquistadors are evil men, Dieguillo, raping and killing at will, and they must be stopped before the whole continent is consumed, as were the islands, before a whole race of people is exterminated.

Thus now I can write that we have the New Laws, which passed by the court in 1542. The New Laws completely prohibit Indian slavery and even disallow the *encomienda*. This is the victory we have sought from the Crown, a sword with which to apply the final remedy, a remedy that should not drag on forever but must be followed up with vigor and be decisive!

Thus, Dieguillo, you can see that we are finally gaining the proper resources for our campaign. It pays to persist in one's commitments, for the justice of our One True Lord turns slowly but it turns.

You will hear a great deal about these New Laws in years to come. They go on and on and will protect every facet of Indian existence and will be the backbone of our decisive campaign.

I hope this letter finds you well and you will consider the importance of the work of redemption for our human condition.

Your friend in Christ,

Father Las Casas

TWO HUNDRED TWENTY-SEVEN. *A NOTE FOR LAS CASAS.*

[Editor's note: What appears to be a response from Diego is found on the back of the three pages of Father Las Casas's letter. Dated in 1546 and titled "A note for Las Casas," it is indecipherable in parts.]

Once again, I reread the good friar's letter, now three years in my possession. I wish I could speak to him. I had the opportunity two years ago, when he came through, but I did not seek it. I had not the heart nor the time for a meeting. Catalina was dying then, and I had not the inclination to shift my attention from her.

…[illegible]…, they were pelting him with stones, hating him as never before. His monks, those that did not desert him right away, could find no food in town and were jeered whenever they appeared on the streets…[illegible]…then, last year, his flounted New Laws were revoked. In Mexico and Peru, the colonists rebelled against the Crown of Spain. "Don't take away our Indians" was one of their banners. The other one was: "Without Indians to work, the conquest means nothing."

Oahh, *guatiao* Las Casas, everything you do is good and yet does nothing! So how am I to respond?

I have no health, I would say. Catalina is buried, I would say. Like the final grains of the *ampolleta*, my remaining suns are counted. Our world as we knew it is destroyed, our people are one in one hundred of what they once were. Such is what I would say.

Of our Indian boys and girls, some farm the land, others have gone back to the bush. Three young *guaxeri* Catalina took in. I have taught them what I know of the tracking cure and they trail the spirit like Taíno…I am proud of those boys…[illegible]…"Each of you teach three more," I told them.

TWO HUNDRED TWENTY-EIGHT. *THEY WILL REMEMBER, MY YOUNG GENERATIONS.*

Fray Remigio is here. He brings me plantain, rice, and beans, and I have my *yucca* patch. Now I give the friar everything, all the pages to put away. It is time he took them. Now I draw this sketch, what my father taught me, the real message of our people. Someday they will remember it, my young generations, someday in dreams its meaning will return to them…[illegible]…that way, because in the black of our eyes we were good…it does not die…

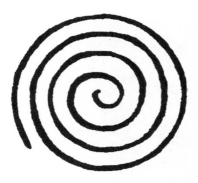

Postcript

The treaty with Enriquillo resulted in the settlement of the Indian community at Boyá, in south central Hispaniola. About four thousand Indian people settled at the free Indian community, where Enriquillo officiated until his death, a year later. The Boyá community persisted, and although intermarriage and migration eroded the Indian jurisdiction, factors of Indian ancestry remain in the families of the region today. Around the time of the settlement with Enriquillo, other Taíno groups in Cuba, Santo Domingo and Puerto Rico sought refuge in the mountains of their respective islands, and thus small enclaves of Taíno ancestors survived, some into the twenty-first century. Of course, the Taíno people, in intermarriage with Iberians and Africans, are a major genetic and cultural root of the contemporary Greater Antillean population. The greater Caribbean islands were under Spanish domination until the end of the nineteenth century. About Diego Colón nothing more is known.

GLOSSARY

adelantado. Spanish military title of forward commander

alguacil. Marshal or policeman

ampolleta. Hourglass filled with sand, turned over every half hour to keep time on long voyages

Anacaona. Taíno *cacica* of the Xaraguá region, sister of Bohechío and wife of Caonabó

areito. (Taíno) Traditional dances and recitations among the Taíno *caciques* and *behikes*

ascendado. The owner of a hacienda, large ranch, or farm

Asturias. Region of Spain

axí(es). (Taíno) Pepper (*Capsicum* spp.)

axiaco. Taíno-derived word, still in use, for a Caribbean pepper- and corn-based soup always mixed in with *yucca*, ñame, and other island root crops

Bahuruku. Mountain range in the southwest peninsula of Española, 150 km of coast and 100 km into land. According to Las Casas, it contained a mountain made of salt. It also contains present-day Lake Enriquillo.

Baibrama. Taíno ceremonial *cemi* and spiritual entity associated with fertility of crops, particularly manioc

Baigua. (Taíno) A plant used by fishermen to drug fish in the water

Baiguanex. Medicine man, or *behike*, of Enriquillo

Baracoa. Taíno word meaning, "existence by the sea," describes a town in the northeast coast of Cuba

barbacoa (barbecue). (Taíno) A method of cooking and drying foods by stacking the raw foods in grates and adding tomatoes, peppers, and other condiments

batéy. (Taíno) A plaza or ceremonial field where *areitos* and ball games were celebrated

Bayamanacoel. Taíno ancestral character who assisted in the creation of the islands by spitting a *guanguayo* on Deminán

Bayamo. A large town in eastern Cuba named for its old *cacique's* name

behike. (Taíno) Medicine man or healer

bejuco. (Taíno) Various types of vines used as medicinal purgatives and as cord rope for tying and construction

Bohekio. *Cacique* of the Xaraguá region of Española

bohío. (Taíno) Home or house; also the island of Española

Boricua. Person or object of Puerto Rican origin

Borikén. (Taíno) "Land of the valiant *cacique*"; Puerto Rico

brujo. (Castilian) Male witch

cacicasgo. Hispanicized Taíno word for the territory or court of a *cacique*

cacique. (Taíno) A regional chief

cagüayo (a). (Taíno) A longish tree reptile; word still in use in Cuba and Puerto Rico

Caiçiju. Taíno grandfather of Guarionex, noted for his prophesy of the coming of the Spanish

caimán. (Taíno) A swamp crocodile endemic to Cuba

cajaya. (Taíno) Shark

Camagüey. (Taíno) Sun-drenched savanna; region, province, and city in central eastern Cuba

caona. (Taíno) Gold

Caonabó. Taíno or Ciguayo chief of the region of Maguana, in Española

caracol. (Taíno) Spiraled seashell

Caréy. (Taíno) Large sea turtle (*Chelonia imbricata*); used here as a personal name

Carib. Caribbean Indian people from the Lesser Antilles, a term chosen by the Spanish for people reputedly cannibalistic

cassabe. (Taíno) Tort made from *yucca* or manioc root; word still in use

Castilian. The language or a subject of Castile, a kingdom (now region) of Spain

ceiba. (Taíno) Silk cottonwood, a sacred tree; name of Diego's first wife

cemi. (Taíno) Wooden and stone statuettes representing various spiritual entities

Cibanakán. (Taíno) A center stone

Çiboney. (Indo-Antillean) A people in central and western Cuba and in the southern Cuban cays

çibucán. (Taíno) Net sack used to squeeze juice from the scraped *yucca*

Ciguayo. A tribe of Indians from north and eastern Española; a captain under Enriquillo

cimarrón. An African escaping slavery who joined the Taíno mountain camps, or *palenques*

Coaybay. Taíno place of the dead

Coatrisquie. (Taíno) A female spiritual leader of rainy winds at sea

cohoba. The ground up dust, or snuff, used by the *cacique*, *behike*, and ni-Taíno to enhance their visions and to communicate with the ancestors and other spirits (*Piptadenia peregrina*); the ceremony of *cohoba*

Cohobanax. Fictional name with the word *cohoba* as root and *nax* added to describe an elder in that ceremony

conuco. (Taíno) A planted field of *yucca* and other crops; an Indian homestead

converso. (Castilian) A converted Jew

copei (copai). A tree on whose broad leaves a message could be written

coxibá. (Taíno) Tobacco plant

Cubanakán. (Taíno) "Center of the island" (of Cuba)

cucuyo (cocuyo). From the Taíno word for the Antillean lightning bug. Oviedo notes the *cucuyo* was used for nighttime travel. A hunter of mosquitoes, the *cucuyo* was also introduced under netting and in *bohíos* at night as a form of pest control.

Deminán. Taíno ancestral character, one of the four directions and four winds, an adventuresome creator of much of the Taíno cosmological world

digo. (Taíno) A plant whose root and leaf produces a cleansing lather used by the Taíno to bathe

dragas. "Little people"; word used by Iberian (Gallego) peasantry

duho. (Taíno) Ceremonial seat or stool low to the ground and fashioned from wood or stone

encierro. The gathering of the bulls prior to a bull run

encomienda. Spanish system of giving Indian villages to specific Spanish conquistadors or grandees to whom the Indian community was *encomended* to be Christianized in return for their land and their free labor

Enriquillo. Taíno *cacique* (d. 1535) whose thirteen-year war is described by Diego in the present journal

escarmiento. (Spanish) A serious warning or lesson

Española. Present-day Haiti/Santo Domingo, variously known as Bohío and Quisqueya and renamed Isla Española by Columbus. The word is also anglicized to *Hispaniola*.

fascineroso. (Spanish) A torrid or agitated person

Fernandina. Christopher Columbus's early attempt to rename Cuba

goeiz (a). (Taíno) "Spirit of (in) a living person"

Gonzalo. A captain under Enriquillo

Guaikán. (Taíno) A remora, pilot fish, or sucker fish; Diego Colón's Indian name

Guamax. Taíno *cacique* of Baracoa area of eastern Cuba

Guamíquina. (Taíno) Chief or head man; the name given to Columbus by his early hosts

Guanahabax. Name combining *Guanahaní*, "the island," and *bax*, "principal man"

Guanahaní. Indian name for the Bahamian island first sighted by Columbus

Guanahaníkan. Name combining *Guanahaní* (the name of the island) with *kan*, Taíno for "center,"(as in Cubanakán, an Indian region in central Cuba)

guanguayo. (Taíno) Spittle of mixed *cohoba* and tobacco juice; spat on Deminán's back by Bayamonacoel

guanin. (Taíno) A shiny metal or copper

guarikén. A Taíno expression, registered by Las Casas, meaning "Come look and see"

Guarionex. Taíno *cacique* of the region of Magua, in Española

Guarocuya. Enriquillo's Taíno name; also, an earlier Taíno rebellious *cacique*

guásima. Cuban "tree of life," sacred to Taíno and their *guajiro* ethnic and cultural descendants

guatiao. (Taíno) Friend, particularly one with whom a name has been exchanged

guaxeri (later guajiro). (Taíno) "One of our humans," or countryman

guayaba. (Taíno) A sweet fruit with high ceremonial importance; guava (*Psidium guajava*)

güira. (Taíno) Gourd (*Crescentia cujete*)

Hatuey. "Certainty of Sun in the Sky"; Taíno *cacique* from Española who fled over to Cuba, warning of Spanish lust for gold

hicara. (Taíno) Receptacle made out of a gourd

hicotea. (Taíno) Freshwater turtle

higüe. (Taíno) "Little people" who normally live around a stream or spring

himagua. (Taíno) Twin

hutía. Rodent of the West Indies (*Solenodon paradoxus*), eaten by early Taíno and present-day *guajiro*

hyen. (Taíno) The poisonous juice of the *yucca* after it's squeezed from the scraped pulp

iguana. (Taíno) A large, edible lizard (*Iguana tuberculata*)

inriri. (Taíno) Woodpecker (*Melanerpes portoricensis*)

Itiba Cahobaba. Taíno female deity, mother of the four creator twins, including the one named Deminán

jaba. (Taíno) Sack or bag

jaguajiguatu. Reconstructed Taino word meaning "fire in the loins"

kaçi. (Taíno) Moon

Kwaib. Term used by contemporary chiefs of the Carib territory in Salybia, Dominica, to describe their people

lucayo. Taíno-derived word for the Taíno inhabiting the small Bahamian islands

macana. War club made of the palm tree

macanear. To hit (common verb in West Indies); from the Taíno word for "war club" or "coral ax," *macana*

Macorixe. A little-documented Caribbean indigenous people identified at various times in Española, Jamaica, and Cuba, noted for their archery

macoutí. (Taíno) "Without feet"; back sack

maguacokío. (Taíno) "Covered men with swords that can cut a man in half with one strike"

Maguana. Taíno *cacicasgo* in south central Española led by *cacique* Caonabó at contact

mahá. (Taíno) The largest nonpoisonous snake in the Greater Antilles

maize. Taíno-derived word for corn; Maisí Point, easternmost point in Cuba
mamey. (Taíno) A tropical fruit
manatí. Antillean sea cow, or manatee (*Trichechus manatus*)
manaya. (Taíno) Stone hatchet
manigua. (Taíno) High grass country; also wild country
mánso. (Castilian) Tame; an Indian living in the Spanish hold
maraca. (Taíno) Rattle made from a gourd
maravedí. Spanish copper coin with limited purchasing power
Marién. A chiefdom and territory of Española
Matininó. Caribbean island(s) reputedly inhabited by Amazonian women
Mencia. Wife of *cacique* Enriquillo, a leader of noble Taíno lineage
naboria. (Taíno) A class of workers, not clearly slaves, that served Taíno society in domestic and field work, likely from earlier migrant groups to the islands
ni-taíno. (Caribbean Indian) The rank of principal people, council of elders, just under the *cacique* families; the more constant form of *Taíno* used throughout history
ñame. Likely Taíno word for edible sweet tuber, or sweet potato; there is dispute as to the Amerindian or African origins of this word.
oidor. (Castilian) A type of judge or "hearer" in the colonial Spanish legal system
opía. (Taíno) The spirit of the human and animals after death
Opiyelguobirán. Taíno *cemi* and guardian spirit of the Spirit World
repartimientos. The act of giving out or splitting of lands with Indians attached to form *encomiendas*
Romero. A captain under Enriquillo
sinrazón. (Castilian) Action, usually brusque, "without reason"
Taíno. (Caribbean Indian) The aboriginal inhabitants of Cuba, Hispaniola, Puerto Rico, Jamaica, and other lesser islands; self-descriptive, meaning "noble" or "good" people
Tamayo. Enriquillo's principal captain
Turey. (Taíno) Sky; also a type of medallion worn by chiefs
Urayoán. Boricua *cacique*, sometimes written as Broyoan, who drowned a Spaniard to test whether in fact the covered men were immortal
xaiba. (Taíno) Antillean freshwater crab (*Callinectes diacanthus*)
Xamayca. (Taíno) Present-day Jamaica
Xaraguá. Territory of *cacique* Bohechio, in southwestern Española
xiba. (Taíno) Stone and woody mountain
xikí. (Taíno) A tree that has a very hard wood
Ya. (Taíno) Strong or vital spirit
yaguasa. (Taíno) An indigenous Cuban duck
Yara. Place near Cuban city of Bayamo, where Hatuey was immolated
Yaquimo. Port town in southern Española; also, Puerto Brazil
Yoruba. Tribal people from eastern Africa, many of whom were brought to the Caribbean as slaves

yuán. A reconstructed Taíno word for "penis," from *iu*, "yucca," the form of the tuber, and *ia* or *an*, "vital force"

Yucahuguama Bagua Maórocoti. Supreme being in the Taíno cosmology. A triple name meaning "One who brings the *yucca*," "rules the sea," and "is without ancestral grandfathers," born of woman only

yucca. (Taíno) Manioc, a primary tropical root crop

yukaieke. (Taíno) Village or settlement

Yunque. A flat-peaked promontory form found near the ocean in Cuba and in Borikén

About the Author

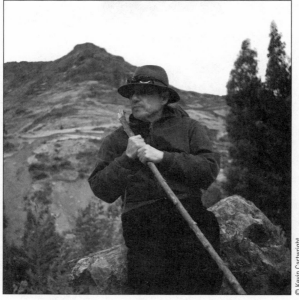

© Kevin Cartwright

Presently a senior scholar at the Smithsonian National Museum of the American Indian, **José Barreiro** is a novelist, essayist, and activist of nearly four decades on American indigenous hemispheric themes. Barreiro is a member of the Taíno Nation of the Antilles.